Praise for ALL THAT MATTERS

2004 TRILLIUM

GILLER PR

NATIONAL

"Choy's effortless style is mesmerizing, and his characters are compelling. Perhaps the most enticing aspect of his writing is the glimpse he offers into the vibrant world of Chinese-Canadian culture. . . . Choy's fluid writing style . . . merges Chinese words and rhythms into the narrative. Non-Chinese readers will learn a lot about the culture and the language without realizing they are being taught."   —*Edmonton Journal*

"Good news for fans of Wayson Choy's memorable first novel, *The Jade Peony*. *All That Matters* . . . is every bit as good as its predecessor. . . . *All That Matters* is a paean to decency and humanity [with] humour, under-statement and precise attention to detail."
                    —*The Gazette* (Montreal)

"A finely crafted novel."   —*Calgary Herald*

"Choy's ultimate gift [is] to be able to employ words like ghosts, curses, blessings, and omens and have even the most analytical of heads nodding with understanding. The Vancouver of the 1930s that Choy has created is where the historical meets the mystical. . . . Choy sustains the balance even as he touches on heavier issues—war, cultural divisions, a mixed-race love triangle. And life, he seems to tell us, isn't so hard to figure out."   —*Time*

"*All That Matters* was worth the eight-year wait because, besides opening a door into a beguiling and largely unknown world, the author grapples satisfyingly with the big questions."   —*Toronto Star*

"Choy's effortless storytelling and believable characters make *All That Matters* an unforgettable window into immigrant life, and a fascinating look at a key period in Vancouver's evolution."   —*Vancouver Review*

"*All That Matters* rewards the reader with a richly textured evocation of childhood in a community as oppressive as it is nurturing. Once again, Choy has created a complex world, peopled with characters you will love as though they were your own family."   —*Ottawa Citizen*

"*All That Matters* is an immensely appealing novel. Populated with captivating characters and laced with a wealth of Chinese lore, the book, short-listed for this year's Giller Prize, is a worthy contender."
                                          —*The London Free Press*

"Choy tells stories that need to be heard."
                                          —*NOW* magazine

"*All That Matters* is a sweet coming of age story. . . . Choy reveals his characters and story so slowly that by the end the reader will begin liking the unlikable and understanding what at first seemed incomprehensible."
                                          —*Winnipeg Free Press*

ALL THAT

Wayson Choy

MATTERS

A Novel

ANCHOR CANADA

Copyright © Wayson Choy 2004
Anchor Canada edition published 2005
This edition published 2012

All rights reserved. The use of any part of this publication, reproduced,
transmitted in any form or by any means electronic, mechanical,
photocopying, recording or otherwise, or stored in a retrieval system
without the prior written consent of the publisher—or, in the case of
photocopying or other reprographic copying, a license from the
Canadian Copyright Licensing Agency—is an infringement of
the copyright law.

Anchor Canada is a registered trademark.

Library and Archives Canada Cataloguing in Publication is available
upon request

ISBN 978-0-385-67879-7

This is a work of fiction. Therefore, any references to actual events
and locales, and any resemblances to persons, mythic, living or dead,
are used for purposes of fiction and are entirely coincidental.

Text design: CS Richardson
Printed and bound in the USA

Published in Canada by
Anchor Canada, a division of
Random House of Canada Limited

Visit Random House of Canada Limited's website:
www.randomhouse.ca

10   9   8   7   6   5   4   3   2   1

*To those who saw me through
a dark time: you are family.*

THE MASTER SAID,
"WITH WORDS, ALL THAT MATTERS
IS TO EXPRESS TRUTH."
The Analects of Confucius

~ *BEGINNINGS* ~

WHEN I HEAR THE SEA WIND blowing through the streets of the city in the morning, I can still feel my father and the Old One—together—lifting me up to perch on the railing of a swaying deck; still feel the steady weight of Father's palm braced against my chest and Poh-Poh's thickly jacketed arm locked safely around my legs. I was three then, in 1926, but I can still recall their shouting in the morning chill, "Kiam-Kim, Kiam-Kim," their voices thin against the blasts of salty wind, "*Hai-lah Gim San!* Look at Gold Mountain! Look!"

I saw in the distance the mountain peaks, and my toes curled with excitement. As I pressed a hand over each small ear to dim the assault of squawking gulls, fragments of living sky swirled and plunged into the waste spewing from the ship's belly, and the sun broke through.

All at once, the world grew more immense and even stranger than I could ever have imagined; I ducked my head to one side and burrowed blindly into Poh-Poh's jacket. Father plucked me off the rail and put me down to stand up by myself.

Poh-Poh did not stop him.

"We are near Gold Mountain," she said, her Toishan words shouted above other excited voices. "Straighten up, Kiam-Kim!"

I watched as Father clutched the rail to hold our place against the surging crowd: he looked ready for anything.

I put my own hands around the middle rail and threw my head back, and tried to look as bold and as unafraid as Father. Poh-Poh glanced behind her. A wrinkled hand shakily held on to my shoulder. I shouted to her to look at the swooping gulls, but she did not hear me.

As the prow rose and crashed, and the *Empress of Japan* surged into the narrow inlet, gusts of bitter wind stung my eyes. At last, to greet the approaching Vancouver skyline, the ship blasted its horn.

"Look there, Kiam-Kim!" shouted Father. "Way over there!"

I looked: along a mountain slope, a black line was snaking its way towards the city.

"See?" Father said, kneeling down to shout above the chaotic machinery clanking away in the ship's belly. "I told you there would be trains."

I laughed and jumped about until the sea air chilled my cheeks. The Old One bent down to lift a thick coat collar around my neck. The air tasted of burning coal.

"Listen carefully, Kiam-Kim," Father said. "Can you make out the train whistle?"

I listened. But I was not thinking of trains.

Grandmother had told me the story that dragons screeched and steamed out of hidden mountain lairs: sweating, scaly dragons whose curving bodies plunged into the sea and caused the waters to boil and the wind to scorch the faces of intruders until their eyes, unable to turn away, burned with tears.

The wailing finally reached my ears. The black line turned into freight cars headed towards the city's row of warehouses and jutting docks. The train engine gave another shriek.

In response, the ship blew its horn again. A shawl of sea birds lifted skyward. Ship and train were racing to reach the same point of land. People behind us applauded.

Father raised his hand to shield his eyes against the dancing sunlight.

"We're here, Mother," Father said to Poh-Poh.

I said to myself, " . . . here . . . ," and gripped the rail even harder.

The long train now disappeared behind a shoreline of low buildings. With my eyes following the great billows of smoke, I heard clearly the echoing screech of wheels.

"The cries of a dragon," said Poh-Poh.

Father said, "Just the train coming to a stop, Kiam-Kim."

But the Old One's voice was so certain that I held my breath.

~ *O N E* ~

WHEN I WAS THREE YEARS OLD, Father, Poh-Poh, and I were sent away from our Toishan village to Hong Kong, sent away by the Patriarch Chen, who was recently a Mission House convert and the head of our clan. As a demonstration of his Christian charity, the old Patriarch had agreed to clear the way for Third Uncle to sponsor us to come to Canada, so that Father, Grandmother, and I, First Son, would have a chance to escape the famine and the civil wars raging in the Pearl River Delta of Kwantung province. Those who could leave Sze-yup, the Four County village district in Southern China, would have a chance for a better existence. Those who settled in Gold Mountain might find work and send back remittances to help the ones left behind; every sojourner would return home when life improved in China.

Much later, I learned that before he had put up the money and bought the documents for us to join him in Vancouver, Third Uncle had to consider the feelings of his dead wife. He consulted Chinatown's Madame Jing, who set up her fortune-telling table in Market Alley and had known him since he first arrived in Gold Mountain. She interpreted the final toss of the *I Ching* coins.

"The spirit of your dead wife approves," she said.

Soon after this sign of approval, American gold and large Mexican silver coins were paid into various hands. Six months later, we sailed on an *Empress* steamer and landed in Victoria, then headed to Vancouver to settle in the Chinatown rooms that Third Uncle had rented for the three of us in a building on East Pender Street, just half a block from his warehouses on Shanghai Alley.

Third Uncle was not my father's brother. In fact, he was a very distant cousin from Sze-yup, connected to us only through our mutual clan name of Chen; his own blood brother had died years ago in the interior of British Columbia. Over fifty, and successful as an import-export warehousing merchant, Third Uncle had been shocked into acknowledging his own mortality. In less than a month, five of his Chinatown associates had died, two from heart attacks, two from the coughing sickness, and one from a stomach tumour. He confronted a chilling fact: he had no family members in Gold Mountain to carry on after him. What legacy, then, had thirty years of his work and investments built? He promptly decided to sponsor a "namesake family" from Old China, a *maaih-gee ga-ting*, a "bought-paper family" that would replace what he himself had tragically lost.

During the long period of civil unrest in Southern China, Third Uncle's own wife and ten-year-old son had met a fearful end. The two were abducted by a peasant warlord and held for ransom. But the ransom note arrived in Vancouver with an incorrect address, the name on the oversized envelope badly blotched by rain, and for three months on the front window of the *Chinese Times* office, the indistinct envelope was displayed, unclaimed. When it was finally opened and read, it was already too late: another letter had arrived from Patriarch Chen to say that a box had turned up, and it held the severed heads of Third Uncle's wife and son. The two decapitated bodies were found in a neighbouring field; mercifully, the bones and skulls were brought together by Patriarch Chen for an appropriate burial, or their ghosts would have wandered hopelessly in the fields and ponds.

Third Uncle wept to think that he had countless times walked past that large envelope. He had even laughed at the awkwardly constructed ideograms, as if a childish hand had struggled with each wavering stroke of the brush: he had wondered who was so ignorant, or so ill-advised, that they would not have hired a street calligrapher to write the words properly. It turned out that the words had been brushed by his own young son. The *Chinese Times* retold this sad story and urged people to check carefully the still unclaimed envelopes taped to the Carrall Street windows: "Some words are made unreadable by rain," the editor wrote, "and some, by tears."

Years later, Third Uncle told me that after the loss of an older brother in Gold Mountain, and then of his own wife and son, he had no intentions of ever again enduring a "blood loss." Further, after receiving the tragic news in the letter from Patriarch Chen, he had been warned by Madame Jing that if he dared to remarry, he would offend the ghost of his angry wife and bring a curse upon himself.

"Your wife feels you deserted her," the fortune teller had said, wagging her finger at him. "She saw you walking by that letter. She saw you laughing."

During the years since that tragedy, Third Uncle kept good company with a few women companions in the Chinatown teahouses, but he never invited any of them to his private rooms in his main Shanghai Alley warehouse. He slept alone there, beside a fading picture of a tall woman and a young boy, and he never remarried.

After thirty years in B.C., and after keeping the memory of his wife and son for so long—though he remembered only a baby the weight and size of a winter melon when he left for Canada, and remembered clearly how he pushed the tiny penis and assured himself the infant was a boy—and shortly after the funeral of his fifth business peer, Wong Ying Si, who boasted that Death would never touch him until his seventy-fifth year, and who died at the age of fifty-three, it was time for Third Uncle, then fifty-three himself and a wealthy merchant with three warehouses, to sponsor a family from his clan to become his own kin. Such sponsorship schemes were not unusual for Chinatown, though only those merchants with enough money could manage them, bringing over to Gold

Mountain their brother's whole family, for example, or a family member of a favourite concubine. Third Uncle quickly arranged with the Chen Association to assist him in sponsoring his paper family.

Arrangements were made through Patriarch Chen back in our Toishan village to settle on the right person for Third Uncle to bring over. He wanted a much younger man who would know some English and would be able to work beside him and help him with his accounts; he would sponsor this man and two of his family members, and pay for the documents and transportation to Gold Mountain. According to the agreement, this paper family would accept him as one of theirs. As a gesture of goodwill, Third Uncle also agreed to donate a large sum of money to the China-Canada Mission House, which the Patriarch favoured.

Father, as it happened, with his gift for studies, had been taught elementary English by the Mission teachers. He had also been helping with their complex accounts, translating the Chinese and English bills and invoices. His mother, my Poh-Poh, had been one of Patriarch Chen's household servants, but now in her sixties, whatever her merits, she held many secrets and was getting too old. Because of the famine and the civil war, Father readily agreed to the overseas proposal and signed some papers, and so we arrived in Vancouver. Father was thirty years old, and Poh-Poh was almost seventy, and I, three. Poh-Poh and I were Father's only two surviving family members; before my second birthday, my mother had died from the coughing sickness.

Ghosts and Old China haunted us, just as they had haunted Third Uncle. Only the stillborn can leave the past behind.

The first three months in *Hahm-sui-fauh*, Salt Water City, we occupied two badly lit rooms on Shanghai Alley, across from Third Uncle's warehouse. A barbershop was below us, and Poh-Poh and I could hear the chatter of men all day. There, Father sat and drank tea with Third Uncle while he was introduced to the community, and men came to smoke water pipes that gurgled in wooden buckets. Women came to visit us upstairs. They came and pinched my cheek and gave me stuffed animals, and soft candies to chew on, and chatted endlessly with Poh-Poh. Sometimes a boy or girl would visit and play with me. Sometimes I sat with Father downstairs in the barbershop and wondered at all the strange faces.

Then we moved into two spacious front-window rooms in a deep, three-storey brick building directly across from the Sam Kee building on East Pender and settled among the clutter of mismatched furniture and a cubbyhole kitchen. I existed there in a noisy jumble of dialects. Middle-aged or elderly faces bent over me, but were quickly forgotten and made little impression. Their concerned chatter, the smell of their seldom-washed bodies, made me wish for playmates my own size.

"Where are Jo-Jo and Little Pot?" I asked, wondering where the servant girls' two boys had gone. "Where is Wah Doy?" Wah Doy was an older boy who played clap-hand games with us in Patriarch Chen's compound nursery. Other laughing faces came to mind. "Where is—?"

"All gone now," Poh-Poh told me. "All left behind."

The musty second-floor apartment opened only to a long, dank hallway. There was no courtyard, no palm trees, no smell of the wet or endless dry seasons, of the dust rising from the ground in swirls. Only the oily smells and train-clanging sounds of False Creek. When I was not distracted by a new toy, Father told me, I whined for my village playmates, for pudgy faces, for hands and feet that pushed against my own and smelled familiar. I must have wished that the world had not changed so suddenly.

Poh-Poh wished, too, for the familiar routine of Patriarch Chen's servant quarters, where she had held me by my squirming, slippery waist in a large porcelain bath bowl painted with birds. In the middle of a walk-about room enclosed by flimsy curtains, she would pour from a jug the lukewarm water that Father had first bathed in. After me, she would climb in and take her turn, talking to me loudly so that no one would walk in on her. I was too young to know any difference, and only wanted to push my nose against her skin. Poh-Poh smelled of the kitchen herbs, of the mint and coriander that she crushed in her palms and rubbed over the back of her neck. In Gold Mountain we washed with a yellow soap that smelled like lye and we never bathed together again; I was stood up in an iron tub, and water poured down from taps with just a twist of the white porcelain handles. Actual doors hook-locked shut, and with no need to chatter loudly against any accidental intruders, Poh-Poh let me splash and babble to my heart's content while she fell into singing to herself tunes that she told me were sung to her by a magician-acrobat when she was a young girl in China.

"Clean up for Father today," she would say to me on days when expected warehouse inventory and supplies hadn't arrived for counting and storage. "On his afternoon break, Father take you for a walk."

Wearing one of Third Uncle's English suit jackets and the scooped Stetson he had bought from Modern Tailors, Father would take my hand and we would walk fifty feet south, behind Pender Street, down Carrall, and see the whole spine of Chinatown pushing against the thriving industrial mud flats of False Creek. Checking his pocket watch, Father lifted me up when I grew tired and pointed out the huge doors that opened up into the back of Third Uncle's warehouse. From the tops of bales and barrels, men waved to Father, who proudly lifted me even higher, urging, "Wave back, Kiam-Kim!"

By four in the afternoon, a fresh sea wind would blow in from the inlet. Until its arrival, the yellow-tinged air often tasted of the acrid smoke and fires spewing from the three- and five-storey-high brick chimneys of mills and refineries. The industrial sites were mostly crammed together under the distant Georgia Viaduct, but they also sat in exile all along False Creek like grim castles anchored deep in toxic black mud. Chinatown children like myself were warned not to go near any puddles, the shallow pools whose rainbow-glazed waters, we were warned, would quickly eat away our skin and leave only our bones behind. Then Father would take me back up the narrow stairs of our residence, and Poh-Poh would give him some extra food to see him through his long shift. I ran to the window and looked down to see Father crossing the street to wave to me before he disappeared into Shanghai Alley.

Our apartment was beside the warehouse district and among the busy narrow byways of Shanghai, Canton, and Market alleys, the three cobbled laneways located between Abbot and Columbia streets. These busy back lanes were enclosed on the south side by the expansive rail yards of the Great Northern and Canadian National railways. On these manmade flatlands of False Creek, freight cars and engines crowded the CPR Roundhouse, an enginehouse with a giant cranking turntable to shift the direction of the trains.

When the air was still and muggy, and gritty with the soot of train engines, Poh-Poh tied a wet cloth over my mouth and nose. After an hour, the damp cloth turned grey.

At all hours, the *foih-chai*, the trains, tugged freight cars that banged together like thunder and shook the windows of our rooms. At bedtime, Poh-Poh stuffed cotton in my ears until I got used to the noises.

"Only dragons playing," she told me. "Lucky dragons."

BANG! BANG!

"Only CPR freight trains," Father said, and took me by the hand one morning to show me how giant boxcars slammed together and shook the ground, crossing from the shipping docks below Hastings to East Pender, rumbling deep into False Creek to disappear into the steaming bowels of the Georgia Viaduct.

When we were alone in our tiny bedroom, Poh-Poh used to whisper to me from her bed: "At night when you sleep, Kiam-Kim, *foih-chai* change into iron dragons—lucky dragons to protect you from white demons. You be like Father: no worry."

Father did not worry about dragons. He had already been set up by Third Uncle to worry about entering numbers into large accounting books, numbers taken from piles and piles of invoices. Poh-Poh told me that Father was now so busy with numbers that he had no more room in his brain to worry about iron dragons.

I, too, did not worry—at least, not in the daytime.

On our afternoon walks, after all, Father had shown me that a train was a train, a solid, whistling, steam-blowing piece of reality. But at night, just before the darkness swept me deeply into sleep, as shunted boxcars went *BANG! BANG!* against each other, and as Father worked on his books under the single desk lamp in the next room, and Poh-Poh, with her knees and elbows cracking every night, as she sank back into her pillowed chair beside my cot, and as my eyelids sank under the weight of unbidden dreams, I felt stirring beside me a steel-plated, steam-hissing grey dragon uncoiling itself. Throughout the night, as the trains rumbled out of the roundhouse and click-clicked across Pender, bisecting the yellow light of street lamps,

I saw dragon eyes flash across the bedroom ceiling and fly into Poh-Poh's ancient head.

Soon after our arrival, Third Uncle Chen—whose business was doing very well—urged the elders in our surname association, the Overseas Chen Tong Society, to support his wish to bring over a female helpmate and companion for my father. He explained to them that Father's only wife had died of the coughing sickness in China when his son was not yet two, and that was why elderly Poh-Poh had come with us to Gold Mountain—so I would have proper family care. Third Uncle and the Old One had discussed these circumstances, he explained. "My good cousin needs help to care for his old mother and his First Son," Third Uncle said to the Tong elders.

The Tong elders were not unsympathetic to the bachelor-men in Chinatown who, more than fifteen or even twenty-five years before, had left behind their families in China and were now unable to bring over those same wives and families because of the 1923 Chinese Exclusion Act. Most of the men were too poor to pay the exorbitant price for the special documents to have their families join them in Gold Mountain. But Third Uncle could afford the expense, and the elders at once agreed to help him with the arrangements. And so one day he came to our rooms and proposed the idea of his buying a *gai-mou*, a helpmate for Father.

Third Uncle did not think a healthy, educated young widower like my father with his small son and elderly mother should live in Chinatown without "properly trained companionship." Besides, hadn't Poh-Poh been clamouring for Father, somehow, to have more grandsons while in Gold Mountain?

"Before I die," she kept saying to him, "I want to see three grandsons."

Even in Gold Mountain, Poh-Poh did not wish to tempt the gods. If she boasted that she would surely live long enough to see three grandsons survive her, Death might snatch me away. Always a price would be paid for expecting too much. But Third Uncle, taking his after-noon tea in our crowded kitchen, agreed with the Old One that more sons in Gold Mountain would be use-ful. After all, more family meant even more help in his warehouse, and I, First Son, would learn to be respon-sible for the new offspring. He ahemed to catch my attention. I looked up from my toy puzzle of the Three Bears. Third Uncle adjusted his glasses and grinned.

"My own brother guided me when I was growing up like you, Kiam-Kim." His Toishan dialect fell into a talk-story rhythm. "My *dai-goh* was like a big tiger. Always looking out for me."

Poh-Poh patted me on the head. "Kiam-Kim will grow up smart and become such a tiger."

Father smiled at the thought.

Third Uncle tapped his pipe against his teacup. *Tap, tap! Enough of his tiger brother!* He reached into his briefcase and handed Father bundles of stapled invoices. "Due the end of the month," he said matter-of-factly.

Father plopped the thick wads on his makeshift desk, an old door braced over two filing cabinets.

"Yes, Chen Bak," Poh-Poh said to Third Uncle, returning to the important topic, as if the idea were new to her. "I die soon. My only son and grandson will surely need a *gai-mou*."

Father frowned at the nonsense of Poh-Poh dying soon, but he clearly liked the idea of a *gai-mou*. He also wanted more sons. Third Uncle showed him a small picture.

"Patriarch Chen say this one available," he said. "Papers can be bought right away."

Behind his glasses, Father's eyes lit up.

"Very practical," he agreed.

Knowing that someone besides the Old One would look after things at home, Father explained he would be able take on extra work in the warehouse office, and he might even do some writing for the local papers.

"This new companion not wife," Poh-Poh said, squinting at the small picture in her hand. Her village dialect sounded tense, foreboding. She put down her teacup. "She never-never to take First Wife's place."

"Of course," Father said, pausing to show his respect for the Old One. "No one replace First Wife."

I wanted to see the small photograph, but Third Uncle slipped it back into his thick wallet before I could ask. My heart sank, but I knew to keep my place and stay silent. This was all grown-up business. Father was now recalling how beautiful my mother had been. That made me wonder if the new woman was ugly, so the ghost of my mother would not be jealous.

Grandmother's wrinkled eyes watered at the mention of my mother. I knew what she was thinking.

Many times she had told me how she had held dying Ma-mah in her arms, gently rocking her on a thin mattress, the small head wheezing its last breath against the deep curve of Poh-Poh's neck.

"All at once, your beautiful Ma-mah still and heavy as stone."

I was not yet sixteen months old, and had been napping on the pillow beside the two of them. As the Old One held and rocked my mother's lifeless body, their two heads nodded above me. Grandmother had shouted for Father to come to the inner room, but he was out in the far courtyard gathering winter melons to take into town to barter for medicine and he did not hear the cries that Ma-mah had died. Distracted by the shouting, the chambermaid from Patriarch Chen's compound rushed to the bedroom; the girl witnessed how I had awakened, with my child's eyes opened wide and gazing upwards. Suddenly I began to burble my own childish talk, tiny arms outstretched to touch the still-warm cheeks, as if bobbing Ma-mah's head were conversing with me, her eyes opened as wide as mine.

Before she fainted, the hapless servant girl swore she heard my mother speaking back to me.

This moment remains with me, for it was told to me by Poh-Poh and by Father, who interviewed the poor servant girl, a story told to me as if, by its retelling, what Poh-Poh and the servant girl thought true would remain forever true, that my rightful and only mother had loved me to the end. Her last words were said to me alone, words now locked away in my child's heart, though I would never be able to recall them. And what did I sputter to her? Did my mother smile to hear my babbling? Would she know that this witnessed last moment between us, told to me again and again, would bind me to her for as long as I live? No one, I thought, would ever replace her.

"In the village," Poh-Poh said, "they still tell this story."

Neither the servant girl nor Poh-Poh knew what I might have said or what I might have heard. They dared not guess, lest First Wife return to curse them. But no one in Patriarch Chen's household, not his two sons or three daughters, or the dozen servants, thought the incident unusual. The villagers insisted that Ma-mah had uttered her very last words to me; when I woke up and responded, she must have died in peace. There was proof enough in the year of mourning that followed her death: her spirit never came back to trouble me. But Father had been busy in the garden and came rushing into the bedroom too late. Father sat beside Ma-mah's shrouded body for a whole day and night. On the second afternoon, at Poh-Poh's insistence, he was pulled away by Patriarch Chen's two ox-strong sons.

Months later, at the Old One's insistence, she and Father went to see a village mystic, who said he had glimpsed Ma-mah's frail figure standing at Father's side; she warned him that whoever dared to replace First Wife would become a curse to our family. Shaken by this portent, Poh-Poh urged Father to heed the future.

I had been told my mother had traditional bound feet, so I could imagine, when she was carrying me in her belly, she leaned on Father for support. When I was much older, I overheard Father tell Third Uncle that whenever he missed my mother being with him, he sometimes felt a slight push against his back, even when there was no wind, not even a draft.

Whatever the story about my mother's ghostly presence, we accepted things as they must be. I learned that she had been the Patriarch's gift to Father and to Poh-Poh, as well, who had been a faithful servant to the Chen household for three decades. No one ever spoke of my mother's history. At her death, perhaps because Father and Poh-Poh both loved her so much, she became somehow irreplaceable. The new companion for Father would have no choice but to keep her place: Poh-Poh would see to that.

"No worry," Third Uncle assured her. "The new woman be told she a *gai-mou.*"

A *gai-mou* would never be named an official wife. She was not a concubine either, but a helpmate. She was a false mother, as important as false papers for our survival in Gold Mountain. She would have duties like a wife, and work as hard to help us all survive as a family.

Father told me that this new woman was to be my stepmother, and I was to be as respectful to her as I would have been to Ma-mah, though this new woman could neither be his real wife nor my real mother. Third Uncle added a saying from the *Book of Rites.*

"Of all the virtues," he said, his eyes rolling above the steel rims of his thick glasses, "filial piety is the first."

Father explained its meaning to me. I listened carefully and accepted what I was told. Over Poh-Poh's black tea and the porcelain cups of Tiger Bone wine, the two men went on talking. Father and Third Uncle agreed, and tradition dictated, that the Old One would determine the new companion's family duties.

"It helps," Third Uncle continued, "that this Chen Siu-diep has had over a year of special training in Patriarch Chen's household." That was the first time I had heard Gai-mou's name. I knew that *Siu-Diep* meant "Little Butterfly."

The three of them smiled to hear her formal name mentioned so casually.

"With her special training," Third Uncle continued, "this woman will accept her family position without complaint."

Poh-Poh's face went ashen. (Many years later, at eighty-three, Poh-Poh recalled this moment and told me how the darkness had almost overwhelmed her.) Her thin lips pressed tightly shut; she felt as if her lungs were being crushed. She released a deep sigh, expelling untellable secrets. Third Uncle asked her if anything was wrong.

"I die soon," she said, and laughed to push away his prying concern. "Your stepmother come soon, Kiam-Kim."

She handed over another sugar biscuit for me to dunk into my watered-down tea and praised my sitting so quietly during all their talk. Third Uncle lit up his pipe. The second-floor kitchen was flooded by the late-afternoon sun, and the painted table gleamed with sunlight. I had been thinking of tiger brothers as my nose crinkled at the strong medicinal smell of Tiger

Bone wine. The shingle-mill whistle blasted into the air to announce the beginning of another shift. Poh-Poh brushed back strands of white hair. Seeing how Father dutifully poured her some more tea, I must have felt, with a four-year-old's acceptance of the only universe possible, that all things were as they should be: when Stepmother arrived to join us, we would be a family in Gold Mountain.

Third Uncle hired an elder to write a letter to Patriarch Chen, promising another large donation to the China Mission House in exchange for arranging Chen Siu-diep's arrival in Gold Mountain.

With Father growing more willing and more anxious to live with a new companion, the secretary-treasurer of the Chen Tong Society agreed to be a sworn witness before a government official that the woman named Chen Siu-Diep applying for "re-entry" had been a former resident of the Dominion of Canada.

Such proof for re-entry mattered, for no new Chinese immigrants were allowed into Canada, even though Chinatown still needed more young women to wait on tables and to work the night shifts in the beds of lonely men. These earlier arrivals, the *kay-toi neui,* the stand-at-table girls, were once easily available. But Chinese bachelor men and common labourers were a glut in Chinatown.

By the late 1920s, Vancouver's rooming houses and rooms-by-the-week hotels were overwhelmed by the thousands of labourers left behind by the collapse of the railroad work camps and by those coming back into town from their seasonal jobs in lumber and fishing. I took for granted the voices of men shouting up and down our apartment-hotel building, noisily stomping up the wooden steps in their work boots. Their voices could be heard on our second floor, farther down the hallway, from behind the locked doors of men with enough luck and money to rent a kitchen-room setup. Whenever Poh-Poh and I left our apartment, her obvious age and my shy stares combined to bring respectful greetings from the lips of even the roughest-swearing men. Poh-Poh told me not to repeat the phrases I heard shouted back and forth. She never explained what they meant, but anytime I repeated them in her presence, she knuckled my crown.

Above us on the third floor, Third Uncle told Poh-Poh, many unemployed men took their half-day turns on narrow cots in divided eight- or ten-foot-square spaces separated by paper-thin hardboard walls or by flimsy curtains. Larger beds were sometimes rented and shared in work shifts of two or three men.

"We lucky we have two rooms and kitchen," Poh-Poh told me, when I asked if I could sleep downstairs in one of the rooms directly behind the tailor's shop, alleyway rooms that were separated by curtains. My short legs were tired of climbing up and down the two flights of stairs, though pushing my way to the third floor was always an adventure. I liked to sit on the top step and listen to the many sounds that came down the hallway until Poh-Poh shouted for me.

On weekends, behind-the-doors muffled coughing was drowned out by the voices of younger men shouting and singing, sometimes mixed with the voices and laughter of women. Poh-Poh's face broke into small frowns: this was no place to raise a grandson. She sighed, and must have longed for the quiet of her servants' quarters back in Patriarch Chen's compound. At times, the rattling and spring-squealing of metal cots, which no one bothered to explain to me, combined with the stomping of feet, shook our overhanging ceiling lights. This made Poh-Poh complain, with bent mouth, that the whole raucous population of Chinatown lived above us.

"They all work hard," Father said. "What do you expect?"

When Poh-Poh repeatedly complained about the weekend noise and about the unwashed smells that drifted into the hallways, Third Uncle stepped in to speak with her.

"Few have any family here," he explained. "Some are even too poor to buy a decent meal. These wretches stay in their rooms so the landlord can't lock them out. Others bring them food."

"Too much noise," Poh-Poh grumbled.

But soon she began to soften her anger.

"Noisy ones eat," she told me. "Quiet ones starve."

Many working nights when Father missed coming home for his supper, the Old One knew he would be taking the customary late meal with Third Uncle and his employees at the Pekin restaurant. Left with extra food, and because there was no icebox in our kitchen,

Poh-Poh would huff up to the third floor with a dish in her hand. If I were not too sleepy, I followed her slow ambling in that dimly lit length of squeaking floor-boards, along the row of single rooms numbered in the twenties, long-term rooms occupied by the oldest tenants. When she could hear any muffled hacking or hemming behind a door, she gave it a gentle but persist-ent knock. If the door opened, even a suspicious crack, the swinging bulb inside would make our shadows dance.

"Such a shame to waste this," Poh-Poh would say, and quickly explain to the bent figure peering out at the one-meal dish that she had just reheated how she had cooked too much for her grandson and herself. A hand would reach out.

"Please to eat well, sir," she taught me to say, slowly and clearly. "Then put the plate by first door . . . on second floor."

One morning I heard a tap-tap on our apartment door. I unlatched the hook, but no one was there. Just as Father stepped over me to go to Third Uncle's office, I lifted up three empty dishes.

"I must be rich," he said. "Your Poh-Poh is feed-ing the world."

"Congratulations!" the Chen elders shouted to Third Uncle when they announced the news that a new woman would be officially joining our family. The tong officers patted me on the head, winked at Father, and laughingly spat their approval into spittoons. Third Uncle stuck his thumbs under his new suspenders.

When told the news of Stepmother's approaching arrival from China, Poh-Poh looked scornfully around the walk-up apartment and pushed her kitchen chair back. She knew from our walks and visits to other Chinatown families that there were houses with even bigger rooms along Keefer and East Pender streets, houses in whose comfortable parlours she had begun to play weekly rounds of mahjong. And where I played with other children and ran from room to room to room . . .

"To have three grandsons before I die," Poh-Poh said loudly, "we need a house like other Chinatown families."

Father flinched. He had already signed papers held between Third Uncle and the Chen Society that he would pay back a large portion of their sponsorship expenses. Monthly payments would begin after the second anniversary of our arrival and last for fifteen years. He looked downcast.

"Why not?" Third Uncle said. "Why not live in a house?"

Father shut his eyes; another lifetime of indentured payments rained down upon his shoulders. But Third Uncle did not hesitate.

"No worry," he said to Father, shaking his shoulder. "You be my family now."

That was true. The birth certificate and immigration documents that Father had used to come to Canada once belonged to Third Uncle's dead brother. Dates had been doctored, of course, to fit Father's age and circumstance, and the brother's embossed picture had been expertly lifted off and carefully replaced with one of Father's. Poh-Poh and I had separate sets of false papers made for us, and all these *gai-gee,* these ghost papers, bonded us as Third Uncle's Gold Mountain family.

Father and Poh-Poh honoured this paper relationship, but Father thought Third Uncle had done quite enough on our behalf. Only Poh-Poh did not think so, and she had the nerve to say this aloud.

"We should have house," she said directly to Third Uncle. "You want more nephews, Chen Bak?"

Father started to say something to stop the Old One from speaking, but it was hopeless. The summer air was sulphurous, tainted by smog. Some freight cars thundered by. Father looked out the window as if lightning might strike him dead.

Third Uncle enjoyed the fact that his paper brother did not take anything for granted. Third Uncle told others that he felt that Father would never exploit the situation. There were those agreements Father had signed, promising to pay back certain expenses; in fact, he had put away some salary to do just that. Third Uncle was impressed by Father's resolve. Poh-Poh was not. She had been thinking of his recent savings, too.

"Use money for house rent," she told Father. To Third Uncle she said, "I work for you, Chen Bak. When Kiam-Kim go to school, I come work for you. Clean your rooms. Cook and wash for you."

"Me, too," I said, catching the spirit.

Third Uncle smiled at our earnestness. He had not made a mistake bringing us to Gold Mountain. His paper family knew their place.

Before the end of our first year living in that second-floor walk-up, Father and Third Uncle came into the kitchen to announce that we would be moving into a two-storey house on Keefer Street, five blocks east of Main Street, and seven blocks away from the noise and smells of False Creek. And I would soon have my fifth birthday in a house with rooms to run in.

The house belonged to the Chen Society. In exchange for a low rent, half the amount to be subsidized by Third Uncle, Father had also to agree to take on the job of the Chen Society's monthly rent collector, as well as to record their list of membership loans and accounts.

"Everyone work hard in Gold Mountain," Third Uncle said. "No worry."

Poh-Poh and Third Uncle encouraged Father to think of the future. In October, when Stepmother would finally arrive from China, she would walk into a pine-board house with three bedrooms on the second floor and with front and back windows that looked onto a bit of property. Third Uncle said he would see that the house was furnished.

"Never mind all that," Poh-Poh interrupted him. "Make sure Gai-mou's ghost papers not cursed."

If ghost papers came from a suicide, or were inherited from a family member who had suffered tragedies, wise people hired monks to exorcise the bad spirits, or risked taking on the ill fortune of others. If the big-nosed immigration demons had been aware, they could have sniffed out the truth, for such papers were deeply perfumed with the lemony smell of ghost-chasing incense.

"You sure papers not haunted," Poh-Poh said again.

"Yes."

"Make sure she bear sons."

"Tell that to him," Third Uncle said, pointing to Father.

"Never mind, Kiam-Kim," Father said, grinning for no reason that I could see. "Just a joke."

"Buy strong bed," Poh-Poh said, poking Third Uncle in the ribs. His pipe went flying. The two broke into laughter. Poh-Poh couldn't stop herself. "Aiiiyah! Buy small bed for me; *big* bed for Gai-mou!"

Third Uncle enjoyed the Old One's cajoling him to do the right things; he felt important, capable. He repeated again that Patriarch Chen had said the woman was twenty years old, healthy enough to fulfill Yook Mai-dang's wish—that is, Poh-Poh's wish—that my new stepmother be strong enough to bear sons. Father was more than ten years older, as he should be, a man of some maturity. It was a perfect match: there would be plenty of sons.

"You soon have two tiger brother," Poh-Poh told me. "And Madame Jing tell me I live to see Number Three Grandson!"

Three was a lucky number, the Old One explained to me, especially where the birth of sons was concerned. In Old China, one boy child, even two boys, might suffer an early death, but surely the gods would not be so cruel as to cut down a third son.

"Two more brother for you, Kiam-Kim," Poh-Poh said, chortling away with Third Uncle. "I boil water."

"This woman will take care of you, Kiam-Kim," Father added. "And she will work with Poh-Poh."

Poh-Poh bowed humbly, lowering her white head. "I die soon," she said matter-of-factly.

She had also spoken those three words before the Tong elders, and they quickly bowed back, their voices rising to waylay the bony hand of death. "No, no, you surely outlive us!"

Everyone laughed. Outside, the B.C. Lumber Mill whistle blasted into the air. Shifts of working men were moving in and out of buildings and factories, tramping into Chinatown cafés and restaurants to dine on cheap meals, or with a numbered chit in hand to pick up their laundry packages. The noise of these labourers barely pierced the thick walls of the main Tong building, built like an Old China temple with a curving roof.

Poh-Poh and Father had come in here to light incense before the sacred gods, to show our gratitude for all that had been given us. After I had made proper bows to each of the five elders, we walked out of the meeting room. At the end of the front hall, Father opened wide two large dragon-carved doors and stepped into the dimly lit assembly hall. At the far end stood a curtained platform with a low curving roof painted bright, lucky red. Long calligraphy scrolls hung down the two side walls. In front of the curtains Father took off his hat and lit two thick candles. Then he yanked on a rope.

Suddenly the fierce God of War, Kwan Kung, towered over me. Three other smaller gods stood behind

Kwan Kung; they gleamed like living beings. Instead of *bai sen,* bowing, I darted behind Poh-Poh's floppy black pants and hid my face. Father and Poh-Poh lowered their heads and mumbled some words.

Dragging me out of the assembly hall, Poh-Poh said, "Gai-mou teach you not to be afraid."

"You teach Kiam," Father said to her. "Tell him your village stories."

Poh-Poh looked disapprovingly at me. Her eyes seemed to say I had better start figuring things out, and her lips mouthed words already familiar to my ears. I repeated them aloud.

"Poh-Poh die soon!"

"No, no," Father said, caught off guard by my audacity. "She live as long as Gai-mou live!"

Poh-Poh, silent as stone, took my hand as Father began to pull shut the big doors to the assembly hall. I quickly looked back. On the temple platform, the two candles burned like tiger eyes. But from this distance, I now could tell they were only candles and stiff statues. This was something I would tell my new stepmother: candles and statues were *just* candles and statues. Nothing more.

"When does Stepmother come?" I asked. "Is she pretty to look at?"

"Grandson, if you be lucky," Poh-Poh said, and pinched my cheek as her voice tightened into a burst of anger, "cross-eyed, pock-cheeked Gai-mou may come . . . *before you die.*"

A dragon door swung towards my face. This dragon was vividly painted, its silvery scales carved so deeply that the crescent shadows shimmered. The bulging head with its sharp teeth seemed to plunge towards my neck. The Death Dragon had come for me! At my look of sudden shock, Poh-Poh yanked me aside until the two huge doors slammed shut.

I felt no relief: the vision of an ugly, pock-faced stepmother hung stubbornly in my head.

In 1928, when I was over five and a half—*six* in Chinese years—and could help Father put away his shoes and stand tiptoe high up on a stool to hang up his coat on the hall hook in our Keefer Street house, and even help Poh-Poh in the kitchen by using a wooden box to reach the lowest pantry shelf, the news came at last that Gai-mou was arriving from Hong Kong in three weeks on the *Empress of Asia*.

I had been attending a kindergarten class in the United Church basement on Dunlevy and could now speak English sentences. At least, I could speak better than half the children there who spoke no English at all. Some jabbered away in such mysterious languages that even Miss Lowe's best English could not reach them with the simplest of requests like "Sit down!" Their broad faces would turn away until she gestured at her own bum, wiggled, and then sat down. We all sat down.

I had told our neighbours' boy, Jack O'Connor, that my new mother was coming to stay with us. Jack was bigger than me, but I didn't think he was as smart: he couldn't speak a word of Chinese.

"What's wrong with your old mother?"

I knew he meant my Poh-Poh.

"I have *new* mother," I said.

His blue eyes said, *So what!* I didn't know why he wasn't impressed; he himself had only one mother to talk about.

"You're a big fat liar," he said.

I told Poh-Poh that Jack wouldn't believe that Stepmother was coming.

"What!"

Poh-Poh was shocked that I had mentioned anything to our neighbours' boy. She barely acknowledged the O'Connors' existence, barely recognized any of the other pale-skinned outsiders, the *lo-faan,* that shared the ragged Keefer Street boundaries of our ghettoed Chinatown. To her Old China eyes, they were all the same: white barbarian ghosts with big noses and funny names like *Oh-kan-nagh.*

The wives of the tong elders had told her the history of white brutes in 1907 yanking the braided queues of the first elders and kicking them down Hastings Street, their white hands bashing Chinese heads and tearing down the shops and laundries of Chinatown. She also knew the kindness of some white faces, of those few who tended the sick of Chinatown, but they were church people, like the China Mission House *lo-faan,* a rare breed of white foreigners who could sometimes speak perfect Cantonese. Then there were those others, so many of them in China, those white foreigners selling opium and taking away Chinese territory.

It was a history that Poh-Poh tried to pass along to me. I listened, but still could not see anything bad in the *lo-faan* that came my way in kindergarten. Even Poh-Poh relented and thought *lo-faan* Jack could play with me. She had accepted that children were not yet like their parents, but would soon grow up and prove their roots to be from one or another kind of tree.

"White come from white tree," Poh-Poh warned me. "Chinese come from Chinese tree."

"White belong to white tree," Third Uncle explained. "Chinese belong Chinese." He also told me about cherries belonging to cherry trees, and oranges to orange trees.

Now I looked carefully at Jack's mother and father. I decided Jack's mother belonged to a bitter tree. Thin-lipped Mrs. O'Connor rarely smiled, but Mr. O'Connor would at least say something about the weather. If they happened to meet, both our fathers would smile and tip their hats and chat for a few moments. They must have come from the same tree.

"Looks like rain," Mr. O'Connor would say.

"Yes, yes," Father would answer. "Rain like yesterday."

Courtesy mattered, Father told me. After all, our neighbours were here long before we Chinese moved up this far east on Keefer. All these rows of pine-box houses, Father explained, were built by white carpenters. He had been reading picture books about Vancouver and showed me the funny people in cowboy hats. There was a time when nearly every Keefer Street house was occupied by an Irish family or by white people who spoke no English at all. But I didn't care about history lessons. "Why is Poh-Poh mad at me for talking about Stepmother?"

"What did you tell little Jack?"

I hesitated. Poh-Poh picked up her chopsticks. Using my best English so that only Father would understand, I half whispered, *"I tell him my new mother coming."*

Before I could stop him, Father translated my words. And before Father could stop her, Poh-Poh's chopsticks snapped, stinging, against my head. The voice grew stern and hard:

"Tell white ears nothing!"

I bit my lip. Father patiently explained to me that white people did not understand Chinese ways. In English, I should refer to Gai-mou as Stepmother.

"Say nothing more," he continued. "Say nothing about our being Third Uncle's paper family."

"Not one word," Poh-Poh stressed. "Or we go back to China on next boat. Starve to death in China!"

I knew that many people in China were starving; that was why I was always told how lucky I was to be able to eat up every grain of rice, how fortunate to be able to chew up every morsel of black-bean chicken and swallow every piece of leafy green.

The next time I saw Jack, he had a few more things to say.

"My mother says Chinamen can have as many mothers as they want, like Solomon the Jew."

I had no idea what any of those words meant. I sensed he, too, had no idea what he was saying. We both shrugged, knelt down, and went on with our serious game of road building.

Having stood for a week watching trucks of all kinds widening Keefer Street with cobblestones and cement, Jack came up with make-believe construction trucks of his own. He showed me how he used the chunks of waste wood that Mr. O'Connor had cleaned out from one of the freight cars to burn in their fireplace. The half-dozen wooden blocks plowed imaginary roads for us, and the triangular ones made zigzag furrows in the small mixed piles of dirt and cement dust. Clouds rose into the air, inspiring Little Jack and me to make louder and louder engine roars. We bellowed out our version of truck horns until we grew hoarse. The thick greyish dust drifted down and clung to our damp faces.

Standing at our front door to call me in to wash up for supper, Father shouted to Poh-Poh in the kitchen that he thought that he was looking at two *lo-faan* boys playing down on the sidewalk. For a moment, he laughingly told the Old One, he wondered where I had gone to.

"I'm here," I shouted, using my English words.

Jack took back the blocks of wood. His mother was stiffly calling for him to come into the house.

With a face as grim and bitter as Mrs. O'Connor's, Poh-Poh threw Father a wet towel to wash me off.

"Not funny," she snapped.

As the Old One stomped back into the kitchen, I struggled against the impossible thought that Poh-Poh and Mrs. O'Connor must have come from the same tree. I pushed away Father's hand and took the wet rag from him to wipe my own hands. The cloth was streaked with dirt, but I hardly cared that Poh-Poh would complain about it. Instead, I kept asking myself what kind of tree would Stepmother be from?

That Saturday afternoon, Third Uncle stopped my outside play and sent me back into the house to tell Father the taxi had arrived to take us to the harbour.

"I'll get the Old One," he said, and called Poh-Poh to come away from the kitchen, where she had been plating sweetmeats and special dumplings to welcome Gai-mou to her new home.

I found Father upstairs standing before his bed, busy with the new bedsheets. Finally, he used his knees to push against the large mattress to straighten everything. I was surprised at how his hand lingered for a long moment over the embroidered pillow that peeped out from the bedspread. When I called to him, he stepped away from the bed and gestured for me to stand beside him. A nod of his head directed me to look at my mother's bamboo-framed picture sitting on the bedside table. Her hair in a tight bun, she had a very pretty girl's face.

"Tell your Ma-mah you will never forget her, Kiam-Kim."

"I never to forget you, Ma-mah," I said, and brushed the picture with my fingers, just as gently as Father had done. He quickly slipped the frame between some silk robes lying in the opened trunk. Just as the heavy lid slammed shut, I noticed Father's eyes were rimmed with tears. His pupils were stinging, as mine were, from the sudden jolt from the camphor in envelopes scattered throughout the trunk to keep away the moths.

Father cleared his throat. "Time to meet Gai-mou." He took my hand, and we walked outside and got into the taxi. Poh-Poh, in her embroidered jacket, was already sitting in the back seat; Third Uncle was beside the driver, listening to the purr of the engine. I shuffled over and sat on Poh-Poh's lap. She commented that I was much too skinny for a six-year-old.

"*Five,*" I said, correcting her with my Canada years. Next year I would go into first grade with Jack O'Connor.

Third Uncle turned to speak but something stopped him. Over my head, the Old One handed Father a folded-up red handkerchief; he blotted his eyes.

"Soot," he said.

I bit my lip, disappointed: Poh-Poh did not even think about my camphor-stung vision, nor did she care about the soot that gritted my eyes, too.

"CPR docks," Third Uncle said to the driver. "Pier A."

My legs tensed, restless with excitement. Third Uncle held up a small photo for me to see.

"This your new *gai-mou,*" he said to me. "Remember how to greet her."

I was seeing Stepmother's picture at last. A small face boldly stared back at me. I was delighted. There were no crossed eyes or pocked cheeks, just as Father had promised me: Gai-mou's head-and-shoulder picture looked fine to me. Maybe even prettier than my mother's small-faced one. I liked her long hair, and the shy smile.

"Enough gawking," Poh-Poh said and poked my cheek.

Father refolded the handkerchief and returned it. I pushed myself back to cross my legs as Father did. Pushed again to get more room.

Poh-Poh knuckled my head. "Sit still, Kiam-Kim."

I did.

The taxi sped up, humming with all our thoughts. To the right of us suddenly appeared the huge hulls of ships and swooping gulls; between the bobbing vessels, rising across miles of cloud-reflecting waves, loomed the North Shore mountains. The air tasted of salt and smelled of tar. Someone was sniffing. I looked up: in the small frame of the rear-view mirror, the Old One dabbed at her eyes. The soot was bad today.

When I first saw the tall, thin woman walking towards us beside Third Uncle , Poh-Poh reminded me, yet again, "This person your father's companion, Kiam-Kim. This not your mother. This to be your *gai-mou.*"

Father took one of the suitcases from Third Uncle, who said, "This is *Chen Siu-Diep.*"

"Your Stepmother Chen," Father said to me.

The planks on the dock dipped and bobbed beneath my feet. Gulls darted into the waves for scraps. Amid the quaking of the boardwalk and the cries of the birds, everyone exchanged formalities, and I bowed politely, three times, to Stepmother. She bowed back.

The tall lady then bowed to Father. He shook her silk-gloved hand and repeated her formal name—

Chen Siu-Diep. Poh-Poh studied her carefully, her eyes unwavering. The dark prow of the overnight ferry made everyone look small. Crowds of people were greeting each other, calling out names in every language.

Before the Old One, my new Stepmother bent her head even lower. Three times. In her wind-blown, long, dark coat with its China-style frog buttons, Gai-mou looked slim and lovely. She turned away from Poh-Poh and bent down towards me. Above the noise of the squawking harbour gulls, she said words I barely could hear.

"This . . . for you, Kiam-Kim."

Gai-mou put a *lei-see,* a lucky red envelope, in my hand. I tipped it open right away. Out slipped a tiny butterfly of Chinese silver, its pair of engraved wings no larger than two pennies. "Can you say my name?" Her Toishan tones were soft, unlike Grandmother's often abrupt sounds, and her voice was sweet.

"Siu-Diep," I said, making my own voice even softer.

"Means 'Little Butterfly,'" Third Uncle said, as if I didn't know. "Very pretty."

"Hold it tight," said Poh-Poh, bristling, her voice loud and as abrupt as ever. "Like this."

I tightened my fist.

Stepmother stood up, and Father shyly took her by the elbow and guided her towards the waiting taxi. People with rolling carts of luggage pushed by them.

Third Uncle Chen looked very pleased, and after saying "Be happy" and waving goodbye to us, he took another taxi to go back to Chinatown to check on the menu for tonight's welcoming dinner at the Pekin. There would be eight tables, seating ten each, he had proudly told Father. The Chen elders, important associates of Third Uncle, and many of his new friends had accepted, including six of Poh-Poh's mahjong ladies, and our neighbour, big Mrs. Lim. Poh-Poh refused to let me ask Jack O'Connor to join us. There would be other children there, she said, like the Yip Sang children, the Chongs and Kees. "Yes, yes, lots of *Chinese* children to play with!"

Third Uncle's taxi drove away. At last, we, too, were headed home.

I sat between the two women at the back and Father sat beside the driver, giving instructions. Stepmother's trunk needed to be picked up at the landing for another customs inspection. She had been, for almost three weeks, languishing in the Customs House in Victoria, which everyone called the human isolation coop, the Pig Pen—the *Gee-ook*—patiently waiting for her official clearance to come into Vancouver. She did not mind me staring at her, wondering, thinking my thoughts.

When the taxi finally turned south, crossing the familiar streets of Hastings and Pender and then turning east on Keefer, a pain started to throb in my hand. The silver butterfly had impressed its shape into my palm. Stepmother looked down.

"I'm happy you like it," she said to me.

"Say thank-you," Poh-Poh said to me, suddenly in her most formal and soft Cantonese tones.

I looked up at the beautiful woman and said, "Thank you, Gai-mou."

Stepmother bowed her head. She was so much prettier than any lady we knew in Chinatown.

Grandmother shifted herself and made me hop onto her lap and sit still. I held my palm out for her old eyes to study the delicate curve of the wings, as if they were poised to take flight.

"This more for a girl," Poh-Poh said, and lifted the silver butterfly from my hand. "I take care of this."

If the piece were more for a girl, and Father did not turn his head or raise his voice to contradict the Old One, I knew protest was futile. I stuffed my empty palm into my pants pocket and sank back, jiggling on Poh-Poh's bony knees as she shifted with the movement of the taxicab. Why didn't Chen Siu-Diep give me a silver dragon? Or a tiger? Those were fierce animals made for tough boys. I tried not to sulk. I tried to show respect.

Poh-Poh asked Stepmother to pass over to me the documents she had carried with her from Canton. Gai-mou slipped a long brown envelope, folded in half, out of her handbag.

I remember the dark-coloured papers sticking out of the opening as she let the envelope fall into my hand, its weight a thousand times the weight of the butterfly. Poh-Poh took it away as quickly as she had lifted the silver amulet.

"These your Ma-mah's documents, Kiam-Kim," Poh-Poh told me, putting the package into Father's reaching hands. She looked at Father. "Belong always to First Wife."

Stepmother quietly closed up her purse and looked straight ahead at her new world, at the distant mountain slopes across Burrard Inlet, and to our right, at the warehouses and buildings with their mysterious signs.

Father and the taxi driver carried the three suitcases into the house. The trunk would later be delivered by one of Third Uncle's friends, who had a small van. Far away from the harbour, and five blocks away from False Creek, here the air was sweetened from the last roses in the O'Connors' front yard.

Stepmother looked up at our pine-board house, so unlike the red-brick buildings surrounding Patriarch Chen's courtyard. Fearful of some misunderstanding of his situation, Father explained to Gai-mou how we rented this house from the Chen Tong Society, and how Third Uncle helped. He offered his hand and helped Stepmother out of the taxi.

She followed Father up the front steps, across the porch, and through the front door. I caught a glimpse of a scarf of pale silk fluttering from her shoulder.

The Old One looked disgruntled: she should have been the first to follow Father into the house.

Stepmother found things confusing at first, though Mr. Ben and Mrs. Annah Chong came to her rescue many times. The couple ran a corner store at Princess and Keefer, two blocks east of us, and Poh-Poh had known their elderly cousin back in a Toishan village.

Mrs. Chong made it a point to drop by between her visits to wholesalers on East Hastings Street. She did most of the ordering for their store. Ben Chong did the books and stood by the cash and watched over their daughter Jenny, who was my age.

The majority of those who settled early in Vancouver's Chinatown came from the same Sze-yup, Four County village district, or spoke related dialects from the Sam-yup, Three County areas, closer to Canton and were therefore considered superior members of Chinatown. Everyone seemed to know someone in Old China who knew someone else closely related to them.

Poh-Poh helped Stepmother to quickly settle in with a group of ladies who, like Poh-Poh, loved to play mahjong. "Get to know others this way," Mrs. Pan Wong told her. "Get to know everyone!" They showed her how Vancouver ladies dressed for different occasions and gave her dresses they no longer fit. They oooohed over Stepmother's slim hips, and their laughing husbands made remarks about Father being seen leaving work earlier than usual to rush home—with Third Uncle's blessings.

As they had done for Poh-Poh, the mahjong ladies gradually introduced Stepmother to everything knowable in *Tohng-Yahn Gaai,* China-People Street—or at least as much as the women were permitted to know. They told her she would soon not notice the bad smells from the mills and refineries when she came into town. Soon she would not even hear the banging trains and whistles. Part of life, they said. Canton and Hong Kong were far worse.

"Buy meat here," Mrs. Annah Chong advised her, pointing to the open counter of Chong Lung's Meat Market. "My cousin never cheat you."

"Fresh vegetables," Mrs. Sui Leong sang out, "best to buy in the morning at Keefer Market."

Mrs. Pan Wong named the best tailors in town, but suggested how clothes were cheaper to buy at American Steam Cleaners. "Left-behind clothes best buy."

The Chinatown clothing, dry goods, and grocery stores were often musty from ceiling-high bales of English cloth and China silks, or pungent with sharp odours of ginger root and herbs and dried shrimp. Carved hardwood-handled scoops crunched into eye-level barrels filled with rice and grains. The scoops made *zzzzz* sounds and spilled their contents onto curving copper pans that hung on balances and swayed like floating sampans above my head.

In Ming Wo, the long, dark counter stretched beyond me. Oak casks of vinegars and soy and wine sat around me like steps, and I stuck out my foot to mount them.

"Don't climb," I was told by one storekeeper. "This morning a boy just like you drowned in a vat of my best liquor!" As proof, he lifted up a small open-tongued shoe tied to the lid. "His mother pay lots of money for damages."

Stepmother sighed, but not as deeply for the drowned boy as for me: I had forgotten my manners.

"Shoe for cats to play with," Poh-Poh told me later. "Cats keep away mice."

Poh-Poh's complaining voice dominated those shopping trips. Later, when I was old enough, she told me how useless it was to argue prices with the Gold Mountain merchants, so unlike the way things were done in Old China. Winning no monetary advantage, she admitted to anyone who would listen how hard it was for an Old Head to get used to new ways. But Stepmother told me Poh-Poh always managed to buy the choicest cut of pork, the fattest chicken, or the last clear-eyed fish in the pail. We ate well.

That year, Third Uncle's stock-and-bond investments had doubled in value. He gave Father an increase in salary.

"You know my accounts," he boasted to Father. "I buy another warehouse with no problem. No worry."

Poh-Poh looked up, fearful that the gods had heard such arrogant talk.

Within a year, our household had found its rhythm. Poh-Poh could lie longer in bed after Father left for work. And Stepmother, already trained from Patriarch Chen's service, did the housework without complaint. Father worked later and later at the warehouse, and I started first grade at Strathcona School. But even though my schooling interested Father, everyone in the family, as well as Third Uncle and the mahjong ladies whenever they visited us, began to turn their focus on Stepmother. She had fainted one afternoon, and had been throwing up in the mornings. Poh-Poh did not take her naps, but kept an eye on Stepmother.

Even big Mrs. Lim, almost as old as Poh-Poh, crossed the street every other day from her rock-perched shack, bringing soups, a mix of boiled herbs and greens to feed Stepmother, she said, to help balance the wind-water humours that seemed to trouble Gai-mou's digestion. For months Gai-mou needed special foods. Poh-Poh told me it was hard for some people's digestive tract to adjust to Gold Mountain water. That seemed true to me, for Stepmother soon grew very big in her tummy and was often sick in bed.

"Soon she be better," Mrs. Lim told me. "Be patient."

"New baby soon," Jack told me, throwing back his blond head as if in great agony and slapping his puffed-up tummy. "Pops out of the belly button."

Jenny Chong was with us that day. She was our age, but pretended she knew so much more than we could know.

"Not from the belly button!" she said. "From the pee-pee!"

I missed the event by sleeping through the whole night. After the girl baby was born, I thought Stepmother would now be a real mother. But she was still to be called Stepmother.

Poh-Poh had heard the church bells ringing during the first morning of the baby's birth. The church people helped the poor in Chinatown.

"Listen," the Old One said, bending her ear to hear better. "Good sign."

And so the chimes partly inspired my sister's birth name, Jook-Liang, "Jade Bell." Father told me the last sound, *liang,* could also mean "bracelet," the name Stepmother herself had desired, Jade Bracelet.

Whether "Bell" or "Bracelet," or both, even baby sister would be raised to call her own mother Stepmother.

Poh-Poh was our family elder, and Stepmother was expected to remember her place as a *gai-mou* in the family; otherwise, Stepmother was warned again and again by Poh-Poh and Third Uncle, First Wife's ghost would take her revenge upon the family. Father did not protest, but some days I saw him pacing back and forth, wringing his hands.

"Say nothing," Mrs. Lim told him. "Let Poh-Poh handle things."

And so she did.

"We lucky to be family here," Poh-Poh said to Stepmother at the one-month birthday dinner Father held at home for the birth of his daughter. The birth was considered a *siu hay,* a little joy, and not the *dai hay,* the great joy a boy baby would have inspired. Poh-Poh sighed. "No one starve here," she said, which meant that we did not have to get rid of the girl child, as was done in Old China. The Old One looked confident. "Next baby be boy child."

Stepmother nudged Jook-Liang closer to her breast.

When Third Uncle was finishing his supper with us in the dining room one evening, and Stepmother was upstairs breast-feeding Liang, I asked Father why Gai-mou sometimes wept at night. Even when she was so tired, why did she clutch at the little baby and seem so reluctant to surrender her to Poh-Poh? Father ignored me.

"Why?" I pestered.

The tears of others had always provoked my curiosity.

"Tell," Third Uncle said, and sucked at his unlit pipe.

"Why not?" Poh-Poh said. She stopped piling up some plates and sat quietly. "Tell First Son."

All this I recall, because for years thereafter, Poh-Poh would remind me of the day that I first understood how certain ghosts had pursued her from Old China. Father shifted uneasily. What, after all, might a six-year-old properly understand?

As if to keep Stepmother, who was still upstairs, from hearing a word, Father lowered his voice. I bent my head towards him.

"Gai-mou knows that a poor family in China, one just as poor as her own family had been, would have snatched baby Jook-Liang from her, and the tiny thing would have been quickly sold or given away to another family. And you, Kiam-Kim, would never have known that she had once been your sister."

"Never?"

"She would never have been given a name," Third Uncle said. "And without a name, she did not exist."

"*Aaaiyaah!*" Poh-Poh interrupted. She looked at the two men before she decided to speak further. "And if baby unlucky, someone palm her mouth and clamp her tiny nostrils. *Like this.*"

My eyes widened as the Old One's palm pressed against her own wrinkled mouth, and her gnarled thumb and slender forefinger pinched shut her nostrils.

"And then?" I asked.

Poh-Poh's black pupils rolled up into her head, and a huge gasp escaped from her.

"Baby die," she said.

I jumped off my seat and ran to Poh-Poh's side. She shifted her knee and let me jump up. A blood-thirsty thrill electrified me.

"Show me how," I said.

Poh-Poh had just raised her palm over my mouth when Father slammed his fist on the kitchen table. The plates rattled.

"Let him know," Poh-Poh commanded. "Life is bitter and hard."

"No!" Father shouted. "This is Gold Mountain. Not necessary for Kiam-Kim to know such things!"

Poh-Poh pushed me off her knee.

It was the only time I had ever heard Father raise his voice against the Old One. Third Uncle started to say something but decided to keep quiet when he heard Stepmother coughing and starting down the stairs. When she stepped into the kitchen, looking famished for her share of dinner, Poh-Poh was piling up the empty dishes. Third Uncle lit his pipe as if nothing had happened. Father looked sternly at me to keep quiet.

I kept quiet.

Stepmother looked too exhausted to notice that anything was out of sorts. "Jook-Liang is sleeping at last," she said.

Father signalled me to offer Stepmother my chair. I jumped off the seat to help clear away the used dishes.

"I bring you hot soup," Poh-Poh said. "Take this, Kiam-Kim."

When I took the large serving plate from her old hand, I wondered at the long finger and scarred thumb, the way they pressed so firmly against the plate's edge. I wondered at Father's scowling face that suddenly turned away from the Old One to look so tenderly at Stepmother in her plain dress. He got up and pulled the chair back for her and pushed it in as she sat down. His ink-stained fingers brushed aside wisps of her hair that had trailed across her damp forehead. The sweet aroma of Poh-Poh's thick, meaty stock drifted in from the kitchen. Stepmother took a deep breath.

"Very good soup," Father said to her. "The Old One make you blood-strengthening oxtail soup."

"Excellent soup for women," Third Uncle said. He puffed at his pipe and shouted in the direction of the kitchen: "Very fine dinner tonight."

Father sent me into the kitchen to help. I could see Poh-Poh had pricked up her ears to hear every word of praise. It was my turn to say something to the Old One, such as "Thank you for the good food," but so many thoughts tumbled through my head that I, instead, silently studied the Old One rushing about, watching as she shuttled plates into the sink. Then, with a deft finger and thumb curving around the bamboo ladle, the same finger and thumb that made Father shout at her, she swiftly poured simmering broth into Stepmother's bowl. My blatant staring at her hand, at the open palm that lifted the porcelain bowl like a baby's head, lifting without spilling a drop, must have trapped her between thoughts.

"Grandson," she said, and staggered against the sink. "Ghosts have followed me here."

As she squeezed her eyes to shut in the tears, pausing a moment before we would step back into the dining room, I somehow understood what the Old One had meant: *life was bitter and hard.* Taking my own small steps beside her, I stared at the steaming blue bowl, the hot blood-strengthening liquid swaying inches above my head.

"Are we poor?" I asked.

Third Uncle laughed. "Not yet."

Here in Salt Water City, he explained, we had a pine-board home with running tap water, a metal stove that ate logs in its grated mouth, and enough dried food stored away in a deep pantry for a month of eating. "No worry," he said. "We keep your baby sister."

In *Hahm-sui-fauh,* Mrs. Lim told me, hardly any girl babies were abandoned, though quite a few were sold to merchant families to be raised as servants, or were traded for a boy baby who would be a greater joy for the adopting family, or—if undesirable and ugly—would be given away, like the children given away by white people. In this city, and in New Westminster, and even Victoria, there were buildings that warehoused hundreds of such children.

Stepmother, too, must have been fretting. She consulted Third Uncle. He told her of his arrangements with the elders of the Chen Tong Society that he himself would see to any additional expenses the girl baby might entail; for sure, he said, our family would keep Jook-Liang. Third Uncle laughed at her Old China fears. Still, all that first month of Liang's life, I remember how Stepmother clutched on to her girl baby as if nothing would separate them.

"No worry," Poh-Poh assured her. "Gold Mountain not like Old China."

Third Uncle expected a boy child, but like Father he did not mind the first being a girl. Uncle wiped his wire-rimmed glasses and told me that Baby Jook-Liang and I must remember how to refer to each other in Chinese, because we were Chinese. Little Sister soon was called Liang-Liang, which meant "Beautiful Bell." In English, however, everything would be made simpler if we matched all our *gai-gee,* our false documents. That was why Liang-Liang would call her own mother Gai-mou: we would fool the demon immigration spies, who would otherwise deport us back to China.

"Remember that in this country of white demons we are undesirables—*Chinks,*" Third Uncle said, "but we are, in fact, a superior people."

Father quoted a Chinese poet and spoke of the Middle Kingdom being "a country as old as sorrow."

That made me think that no one ever laughed in Old China. I was glad to be in Canada.

"Kiam-Kim, never forget, *ney hai Tohng-Yahn,*" Father said. "Never forget, you are Chinese."

The way Father stared proudly at Third Uncle, who was showing me large picture books with ancient

Chinese temples, and the way they both turned to study each page, telling me tales of monks who could snap steel rods and smash stone boulders with their bare hands, made me sit up straight in my chair. Even Stepmother looked up at me from her breast-feeding, as if it would be impossible, if not madness, to be other than *tong-yung*.

"Baby be Chinese, too," she said. "*Tohng-Yahn* is best."

I looked at her feeding Liang-Liang and reasoned that if, instead of having given me a skimpy butterfly when we first met, she had put into my palm a silver dragon with five claws, or even a tiger with fierce eyes, a great joy would now be sucking at her breast. And Father and Third Uncle would have lit firecrackers. Poh-Poh would have demanded Third Uncle pay for a first-class banquet at W.K. instead of dinner at the Pekin. From a red baby's cap would dangle countless gold trinkets; twice the number of red-dyed eggs would sit on our best dishes, and many more pink-dotted dumplings for many more guests. My lip curled.

"Kiam-Kim?" Stepmother beckoned to me. She shifted Jook-Liang onto her knees. "Would Big Brother like to hold her?"

I quickly realized that it was useless to keep wishing the girl baby would go away. I finally got used to stroking the brown eggshell forehead and pushing the rubber pacifier between the tiny cupid lips to keep her quiet.

"Gently," Stepmother said to me.

I tried again. Baby fingers grasped my thumb and held on tightly.

"See how she likes First Son," Father said.

I pushed away from the cradle. With so much to discover in my own world, I did not mind sharing Poh-Poh and Stepmother with her. Father spent as much time as he could with me, and when he came home early he always gave me his hat to hang up on the small hook beside my own coat. In the beginning, the two of us would go for walks before the darkness came. But soon, as he took on more part-time work in the restaurants and warehouses of Chinatown, helped Third Uncle and other merchants with their invoices and accounts, studied English books in the Carnegie Library, and worked on his English with the minister from the United Church, Father was rarely at home when I was awake. Arrangements were made: other men and women, kindly acquaintances of Third Uncle, mostly elders, took me out for walks. Father taught me to recite their proper names while standing at attention; I mimicked appropriate greetings with a bow and learned how to accept small red-enveloped gifts of lucky money without rudely opening them to peep at the contents.

"Too generous," Poh-Poh would protest on my behalf.

"Too kind," Stepmother would instantly say as I held the *lei-see* in my hands for a respectful few seconds and lowered my head before another tall or squat newcomer to our house. Father was pleased to hear that I was considered polite and smart and gave others the pleasure of recalling their family life in Old China.

Poh-Poh had taught me to feel with my fingertips during the exchange of lucky money and my humble thanks, to discover whether coins or crinkly bills sat inside the red folds of the *lei-see*. She said this would help me resist tearing open the flap. It was a trick she had taught the grandchildren of Patriarch Chen himself.

"Lowly children," Poh-Poh said. "All girls."

I didn't care. I wanted to know what were the consequences if my fingers felt a coin or a bill. Poh-Poh laughed at my impatience. A ten- or twenty-five-cent coin meant I might keep it in my own piggy bank. A fifty-cent coin or any folding money meant Father or Stepmother took the *lei-see* from me.

"For your education," I would hear them say.

Of course, to open any *lei-see* in front of guests was very rude and would expose my lack of manners. Worse, Stepmother warned me, whoever gave me a coin, however generous, would feel that they had *suk-mein*, lost face, in front of anyone else who might have slipped me folding money.

"Father would lose face, too," she said. "Guests would shake their heads and say, 'What an impatient and greedy First Son!'"

"Yes, yes," Poh-Poh chimed in. "People would say, 'Has this greedy grandson of yours *mo li*—no manners?'"

The world, I discovered, was filled with such refinements, and to have *mo li* meant not only to lack manners but to have little sense of social ritual, thus bringing a bad reputation to one's family. Poh-Poh's brows furrowed at the tragic thought that her grandson might have been born an idiot with *mo li*. She quoted something from Confucius, "Follow the Right Way." This was the highest authority, to warn me to be on my best behaviour. The classic four-word proverb meant nothing to me, but the Old One's warning tones as she pronounced each word so precisely spoke volumes: Confucius was High Authority.

Lucky money was a social ritual I liked. Whenever my longings began to run away from Old China ways, lucky money brought them back.

"What're those red things?" Little Jack asked me once, when I was showing off how many lucky packages I had collected from a dinner party at the Pekin celebrating Poh-Poh's and my birthday. It hadn't mattered that our birthdates were days and months apart; Father felt it was time to honour the Old One, and Poh-Poh said I should have my share of joy, too. Everyone gave me a toy or lucky money. Afterwards, the lady guests came to our house to play mahjong, and the men went someplace to gamble and drink. My pockets were bulging with *lei-see*. I got tired of playing with the other children and looked out the front window, and I saw Jack staring at me from his porch.

"Look what I got," I said, showing a fistful of red *lei-see* packages. "Bet you don't have any."

Jack came closer to see. I held my fist out and offered him one. I checked with my fingers that only coins were inside. Otherwise, Father or Poh-Poh would be mad at me. All at once, Jack laughed and tore open the envelope.

"Hey, it's money!"

"No," I said, "it's lucky money."

"You bet it is," he said, holding up two fifty-cent pieces.

Then he ran into his house. There was nothing to do but go back into my own house. A few minutes later, there was a loud knock on our door, and Stepmother saw Mr. O'Connor's tall, lanky figure shadowing our parlour window. Everyone stopped playing mahjong and stared quietly at the front door. Stepmother hesitated to open it. In the dining room, Poh-Poh glanced at Jenny Chong's mother, who spoke English. Mrs. Chong got up with a heavy sigh and went down the front hall. She was always interpreting for Chinatown residents.

"Yes?" Mrs. Chong used her customer-service voice with Mr. O'Connor. "May I please to help you?"

"Your boy gave my son this money," Jack's father said. "Should he have done that?"

Mrs. Chong could see the torn red envelope and the two coins peeking out.

Poh-Poh looked hard at me. Stepmother stood up from the parlour table and shook her head.

"You gave lucky money away?" Poh-Poh said, in Toishanese. I could see Jack's father was wondering about the Old One's serious tone. "Now you tell that foreigner what you mean by that."

Poh-Poh got off her chair and pushed me forward down the front hall. Mrs. Chong stepped aside. Jenny Chong came running out from the back to see what was the matter. She was always a Nosy Parker.

"For Jack to keep," I said to Mr. O'Connor.

The tall man looked past me to see how Stepmother or Poh-Poh would respond.

"Play cards," Poh-Poh said in Toishanese, and the other ladies immediately began pushing the tablets noisily around the table, ignoring the situation at the door.

Stepmother watched me step back. Mrs. Chong shut the door.

Then the noise of the clicking game resumed in both rooms. No one said anything to me as Mr. O'Connor's figure left our porch and descended down the steps.

Jenny Chong said, "Give me one, too."

Mrs. Chong reached out and slapped her daughter's head. None of the ladies in the room took notice.

When I was put to bed, Poh-Poh wagged her finger at me. "Only a fool give lucky money away! Are you a fool?" Shortly afterwards, Stepmother's shadow crossed my bed. I shut my eyes and refused to acknowledge her. She tucked me in and slipped some extra coins in my palm.

~ *T W O* ~

POH-POH WARNED ME THAT I was no longer the same *Tohng-Yahn* boy she took by the hand when we first struggled up the crowded third-class gangplank in Hong Kong to board the CPR steamship to Vancouver. "You old enough now to keep secrets."

Grandmother was right. I was eight years old that fall of 1930, as I stood waiting in the doorway of our cramped, stuffy Chinatown kitchen to help her wash and prepare the vegetables. The door jamb had lines that Father pencilled on to record my height. Father had said that when I reached a certain height, I would be trusted to know more, to know family secrets that even my very best friend, Jack O'Connor, could never be told.

"I'm taller now," I said, looking as grown-up as I knew how. "I'm bigger, too."

The Old One laughed.

"You not *Tohng-Yahn* like before, Kiam-Kim," she said, displaying her old know-it-all village manner and shaking her wrinkled head at the fierce-faced, nearly cross-eyed Kitchen God stuck on the wall. Even *he* agreed. Poh-Poh unhooked Stepmother's flower-printed apron from the doorknob. I looked at the dangling garment and took a step back into the dining room. Poh-Poh shook her head again.

"You not *Chinese* like before. Now you just a *mo no* boy, a no-brain boy!"

Poh-Poh did not mean that I didn't have a brain; she meant that I didn't have the right kind. One day when I sat in my room, bent-mouthed and feeling crushed, Stepmother told me to pay no attention.

"When you count up Father's invoices to match up his bookkeeping entries, what does the Old One always say?"

I thought for a moment. "Poh-Poh says, 'Kiam-Kim has a Number One Brain.' Then she pulls my ear."

"Yes, yes . . . ," Stepmother said. She sighed. "To keep First Son humble."

I protested and punched my pillow.

"Father always laughs."

"You must laugh, too!" A delicate hand brushed away my tears. "Yes, laugh. Then you have a *Tohng-Yahn no,* a Chinese brain like your Poh-Poh."

Stepmother smiled when I got her meaning: never take Poh-Poh too seriously. Smile. Laugh. Stepmother herself barely reacted to any of Poh-Poh's abrupt suggestions: "Steep tea longer." "Fold sheets this way:

tight-tuck every corner." "Hold the baby . . . *firmly.*" "Eat more meat."

To each command, Gai-mou would respond with a faintly pleasant smile, as if Poh-Poh's take-charge voice should not be taken too seriously. After a moment, she would submit to Poh-Poh's way: the green tea was steeped longer; bedsheets were stretched just so and all four corners stiffly tucked in; the baby *firmly* held; and, finally, another morsel of meat was politely swallowed.

"*Ho, ho!* Good, good!" said Poh-Poh, satisfied that Gai-mou had not disregarded her. However, even as the Old One increased her pushy ways with me, Stepmother began gradually to fold the bedsheets in her own way. In the midst of her breast-feeding my sister, she lifted Liang-Liang to burp, not as *firmly* as Poh-Poh would have liked: the tiny head limply propped over the towel-padded shoulder and slowly slid down again to feed. Stepmother was doing more and more things in her own way.

Mrs. Lim remarked on how the dinner table was set. Poh-Poh said, waving her hand dismissively, "Gai-mou work too hard to do everything right."

Eventually, even Father noticed that certain habits had changed in our house: now the Old One folded her own sheets exactly in the way Stepmother did, with three corners tightly tucked in but with one inviting corner flipped back.

Father was relieved to see that the two women got along most days, though once I saw him wink at Stepmother as if they had agreed upon a secret strategy to use their Chinese brains to contain Poh-Poh's abrasive inclinations—using the kind of brains I lacked. But if the right grey cells hadn't yet bloomed inside me, at least I was now taller than the last pencil mark scratched on the door post: taller and bigger and able to keep a secret. And too tall to travel free to Vancouver Island.

"We're going to the Chinatown in Victoria to get you and Liang a new brother," Father had said that morning.

"There will be two sons in family, Kiam-Kim!" said Poh-Poh. "Two grandsons!"

"It's a secret," Stepmother said.

"No one else must know," Father explained, "or the government officials might give us trouble. Understand?"

I tried to argue that I should go to Victoria instead of Liang-Liang.

"Liang small enough to ride no charge," Poh-Poh said, but I—*oh, a big boy like our First Son*—would have cost the family an exorbitant full fare. "Father not rich," she concluded, "so you, Kiam-Kim, sacrifice yourself and stay home."

"Final decision," said Father, lowering his glasses.

I sensed they must have known the secret for a long time, waiting until they were ready to leave to tell me. Still, I was keen to probe for more information.

"*How* am I going to get a brand-new brother?"

Stepmother nudged Father.

"Well," Father said, snapping shut his leather brief-case. "*How?* First, lots of boring paperwork. Documents still to read, blank spaces to fill out, to sign."

"Yes," Stepmother said, her delicate lips barely

moving, half whispering her words. "Too much . . . documents."

"Then?"

"If everyone . . . agrees . . ."

"Then, Kiam-Kim, if things work out—" Father stared steadily at Stepmother's back "—if everything *agreeable,* your new brother soon join the family."

"Who is he?"

"He's four years old, Kiam," Father said. "Half your age."

"He'll be your Second Brother," Stepmother said. "Won't you like that? I think that I—I might like that."

Father caught her eye and seemed pleased.

"Second?" I asked.

"Number Two," Father said. "You be First Son, *Dai-goh,* you be Big Brother to him."

"You be *boss,*" Stepmother said, repeating how Third Uncle told me that in Canada being "boss" or "Number One Boss" was best, like my being First Son.

"What if Second Brother doesn't want to join us?" I asked.

"Don't worry so much," Stepmother said.

"And it's a—a *secret,*" warned Father. "Can you keep a secret?"

I stood up straight and nodded. A shuffling sound was coming from below the staircase.

"Kiam-Kim!" Poh-Poh shouted up at me. "Too many questions!"

I carried Stepmother's small suitcase down the stairs so she could carry Liang, twisting with excitement. In the hallway, she put Liang down and put on the second-hand wool coat that Mrs. Ben Chong had picked out for her at the China Relief Bazaar, the one held every three months at the Mission Church. Father opened the front door. In the sunshine, a taxi stood waiting at the curb; the driver stepped out and opened the trunk.

My head began to buzz: *what if I shoved my way into the trunk and refused to leave it?*

"In China," Father began in formal Cantonese, "a First Son cheerfully fulfills his filial duty."

The bleak, lecturing tone made it clear that staying home and assisting Poh-Poh were among those cheerful duties.

When the three of them left in the taxi, and the front door closed behind them, I thought, *Vancouver is not China!* and began to sulk.

"Come," Poh-Poh commanded from the kitchen. "I give First Son a taste of plantation cane."

From the blue bowl on the kitchen table, I took one of the soaking brown pieces she was using in her cooking and began to gnaw on the chewy stump. Instantly, a thin line of cloying liquid ran down my chin.

My own Number One Brain, Chinese or not, suddenly felt mired: I had been ensnared by a finger-joint of sugar cane, lured back into the kitchen where Poh-Poh's treacherous white crown had been waiting to outsmart me. When she reached for the flowery apron hanging on a hook, I grimaced, but it was not compelling enough to distract her weathered hands from flinging the apron into the air like a net and quickly catching the flaps around me. I yelped, but a relentless palm twirled me around; lightning fingers snatched away the chewed-up cane, tossed it back on the kitchen table, and knotted the double-folded apron tightly around my waist.

Bluebells and violets, red and yellow roses, and swirling pink petals cascaded in repeated patterns all the way down to my bare knees. I looked like a meadow in bloom. It was useless for me to smile, hopeless for me to grin, and futile for me to laugh: a wily old Fox Lady had trapped her innocent victim in an oilcloth apron of sissy flowers.

Poh-Poh lifted up my shirt sleeve to study the bony appendage of my arm, just as I would have inspected a held-up limb of one of those large, squirming toads Jack O'Connor and I regularly caught at MacLean Park. Or just as the famished Fox Lady would study its prey before . . . before I knew what was happening, a knobby thumb and forefinger encircled my wrist. Grandmother made a pitying face and took on the talk-story voice of the disappointed Demon Fox,

"Have bigger shank bones in soup pot!"

That was when I should have laughed at the silly joke, remembering that that was what the lip-smacking Fox Lady always declared before she locked away her struggling main course to be fattened up. Instead, a scowl stretched the corners of my mouth and I pulled back my skinny arm. But I knew it was pointless for me to resist: Poh-Poh would have her way.

Father had that afternoon warned me to be on my best behaviour and to help the Old One prepare the *sui-yah,* the late-night dishes, for her party of mahjong ladies. "Keep busy tonight," Father had advised me. "Obey your grandmother and keep the family secret."

I knew there was nothing else to do but to observe Poh-Poh, apron-wrapped in the kitchen, in the midst of a squadron of pots and pans being heated on the stove, surrounded by bowls and plates loaded with the food that she had chopped and sliced all afternoon, and obey. And keep the family secret.

Poh-Poh herself looked unnaturally plump, with her long white apron tied over her blue-quilted jacket and black Old China pants. Between her rolled-up ankle stockings and the edge of those pant legs, I glimpsed her long johns. In the early fall, with the North Shore mountain winds coming down into Vancouver and the constant fog rising from Burrard Inlet, she always felt vulnerable to drafts and chills. Still, with her hands slapping pot lids shut, her sturdy body shuffling the unprepared carrots, turnips, and leafy greens, bringing out the platters of raw meat and chicken wings from the icebox outside on the back porch, Poh-Poh wheeled back and forth like a bun-haired dervish.

"I save carrots for you to do," she said.

Then she took the greens and chopped away with her cleaver, lifting each mound of vegetable with the flat of her blade and sliding exact portions into ceramic bowls; finally, she slapped the meat down and minced with the blade faster than my eyes could see, the rhythm of her chopping and mincing beat-beating like a drum on the cherrywood block. My sulk vanished. Any thoughts of a new brother receded. I was captivated.

The climax came when the Old One grabbed the cleaver to hook the anvil-handle of the peep-grill, snapping the iron cover up to study the licking flames in the roaring belly of the stove. Hot enough to heat the rooms and, later, to sizzle the food. All at once, she pulled the blade away and the iron grill landed with an ear-shattering *BANG!*

I jumped.

In all Poh-Poh's stories, the clever children escaped the clutches of the ravenous Fox Lady and came back to the village to warn others. I thought of telling Jack O'Connor to be very careful of old ladies who offered him sugar cane, who would wrap him in a shroud of flowers and fix their beady eyes on him.

"Keep busy," Poh-Poh said. "Taste this all-day melon soup."

She handed me a small bowl of steaming amber. Somehow, her *Tohng-Yahn no* had read my long and wistful face: my brain cells had been wondering, while I waited for the soup to cool, how I could tell Jack O'Connor the family secret.

"Taste now," said Poh-Poh.

The soup tasted like warm chicken broth. Pieces of salty melon pulp burst into tangy sweetness. It was perfect. I tipped the small bowl and slurped up every crystal drop.

"Maybe," I said, "too salty."

"Bullshit," Poh-Poh said, using one of the half-dozen English words she had picked up from Third Uncle's labourers. She snatched the empty bowl from my hand before I could ask for more.

Acting grown-up, I said, "Not nice."

"Shut up," she said in English, without a trace of accent.

Satisfied with her orderly fleet of plates and utensils, her eyes glowing from the heat of the stove, Poh-Poh loosened her apron to fan more heat into the dining room. She asked me to thump the sawdust chute feeding one end of the stove.

My fists battered the galvanized sides until the load of sawdust inside made a gradual *whoosh* as it slid down towards the flames. Poh-Poh then directed me to wash my hands in the sink before I tackled my next job. I stood on tiptoe and reached over the deep metal basin and wrung my fingers under the cold tap water. Poh-Poh roughly dried my hands on a length of clean towel that hung on a wooden roller beside the back door.

"Stand on this," she commanded. With a slippered foot she shoved sideways against an empty crate until it banged into the deep metal sink. Everything smelled of sauces and crackling firewood. She handed me back the half-chewed stump of sugar cane.

As I sucked, I looked down at the colourful label covering the slats of the crate. Between slurps, I read out loud: "Bee-Seee Ap-ples."

"Too smart," Poh-Poh said. "Stand up."

"Frae-sir Val-leee Eee-daan Farm."

Using my best English, and pronouncing carefully, I told Poh-Poh, "The Val-lee is the food bas-ket-*lah* of Vancouver," just as my teacher at Strathcona had taught us. By the end of Grade 2, I knew more about British Columbia than I could ever remember about China.

"You *mo no,*" Poh-Poh repeated, after I badly translated into Toishan the idea that Fraser Valley Eden Farm was "the Big Paradise Apple-Box of Upside-down Mountain."

"Nonsense," she said and snatched the acid-sweet cane from my lips.

However they were translated, Grandmother took no pleasure in the *faan gwai* English words, the foreign demon words, though she was clearly jealous of my expert ability to read the complex labels of apple crates and grocery tins. I could even read the Grade 3 Look-and-Learn books like *This Is the House That Jack Built.* (Jack O'Connor knew that one by heart.) But instead of commending me as Stepmother and Father did, the Old One fretted over how her grandson squinted and stumbled over flimsy Chinese textbooks yet somehow could read, even with one eye shut, page after page of rhyming English words; she complained how her no-brain grandson could pivot a pencil into ten English sentences faster than he could daub a brush over just one single Chinese ideogram. Worse, she wrung her hands and warned Third Uncle and big Mrs. Lim, who only sulked to hear the latest news about me, that First Son was muttering more Chinglish than Chinese.

She begged of them, "What will happen to my grandson? What will happen to Kiam-Kim?"

I thought Poh-Poh took things too seriously. Whenever I looked in the mirror and saw my narrow eyes and pug nose, there was no escaping the fact that I was my father's son, and I would always be her grandson. She and the elders often worried about children like myself, whom they called *juk-sing*, bamboo stumps, who were sturdy outside but held a hollow emptiness within.

Sometimes Poh-Poh held me by my shoulders and looked into my eyes as if she wanted to drill deep inside me, to see if anything of value was filling up that hollow domain. I would speak to her, say something that was using my very best half-Chinese, half-English sentences, and she would choke and choke at the apparent absurdity of my statements.

At those times, I thought of all the wrinkle-faced people, white-haired people with furrowed brows from Eastern European countries and from Italy, who sat on their porches and on the steps along Keefer Street, and how sadly they sometimes looked upon the lot of us white and yellow kids romping together on the streets. Their disapproving glances and shouts for their grandchildren to rejoin them on the porch made me think they all longed for us to be among our own kind, just as they once were: children of a single language and a single community.

"Fraser Valley . . . ," I said even louder and kicked the box hard. "Eden Farm."

"Kiam-Kim," Poh-Poh warned, "you soon forget—*you China!*"

I started to protest. She bowed her head and began dabbing her eyes with the corner of her white apron.

"On—onions . . . ," she said.

Just as she turned her back to me, I snatched the chewed-up sugar cane and stuffed it in my mouth to suck out its last bit of pulpy sweetness. Then I loudly and rudely spat the stringy fibres into the compost bin.

"I'm finished," I said and jumped off the wooden crate.

"You clean and cut carrots for me."

She did not even turn around. I picked up the dull scraping knife and pulled up a chair. The carrots were thick and twisted. Her old chin rose to beg the tolerance of the Kitchen God for the salvation of her *mo-no* grandson.

The wild-eyed Kitchen God was only a picture on a placard, an ancient warrior printed on a small poster stuck just above the stove, but she mumbled something to him. Scraping away, I mumbled something, too.

"Careful," Poh-Poh said. "Tsao Chung hear you."

I made a face at Tsao Chung and didn't even care if all my few Chinese brain cells withered away.

She lifted her know-it-all eyebrow. "You ask for more blessing or trouble?"

At my look of surprise, she burst out laughing and left me by myself in the prickly heat of the Kitchen God's kingdom.

As I yanked the green, ferny tops from the knobby carrots, my head began to work out the things both Third Uncle and Grandmother taught me that would either bless me or trouble my life.

Between hacking into spittoons, the elders were always proclaiming ten thousand this or ten thousand that. "Ten thousand blessings!" Third Uncle would exclaim if his business went well; then, Poh-Poh would laugh and warn him, "*Aaaiiyaah!* Ten thousand troubles!"

Sure enough, the stock market crashed. Ten thousand troubles landed upon our doorstep.

Grandmother explained to me that her words were meant to chase away the envy of the gods, but she had not been present to utter the right incantations when Third Uncle boasted of his growing bank account over business lunches with the H.Y. Louie and the Yip Sang merchant families. Women were never invited to those lunches. Poh-Poh told me how in America some months ago men jumped out of buildings when the value of investments dropped. Third Uncle had even thought of killing himself, but Poh-Poh reminded him to think of his new family in Gold Mountain. As a family, Father assured him, we would survive. Third Uncle joined the merchants for their regular luncheon.

"They never invite women," Poh-Poh explained. "No woman die for money."

The last carrot waited to be scuffed and washed. The idea of having a new brother sent my mind searching for blessings.

Whenever anyone offered Chinatown children candy, we were taught to refuse at least twice, so one would be humble and worthy of a final third offering. Whenever I expected too much, like lots of lucky money at New Year's, I would walk past the small

Goddess of Mercy in our parlour, behave as if I didn't care how much lucky money I might get, that I wasn't greedy or grasping. I wanted only luck.

Big Mrs. Lim always told me that the gods and ghosts look for ways to trick you. It was no use my saying I never saw any gods or ghosts; apparently they were everywhere. I was in even more danger, she warned, because I did not see them. Other children saw them, she told me and Poh-Poh, like the Lon Sing twins, who finished each other's sentences, and the Chiangs' little girl, who went mad with hearing ghost voices and fell into a coma and died.

"Expect nothing," Father told me, "and anything that comes will be a gift."

"Be patient," Stepmother had cautioned me that very morning. "Keep deep longings to yourself."

I thought of what everyone had said to me when I got all *Excellent* on my first report card.

"Even white people say," Third Uncle said, "'Never show poker hand.' Pretend you got *Needs Improvement.*"

Mrs. Lim warned me not to strut too much. "The cocky rooster makes the best soup."

Grandmother told me that when I was a baby in China, whenever she took me outside, she complained out loud of my wretchedly pinched eyes and snot-running nose, so the gods would not be jealous and snatch me away.

I fought down my excitement: I would set an example for my promised Second Brother when he disembarked; that is, I would be openly disappointed with him. But why would any jealous god worry about me as

Number One Boss? What example was I, wrapped in a flowery apron, wearily scrubbing carrots and wiping at my nose with the back of my wet and skinny wrist?

Poh-Poh stepped back into the kitchen. She had oiled and neatly primped up her hair with her jade hairpieces. I lifted the long knife, as she and Stepmother had taught me, and began slowly, carefully, slicing the carrots at an angle. Grandmother ignored me until she noticed my runny nose. She took a tissue from her sleeve and made me blow three times. She washed her hands, then began wiping the wok with a tiny mop soaked with cooking oil. My eyes glazed with thought. Between her humming a singsong tune, she broke into comment whenever she felt like it.

"Kiam-Kim thinks too much," she told the Kitchen God, her tune faltering between some nonsense lyrics. "*Aaaiiyaah,* what proper girl will ever marry my worthless grandson!"

I reminded myself that the so-called Kitchen God was only a small, heat-curled poster pinned on the wall. He looked like a warrior in one of my floppy Chinese comic books.

"At the end of this year, Kiam-Kim," Poh-Poh went on in her lecturing tone, "the Kitchen God Tsao Chung will tell tales about the family."

I knew that. I handed her the plate of cut carrots.

"Tsao Chung soon fly back up to Heaven to the Jade Emperor."

I knew that, too. During the last week of the year, after smearing the paper lips with a dab of honey to sweeten his words, Grandmother had Father walk out the back porch and set Tsao Chung free by burning him up in a clay pot in front of all the family. Transformed by the fire into smoke, Tsao Chung began his journey to Heaven to report on our family. Last year, as Poh-Poh solemnly followed the rising vapours, Father nudged me and winked. Then he threw the ashes into the air. Poh-Poh stared at the fragments, never looking away until every bit of ash vanished skyward. By the second week of the New Year, a new Kitchen God would be pinned in the same place.

Later that day, Father told me how—scientifically— it was only smoke. Overhearing this, Third Uncle said, with some reluctance, "Sometime smoke, Kiam-Kim, and sometime not."

Next door, at the O'Connors', there was nothing like a Kitchen God. But as I waited in their front hall for Jack to come out to play, I saw hanging askew a wood-framed picture of a white lady in a blue dress. In their tidy, uncluttered kitchen, Mrs. O'Connor made Jack and me hot dogs in the only pot that I could see, and Jack told me that the lady in the blue dress was the Blessed Virgin Mary. She had the Holy Baby Jesus in an old barn crowded with livestock. Mrs. O'Connor said it was all true, and crossed herself.

I told Poh-Poh and Stepmother about Blessed Mary and her having a baby right there in a cowshed. I told them about all the creatures surrounding Baby Jesus, all the chickens and ducks, the sheep, the cows and pigs, including, best of all, the three hairy men and their three camels. Poh-Poh thought a moment.

"Not too clean," she said finally.

When I told some of the other Grade 3 white boys about Tsao Chung, they all laughed at me. Jon Wing, whose father's store sold the images wholesale, said nothing. One of the Italian boys shoved me aside, but he said something that made sense to me. That afternoon in the kitchen, I repeated the boy's words to the Old One.

"Poh-Poh, the Kitchen God—*just a piece of paper!*"

"Kiam-Kim, you be careful what you say. You clean up now," she ordered. "Put out chopsticks and best dishes on kitchen table, all ready for later."

I quickly scrubbed the empty colander. Then, wiping my hands, I jumped off the apple crate, climbed up on the chair, and lifted from the lower shelves two sizes of our best plates and bowls. Then I dipped into the lower drawer for the chopsticks. Everything clattered into three stacks bristling with serving spoons and eye-poking chopsticks.

"What's that?" Poh-Poh asked.

Gentle knocking drifted from the front door, but I kept busy, carrying the dishes to the pine board that Father had put up as a serving shelf. *I'm too busy,* I thought, and gathered the spoons into one bowl; the chopsticks I plunked into a glass, just as Stepmother would have done.

The Old One had no time for my stubbornness. She tossed her flour-bag apron over the broken-backed chair by the doorway and shifted the stockpot away from the direct heat. Thick pork bones bobbed to the surface. Her lightning-quick eyes appraised bowls and plates of raw and semi-cooked ingredients, all placed in a certain order for the stir-frying. Finally, Poh-Poh reached over and wiped her hands on *my* apron. "Who answer your door, clever boy," she said to me, "if no one marry you!"

I didn't care.

She hurried out of the kitchen, her quilted jacket dancing on her shoulders. I looked past the Old One as she opened the door. Two tiny ladies bustled in to escape the fall dampness, Mrs. Pan Wong and Mrs. Hin Leong, their voices happily chirping above Grandmother's humble greetings.

Grandmother shouted back at me, "Watch the soup pot!"

Minutes later, she scurried into the kitchen with a small bag of oranges and two wrapped parcels. There was a parcel of two cooked chicken breasts from Mrs. Wong, who always brought the same thing. Crunchy-skinned barbecued pork fell out of the second parcel onto a serving dish.

Poh-Poh stood at the loaded kitchen table and wiped her hands on the dish towel. Everything was in place. Except me.

"Sit," Poh-Poh said to me, frogging the row of silk buttons on her jacket. "Read."

I knew she meant the Chinese First Word books lying dead on the corner stool, just as Father had left them.

Turning her back on me, she lightly touched the greyish bun of her hair and adjusted a cloisonné barrette. I yanked off my flowery apron, threw it aside, and advanced towards the textbooks as if I were going to

lift one up. Satisfied, the Old One ambled away. I
ducked into the pantry.

There I sat on the cool linoleum floor under the
glowing lightbulb. I pushed aside the family rice barrel
and reached behind for the comic book that
Stepmother had slipped me that morning.

"Don't tell Poh-Poh," she had said.

These China-made comics were stitch-bound booklets. Their sixteen pages depicted in vivid, detailed
drawings how ancient Chinese warriors had fought the
early Mongol invaders. There were five booklets in the
series, each with running panels of detailed drawings
and captions below in Chinese. Even if you could not
read the Chinese, the drawings were so elaborate anyone could follow the story. Even Jack. We both traded
our comics and read them. He said he read them on
the floor in the parlour and in bed. *Terry and the Pirates*
was the best. We sometimes read comics together in his
house, but Poh-Poh never wanted me to let Jack into
ours. Playing on our porch one summer day, he had
asked Poh-Poh what smelled so rotten in our house. I
translated. Poh-Poh had been making a herbal soup.
The front door slammed shut in our faces.

"*Mo li,*" she told me later. "No manners."

Mr. O'Connor said that the Chinese comics
had more details in them but the writing was all
"chop-chop" to him. Jack made a face and pretended
he could read Chinese. I could make out only a word
or two myself.

Jeung Sam was number three. Father had taught me about the Chinese heroes of the first two books, how each of the five warriors were like today's soldiers fighting against the evil foreigners who were dividing up China. The dog-turd Japanese. The demon Russians. The big-nosed British. I was supposed to enjoy number three only after finishing my chores for Poh-Poh and after I made sure I read my Chinese-school homework.

"I promise," I said to Stepmother, remembering how the Old One laughed at these comic heroes that Father thought were so important for me to discover.

"No one kung fu any more," Poh-Poh said, pushing her fists into the air. "Spears! Swords! Useless! Today, one bomb kill everybody!" The war news from China had been terrible.

Poh-Poh reminded me that comic books were bad for young eyes.

Now I leaned against the wooden slats and flipped through the first few pages of the comic. Here were drawn the usual Chinese words on the huge banners of the fighting armies: *North. East. Tiger* . . . and the adventures began . . .

That bit of reading would be, I reasoned, my Chinese homework.

I studied the dramatic panels, the wave of arrows in the air, the swords dripping with blood, easily figuring out the good guys from the bad guys with their snarling dark faces and slit Mogul eyes. I found myself stage-whispering sounds to mimic the flying arrows and slashing swords, marvelled at the trickery of friend and foe, and cracked my knuckles as the enemy broke the legs of the captured hero. I gulped at his dying, and heard his challenge for others to come forward, not to save him but to "Come and save China!"—the same words Father wrote in his newspaper essays, the words he taught me to write out—the final cry of a victory in defeat.

"China never lose," Father said. "Always be Chinese."

I looked up and remembered where I was. In the yellowish light of the pantry I could hear rising voices, impatient voices.

From the parlour, Mrs. Pan Wong and Mrs. Sui Leong were talking anxiously with the Old One, all three waiting for their fourth partner. They were cracking red melon seeds and tsk-tsking over and over about how late, as usual, Mrs. Chong was.

When I had read twelve pages—another hero, this one a master of archery, now perched on a double-spread cliff ready to plunge into the raging river below—Poh-Poh's firm voice rose above the other two.

"Well, this is more than Chinese time to be so late."

I heard a bustle of rattling paper bags being opened. I imagined packets of candied plums, sugared ginger, dried prunes being exchanged. They were relaxing into serious talk, sitting back on the cushions, not waiting for Mrs. Chong. Mrs. Pan Wong started to speak, and Poh-Poh abruptly said, "Shh—the kitchen!"

Now there came whisperings. I listened closely, imagining three heads bowed towards each other.

Huddling spies. I thought I heard my name pitched dramatically, *Kiam-Kim . . . Kiam-Kim,* but I couldn't make out anything else. The murmuring intrigued me.

Grandmother, from where she sat in the parlour, could partly see the empty stool. She demanded I come out. *Right now!* I refused to answer. Abruptly, her tone sweetened. Perhaps she remembered her promise to Father to be patient with me.

"Come out, Kiam-Kim," she said. "Come and join Mrs. Leong and Mrs. Wong for a visit. They want to see you."

I slipped my comic back into its hiding place and stood up. As I walked towards them, Poh-Poh offhandedly mentioned that Grandson would be helping her cook each dish for the *sui-yah,* that Grandson had even helped her prepare the many ingredients.

"Such a smart boy already!" Mrs. Wong said. "Some lucky girl will catch him!"

Mrs. Leong said, "If only my eight-year-old could do a tenth as much!"

She was talking about her Winston, a fat boy with a thick head. He failed English Grade 2 and was taken out of Chinese school for throwing ink at some of the younger girls who laughed at his stuttering. Mrs. Leong bit her bottom lip. Mrs. Wong knitted her thinly drawn eyebrows.

It was inspection time. Glittering, appraising eyes took in everything. Poh-Poh reached out and tucked my shirt in. I felt I was going to be sold to one of the ladies, just as the bad children back in China were sold at the whim of an elder. The two ladies on the chesterfield broke into even broader smiles. Mrs. Wong pulled me closer to her. What a good grandson. How tall, how always considerate. Under the parlour lamp beside her, Mrs. Pan Wong's gold tooth shone like fire. The Old One's eyes registered *enough, enough.* She was more anxious to play mahjong, to get on with the business of the evening.

"Check on the chicken-melon soup," Poh-Poh said. "Use the metal spoon carefully."

I knew what she meant. Stand on the apple box. Lift the pot lid and peek in to see that the liquid was not bubbling over.

It wasn't.

"I'm getting a new brother," I said just to myself, and, to pass the time, banged on the side of the stock pot with the spoon and a chopstick. The banging did my talking for me: *New! new! new! new!* The pot lid tilted, the golden liquid hissed and bubbled over.

Poh-Poh stormed into the kitchen, her back hunched up beneath her quilted jacket, bent knuckles ready to land on my crown. "You study your school book and listen for the door." With stinging precision, her knuckles landed. "Mrs. Chong come any minute now."

She straightened the 100 per cent Canada Wheat apron hanging over the chair. As I rubbed my head, the flaps of the white apron wavered like two ghosts.

"Did you say something, Grandson?"

"Nothing," I said, dropping the spoon and chopsticks.

"How clever," the Old One said, "to say *nothing*."

Giggling rippled from the front room.

When finally Mrs. Annah Chong arrived at our front door, she apologized, using her formal Cantonese to win back Poh-Poh's good grace.

"*Jan-haih mh-hoh yee-see la,*" the tall woman said. "How thoughtless of me. Arriving so late. You must think I am so ungrateful."

"*Mh-hoh haak-hei,*" Poh-Poh said, echoing Mrs. Chong's formality. "Don't stand on ceremony. Let my grandson take your lovely fur coat."

As I stepped up to do so, Mrs. Chong slapped her purse into my hands and hurriedly unbuttoned her coat.

"Thank you, Kiam-Kim," she continued in Cantonese. "You're such a good boy, so smart looking, so tall! Grandmama must be feeding you her best cooking."

I smiled, but knew I was not to say anything. Mrs. Chong swung her thin arms out to let her heavy coat slide away from her. The coat smelled faintly of mothballs; two beady-eyed foxes dangled from the collar into my nose. I grabbed one corner of the dark garment just before it hit the floor and was surprised to see Mrs. Chong's daughter, Jenny, standing right behind the curtain of fur. The coat knocked the purse from my hand; Jenny was quick to catch the strap. Her eyes narrowed at me as if I were stupid or clumsy. Or both.

Tonight was for Poh-Poh's ladies only, a chance to get away from the rest of their families, especially from their crowded households of live-in namesake cousins and roomers, and from children the likes of Jenny Chong and me.

Except I got stuck as kitchen help and doormat.

"Remember to help Poh-Poh greet the guests, Kiam-Kim," Stepmother had said. "You be the man of the house tonight."

When Mrs. Chong walked by and absent-mindedly patted my head, I remembered to be like Father. I stood taller. Girl children, like Jenny Chong, first-born or last-born, hardly mattered. I ignored her.

Jenny's lips curled when I said my formal greetings to her mother. "*Chong Sim, nei ho ma?*" If she smiled, she might not have been so ugly.

Mrs. Chong gave her a stern look, her pencil-drawn eyebrows curving upward, her dialect slipping back to her Toishan village origins.

"*Mo yung neuih* upset her father! Useless girl! Three times this week!" Mrs. Chong dragged Jenny into our parlour, grabbed her thin shoulders, and shook her in front of everyone. "You behave! Dai-mo send you away!"

She called my grandmother Dai-mo, Great Mrs. or Great-aunt, because Poh-Poh, in her seventies, was the oldest of her crowd. Mrs. Chong brushed back a strand of her hair as if she were regaining control. She pushed Jenny down on our long sofa and glared at her.

"Stay here and die," Mrs. Chong said, throwing

some school books at her. She sighed and walked into the next room to join the mahjong group.

"*Say neuih,*" Mrs. Chong said, her arms opening up to her three friends for sympathy. "Dead girl, I have a dead girl for a daughter."

Two stiff-necked foes were left behind in the parlour.

Jenny looked up at our Great Wall of China calendar. She sat rigidly in her bright red dress, a dress topped with a ruffled collar. When she turned back to glare at me, the ruffles shifted like a stupid clown's collar.

I could see no interest or mystery in girls like Jenny. If I laughed, even smiled, she would have told Poh-Poh. Then I would be sent right up to bed without even a taste of the late-night supper. The two bowls of *jook* I had earlier would hardly keep me from hunger. I glared back.

Jenny Chong was almost eight, but skinny in the way most Chinese girls were, stretched too tall for her weight. Her braided pigtails were tightly pinned up and ribboned, and her nostrils visibly flared. She dared me to look away. I found it hard to keep my eyes focussed on her, so I glanced at the four women, who were babbling again. They were admiring Mrs. Chong's embroidered silk *cheongsam,* as if her tardiness hadn't mattered at all.

"I wear special dress for special party," Mrs. Chong said.

Then there was that pause again, a sudden and important silence.

"Grandson," Poh-Poh called out to me, "come and get the game table ready."

I slowly walked away from Jenny to make it clear that she, a girl, wasn't the one who made me leave the parlour.

"Grandson!"

I went to the hall cupboard and took out the game case.

Mrs. Chong smiled at the three ladies already sitting at the fold-away card table parked just a few feet from our round oak dining table. The tall woman stood as if she could barely move, still fuming over whatever had happened at home. She took out the lucky ashtray she always carried to these parties and parked it on her right side. It was a tiny thing, shaped like a flower. Poh-Poh handed me a coaster to put under it. Finally, Mrs. Annah Chong sat down.

"Just relax, Ann-nah," Poh-Poh said, and pursed her lips to signal the other two ladies to remain silent. But they purred with curiosity.

"Annah, may I ask what your lovely daughter has done to upset you so?" Mrs. Pan Wong's Sun Wui village dialect sounded delicate, more diplomatic than familiar.

Mrs. Leong caught Grandmother's warning look, too, but ignored it. "What could such a beautiful daughter have done to her poor mother?"

"Oh, Leong Sim," Mrs. Chong said, lighting up a Sweet Caporal, "you are too thoughtful." She blew out the match. "Me? I suffer in silence. Please, let's ignore my useless daughter."

I liked the way Annah Chong would inhale so deeply that her cheeks formed indentations; when she exhaled, they ballooned out. A puff of smoke rose into the air.

The Kitchen God, I thought.

"Grandson," Poh-Poh said, "we're ready to play."

I lifted the leather case of playing tiles onto the table and slipped out the tray with the counters, shook out the two dice and the four-wind disc. Mrs. Wong smiled at me.

"What a good boy," she said. "So tall."

The ladies began throwing dice to see who would start breaking up the tiles.

"You start, Sui Leong," Poh-Poh commanded. "You East, Pan Wong, you sit across."

I stepped out of the way.

The four ladies began shuffling and palming the ivory tiles, turning them face down, stacking the pieces into two-tier walls. Their gold and jade bracelets tinkled like bells.

I sat at Father's small oak desk, facing the gaming table, and turned my attention to my Meccano set, hardly looking up at anyone. I was building a Ferris wheel, like the one shown on the battered box that Third Uncle had bought me from the Strathcona School bazaar.

"It's an Advanced project," Father told me, "recommended for big boys, twelve and up."

"I can do it," I said.

"There's some pieces missing," Third Uncle had told me. "You do your best, Kiam."

"Very smart Grandson," Poh-Poh said, out of the blue.

With a quick flip of her forefinger, Mrs. Chong discarded a tile. She and Poh-Poh smiled across the table at each other.

Between one of the mahjong rounds, while the tiles were being shuffled, Mrs. Chong finally broke down. A cloud of cigarette smoke streamed into the air.

"My heart is too heavy," she began. "I must tell you, dear friends."

"Tell, tell!" Mrs. Wong said. "You know we all care for your happiness."

"Yes, yes," Mrs. Leong said. "If the women of Chinatown don't care for each other, who will?"

"Well . . . ," Mrs. Chong began, putting down her Sweet Caporal, "my worthless daughter threw a book at her father."

"Poor Ben Chong!" Mrs. Leong leaned over to hear more.

Mrs. Wong shook her head in disbelief. "Attack her father!"

Jenny's mother gravely bowed her head. "That's why, Dai-mo, I thought it best I bring this useless girl with me."

"No worry, Annah," Poh-Poh said. "She really is good girl. Has tiger spirit."

"Tiger, yes, but *good*," Mrs. Wong said, and her pudgy hand reached out to touch Mrs. Chong's sloped shoulder. "Your daughter is plenty smart. How could she—?"

"Let her rot by herself," Mrs. Chong said. "*Say neuih! Mo yung neuih!* Dead girl! Useless girl!" She lit up another cigarette.

Mrs. Leong and Mrs. Wong clucked their tongues at this news of a mere girl daring to throw anything at anyone, let alone a book at her father. One of Ben Chong's many jobs, aside from working in his own corner store, was keeping sets of accounts for Chinatown's smaller, and more and more often failing, businesses. In their upstairs office, where I had visited a few times with Father, big metal-clipped volumes lay about. I imagined one of those inches-thick account books, two feet wide, being heaved across the room. They could knock out a man with one blow. Mouth open, I looked at Jenny Chong. She looked so thin, too thin.

Grandmother noticed my astonishment and said, "Annah, may I ask—?"

"Yes, yes, Dai-mo, ask me."

"How large was this book that your daughter threw?"

"Well, of course," Mrs. Chong said, exhaling, "it was only one of those school scribblers."

"A scribbler," Poh-Poh said, pausing thoughtfully, looking directly at me, "is hardly a book."

I squeezed my lips together, tried not to laugh. A scribbler was smaller than a comic, would barely flutter a few feet in the air.

"But what a thing to do!" Mrs. Wong said, fanning the fires. "Such spirit!"

"We needn't give this another thought." Grandmother tapped the table. "South?"

After almost two hours and nearly completing the round, Poh-Poh called me away from my wobbly, nearly finished Ferris wheel to get the wok ready. Mrs. Leong complimented me on my skill. I sighed. For sure, there were some Meccano pieces missing, but I had done my best. Poh-Poh told me to hurry and heat up the large wok.

I wiped the curved bottom as I had been taught to do, then lifted one of the stove tops to set the pan in. I slid the handle on the grate. The stove stirred awake and flames began to lick the wok bottom.

"Everything all cut and ready," Poh-Poh said, pushing Mrs. Leong back into her seat and insisting she only needed me. "Just need ten minutes to stir-fry."

In front of our wood-and-sawdust stove, Grandmother handed me Stepmother's flowery apron. I folded and tied it around my waist just the way Mr. Ding Wong the butcher would, or the waiters at the Hong Kong Café.

Poh-Poh seemed pleased that I did not have to be told twice to follow any of her instructions. When she ordered, I handed her the tin pan of marinated chicken pieces and the flat of pork cubes out of our wooden icebox; passed her the bowls of bean sprouts and soaked mushrooms; tossed her the soy bottle and sesame oil when she nodded towards the pantry and the small dish of *dao-see*, black-bean sauce, with the tablespoon of starch when she said, "*Din-foon.*"

She had taught me well, as she had promised Father

she would, so that I would survive in Gold Mountain among the barbarians who boiled greens into mush and blackened whole chunks of meat the size of a man's head, and carved the dead thing and ate whole slabs employing weapons at the table.

"He will teach Liang when I gone," she told Father.

One after another, our serving plates filled with different dishes. Then I stood back from the wok as Poh-Poh threw in a splash of water to steam the last of the greens with crushed ginger and garlic and a final plop of oyster sauce.

Tonight, at the Old One's gathering, I was supposed to be on my best behaviour. I was. Still, in the midst of all the activity between Poh-Poh and myself, I thought Jenny Chong should be here, too, not sulking in our parlour. More than I did, she belonged in the kitchen. She should have been whipped, the way Poh-Poh was whipped when she was a servant girl in Old China, with thin bamboo rods that etched hairline scars forever on her back.

The melon soup was now at full boil. Five steaming plates were piled with greens and meats.

"We serve now," Poh-Poh said. "Why you look like that?"

"Nothing," I said, still fuming about doing all the work when Jenny could have helped.

"Take off your nothing apron."

I obeyed. She pointed to the cloth napkins. I folded the napkins, then picked up the chopsticks.

With a pot holder, Poh-Poh lifted the hot dish of beef and greens sprinkled with herbs, all steaming with flavours and glistening from the sesame oil. Grandmother clanged her ladle against the wok.

"Everyone please help!" she said, and the three ladies rushed into the kitchen, exclaiming over the delicious smells. Mrs. Chong filled blue-and-white bowls with rice, and scrawny Mrs. Leong and pudgy Mrs. Wong, holding tea towels against the hot platters, carried the remaining pie-plate tin and porcelain dishes past Grandmother's surveying eyes. I counted out enough napkins for everyone and picked up the porcelain soup spoons, just as I always did for Stepmother at dinnertime. I slapped a napkin, chop-sticks, and a spoon down in front of each empty chair. Adding me to the table, there were five chairs. But there should have been six.

I caught a glimpse of Jenny Chong looking as mean as her mother. Her eyes narrowed again, daring me to stare one second longer.

Poh-Poh pushed me aside. "Watch out for the soup!"

And when the lid with the lucky red-and-gold crests was lifted off, the golden brew steamed majesti-cally. Crystals of melon lay in a rich broth. The air smelled of crushed ginger. Everyone sighed with delight. Summer melon with chicken and sweet pork in chicken-feet stock was one of Poh-Poh's specialties. Mrs. Chong had grown the prized melon in her back-yard garden, and Mrs. Leong, the herbs. Mrs. Wong, the butcher's mother, had contributed the pork bones; she made sure they were thick with meat.

"People still eat," she had said, "but they don't buy so much any more. Stingy times."

To signal the beginning of the meal, Poh-Poh dipped her chopsticks down into the communal soup bowl and gracefully lifted away the largest pork bone. Thick, tender-cooked pork slid away and fell back into the fragrant broth. Everyone began to chatter, drifting into the deep comfort of their village dialects.

"Perfect," Mrs. Leong said in her Sam-yup manner. She reached over with her chopsticks and graciously took the bone from Poh-Poh to put onto the bone plate. "Everything perfect."

"*Sik-la!*" Grandmother commanded. "Eat, eat, eat! Don't stand on ceremony!"

"You and your grandson, *daiyat!*" Mrs. Chong said. "Number One!"

I suddenly felt proud that I belonged there with Poh-Poh—the Number One assistant to the culinary celebrity. Clicking chopsticks rose and fell, and the clink of porcelain spoons in the large bowl made a happy chorus. Grandmother picked up choice pieces of chicken and pork with her ivory chopsticks and generously put them into the rice bowls of her friends.

"Take this one," she would urge, "this is best."

Each guest would feign refusal, smiling all the while with pleasure. Finally, everyone was left to eat the portions fate had left facing in his or her direction, like sections of a pie. To cross over your section was rude, unless you wished to give away a good piece from your own portion to someone else. Because I was a growing boy, I was often given good pieces. Mrs. Chong lifted a leafy stalk into my rice bowl.

"Be big and strong for my useless daughter," she said. "Ten thousand blessings!"

"Here, Kiam-Kim," Mrs. Wong said, "this morsel of chicken will help you grow up even bigger and stronger."

"You be good friend to Jenny," Mrs. Leong said. "She need good friend."

The women all laughed, as if they were sharing a secret.

"Eat, eat," Poh-Poh said to me before I could think.

Through the waves of savoury steam, I stole quick glances at Jenny Chong. Grandmother noticed me looking.

"Come—come in and eat, Jen-Jen," Poh-Poh called out. "Kiam-Kim, bring the kitchen chair."

Everyone turned to look at Jenny Chong in the parlour. She sat with her hands in her lap as if she had been frozen in ice. Just below her chin, below the ruffles, a pinkish flower was pinned to her red dress; I watched to see if it moved. It didn't: she was stubbornly holding in her breath. Her two thick pigtails shone like plaited rope under the parlour lamp.

"No, no, no!" Mrs. Chong said. "Leave my *mo yung* daughter alone. Nobody wants a useless daughter to spoil our dinner!"

"Stop staring, Kiam." The Old One shoved me back into my seat. "Eat."

The chair I had slipped between Mrs. Chong and Mrs. Wong sat empty. Now I had a direct view into the parlour. Jenny Chong turned her face away, as if she had better things to look at than a bunch of monkeys feeding their fat faces. She pretended to read.

"Soup very hot," Poh-Poh said. "Careful, Mrs. Wong."

I picked up a piece of chicken, moist with flavour, and held it up to see if I could catch Jenny Chong's attention. I wanted her to notice, to get up and join us. I chewed and swallowed. She took deep breaths; the pink flower on her dress shifted up and down. She was peeking at me. I picked up an even nicer piece. I made a show of slowly chewing and swallowing the meat. I picked up a length of bok choy with my chopsticks and let it slip gradually, lusciously, into my mouth. I thought Poh-Poh should also see how much I enjoyed her cooking, but all the ladies hardly noticed me. Mrs. Chong went on talking about whose Pender Street business might fail next, and the others nodded sadly. In between the nodding, the women slurped their hot soup and complimented the Old One on her cooking.

"Nothing at all," Poh-Poh responded. "So simple to make."

I moved my chopsticks over the glistening mushrooms studded with crushed peanuts and seasoned with soy, and the fresh-picked green beans and savoury fried onions. My smiling face and my broad table gestures were all saying *delicious!*

I chewed with even greater mouth-watering, Charlie Chaplin intensity, desperate to catch the eye of someone starving to death. She should come to the table, I thought, add to Poh-Poh's joy.

Jenny Chong's head turned slightly. She looked at me from the corner of her eye. I imagined her stomach growling with hunger, a tigress's empty belly, her mouth salivating, her eyes the eyes of a huntress. Her jaw moved slightly, as if she were chewing.

I gobbled down some rice like a hungry bear. I took up my spoon and royally dipped into the communal bowl. The mixed pork and chicken broth was savoury with sweet dried shrimp and greens. I slowly tipped the brimming porcelain spoon and caught a square of melon.

I only meant to slurp gently, but the heat of the melon caught me off guard. I gulped, gasped. Everyone stopped talking. I sputtered, a trail of glowing liquid dribbling down the corner of my mouth. Jenny Chong stared wide-eyed. Knuckles rapped my head.

"Stop showing off," Poh-Poh said. "No one wants you!"

Beneath the stinging pain, through the waves of half-swallowed heat that made my eyes tear, I saw a grin break out on Jenny Chong's face.

After dinner, when all the ladies had helped Poh-Poh clear the dishes away, the women persuaded Mrs. Chong to let Jenny out of the parlour.

"She only a child," Mrs. Leong said. "She learn her lesson, yes, yes."

"Too much discipline," Poh-Poh said, "can spoil the lesson."

"And not enough discipline," Mrs. Chong sniffed into her flowery hanky, "spoils the child."

Poh-Poh and Mrs. Wong stared at Mrs. Chong until she relented. She got up, knuckled Jenny, and sent her smarting out of the parlour.

"You go help Kiam-Kim clean up," she commanded, and pushed her dead girl in the direction of the kitchen.

Poh-Poh suggested that Jenny help me rinse the dishes to be washed later. In the kitchen, she quietly offered some soup to Jenny, but Mrs. Chong stood guard at the doorway.

"Let her starve," she said. "Let this *mo yung* girl earn her keep like we did in Old China. Who gave us good soup?"

"Every child spoiled here," Mrs. Pan Wong said. "My two grandsons always they beg for candy and Coca-Cola! They die soon, poisoned!"

"You show Jen-Jen what to do," Grandmother said to me.

"A fine, fine First Grandson, your Kiam-Kim," Mrs. Chong said. "Oh, why am I cursed with such a daughter!" She pushed up her silk sleeves and went back to the mahjong table, all set up for another round.

Grandmother shut the kitchen door behind her and left the two of us by ourselves.

Jenny stuck her tongue out, then turned to the platters of leftovers. She picked up some chicken and vegetables with her fingers. Through the door, I could hear the loud clicking of the mahjong tiles, the muffled chattering of satisfied voices rising with pleasure and complaint.

"What job do you want?" I said. "Rinsing or stacking?"

"Shut your mouth," she mumbled. She picked up a pair of chopsticks and started chewing on a piece of chicken, then she dashed in some rice. A grain of rice stuck to her chin; she ignored it. She tilted the soup bowl to scoop up what was left. Piles of dirty bowls and plates sat on the galvanized wash counter.

"I'll get the sink rack ready," I said.

I always liked doing this orderly chore. I could see what was done and what was not done. I didn't have to wait for Jenny Chong.

After Baby Liang's arrival, rinsing the dishes was one of the jobs that Poh-Poh and Stepmother insisted I do. Only the dishes, though, not the knives or the pots and pans. I was five then and used to stand on a wooden stool to reach counter height, doing very little but passing along plates and utensils. It was like a game. I sang songs I learned from the Chinese United Church kindergarten and rattled the plates like cymbals. But now I was older, and I stood on a sturdy wooden crate to do the job.

"So," Jenny said to me in a stuffy voice, "start."

I decided not to. She was tall for a girl, but no taller than I was. I went to the back porch and got another crate.

"What's that for?"

"You," I said. "You rinse. I stack." Rinsing was really more fun, and so I thought she might prefer it.

She sneered. "Put this box on top of yours," she said, "and you'll *maybe* reach the counter."

I ignored her. She paid no attention. She stepped up on the box, brushing back her hair. She had unbraided half of one pigtail and must have been playing with it all that time in the parlour jail. It was messy. Her pinned flower looked wilted up close, but now I could see it was only scruffy pink tissue paper. She tried to turn on the brass tap, but there was a trick to turning it.

"Let me," I said, and stood on tiptoe on the edge of her box and reached over to the tap. The water started to trickle out. I turned the tap a little more. I would let her decide how much water she wanted.

The sneer never left Jenny Chong's face.

"So," she said, "why are you doing this sissy job?"

"This a man's job in all the Chinatown restaurants."

"*This*"—she waved her arms—"a restaurant?"

Stepmother said I was not to fight with girls, even if they teased. Even if they started it. And even if they deserved a sock in the mouth.

"My sweet mother says you do just about everything"—Jenny Chong held her nose in the air and shut her eyes like a snob—"*just perfectly.*"

"That's right," I said. "I'm not a *mo yung* girl like you. I'm tough."

"Tough?" She stepped back, looked at the stove, at the steam rising from the stock pot. "Bet you don't dare stick your hand into that."

"Put on an apron," I said. "There. On the hanger."

She hopped off the box. "You put yours on," she said. "You think you're so smart."

She threw a half apron at me and took the full apron for herself. She stared into the sink at the dirty pots and pans stuck with rice and food, the upside-down greasy wok lying on top. I could see she didn't want to go near them.

"We don't have to do anything with those," I said. "Just rinse these dishes for Poh-Poh to wash later."

"Shut your mouth," she said.

With my bare warrior hands, I could pick up Jenny Chong, spin her in the air like nothing, and toss her out of the kitchen.

Poh-Poh's voice startled me.

"How come I don't hear the tap running?"

Mrs. Chong shouted out from the dining room, "Get busy, *mo yung!* I send you away. Send you away soon!"

Being sent away did not seem to scare Jenny. Her eyes boiled with anger. She grabbed the brass tap and twist-turned it violently.

I should have known to step back, but it happened so fast. A watery burst hit the upturned bottom of the wok and curved up in a sudden arc. A wave splashed full in my face. Eyes blurry with water, I pushed Jenny off her crate and blindly turned the tap.

I gasped. I was soaked, from shirt to pants. Jenny Chong, apron thrown over her head, could not stop laughing. Too loudly.

"What's that dead girl doing!" Mrs. Chong shouted, and we could hear her chair screech back.

Jenny's hands went to her eyes, and her face contorted with fright. We both held our breath.

Through the partly open door, we heard Mrs. Leong saying, "Don't be so upset." We heard someone get up, holding back Jenny's mother.

"They're only children," Mrs. Wong said. "Children *play*."

For a second, I wasn't sure what to do.

"It's me!" I called. "I made a funny joke!"

"A miracle," I heard Poh-Poh say. "My grandson is clever enough to tell a joke."

Mrs. Leong chortled. "Oh, they get along good, very good, those two children."

Mrs. Wong laughed. But Jenny's mother kept muttering. "Send her to strict Catholic school! *Useless dead girl!*"

Her chair scraped again as she sat down.

The mahjong game continued, tiles clicking and crashing. Jenny sighed with relief. My quick thinking had saved her skin. She caught me looking at her and quickly made a little cough, covered her mouth, then reached down and roughly rinsed off another plate.

"Big hairy deal," she said, and shoved the plate at me.

I decided to say something that would really catch her off guard. The wood stove crackled. "I'm getting," I half whispered, "*a new brother.*"

She looked around, as if someone might overhear us, and whispered back to me, "It's a *secret*, isn't it?"

"Yes," I said. "It's a big, *big* secret."

She smiled for the first time. "You *mo yung say doi.*" Her lowered voice made each word sound triumphant, her thin, bloodless lips curled into a sneer. "You useless dead boy," she said. "You *shouldn't* have told me."

The Kitchen God glared.

The Kitchen God must have laughed at Jenny Chong's thinking she had tricked me into giving away the family secret and that I would be punished. The joke was on her. Nothing happened.

Within a week of the papers being signed, every one of the mahjong ladies knew all the details. Those agreement papers had been signed in Victoria, but my Second Brother was coming from Kamloops, far away in the Interior. I marvelled at how the papers and the boy were miles apart. I remembered that the immigration papers that brought Stepmother over were a whole ocean apart to begin with.

Stepmother said that we could not go to the train station to get Second Brother. A tong official would be with him on the train. With another mouth to feed, Stepmother told Father that they could not afford to stop working. The money mattered more than ever now. Poh-Poh and Third Uncle agreed. He had to work that afternoon, too.

"I pick him up at the station," the Old One said.

"I'll go, too!"

"No," Father said. "Too much confusion for your new brother. Poh-Poh will go in a taxi. She knows the tong elder who will be with the boy."

"You be patient," Poh-Poh said to me. "I bring him home."

Stepmother took me aside. "You forget something?"

"What?"

"You fix up your room for him. Move your bed over. We discussed this."

In protest, I pushed my hands down to my side.

"That be your duty," said Father.

Third Uncle tapped his pipe. "Don't you want to be Number One Boss, Kiam-Kim?"

They all looked at me across the dining-room table. Beneath the tablecloth, I pushed my fingers out like a boxer in training.

"Yes," I said, and tightly clenched my fists. Ready for anything.

~ *T H R E E* ~

POH-POH SAID, WHEN SHE CAME BACK from the
train station with him, "This is Jung-Sum, your
Second Brother."

She pushed a small, dark-skinned boy into our
front parlour. His hair glistened and smelled of
Wildroot. His shirt collar, starched, was encircled by a
glimpse of blue sweater, both protruding above his ill-
fitting dark jacket. Everything sagged over his bony
shoulders. His big-eyed head stuck out like a scare-
crow's on a broomstick. All he lacked was a straw hat. I
tried not to laugh.

Liang-Liang, with a pink bow in her hair, clung to
Stepmother's skirt. She stared at Jung-Sum and apparently liked what she saw. She smiled shyly.

Poh-Poh shot me a warning look. She had
informed me the day before that there was no way to get
rid of him once we called him family.

"You grow to like him," she said, and looked at Stepmother. "Everyone soon like him, just the way we like Gai-mou. We family."

When Stepmother removed his outer jacket, he looked even more puny, not the rough kind of *Our Gang* picture-show kid I had expected to get.

Though I knew he was only four, half my age, it was still a letdown to see that he barely stood a head above my waist. Below his short sleeves, his elbows stuck out like doorknobs. He looked back at the grown-ups with darting eyes, as if demons were going to pounce and gobble him up. I thought of Poh-Poh scolding the chicken man about his grizzled birds, *Too skinny for soup bones!* Or maybe he was looking for his mother and father. I wondered why they didn't keep him, why they gave him away.

Liang shook her Raggedy Ann doll at him. He jumped.

Father pushed me forward. "Introduce yourself," he said.

"I'm Kiam-Kim," I said. "It means 'proficient.' I'm smart."

He whispered something to Poh-Poh. She stooped down, and they began talking in a funny dialect. Then Stepmother showed him the kitchen, the pantry, and the dining room, with Father's desk in one corner. He stopped to look at the Meccano Ferris wheel I had left there.

"Jung-Sum speaks Hoiping," Father said.

"I speak *English!*" a thin voice squealed from the next room. "I speak *goot* English!"

"Take Jung-Sum up to your room, Kiam-Kim," Stepmother said. "Take his suitcase with you."

"Go with First Brother Kiam," Poh-Poh said. "We call you down for *dim sum.*"

Dishes rattled behind us as he followed me upstairs. I threw his battered suitcase on his bed and motioned him to sit down. The springs squeaked. The iron fold-away cot smelled rusty. Father said Jung-Sum had to share the bottom two drawers of *my* five-drawer dresser and half *my* closet space. That was the way it was.

"Where you're sitting," I said. "That's where you sleep."

As he sat back, his trouser legs rode up. In summer short pants, his stick-thin legs, like a girl's, would be embarrassing. At least he wasn't a chatterbox. He didn't even bounce on the cot to test the springs, the way I remember testing my big bed when I first got it.

"I'm your *dai-goh,* your big brother," I announced. "You have to be tough to be my baby brother."

He nodded.

Jung-Sum wasn't what I wanted for a Second Brother. I had imagined getting a boy like me when I was three, standing by a moon gate in that last picture taken in China; I was big and strong, fed lots of good food to prepare for the weeks-long overseas journey to Gold Mountain. I wanted a chunky little boy to boss around, the way everyone bossed me around. But Jung-Sum looked so small, so hopeless. It would be like bossing around Baby Liang. Not much fun.

Still, I had responsibilities that I couldn't avoid now. As Jung-Sum's new *dai-goh,* I should set down some rules, show the squirt right away who was boss.

His fingers slithered over to the worn suitcase handle, as if I might grab it.

"Let me see how tough you are," I said. "Stand up."

He sat there looking confused.

I put two stiff palms under his arms and stood him up. I made a fist in front of his face and waved it like the boss boy in the *Our Gang* pictures. I gestured like a shadow boxer so he'd know what was going to happen next: I punched him in the stomach. *Just hard enough,* I thought.

I expected him to cry like a baby, but he didn't.

I picked up the red crayon I had taken from Liang's toy box and drew a line across the linoleum floor. Told him to keep to his side. He nodded. I put crayoned X's on the two drawers that were his. The bottom two. He understood.

He looked up at the torn calendar on the wall. It had a picture of cowboys rounding up cattle.

"You like cowboys?" I said.

He nodded. He opened his suitcase and pointed at a worn stuffed doll. I picked it up. It had on a darkly stained cowboy outfit, but only the broad brim of a hat clung to its stitched head. I looked closer. It looked as if someone had tried to cut off the hat but gave up halfway. The stained label said *Tom Mix.* I put it back down. Second Brother would need a lot of bossing around. I was about to tell him there were bad and good cowboys, when Poh-Poh called us down to eat.

Later that evening, when he was trying on one of my old undershirts, I inspected him some more.

He pulled away his sweater and yanked off his shirt. I was prepared to laugh at his exposed cartoon skeleton, but when he turned away, I noticed red lines running over his back, as if Long John Silver had tied him up and had lashed him a dozen times.

"Don't move," I said. I traced my thumb along one of the darkest lines. The thin, deep line began at his bony right shoulder and went diagonally across the tip of his spine.

He hardly flinched.

"What's this?"

"Ba-bah hit me," he said.

I shouted for Poh-Poh and Stepmother to come upstairs. The Old One took one look and said, "*Yes, yes, the belt,*" as if she had expected to see such marks. Stepmother stood by the doorway carrying Liang-Liang in her arms. Only Sister was alert to the newcomer and stared pensively at him.

"Jung-Sum," Stepmother said, "Third Uncle is downstairs. He brought some dumplings just for you to eat later. Some friends left us clothes for you, too. Come down and see."

"One minute," Grandmother said. She had been studying the criss-crossing lines. "Wait."

Stepmother and I watched in silence while Poh-Poh came back from her room and applied one of her special ointments on Jung-Sum's back. No one had ever hit me like that, the way Poh-Poh had been hit when she was a slave girl in China. I only ever got knuckled, and once at school, three straps on the hand for spitting.

I thought, *He's tough.*

The Old One said to him, "Put on undershirt and your green sweater. We go downstairs now."

Poh-Poh offered her hand, but Second Brother ignored it and waited for her to walk out first. Poh-Poh shrugged and gave Stepmother a pleased look as she passed. Their small footsteps on the stairs made the same sound, like an echo.

I didn't move.

Stepmother stood in the doorway, looking at me. Sister Liang was now clinging to her dress; her cloth doll hung upside down from her tiny fist.

When the Old One led my new brother into the parlour, I heard Father shouting out a welcome. He and Third Uncle were drinking Tiger Bone wine. Father's voice rose above Poh-Poh's laughter. "A toast to my new son—to Jung-Sum, who will be the Second Brother of my First Son, Chen Kiam-Kim, and Second Brother to their Only Sister Jook-Liang!" Glasses clinked. There was another toast to Poh-Poh and to her three grandchildren.

"I long for three grandsons," she cried. "Then I die soon."

Laughter rumbled up the staircase.

Sister Liang ran into the room and plunked herself down on the fold-out cot.

"Your new brother's cot doesn't take up too much room," Stepmother said at last.

I sniffed.

"You hardly use all those drawers, and the closet is big enough for three boys."

My mouth would not unbend.

"*Why?*" I asked.

"Father and Poh-Poh wanted another boy in the family."

"Why didn't his own mother and father keep him?"

"They're dead," Stepmother said.

My fists tightened.

"Both of them?"

She took a deep breath to say it all at once. "Jung-Sum's father drank too much. He came home and killed Jung's mother, then he killed himself. Some men are driven by demons."

I imagined the truth of that, but I wondered how that might happen, for one to be so driven by demons as to kill himself.

"You saw the marks on his back. He wasn't lucky like you, Kiam-Kim."

Father called for us to come join him. Stepmother went to my dresser and tossed me a sweater.

"You have a good father," she continued.

I put my head under the sweater. Her soft voice penetrated my ears.

"You have a good *nai-nai* like your Poh-Poh. This boy has no one."

"No one?" I pushed my arms through the wool sweater and wondered what it would be like to have no one.

Liang turned over on the cot and mimicked my voice: "*No one?*"

"Unless we take Jung-Sum in"—Stepmother sat down beside Liang and began to retie her ribboned hair—"no other family in Chinatown will take him."

Poh-Poh had come up the stairs to see what was holding us up. Liang clung to her Raggedy-Ann doll.

"Why not?" I asked.

"Some people think Jung-Sum is cursed," Stepmother said. "Not lucky to lose a father and mother that way."

A history, brief as breath. There were no more details left to tell a boy like me.

"Why *us*?"

"Father knew his father," Stepmother said. "They were boyhood friends, students together back in the village."

Everyone in Chinatown seemed to know everyone else. You only had to say your surname, mention any Kwangtung county—*Sam-yup, Sze-yup, Chungshan, Heungshan*—even mention *Canton, Hong Kong,* speak any of the city or village dialects—and smiling strangers would link you to a chain of kinfolk. In a hostile country like Canada, anyone having the same last name was enough: *we Chinese together.* But Father had known Jung-Sum's father: before the time of demons, the two had been friends.

"Good to have another grandson," Poh-Poh said. "He can grow up and work. Earn money."

I tried another tack. "Do we have to take him . . . forever? *For keeps?*"

Stepmother barely paused. "Yes, just as your father and your Poh-Poh took me in."

I thought, *I, First Son, took you in, too.*

"Kiam-Kim." Stepmother's eyes were clear and firm. "What is the right thing for us to do?"

I unclenched my fists. I did not know what to think. At last she asked me what I did not want to be asked.

"What shall be Jung-Sum's luck?"

I was not surprised when Stepmother reminded me that good luck was always connected to doing the right thing. She wanted us to be lucky, wanted Jung-Sum to be lucky. She told everyone that even when others did the right thing for her, even when she did the right thing for others, her fortune was often "a bitter luck."

Whenever Poh-Poh would say "Luck is luck, however imperfect," Stepmother would remain silent. Poh-Poh would remind her, "You lucky be in B.C. Plenty to eat in Gold Mountain."

Stepmother closed her eyes.

When I asked Poh-Poh why she always insisted Stepmother was so lucky to be living in Chinatown, the Old One would tell me how there had always been so much starvation and famine, so many bandits and wars in Old China, that Old China we had left behind and could barely remember.

"Ten *times* ten thousand die," she said, jabbing ten fingers into the air. At my bloodthirsty urging, Poh-Poh would tell me again and again of the bodies in the Canton laneways, the carcasses pushed into gutters, to be dragged away by coolies before sunrise. "Many times, Kiam-Kim, I lifted you up, and you hold your baby nose like this."

Grandmother laughed when I pinched my nose to keep her company; yet something of that time would come back to haunt me. Her vivid retelling made me feel again how my face had been swathed with thick cloth, and I would see myself toddling down crowded Canton streets, and just as Poh-Poh would put her hands under my arms to pretend to lift me up over imaginary, smoky debris, a remembered smell of cadavers in the summer heat, an acrid, putrid aroma, would suddenly burn the back of my throat. "That smell I never to forget, Kiam-Kim," the Old One would say. Though I always swallowed at the end of these talk-stories, my small ears were eager for more.

"Tell me again about you and Father!"

"*Aaaiiyaah* . . . I tell!"

And she would begin long before my own history, in an even more terrible, tragic time, when she gave birth to a boy-child who was to become my father.

Poh-Poh always bit her lower lip when she told me these stories of her raising father in Patriarch Chen's household, of their survival together in the Chen family compound. And to show me how desperate those times were, she tongued her lower lip to show how the taste of her own blood nourished her and the baby, my father, when there was barely enough to feed all the Chen family members. Fortunately, Patriarch Chen had three farms back in Toishan county. All the clan and their servants went back, and they all toiled and grew what little would grow in the greyish soil, and servants like herself survived mainly on shrivelled root vegetables. After many years, Father became a man and married the tiny woman who would become my mother. "She so beautiful," Poh-Poh would say.

Only two photos remain of those times. One Father had kept by his bedside—Mother's wedding photo. The other, Poh-Poh had kept for me. It shows a small woman with a baby in her arms, sitting on a bench before a moon gate garden. The Old One would only say, "Here is your mother and you."

In the sepia-tone picture, my mother's bound feet are lifted behind her *cheongsam,* as if she were floating on air.

I remember rummaging through the Old One's trunk one afternoon and finding a pair of tiny flower-embroidered cloth shoes, barely three inches long, like boots for a toddler.

Poh-Poh said, "Your mother wore those lotus shoes."

She tenderly took them from my hands and tightly closed the lid. From the way Grandmother held her bent head over the wooden trunk, and from the look in her eyes, I sensed enough darkness not to ask any more questions.

Even Stepmother knew not to ask too much. At the end of these talk-stories, she stayed silent, as if whatever she herself knew could not matter much. Her silence made me think that only Grandmother kept all the stories of our family, and only the Old One decided which were to be told.

Among the elders of Chinatown, there was always an understanding that some things could never possibly be told, that what mattered was that one had done whatever had been needed to survive. Doors and windows were shut on the past and should not be opened. In the end, even Poh-Poh agreed, only luck truly mattered.

"Better be lucky than smart," she said.

Stepmother saw my confusion. Just do the right thing, Kiam-Kim. Remember to do what is right."

"Oh, yes . . ." Poh-Poh's voice quavered as she shut her eyes. "Only . . . the right thing."

The Old One lowered her head. She looked as if she were deep in prayer, like the ladies at the Good Mission Church.

"Are you praying, Poh-Poh?" I asked.

The Old One covered her mouth to stifle her laughter.

For the first two months, Second Brother didn't say very much. He listened, the way Liang did, open-mouthed to Poh-Poh's stories about the Monkey King and Pigsy, and played with Only Sister in the backyard under our watchful eyes. He sensibly obeyed Father and Stepmother, but he always studied me from the corner of his eye.

By the time he was five, I realized he wanted to be what his First Brother was: tough. I let him slug me a few times and told him not to hold back. But he was too scrawny to hit with any force. I told him if he was going to be as skinny as an alley cat, then he had to learn how to fight like one.

"I'm tough!" he said, wildly throwing up his fists for a fight.

As he slugged away, I hauled him up in the air and spun him, squealing, like a propeller while Liang jumped up and down shouting for her turn. Then we all got scolded by Poh-Poh for waking her up from her nap in the rocker. I told her we were being tough.

"Tough not noise!"

Jung and Liang-Liang tolerated my bossy ways when I followed Stepmother's and Poh-Poh's instructions to tell them to tidy up their toys or, whenever we went walking down Pender, to stick by me while the women went into the shops. Liang always wanted to hold Father's hand if he were walking with us, but otherwise she reached for my thumb and yanked on it for me to slow down. Other times, at home, when Jung decided to make monster faces and chase Liang giggling down the hall and through the parlour and back into the dining room where Father or I were working with our pencil or brush, with a quick glance up at me and then at the two romping through, Father indicated my duty.

"Father and I are working," I would say, taking on as best I could Father's solemn tone.

"We're having squealing matches!" Jung would protest.

Often I would have to catch Liang and toss her hollering and laughing onto the sofa. Jung would climb over me to save her, and we all three would end up in more horseplay. But that didn't last. Father gave me a stern lecture on setting an example.

"How can they be well mannered when First Son behave badly?"

Poh-Poh said, "Maybe Jung-Sum take charge."

Jung jumped to attention.

"No, no," he said, "Dai-Goh stay Number One. He take care of us all the time!"

I had been teaching him how to take on the two playground bullies that had started teasing him for being a "skinny Chink."

"Hit or run," I told him. "Or just run. No use being a fool if you're outnumbered."

Jack was in the backyard with us and put in his two cents.

"If you're outgunned," he said, "first kick them in the balls *and then* run!"

It didn't sound fair to me, but from the street games we played, Jack knew that Jung was a fast runner.

"What do you say, Dai-Goh?"

I shrugged. I didn't want to sound weak in front of Jack. "You figure out what you can get away with."

Jack elbowed me out of the way. He looked Jung squarely in the eye. "Can you kick as quickly as you can run?"

"Sure," Jung said.

"Kick high to the balls?"

"I guess so."

"There's your answer, pal! No one chases after you when you kick them there."

After supper, Jung took me aside. "Was Jack right, Dai-Goh?"

As Big Brother, I knew I had to give him a good enough answer. I sucked in my cheeks the way Third Uncle would do whenever he was thinking about something.

"The bully picked on you first," I said, "so I think you should kick and run—if you can. You decide."

Liang overheard us.

"I bite," she said.

We asked Father what was the right answer.

"Run away is always better," Father told us. "No one hurt and no one in any more danger."

"But what if I feel hurt?" I said.

"In Gold Mountain *outside* always hurt. But *inside*"—Father patted his heart—"no one can touch if you strong and proud. *Inside* matter more. You decide."

Jung nodded. I thought of the scars on his back. The outside. Second Brother's inside smiled up at me.

"Yes, yes," he said, in the enthusiastic way Poh-Poh always repeated herself if she was in agreement. "I decide."

By chance, Father had used my words. Jung looked up at me as if I were the smartest boy he knew. Liang came running at him again, trying to make him chase her.

"Play quiet," he said. "Dai-Goh and I talking."

Father and Stepmother were rarely home long enough to entertain the three of us. Stepmother left the house at five each morning, picked up by a co-worker in a truck and taken to Keefer Wholesale Grocery. There, alongside other women, she sorted and trimmed vegetables and rinsed countless heads of lettuce and cabbage before they were sent to over a hundred Chinese greengrocers. When she came home, Poh-Poh would rub Stepmother's water-wrinkled hands, and every two weeks she would treat them in a pan of warm paraffin. Father massaged her neck and back. And big Mrs. Lim taught me how to wrap the teapot with a towel when she made a special herbal tea for all of us, a revitalizing tonic she used to make for her one-eyed husband. Sometimes Poh-Poh added a little bit of grated ginger.

"Good for *che* energy, Gai-mou," Mrs. Lim told us as she placed two fingers on the nape of Stepmother's neck. "Need heat inside here."

Che was important for good health. I took a sip or two of the bitter stuff with a spoonful of honey and could feel my muscles growing. Jung-Sum took a sip, too, and made a face. Liang stuck out her tongue and ran away from any attempt to give her a taste.

Father could have engaged us with many of his stories of Old China, but he was always busy in pursuit of one part-time job after another. He was helping small storekeepers with their accounts, waiting on tables when he had the time, and writing letters for the uneducated elders and unemployed labourers who sent lies back to village families, often evading the truth about their despair and sinking funds. Father was also kept busy at Third Uncle's remaining warehouse, filling in customs documents and invoices and always dealing with Third Uncle's panic over the account books and their diminishing numbers. Between jobs, Father wrote a few articles and filed interviews for some of the

Chinese-language journals. He and Stepmother used every earned dollar to keep us fed and clothed, and saved the pennies because one day, he told me, I would have to finish my education and take over as First Son and do my share. How hard he worked and studied his English books was how hard I should always work.

Father often came home too exhausted to think of telling fables to us. When we asked for them, he laughed and said he counted on Grandmother to be the family storyteller. Then he winked at Stepmother, who always protested that she knew only some Christian Bible stories preached by Patriarch Chen.

"Impossible to believe," she said. "Whales swallowing up people and spitting them out alive!"

And so there was only Poh-Poh to be counted on to tell the Old China tales to us. They were the stories she had told Father when he was a small boy and Father said they would be the same stories we would one day tell our own children. I didn't think that would happen: if Stepmother found the Christian stories too far-fetched, and Father didn't think the Old China stories were worth his own time to tell, then why would I tell anyone, Jack O'Connor or stubborn Jenny Chong, let alone my own future children, about the dragons and devious Fox Lady and the talking pigs and monkeys on sacred treks that once lived in Old China.

When I was almost ten, I stood with one foot deep in the rippling waves of Poh-Poh's storytelling while my other foot stood firmly on dry ground. I would watch over my siblings, catch them if they slipped into Poh-Poh's beguiling waters, as I had often slipped in my dreams, half believing trains to be iron dragons. I decided that one of my duties would be to explain to Jung and Liang what was real, what was true, in Gold Mountain, just as Father had done for me, taking me to the echoing CPR Roundhouse where the ear-shattering train engines were shunted and turned around to head back east. I would turn my siblings around to see the world as it truly was. Show them at the proper time that the world was scientific and solid, just as Miss Kinny, with her chemistry demonstrations, had confirmed to us at school. Yet when the talk-story mood entered into our day, it was hard even for me to resist.

"This story true . . . oh, so long ago . . .," the Old One always began.

"Dragons and talking monkeys!" I demanded. "They really true?"

"Not so true today," Poh-Poh would say, a little disgruntled at my challenge. "But very true a long, long time ago in Old China."

Jung-Sum crossed his legs and pushed me aside. "When was that time, Poh-Poh?"

The two at her side wanted so much to hear the story, they shifted restlessly on their bums.

"When?" Liang repeated.

"When ancient dragons and talking monkeys ruled the world, oh, way even before I was born . . . just ask Mrs. Lim."

Jung-Sum's eyes shone with amazement. I knew it was useless to argue over details at such a moment. Besides, I still wanted to hear the stories, so that, late in bed, as Jung-Sum tossed about and the flimsy curtains shifted gently with possibilities, I could sense the wonder that must be visiting him in his dreams, the time during which fierce dragons and birds of paradise all had appeared before me, too. During those years of my dreaming, Father said that from his own bedroom he could hear me shouting in my sleep.

"What did I say?"

"You said, 'Poh-Poh, talk-story!'"

Stepmother smiled when she was told this. She must have thought that was my Chinese brain starving for more stories.

No, I would be patient with Second Brother and Only Sister: they, too, would need a Chinese brain, or be forever *mo no*.

Late one afternoon, as the skies darkened, gossiping Mrs. Lim said that her back was telling her that a rainstorm was headed towards us. Though we might be scattered with our toys and books in separate rooms, Liang and Jung could be summoned at once for talk-story time like hungry dogs to dinner.

I took my time.

"*Fa-dee lah! Fa-dee lah!,*" Poh-Poh called out to me. "Hurry! Hurry! I talk-story now."

The Old One's clearing her throat and shifting in her seat would quickly settle down the two youngest beside her in the kitchen, knee-clinging Only Sister and stool-perching Second Brother Jung. Then came stand-alone me. I leaned against the doorway, as if I was not going to be fooled like Liang and Jung, who would be swallowing every word Poh-Poh spoke.

Our largest teapot sat between big Mrs. Lim and Grandmother. This was going to be a long story.

"I tell story about Mistress Mean-Mouth," Poh-Poh began, making a shuddering gesture as if a demon had just walked into the room.

A wild wind knocked against our kitchen window. Mrs. Lim rubbed her back and sighed.

Slam!

Everyone jumped. I had left the front door unlocked again.

"A house that welcomes thieves," Mrs. Lim said. "Get me a cushion from the sofa, Kiam-Kim."

"I talk-story," Poh-Poh said again, ignoring me. I rushed out to lock the front door and came back with the cushion.

Mrs. Lim pulled in her chair and settled down on the cushion. "I listen." With her thick palm she pushed aside the flour sack of carrots and turnips on the table, moved the bottle of pickled cabbage, and reached into the half-filled bucket of unshelled peas picked from her garden. She and Poh-Poh both began shelling the peas, dropping them into a porcelain bowl. The Old One tossed aside the green shells, working quickly. Mrs. Lim picked out a thick carrot from the sack, wiped it clean with the dark sleeve of her wool sweater.

"Fatten up, Jung-Sum," she said.

Jung caught the carrot in mid-flight. At six, Second Brother was now more lanky than thin. He bit into the carrot like one of those cartoon rabbits. Mrs.

Lim wiped a smaller one for Liang to chew on, but she saw nothing to offer me. I hated raw carrots anyway.

All this delay and settling down was meaningful. The story was to be a very special tale and required dawdling about to build up the suspense. An old trick.

Poh-Poh sighed, her mind settling in to talk-story. Only after the third and final sigh would she begin. But we were to sit still and wait respectfully. Even Mrs. Lim, whose very breathing grew quiet, slowed down the shelling. We sat while the Old One tilted her small head and brushed back the white strands. She gave the two youngest a sidelong glance, a warning to sit still, or absolutely no three-sigh-story would be told.

Big Mrs. Lim picked up the teapot and filled two china cups for herself and Poh-Poh.

I was growing impatient. From the corner of her eye, Poh-Poh caught me squirming and smiled.

In China, Father had explained to me, storytellers rattled noisemakers or knocked wooden clappers together, but even when a good crowd had gathered around them, there was always the waiting. The more famous the storyteller, the longer the wait. And three-sigh storytellers were the most desirable. With the loud second sigh, the hushed crowd understood more coins were required. Coins clinked into his cap to encourage the third sigh. With a satisfied glance at his cap, and only after the last exhalation, he would begin the story. Father said that a poor teller of tales would need to begin right away, even before he sat down, or everyone would depart. Poh-Poh was a three-sigh storyteller, and our coins to her were our squirming impatience for her stories of Old China.

Poh-Poh sighed a second time. Mrs. Lim put down her teacup. Both women studied us to see whether we were ready.

Excited, Jung snapped at his carrot. Liang pretended to chew, merrily displaying her missing tooth. The Old One looked at each of us. Satisfied, she gathered her breath, summoning up the third, crucial sigh. I sank back against the doorway.

"Don't stand like useless boy," Poh-Poh said to me instead of sighing. "Sit. Clean turnips. Grown-up job, Kiam-Kim."

She plopped into my hand her favourite rasp, a curved blade with a rough sandpaper surface that she wielded like a weapon. Until that day, I had never been allowed to touch it. Too sharp, too dangerous. She shoved a large tin bucket my way and upended the flour sack with a bang. Liang jumped. Head-sized turnips and thick carrots tumbled out, rattling the sides of the galvanized bucket. Dust rose in the air.

I sat myself down on the extra crate.

"You know what to do?"

"Yes," I said, having seen her use the razor-sharp weapon with a sculptor's ease, carving a winter melon. Jung-Sum looked at me with envy. I had almost forgotten there was a story to be told. Poh-Poh's third sigh came at last. She had been waiting for me to do my part.

I reached for a large turnip and leaned it against the lip of the pail between my knees. The hardened dirt from Mrs. Lim's backyard flew off the root. The kitchen smelled of earth and pods. I was doing a man's job. Everyone watched me. Then Liang shuffled restlessly in her chair and cried out for the story to be told. Jung chewed on the end of his carrot and nodded, *yes, yes!* Mrs. Lim laughed and said I was doing a good job on those turnips: "Just like my dead one-eyed old man used to do." All this talk teased us into unbearable anticipation.

Finally, Mrs. Lim poured more tea and urged Poh-Poh to begin.

Silence.

We heard an incredible *fourth* exhalation, Poh-Poh's signal that this story, rare and surely to be fantastic, was a most important one. Liang and Jung stopped wiggling. Distant thunder sounded. The room darkened. We held our breath. Mrs. Lim reached over and snapped on the light. Shadows darted away. Unable to stop my Chinese brain, I thought of ghosts.

With eyes closed, her head titled back, the Old One began.

"Once upon a long ago in Old China, in the time of my slave years . . ."

She put down the bowl of peas and lifted Liang onto her knee. She turned Liang around to show Jung and me how she was taught to comb the waist-length hair of the young mistress, who lived like a royal princess.

"Hair down all the way here," she said, patting Liang-Liang's bum. "Face like pie plate. Every time I be with her, I see the two corners of her mouth go one way, *down*-way. Like this." Poh-Poh pulled at the corners of her mouth. "When she carp at me, her words so *mean* to me, so cruel, the words drop like stones into my heart."

Poh-Poh was warned not to pull at hair tangles or she would be beaten with a slim bamboo cane.

"Mistress Mean-Mouth, oh, she always yelped if I tug too hard," Poh-Poh said, tugging gently at Liang's hair. "My little hands carefully, *very carefully,* pull down the long comb, one slow, gentle stroke after another. Pull comb, *once, twice,* my hand shake. Tremble."

But the comb was magical, we knew.

"Tell about the comb," Mrs. Lim prompted.

I could see Liang's eyes light up. Jung held his breath.

Decorative carved creatures were entwined around the rosewood handle of the oversized comb—two life-like serpents with fierce dragon heads, with inlaid pin-point gems for shiny eyes. Most marvellous of all, in the night, when everyone was asleep, these serpents moved about, their tails slithering.

"Oh," Poh-Poh said, catching the tilt of my doubt-ing head. "I tell you how I know this."

In a dream one night—one of those nights when she had been beaten and sent to bed without food— one of the two serpents spoke to Poh-Poh and granted her a single wish. With a child's hopeless misery, Poh-Poh clutched her stone pillow and wished the Mistress a terrible death, never to bother anyone again.

"I wake up and grab the comb. I look—" The Old One barely smiled, wetting her lower lip." One serpent tail now over *here,* the other one over *there.* Not by the end of the handle. Both tails inches away from where they once reposed."

"How come, Poh-Poh?" Jung asked, his eyes wide.

"Yes, yes, I asked that, too," the Old One said. "I asked the Number Two house servant. He tell me the rare rosewood comb once carved by a magician. Fine teeth sliced from ancient turtle shell. 'You get your wish,' the old servant told me. *The Mistress will die.*'"

Jung twisted his leg around the stool. "Is that truly true?"

"Of course!" Mrs. Lim said. "In China, witches and magicians everywhere."

"No," Jung said. "I mean the comb."

Mrs. Lim looked at Poh-Poh. The two women shook their heads in disbelief. How could a child doubt the truth?

"Comb had two serpents," Poh-Poh said. "Oh, yes, yes. I never to forget."

"Yes, yes," Mrs. Lim said. "A Chinese comb is not a five-cent Woolworth comb! Many combs with serpents made in China. Why should your Poh-Poh not say so?"

Jung nodded. He watched the Old One drop more peas into the Blue Willow bowl.

"Why wasn't the magic comb made of—*gold!*"

"Because made of rosewood," Mrs. Lim said. "Who can change wood to gold?"

"Ah, yes," Poh-Poh said. "If that was possible, I would be rich with gold, with jade, and have by my side today six more grandsons."

"If we can change the past by lying," Mrs. Lim said,

helping herself to some raw peas, "these will change to pearls." Mrs. Lim put a few into Jung's hands. "See? *Still* peas!"

Jung stared at the green spheres, then bit into one. *Peas,* for sure.

"Tell what happened," Jung said, chewing slowly. "Poh-Poh, tell what happened."

I stopped scraping. There was perfect silence. The turnip in my hand seemed to be listening, too.

A sigh.

"Every morning, first thing, I comb her hair. If Mistress yelp, she call me *cat-bitch,* slap me hard. Lash me with her bamboo cane. Every night I sleep on the kitchen floor, I clutch the magic comb and wish her dead. Every night, with the comb beside my stone pillow, I hear the hiss of snakes. *Ugly cat-bitch!* Mistress Mean-Mouth yell at me. Every morning, her thick hair snag and snarl: she hit me again and again."

"What did you do?" Liang asked, clutching at Poh-Poh's elbow. "Did you trick her?"

It was a question I wanted to ask. To survive in this world, Third Uncle once warned me, you had to know that demons and even good ghosts used trickery to test your character. Demons you had to outwit; with good ghosts you had to prove your character a worthy one. But human trickery could go either way. Liang knew from Poh-Poh's stories that deception often meant survival. I knew that a ghost or demon would soon appear. Always at the last minute.

"Trick her?" Poh-Poh smiled. Her voice fell into a

whisper. "One day, the cook told me to soak the comb overnight in the wide-mouth jar sitting on the shelf above my head. The deep jar was filled with pure cooking oil. 'Be sure always to wipe the comb off,' he instructed me, 'then use it on the Mistress.'"

I asked, "Did it work?"

"Slowly, slowly"—the Old One's small, wrinkled hands drifted up and down—"with trembling hand I pull the comb through the Mistress's hair. Her long fingers tightened on the cane, ready to strike me if I slipped. But the combing went as smooth as wind. No more knot. No tangles. And by the fifth day, Mistress's hair shone like black silk in the morning light."

"Good, good." Jung laughed.

I said, "Then what happened?" Caught!

"*Aaaiiyaah.*" Poh-Poh's voice faltered. "One day there was no fresh cooking oil to be found. The big jar was empty. Not a drop. At the great Full Moon banquet in the main hall the night before, so much food was cooked, the three family cooks had used up all the oil. All that was left was thick grease, thick, brown syrup left in a deep pan."

Liang clutched her hands. "What you do, Poh-Poh?"

"I don't know what, Granddaughter. I only nine years old like Kiam-Kim."

Poh-Poh held my eyes for a moment. She looked to see that I was using the rasp properly. The Old One smiled.

"You see, I only know to push the rosewood comb into the pan, hard, like this, and let the dragon-headed serpents sink slowly into the thick, brown grease. As the handle slipped downward, Jung-Sum, I thought jew-elled eyes winked at me. The next morning, after I wiped the comb over and over again, the rosewood gleamed darker, the serpent coils so slippery. Then I saw that the two tails were fixed again by the edge of the handle, just as I had first seen them. I nervously go to comb Mistress Mean-Mouth's hair. The comb teeth slipped through even more easily . . . so *smooth*. The long hair shine even brighter, brighter than silk. Shine like polished imperial ebony."

Liang shut her eyes against the brightness.

I wanted to shut my eyes, too, the way I used to, so that Poh-Poh's world came alive in my head, more real than anything I saw or felt with my eyes open. Though I knew better, I couldn't resist.

"But her hair *smell*," Poh-Poh said, curling her fingers as if she held long silk strands of dark hair. "Smell like yesterday's great Full Moon banquet! Smell like splendid Peking roast duck, crispy-skin pork, fried quail, stuffed breast of pheasant, and fat-braised oxtail. Mistress Mean-Mouth sniffed the air. Her nose bounced back and forth like a squirrel, *sniff, sniff.*

"She said, 'I'm hungry. Get me something to eat!'

"All the poor people in the town were dying, starv-ing, but she could eat as much as she wanted, like a royal princess. This rich family shared nothing with the poor. Nothing."

"What did they do with leftovers?" Jung asked.

"Leftovers?" Poh-Poh looked sad. "You think they give even to slaves like me?"

"They feed leftovers to their dogs," Mrs. Lim jumped in. "Then, Jung-Sum, they cook and *eat* the fat dogs. Servant-slaves eat rice gruel. Maybe lucky to suck on dog bones."

Liang gasped.

I laughed with squeamish glee. But I knew that, in Poh-Poh's stories, a just punishment followed injustice. Mistress Mean-Mouth and her family had chosen their luck.

"All morning the Mistress eat and eat. One hour after lunch, she run her fingers through her hair. *Sniff, sniff.* She want to eat again. At night, even after the servants had cleared away an eight-course family dinner, she still smell *food. Sniff, sniff.*"

"Her stomach *growwwwl.*" Poh-Poh patted Liang's tummy. "She demand all the servants bring her more and more food. She go to bed. She eat. She shake her long hair and, guess what? She want more food! More ox smell, more chicken smell—more food!"

"More pork smell!" Liang shouted.

"More roast duck!" Jung joined in. I held my nose in the air and sniffed and sniffed, laughing with Mrs. Lim. We began sniffing; even Mrs. Lim raised her nose in the air, her nostrils flaring with indignation.

"Finally, I go to my own bed." Poh-Poh lowered her voice. "Every day, from spring to fall—to winter— the Mistress get fatter and fatter . . . and *fatter.*"

We looked at Poh-Poh's big friend.

Mrs. Lim laughed. "No, no, ten times fatter than me!"

"As round as this kitchen table?" Liang asked.

Poh-Poh nodded *yes, yes,* and emptied the brimming blue bowl of shelled peas into a clean pot.

I sat up, and my knees knocked against the bucket of turnips. They rolled about like decapitated heads and carrot noses. Mrs. Lim put down her teacup. I held the bucket still.

"First thing in the morning," Poh-Poh began again, "I get up as usual to groom the Mistress. Her eyes strangely shut tight, her mean-mouthed head as dark as that turnip." She pointed. "I climb up big bed, tug hair, yank *one, two,* and then *harder!* The hairy head, heavy like turnip, fell over on my knee. Suddenly, from beneath her winter quilt, I hear bubbly, *burbling* noises. I lift up autumn quilt. *Aaaiiyaah!* I scream. Her stomach split wide open, belly gaping like this—" Poh-Poh unbuttoned her quilt front and pushed aside the flaps, her thin fingers danced madly, twisting and turning. "I see hissing worms on the bed—worms and twisting *guts.*"

Liang shrieked.

Poh-Poh's eyes rolled, her head plunged backward. "Mistress Mean-Mouth"—she sighed—"*dead.*"

Jung clapped. I clapped, too, imagining the bed splashed with gobs of burbling intestines.

At my clapping, Jung must have felt the story was as true as the Old One wanted him to believe it was. I knew he was thinking of his own life, of the belt that had fallen upon his back.

The rain began to pelt the back porch.

Jung tugged on my sleeve, and I shuffled over with the bucket and leaned against the stool. His hand, settled against my shoulder, and my tongue could not speak.

Liang grasped the Old One's fingers.

"Tell, Poh-Poh," she said gently. "Tell how she look in the coffin."

Liang had stood with Jung and me one afternoon and watched a coffin being carried out of the Mission Church. The coffin had a polished brass top and shone like gold.

The Old One sighed. "She— Her hair so shiny, the hair I combed for months and months—"

Grandmother looked away, her eyes glistening. She hugged Liang to her. "Oh, Liang-Liang," she said, "she looked . . . *beautiful.*"

I saw a shadow cross the Old One's brow. Liang and Jung-Sum were too young to notice anything. I wished I hadn't—it threw me off, made me feel that I had sensed something impossible, something invisible yet . . . *there.*

Mrs. Lim broke the silence, "No use to curse the dead, Chen-Poh."

The Old One bit her lip. "At—at her funeral," she said directly to Mrs. Lim, "everyone said, 'Look, look how lovely her hair is.'"

The two women began talking to each other as if no one else were there.

"And I smiled to myself," Poh-Poh said, "proud of that beautiful, burnished hair. The other servants said, 'Look how lovely her tiny bound feet are.' But I not envy her tiny bound feet, not envy her shiny hair."

"Old One," Mrs. Lim said, "better to forget those

days. The mistress die so long, long ago."

"She dead, yes, yes"—she put her arm around Liang—"and I still live."

Liang kicked her feet. "What happened to the comb?" she asked.

Grandmother shook herself, as if shaking away a ghost. Mrs. Lim urged her to go on with the story.

"When I—" Poh-Poh began, "when I was sold a second time, I hid the comb in my jacket and took it with me."

Liang squealed with excitement. But something wasn't being told. My knees shifted, rattling the bucket of carrots and turnips.

"And then what happened?" I asked.

"I made last wish, Kiam-Kim. I stood on sampan taking me to second owners. I wished one last time"—she threw her hand out—"and tossed comb away into Pearl River."

Mrs. Lim nodded, her dark eyes tracing the comb's descent into the waves.

Our eyes followed.

We knew from other tales about the adventures of the Monkey King and the treacherous Fox Lady that it was dangerous to carry with you magic items whose luck you were uncertain of; foolish to think such magic might not harm you in the end.

"Yes, yes," Mrs. Lim said, "best to get rid of the comb."

"The wish, Poh-Poh," Jung said. "What did you wish for?"

"A secret," the Old One said. "But I promise I tell

it to First Son when right time comes. Then, maybe, he will tell you."

I squirmed with impatience, but Mrs. Lim put a finger to her lips. *A secret for now,* she was saying. *Be patient.* In my bones, I knew there was no way I could ever force a secret from the Old One.

The two women closed their eyes, remembering the past, or perhaps, as I did, imagining the rosewood hair comb floating upon the waves, a pair of beady-eyed serpents splashing out to sea. The rain fell harder. I thought of the dust on the sidewalk washed away. The rasp rested against the bucket.

The two ladies sat motionless, breathing deeply, eyes shut.

No one could ever know everything the two of them knew, close friends since their first neighbourly meetings in Old China days. When I looked down at the large turnip Poh-Poh had pointed to, I could see again Mistress Mean-Mouth's head lolling against my knee. But I also heard Father warning me again, "Don't believe all those Old China stories."

"Poh-Poh," Liang said, "tell what happened afterwards."

The Old One opened her eyes. "I told you. I was sold one more time."

"Then what happened? Did the Monkey King come?"

"No, no. Finally, a good Canton family took me in."

Liang snuggled against Grandmother's quilted warmth. Jung-Sum gazed into the air.

"I bought and sold *three* times. Three times lucky!

Then I birth a son for the Chens, and this son, well, he became your father!"

A lucky ending.

"Lucky like you, Jung-Sum," Mrs. Lim said, splitting open the last pea pod. "You a Chen, too!"

Jung-Sum untwisted his legs from the stool.

I wondered if my adopted Second Brother had ever been told such tales by his own mother. I wondered if he knew his mother had been unlucky to marry a man pushed by demons, a man who would abuse Jung-Sum, murder her, and kill himself, mysteriously leaving their son behind.

I thought, too, of Stepmother sweeping the rooms upstairs; how in Old China, Grandmother and she had been luckily rescued by the Christian Chen family. I thought of Only Sister, how Stepmother held her so tightly those first few weeks, afraid her girl-baby would be taken away. How Liang-Liang gurgled and smiled, not understanding her luck. I was the First Son and China-born, my mother dead. Did that make my luck different or the same? Was her ghost still in my head?

Would my siblings ever think of their luck at all? And what ghosts, if any, would come to live inside their heads?

Only memories.

Even after I got up, the two of them had not moved. Liang, still stiff with enchantment, clung to Poh-Poh, and Jung-Sum sat wondering. I wanted to tell Second Brother what was real. Trains were only trains, as Father had taught me. Combs were only combs, nothing more. He was older; he would understand. All at once Jung's knee pushed against my back, his heated hand clutched at my shoulder, and I saw again his hopeful eyes; I knew then that saying the obvious would be careless of me, that both Liang and he would suffer. Something had been taken away from me. If I said anything now, something in them, too, would perish.

"Time to cook supper," Poh-Poh said. She turned to me. "Take the two with you, Kiam-Kim."

But I wanted to leave them there, leave them between the two women brewing with story.

One morning before he went to the *Chinese Times* office, I asked Father about Mistress Mean-Mouth.

He told me that in the real story (so the oldest of Patriarch Chen's sons told him) the first mistress Grandmother had served as a slave-child had died in agony during the night, of an internal rupture, perhaps from overeating. Poh-Poh had not seen the doctor cut her mistress open. No one in the household had thought to wake her up and warn her to stay away.

Well, maybe her appendix burst, Father suggested when I insisted on knowing more, or maybe the mistress died from a poison. To be poisoned by a family rival or by a spiteful servant was not uncommon in those days. In fact, Father said, the Imperial family kept official food-tasters to guard against such poisoning.

"Maybe Poh-Poh poisoned her," I said.

"Frankly," Father said, laughing, "I don't know what the Old One is capable of." When he caught the dark, proud look on my face, he stopped laughing.

At once I saw the young girl that was Poh-Poh reach for a small packet of poison and shake the dark powder into Mistress Mean-Mouth's steaming soup.

I would have poisoned her, too, I thought. *Poisoned anyone who was mean or nasty to me.* I tried being a detective, like Dick Tracy, told Father some of my ideas. He laughed.

"Don't think too much about their stories," Father said. "You're getting too old for that."

I asked him if he knew what Grandmother had wished for when she threw the comb into the Pearl River.

"Her secret," Father said. "Just her Old China ways." He put down his briefcase and looked straight at me, as if to say it was foolish to guess about such wishing. "We in Canada now."

"Yes," Stepmother said, helping Father with his coat.

"Maybe soon we have another grandson for the Old One," he said. "Make her old age happy, make her forget those unhappy days when she was a servant and had no family."

Stepmother said nothing.

One spring morning we were preparing for the next day's Ching Ming Festival, the day everyone in Chinatown visited the gravesites of family or namesake members and burned incense and paper money for the spirits to spend in their next life. We also carried plates and bowls of token foods, like chicken and pork, oranges and other fruit, and bowed three times to show our respect. I mentioned that we had run out of the dark soy sauce.

"Lucky you have smart grandson!" said Mrs. Lim, wiping her wet hands on Poh-Poh's handy apron.

"You go, Gai-mou," said Poh-Poh when she noticed Stepmother's wan face and tired expression. "Get some exercise. Enjoy yourself. Buy sweet buns from the Royal." She reached into her porcelain steamer bowl, high on the shelf, and handed Stepmother some dollar bills.

The two older women had been busy preparing the chicken and pork, checking through the pantry for ingredients. Mrs. Lim had coated the chicken with dark soy in a special way, so that the roasted skin would turn crispy and taste of salt and ginger, exactly the same way her one-eyed husband had liked to eat it. Some other ingredients were running short, and Poh-Poh sent Stepmother and the three of us children to pick up some things from Chinatown.

"Go, go, go," Poh-Poh said, rushing all of us out of her and Mrs. Lim's way.

"Get fresh air," said Mrs. Lim, and I noticed how she sweetly patted Stepmother's tummy. She and the Old One burst into knowing smiles.

"Buy sweet buns," Poh-Poh said again.

Stepmother blushed when I patted her on the gut and asked if something was wrong. Her belly was pushing against her simple dress. But that wasn't too surprising. At supper, Father had pointed out that she had been eating much more than usual and had been drinking lots of tea with Mrs. Chong. Before she could answer my question, Poh-Poh came chasing us to leave the house. We rushed out the door, my head filled with thoughts of treats to be bought from the B.C. Royal bakery.

But as we stepped onto the sidewalk, another thought came to me: Stepmother was going to have a baby. *A secret,* I thought. Something children were not to know about, but to know just the same. Perhaps to say anything more would bring bad luck. Signs were everywhere for me to see and *not* see: Stepmother had blushed, Mrs. Lim had patted her belly as one might pat an eggshell, and Poh-Poh had rushed us out as if to say, *Pay no attention! Not for children to know!*

I watched for more signs. How did such things happen? Babies like Liang must have come from the tummy of Stepmother at night. After Liang was ours, I remembered, Stepmother's middle flattened out again. Jack and I had seen an alley cat drop slimy kittens from its backside. I felt queasy and stupid and wise all at the same time.

At the end of our walk into Chinatown we stood at Pender and Main and waited for Stepmother to return some mending to Gee Sook at American Steam Cleaners. Jung took a tennis ball from his pocket and played catch with Liang. I got to dash into the road and retrieve the ball a few times, the cars honking at me as if I were in danger. Finally, Stepmother came out. Gee Sook shook his head at me.

"No play on the road," he said. "Little boy killed there last week. Right over there. Head crushed by truck."

He pointed at the corner where I had dashed out. Jung's eyes widened. While Stepmother exchanged some last words with Gee Sook, Liang huddled against Stepmother's skirt. A truck honked and Stepmother jumped. I thought the baby inside the tummy must have jumped, too, but I pretended that I didn't think such things. I would let everyone tell me whatever they wanted me to know. What was the use of knowing anything more than I should know? Best to let things be, as Poh-Poh often advised Mrs. Lim.

Gee Sook was a kindly man, but he had told me once too often about the dead boy killed at the corner of the road. I counted on my fingers how many boys had died *right over there,* and ran out of fingers to count on. The cautionary story still had its effect over Jung and poor Sister Liang, but to me, bad and unlucky little boys were dying every week in Chinatown. Even Mrs. Chong said so. Yet whenever we went to the cemetery to pay our respects at the Chen Tong Memorial, I never saw any little boys buried there.

Finally, we made our way into the heart of Chinatown, along Market Alley and Columbia. Between the gaps in the buildings I could see the campfires blazing along False Creek. The smell of smoke and stagnant water drifted up towards us. Jung and Liang tugged at Stepmother to slow down while they watched a long train slowly cross Pender Street, headed for the CPR Roundhouse. Men walked with their heads down, their caps pulled over their foreheads as if to avoid looking at us. We were a family shopping together, a reminder of what they did not have. In the grey afternoon light, the striped green awnings over the street stalls sagged wet from the morning's rain.

"Everyone so unhappy," I said. I was thinking of the pictures in Father's copy of the *Herald* that showed the shopkeepers smiling. It was an article about "yellow labour" and city health standards, about Chinatown grocery stores and open live-chicken cages and why they should all be shut down.

"Yes, yes," Stepmother said, but before I could explain myself, she turned away from me to demand that Mr. Wing check his scale again. Jung-Sum raised himself up on the outdoor counter to look. The balances swung in the air, then settled.

Stepmother looked discouraged. How could this balance be correct? There were now even fewer pockets with cash to buy the special imported food from China—shouldn't things be cheaper? "Why so much!" she demanded.

"Piracy in the China Seas," Mr. Wing noted. "Japanese invasion. Famine. Civil war . . ."

The balance stood still. Mr. Wing shrugged. The weight was correct. The price of Hong Kong salted fish had tripled.

"Buy it or leave it," said Mr. Wing.

When Stepmother looked so downcast at the coins left in her palm after giving over a whole dollar bill to Mr. Wing, Liang volunteered to carry the small newspaper-wrapped package herself.

"Soon the family sell you to buy food," Mr. Wing joked to Liang.

When the husky man caught the fury in Gai-mou's eyes, he quickly retreated to the other end of the stall.

Liang looked up at Stepmother.

"No one sell you," said Jung.

"No one," I said, catching on to how Liang-Liang was trembling.

Stepmother knelt down and held the little head against herself. "No one sell you . . . no one sell you." But Liang's tears would not stop.

I picked up the dropped package of salted fish.

The next day, Stepmother said she was not feeling well enough to go with us to Ocean View Cemetery; she asked that Liang stay home to keep her company.

The Vancouver rains had started again, and Father agreed with Poh-Poh that Stepmother would be vulnerable to the graveyard dampness. Mrs. Lim, dressed all in black, said she would make some herbal tea for Stepmother when we all returned. Poh-Poh said Gai-mou should be sure to eat some of Mrs. Lim's cemetery chicken, which would be brought right home with the pork and the fruit after the ceremonies.

Third Uncle's van puttered up and his driver honked. Impatient, Third Uncle ran up to our door and knocked loudly, as if we were all deaf. Bachelors, complained Poh-Poh, never understood how long it took to dress a family for an outing.

At last we piled in for the long drive to Ocean View, the men carrying large umbrellas over the women's heads as they took the two side seats; Jung and I lugging the two boxes of foodstuffs into the back of the van; Father holding on to the sticks of incense and the box of Eagle matches; and Third Uncle carrying the two bags of token Hell money for the spendthrift dead.

Staring out the back window, I could make out Stepmother standing in the parlour window, holding Liang in her arms. I watched them through the light curtain of rain until the van jerked and pulled away.

"Sit down," Third Uncle commanded me. "Last time, a little boy fell out of this van and smashed his head on the road."

We never again shopped at Mr. Wing's stall.

Grandmother and I were sitting on the porch on two mismatched kitchen chairs. Now and then a brisk, chilly wind blew down from the snow-topped North Shore mountains and rustled the pages of my comic, and Poh-Poh pulled her thick woollen sweater tight around her shoulders. Pink and yellow flowers were in full bloom in the O'Connors' front yard, and the tendrils of bean and pea plants in our own yard were already tied to thin bamboo stakes. It was hard to focus on *Mutt and Jeff*, but Poh-Poh insisted that I sit and wait with her.

"Maybe some good news," she said, shifting her feet about on the wooden porch. "We wait." Stepmother and Father had gone to visit Mr. Gu, the old herbalist on Columbia. Stepmother had been waking up in the morning drowsy and sickly, and Father had been acutely sensitive to her moods and bringing her tea in bed. The mahjong ladies brought her gingered soups. Big Mrs. Lim was especially interested. Across the street, from her wooden shack perched high above a rockery, big Mrs. Lim hollered down at us, "Any news?"

Poh-Poh told me to wave and answer back.

"Not yet!" I shouted, and in that instant the Old One sat up. Down the street, we could both see Father and Stepmother in their long coats walking towards us.

"*Fa-dee! Fa-dee!*" Poh-Poh shouted at them. "Hurry! Hurry!" But just as suddenly her strained, impatient voice turned to concern. "No hurry! No hurry!" she cried out. "Take time! Take time!"

Poh-Poh snatched away my comic and pushed me off my chair. "Go down and help Gai-mou and Father," she said. "Take shopping bags from Father and take purse. Hurry!"

I scurried down the steps and ran the half block to meet Father and Stepmother. I took her purse, and Father, his face flushed, handed me the two bags of groceries so he could take Stepmother by her elbow. Stepmother leaned heavily on Father; her brow glistened. I walked beside them.

From the porch Poh-Poh began her urgent singsong questioning. "Yes? Yes?"

Mrs. Lim stomped her way over towards our house. She seemed to jiggle with questions but only repeated over and over the Old One's same singsong query: "Yes? Yes?"

At last, halfway up our six porch steps, Father responded: "Yes! Yes!"

Stepmother sighed loudly enough to hush up everyone. We all followed her into the house. To my surprise, instead of walking directly into the dining room or kitchen, everyone settled themselves in the parlour. Stepmother sat in the sofa chair, breathing rapidly, her face red from the sun or from exertion. Father held her hand and explained there were no taxis available. Some white labour groups were on a kind of strike, protesting against the Chinese fruit and vegetable merchants. The roads in and out of Chinatown had been blocked. The angry crowd of shouting men had parted to let them walk through.

"We don't pick on ladies," one of the white men said to Stepmother.

From her rocker, Poh-Poh waved to Mrs. Lim to sit herself down on the chesterfield.

In the silence, each one of them took a deep breath.

Stepmother dabbed her brow with her lacy handkerchief. She took pride in all the family's white handkerchiefs, washing them twice, bleaching and ironing the plain ones for Father and us kids, and always taking the time to press and starch the lace edges of the fancy Irish linen ones sold cheaply by Ben Chong at their corner store and used by her and Poh-Poh and all the mahjong ladies.

They were all waiting for Stepmother to say something. I couldn't resist repeating the query that Poh-Poh and Mrs. Lim had shouted.

"Yes? Yes?" My voice squeaked. "Yes? Yes?"

Father burst out laughing.

Playing in the backyard, Jung-Sum and Liang must have heard him through the open window, and they came running up the back stairs, dashed through the kitchen and dining room, and jumped into the parlour to join us. Often someone would have brought a box of dumplings or dried plums to share. But there was none today. The two looked confused. Father was still laughing, but the three women were silent. Poh-Poh sat up straight. She looked steadily at Liang-Liang and Jung, and then slowly her dark, sharp eyes landed on me.

"You soon have new brother," she said.

"So!" exclaimed Mrs. Lim. "Mrs. Ben Chong and I never wrong!"

"Never wrong," said Father.

"Yes, yes," Mrs. Lim said, "this time a new boy baby!"

I looked at Stepmother, who looked worried.

"Maybe a new sister," Father said quickly.

"Brother," insisted Poh-Poh. "What did herbalist say?"

"Maybe a boy," Father said. "Maybe not."

Mrs. Lim fidgeted. "We old women know better."

Everyone turned to Stepmother. With an ebbing smile she patted her tummy and said nothing.

During the next few weeks, as Stepmother's belly grew slightly rounder and she stayed home from all her part-time shifts, the mahjong ladies—Mrs. Leong, Mrs. Wong, and Mrs. Chong, and the others—visited us regularly. Third Uncle promised a celebration banquet when and if my new brother arrived.

When we were shopping together, I grew used to seeing others' tiny smiles of appreciation mingled with envy and grew accustomed to the good wishes that followed Stepmother's response to their hints of concern.

"So sure a boy, Chen Sim?"

"Everything well. Most kind of you."

"How nice! A boy baby!"

I wondered how it was when I was in my own mother's tummy in Patriarch Chen's compound in Old China. Was the tiny woman with her bound feet greeted with as much seeming warmth and concern? I asked Poh-Poh and Father for details, but they both said, 'Yes! Yes! Of course! Of course!' and turned abruptly away from me, stifling further questions. After all, I had little gold baby bracelets and a few jade amulets to prove how much I had been expected. Those would be for me to pass along to my own son one day, Poh-Poh told me. She kept everything in silk sachets, along with the silver butterfly Stepmother had given me, the silver butterfly given to Stepmother herself at her birth. Girl babies did not always get gold trinkets. All I knew was that I must have been a wanted baby, just like this new brother of mine.

With Third Uncle's return to financial stability and with his stated happiness over the news of his sponsored growing family, this boy child would not starve or ever feel unwanted. Every day, Poh-Poh kept stubbornly to the idea that Stepmother was bringing her the wished-for third grandson, though she was diplomatic and very careful only to whisper about the matter. For example, before the big ears of the Kitchen God, we were all warned to say nothing about the Old One's desire for more grandsons, not even to hint at her long-ago talk-story wish, though as she mixed, mashed, and stirred the blood-strengthening dishes, she often, and somewhat casually, invited fierced-face Tsao Chung's blessing for Stepmother's good health.

"If Heaven grows jealous . . .," Poh-Poh said, and shut her eyes tight against the possibility.

If any of the gods grew jealous, she insisted, shaking her white head, the birth would go awry. Even Father cooperated by urging all of us children to respect things as they were, to say nothing ever about Stepmother's condition. Not to anyone. Especially not to Jack next door, even though all of Chinatown seemed to know about Stepmother's situation.

"As in Old China, as in England where the King and Queen of Canada live," Father said, "respectable women in Vancouver do not leave the house."

"No," added Mrs. Lim. "Not after their tummy grows to a certain size."

"Children do not talk about these things," Mrs. Chong pointed out.

"Very *mo li* to do so," insisted Mrs. Leong.

In those summer months of 1933, Stepmother's tummy grew bigger and bigger, and she stayed home just as Father had told us she must. And we three children said nothing, just as Father and Poh-Poh with her stern looks warned us not to.

Women friends brought Stepmother sachets of mixed leaves and bits of prune to brew pink-coloured teas, and jars of vinegared pigs' feet soup to reheat. A small pile of baby clothes sat unwrapped in her bedroom. The wooden crib was brought down from the attic and thoroughly washed. Bachelor Gee Sook from American Steam Cleaners sent over eight baby-sized cushions sewn from, and stuffed with, discarded fabrics. Eight was a lucky number.

"Best cushion!" he declared, handing them over in a Woodward's shopping bag when Father went to pick up his suit jacket.

Poh-Poh prepared dishes especially for Stepmother.

"This dish help make boy-baby," she would say, setting down a shallow plate of sweetened turnip mashed with carrot and long-stemmed pea pods—which Liang and Jung got to sample—or a bowl of ginger-laced broth made of pork and chicken stock, which I tasted.

At the centre of all this attention, Stepmother smiled politely, laughed graciously at the jokes, and said little more than she needed to. Whenever Father felt a draft, he wrapped extra sweaters around her shoulders. When she was napping, he told us to play quietly outside. If it was raining, as it did most days that year, we were made to sit and read our school books or help Liang colour her pictures. Father seemed proud of Stepmother's silences, the way she sat and knitted, hummed tunes and complained little, except about a backache or two. All of us were caught by the gentle way she ruled us. Soon, Poh-Poh even made sure the handkerchiefs were all washed twice, and pressed and folded exactly the way Stepmother preferred.

No one asked, and I dared not think, "What if the baby were a *girl?*" How that troubling thought must have swirled about in Stepmother's mind but she kept calm, at least outwardly.

The Old One took me to the tong hall temple to burn incense before the statues and to ask for luck and blessings. She chattered away about Stepmother's condition—"such a humble, useless condition"—then said her deepest thoughts to herself, in a prayerful manner. Poh-Poh told me that the gods were listening most of all to her silences.

I had been looking for two empty boxes to put the Spencer's First Quality English Tea in—each bundle of six ounces a gift, one for Jung-Sum's Grade 2 teacher, Miss Jamieson, and one for my Grade 4 teacher, Miss McLean—when I noticed sitting on the pantry shelf between tall jars of dried fruit a green velvet box with a cracked red seal and an embossed gold dragon. Something rattled inside, but the lid would not open for me. The Old One raised her eyebrow and took the box away from me.

"Women only," she said.

The second week into December, Stepmother complained of severe cramps. Poh-Poh gave me the green box to take to Mrs. Lim.

"She know what to do," Poh-Poh said.

For two days, Stepmother could not even get out

of bed. Poh-Poh or Mrs. Lim stayed beside her. Father slept downstairs on the chesterfield. One morning I peeked into the big bedroom and saw the dragon box sitting on the small table. Its lid was off. I stepped in to ask Stepmother if I could get her anything. She shook her head. Poh-Poh felt her forehead. I inched my way closer to the small table. I noticed there was something like pebbles in the green box, many-coloured stones. I got Jung-Sum up and we got ready for school.

Liang shook Father's head to wake him up. He had to work the late-morning shift at Third Uncle's warehouse.

"After you finish at Strathcona today, go right to Chinese school," Father told Jung and me. "Don't bother coming home for your snack."

He handed me thirty cents to buy something to eat and drink from the Hong Kong Café. I knew we would buy some of their egg tarts and maybe a soda to share.

That night after Chinese school, when we pushed open the front door, Third Uncle ran up to us.

"Go see your new baby brother," he said, but he looked worried. "Ask Poh-Poh to let you see him before it's too— No, no, go see!"

I beat Jung-Sum up the stairs and stood breathless before the bedroom door. A little bundle lay on Stepmother's shoulder. Poh-Poh was changing something on the bed. When I walked up, before the Old One noticed, I caught a glimpse of red droplets along Stepmother's exposed belly. Poh-Poh quickly lifted the bedsheet over the nakedness. The soft voice that welcomed me didn't seem to mind.

"Come closer," Stepmother whispered. Her eyes were half closed. Her hair lay matted on her forehead. Poh-Poh gently pushed back the baby's blanket to finish wiping its limbs with a wet cloth.

Jung pushed me aside.

We both stared at the tiny, wrinkled-faced baby. It looked scrawny and unhealthy, like a black-haired plucked chicken. Then Father came upstairs with Mr. Gu, the herbalist. Jung and I were ordered out of the room.

Poh-Poh left with us. She had to change the pail of brownish water.

"What's his name?" I asked.

"Too soon for name," Poh-Poh said.

When we were halfway down the steps, the baby's wail rose into the air and turned the Old One's head.

"Name soon," she said. "Very soon."

The wailing went on. Poh-Poh looked relieved.

One month later, after considerable fussing by everyone, by Mrs. Lim with her potions and ointments, by Mr. Gu with his herbs, and by the mahjong ladies with their advice and with their share of special recipes for Poh-Poh to consider for Stepmother's recovery, the baby boy had survived long enough to be given his official name. Third Uncle made sure that the herbalist approved. He even had the baby poked and prodded by a Western doctor.

"Chen Sek-Lung," Father said at last.

All at once I thought of the stony pebbles that I had glimpsed sitting in that beautiful green box. *Sek-Lung*—"Stone Dragon." Before I could ask anything about the name, Third Uncle was already thanking Father for considering his humble suggestion. The name had reminded him of the carved long-necked stone dragon at Prospect Point that looked across the sea towards China.

Poh-Poh was asked if she approved of the name.

"Of course, we discuss this name with you first," Third Uncle told her. Father smiled.

"Is Chen Sek-Lung acceptable, Old One?"

Poh-Poh smiled back. "Yes," she said.

~ *F O U R* ~

THROUGHOUT MY ELEVENTH AND twelfth years, everything focussed on English and Chinese school work, and I also grew busy with new duties—I now routinely went with Father for an hour or two on Sunday afternoons to Third Uncle's Shanghai Alley warehouse, where, under the towering ceiling, I pulled along a handcart of account books. At every one of the three storage floors, I clambered over stands of huge boxes and shouted out their code numbers while Father checked off the inventory list. When we were finished, we would go to one of the noodle houses on Pender with some of his friends and some elders.

Certain Saturdays, after I finished my morning Chinese classes, Jung-Sum and I met at Gore and Pender and took turns carrying the grocery bags for Stepmother. Poh-Poh would be home with baby Sekky, cooing over him every waking minute.

Second Brother and I also took regular turns filling up the sawdust pails ready for feeding the chute on the side of the kitchen stove. Chopped logs had to be piled neatly beneath the back stairs, then covered with a large canvas tarp. We were also assigned to help Mrs. Lim with her load of logs when she couldn't find anyone else who would, for ten cents an hour, carry them up the two and a half flights of precarious stairs to her little house. The money was paid in an envelope to Stepmother or Father, who always said, "For your school books."

Mrs. Lim fed us well during those lugging sessions, calling us good grandsons and telling Poh-Poh how we were building up our muscles.

"Good for fighting," said Poh-Poh.

Though my time with Jack O'Connor was restricted, we still managed to meet up for sword fighting, acting out Robin Hood episodes in his backyard, or climbing over each other's porch like Sinbad the Sailor jumping from one prayer tower to another.

One morning, before a shopping expedition with Stepmother, Jack was showing off to Jung-Sum how he could swing like Tarzan from a thick rope we "found" near the ice house and which we had securely tied up to our porch. Jack now decided to tie the rope even higher. He climbed up to the roof and knotted it around one of the metal anchors bracketing the eaves.

"See if it'll hold," he hollered down to us.

Jung and I pulled down with our whole weight, and the rope held. Then I tossed the end of the rope to see if it would reach the O'Connors' porch. It swung like a loose snake and easily crossed to the other side. I figured that Jack would have to fly through the air at a harrowing angle to avoid banging into our corner post. I leaned over the bannister and warned him about the angle.

"Don't wet your pants," he said. "I can see that post from up here."

"Let me go next," Jung-Sum shouted up, just as Jack flew into the air with his Tarzan yell.

For a few exciting seconds, everything was going aces. Jack's lanky body came swinging down in a perfect arc, but suddenly he realized gravity had taken over, and he had only a split-second to jerk himself out of the way of the post. His foot lifted, his hips swung sideways, then his whole body angled out of kilter like a piece of lumber. He missed the post and went swinging down as planned. Jung's mouth fell open. I was about to yell 'Watch out!' but before a single word could escape me, Jack went flying across and into his own porch and crashed through the front window.

Afterwards, Jack told me that he wasn't the one doing all the screaming, it was his mother. "She gets hysterical," he said.

She'd been sitting having tea with a friend when two feet came hurtling at them, followed by shattering panes of glass and Jack himself, thumping down hard onto the shards, his limbs entangled in curtain and rod.

Jack required stitches just above his knee. That impressed Jung even more.

The next day, the rope still tied to our roof, Father made me walk over with Jung-Sum and apologize to Jack's parents. Father even offered to pay a share of the damage. But when Mr. O'Connor walked outside and saw Stepmother carrying diapered Sekky onto our porch, he told father to put away his wallet.

"Jack's big feet and thick head were the main problem," he said. "My boy has absolutely no common sense."

Jack was not allowed out for two weeks, but later he had fun showing off to the gang at MacLean Park the Frankenstein stitches on his leg. I thought Jack limped a little more than he needed to, but his injury made us both the centre of attention.

"Kiam was ripped up a bit, too," Jack would boast for me in front of the gang at recess. He gravely indicated an area near my groin. "But his granny won't let anyone see."

I kept my mouth shut. I wasn't sure whether I should have limped a little, too.

"You have to give them some blarney," said Jack when we were on our own. "Makes life interesting."

Later, I asked Father what Mr. O'Connor meant by Jack's having no common sense.

"That means," said Father, "*mo no!*"

That made me feel good. Jack and I both lacked the same thing.

By 1935, shadowy men and darker events edged the ragged borders of our life in Chinatown. More and more hobo shacks and corrugated-tin lean-tos were being built in small enclaves along False Creek.

"Very bad," Father said as he and Third Uncle looked out from the third-storey warehouse window and observed the hut-like humps growing around the distant steam ducts and heating vents under the Georgia Viaduct.

"Never go there," warned Third Uncle.

Mrs. Chong claimed that at least two hundred unemployed men were living in those hovels, cooking over open fires and sharing pots of gruel salvaged from the slop pails of Chinatown restaurants. Segregated areas were now populated by Chinamen who had lost their seasonal jobs and who could no longer afford sharing a shift-time room, often just a bed with three or four others taking their turn to sleep; dozens had already starved to death, their bodies found in the rooming houses in Canton Alley, in the weekly-rental hotel rooms along Hastings and Main Street, and in the deserted alleyways.

"Those place stink with death," said Third Uncle.

He was on a committee of merchants and land-lords, part of the Chinese Benevolent Association, who volunteered to open up their warehouses, base-ments, and backrooms to shelter and feed some of the homeless.

The Vancouver Health Board was set to condemn Chinatown's efforts. Men and women were coughing all night; many coughed up blood.

Father and others from Chinatown joined a com-mittee set up by a United Church preacher to organize some soup kitchens. Late at night, Chinatown restau-rants brought out unsold soup and soon-to-be-spoiled food to serve to lineups of waiting men. The rule was quickly established that no one would come to the front of the Chinese cafés or restaurants and frighten away the paying customers. One came to ask for food only in the back alleys, and only after dark. Even the unwashed white faces came to understand that. No one was turned away.

Father told me the Canadian government would offer the hungry men and some women their fully paid passage back to China, but only if they agreed to surrender their original documents and sign a contract that said they would never return to Canada.

"They all come to Gold Mountain with hope," Third Uncle said. "They work hard for ten or twenty years and leave with only what they can carry back in one suitcase."

I remember going with Father to the docks to wave goodbye to a group who had accepted the free passage. Hundreds of men and the few women who saw no more future in Gold Mountain, carrying no more than a smelly duffel bag or a battered suitcase, often dressed in second- and third-hand coats, all of them sadly pushing their way up the gangplanks.

"Why not starve and die in China?" said one old man to Father. He bent down and shook my hand and wished me well in Tin-Pot Mountain. His stumpy hand felt funny, but I knew better than to back away. Father had warned me about such hands. Old Beard had first helped to clear the forest for the railroad tracks; he lost a few fingers in the shingle mill, yet with his hooked fists he had hauled nets on salmon boats until he could do so no more. Jobs vanished from the West Coast, and jobs fit only for the labouring Chinese were the first to go.

"Why not die in Toishan?" asked Old Beard. "Why not be buried back home? You remember that, Kiam-Kim. You Chinese."

Poh-Poh understood. Old Beard's bones would not have to wait their proper return to ancestral burial grounds. His ghost would not have to wander in Gold Mountain crying out for his Old China ancestors.

Elderly men that Poh-Poh once fed at our second-floor apartment came to our Keefer Street house to say goodbye.

"I never to forget you, Kiam-Kim," one said to me. "How tall you be now!"

"Take care of Poh-Poh," another said. "Listen to your good father!"

When Stepmother invited them in, pushing Only Sister aside to make way, they shook their heads.

"I not too clean," some would say, perhaps catching Liang-Liang wrinkling her nose at the smell of their unwashed bodies.

Stepmother told me that it might break their hearts to see how all of us lived in a house, how we were living as a family in Gold Mountain. Some of the men patted Jung-Sum on his head and gave him and Liang-Liang a handful of candies. I sometimes got a red packet with their last coins enclosed.

"For school," a few would say.

I would refuse, three times, and three times the *lei-see* would be pushed back into my hand. Then they would turn from our door and walk slowly away, or Father would walk with them down the porch steps, promising to see them one last time at the docks.

"I say goodbye now," Poh-Poh would say from the front door, carrying Sek-Lung in her arm. "I die soon."

The men would protest, but then they would laugh along with Grandmother, shaking their heads sadly at the same time; after all, whether young or old, they joked, who could live forever?

Later, I was told that some sickened and died in the fourth-class hold of the slow steamers that took them back. Others jumped into the ocean, unable to bear the shame of going home with less than nothing in their pockets.

Beside a few obituary lines published in the Gold Mountain newspapers, some formal names were noted under the heading "Missing at Sea."

"Who's that name?" I asked Father, who was reading the list aloud to Poh-Poh. They were both commenting on the last formal name, as if they had known the person very well.

"Old Beard," said Stepmother. "Do you remember him?"

If I hadn't been so busy being protective of him, I would almost have been proud of Jung-Sum.

Father constantly emphasized that we all had to take care of one another, and the oldest son would always be the one the family members would most depend upon. Stepmother taught me that Jung-Sum and Liang would pay attention to my example, and so I was to do my very best in school.

As First Son, I had a responsibility that weighed

heavily on me: to set an example, to never let the family down, to never give them cause to be ashamed of me.

"What's ashamed?" Jung-Sum asked me.

"It's when you do something bad and—and . . ."

"And everyone wishes you weren't part of the family," said Poh-Poh.

Second Brother shivered.

"No worry," Poh-Poh said. "We raise you up to be good. Never to shame the family."

But Jung-Sum insisted on hearing examples of shameful behaviour.

"You murder someone," explained the Old One. "That very shameful to family."

"How about stealing?"

Poh-Poh thought a moment. She guessed what Second Brother was thinking: the Old One often put extra "samples" into her shopping bag at Mr. Lew's vegetable stall when he put out dried fruits, salted greens, or fresh peas for customers to taste or sniff.

"Big stealing," she said finally. "Big stealing very bad."

"How big?"

"Too many questions!"

Stepmother smiled at the Old One's impatience. Wrinkled eyes caught her looking too comfortable.

"What do you say, Gai-mou?"

"When you do something bad," she answered, "something inside will tell you."

"That's what Miss Schooley tells us," I said. "Except very bad people don't know how to tell right from wrong. Miss Schooley says they don't have education."

Poh-Poh nodded, grateful for the change in subject. "Study hard like Kiam-Kim," she told Jung and Liang, then set down a cup of tea beside me as if I were to be respected as much as Father was respected behind his pile of notebooks and invoices.

"The oldest branch bear the most fruit," Mrs. Lim once said to me.

I thought she meant to compliment my stature as First Son, but as was the way of village women, the saying was to warn me of the unspeakable burdens that lay ahead. Third Uncle later revealed to me that when Mrs. Lim's only brother, many years older than her, was in his thirties and none of his three brides had produced a single child, he hanged himself from a courtyard tree. Then her family sent Mrs. Lim away to be a mail-order bride to a desperate stranger in Gold Mountain.

I asked Poh-Poh why Mrs. Lim's brother didn't pick up a son like we had Jung-Sum. After all, children were bought and sold in Old China.

"Too proud," she said, turning away from me with a look that disturbed Stepmother and puzzled all of us, especially Jung-Sum. Poh-Poh reached out to him and took his hand. "Never worry. You be family with us," she said. "You hear what I say, Kiam-Kim?"

I nodded, sipped my tea, and turned back to my textbook.

The Depression soon set me free from my work duties at Third Uncle's warehouse; it was considered inappropriate for children to be doing work that an unemployed man might do. Children in Chinatown never starved, for the Benevolent Society kept track of the Tong families. And Father and Stepmother had part-time work offered to them, however menial.

I was at liberty to play.

Jack had started to go to the Hastings Gym for boxing lessons. He was a few months older than me, taller and heavier than I was, and he qualified for the twelve-to-fourteen Second Junior Level.

I took Jung to the gym to watch Jack. At night, I would walk into our bedroom and catch him boxing with his shadow. Skinny arms flailing, he looked comic in the beginning, but he quickly caught on. At first his fists thrashed away at the air. Jack and I would position his elbows to stick out at a certain angle. Tell him to punch from there.

"Imagine a guy in front of you, Jung," Jack said. "See his ugly nose?"

Jung-Sum nodded. Jack pointed in front of him. Gave me the signal.

"Ready," I said. Jung shifted his weight. "Aim."

Jack put his lips right next to Second Brother's ear and barked: "*FIRE!*"

Battering rams slammed into the air. One-two, one-two. Jung's eyes lit up; his bony shoulders heaved with every whiplash wallop until finally Jack grabbed his wrists and shook one tiny fist into the air.

"Knockout!"

Jung collapsed into Jack's side.

Jack's father got him started at Hastings Gym, in tribute to his pal, Jimmy McLarnin, the gallant neighbourhood boxer who knocked out Young Corbett III in 1933 and took on the title of World Welterweight Champ. A picture of Mr. McLarnin even hung on one of the walls at Strathcona School, where he was once a student. At the Hastings Gym, the champ's newspaper pictures were prominently displayed in the manager's front office. Every one of them caught McLarnin's left fist poised to strike the final, skull-cracking blow. But Mr. O'Connor had a special photograph.

"That's Jimmy McLarnin," Jack said, pointing to a picture in a frame that he took from his father's dresser. "And that's my dad."

Mr. O'Connor looked much younger in his sharp fedora, and proud, as if he knew he was standing beside a future champion boxer.

Jack put their RCA in the front parlour window so Jung and I could hear the Saturday games: baseball in the daytime and boxing matches sometimes at night. His father listened to them at a Hastings Street pub and would discuss the highlights with Jack later in the evening.

We crouched down and strained to catch the fade-away American baseball broadcasts, three heads bumping like coconuts. Sometimes Jack and I did push-ups during the commercials for Burma Shave, pushing up and down with the rhyming jingles. Jung would stoop and count with us, pumping himself up and down like the heroes who ate Wheaties, the Breakfast of Champions. Jung begged Father to buy Wheaties instead of the oatmeal Poh-Poh would boil for the family.

Jung-Sum began to grow taller, faster, stronger. His habit of cheerfully eating everything and asking for seconds, even thirds, made Poh-Poh and Stepmother feel like happy matrons, but Father wondered if his children would eat him into the poorhouse.

Father wasn't wrong. Some days, there wasn't enough food on the table. As I caught on, I told Jung he ate like greedy Pigsy. Poh-Poh knuckled me.

"I tell him when to eat or not eat," she snapped. "Jung-Sum, hold your tummy in. Tight, like Kiam. See?"

I sucked in my stomach.

"You feel full in two minutes," Poh-Poh said. "You eat more, Sekky!"

Jung-Sum did feel full, and Baby Brother ate more of the food Stepmother chewed first and then, with mushy dabs on her finger, slipped into his mouth. But we all worried: Sek-Lung slept more than Stepmother thought he should, and in his sleep, his breath was raspy and unsteady. Dr. Chu said he was having some lung problems and we should track his growth and watch that he did not catch any drafts. At night, I could hear Stepmother pacing back and forth, calling out his name as if to call him back from some dark well. Father would take his turn, but neither would sleep until Sek-Lung was breathing well again. Some nights, Poh-Poh took over, and she woke me up to bring the bowls of steaming water that smelled of eucalyptus, and the Old One would hold his little head high over the vapours. Finally, Dr. Chu said that he was getting stronger. Sek-Lung began to chatter, grab at things with his fists, and one day he stood up and yelled for a toy. We all ran to him and clapped, and he laughed as Father picked him up to gently swing him by his arms. Stepmother cried, and Poh-Poh beamed. Liang even said she would make doll clothes for his toy bear.

Father found time to take Jung-Sum and me to visit various tong halls while he interviewed Chinatown politicians for the community newspaper. Some were just street-level reading rooms, like the ones along Columbia Street, where the elders sat around smoking and talking. The larger family association halls were on second or third floors, up long flights of wooden stairs that you climbed from the street, finally to stand before latched swinging doors that opened up to vast assembly rooms.

During those visits, Father would tell a friendly elder to take charge of us. "Teach my unworthy sons to be Chinese," he would say.

The elders would laugh, call us *juk-sing,* hollow bamboo stumps, then ease into telling us stories of their young lives back in China, how they, as I should, bowed three times before the tall gleaming statues of Buddha or the grinning Gods of Fortune and Longevity. We were given fresh fruit from red-and-gold-rimmed bowls and sometimes a penny or a nickel if we had been especially attentive. When no one around cared to give us attention, Father would let us wander about.

I always hunted up the older boys trying out for the kung fu teams at the other end of the hall. Then a bunch of us would talk sports with Quene Yip, the Chinatown soccer champ.

Some of the elders appreciated how Second Brother stood in the central halls to study their exercise routines. He mimicked their movements, so Old Sing taught him a few Tai Chi routines.

One day, left by himself, Jung decided to practice a Tai Chi routine while standing ten feet up in the air on the edge of a six-inch-wide plank some workmen had been using to paint the ceiling. Slowly stepping forward, he angled his one foot and turned while lifting his other foot in the air; he bent forward, his head up, hands praising Heaven. He told me later he was playing the Monkey King crossing the sacred rope bridge, just as Poh-Poh had told the story. But he slipped, tipped over the narrow beam, and everything—plank, paint cans, tools, flailing boy—fell with echoing explosions.

I realized, then, how everything taught to Jung, he wanted to make more dangerous. He wanted to be like Jack O'Connor.

Poh-Poh told me one day how Jung-Sum lifted two buckets of nails at Ming Wo's hardware store when Mr. Wong, the proprietor, dared him to act like a man.

"He not like you, Kiam-Kim," Poh-Poh said. "He tougher."

"So what?" I said.

"So you—you be clever! Watch out for him!"

Everyone noticed Jung. With all that attention, I started to feel as if I, too, were important in some odd way, that his toughness made him my worthy Second Brother.

We were a crowded house, everyone sleeping two

to a room, but for the most part things were comfortable. Poh-Poh occasionally mentioned how Liang was filling up their bedroom with her dollhouse and toys, but she didn't mind too much. Liang said the Old One snored too loudly and the herbal medicines she concocted from ancient recipes were stinkysmelly. Everyone shushed her up. Father sometimes said he could turn the small storage room at the end of the upstairs hall into a room for Liang. He would burn all the junk he had kept from our first years in Vancouver and donate to the homeless shelter all the extra furniture and hardware we had been given by the Chen Association to start our home. But it remained just talk.

One morning, Liang climbed her way onto a footstool balanced on top of a chair. Stepmother caught her just as she was reaching for one of the mysteriously labelled bottles, filled with paper-thin slices of deer horn and roots, sitting between the tins of smelly, dark powders on the second shelf. When I came home that day, the storage room was empty. Third Uncle had sent his van over, and two of his workers took everything away. In the backyard, Father had lit a fire. I saw fragments of notebooks and old newspapers, bits of cloth and legs of broken furniture poking out from the flames.

That weekend I helped Father clean the floors and walls; finally, we carried Liang's furniture into her very own room. She squealed with delight and did not mind that the space barely took in her tiny dresser and pallet.

"Just temporary," Father told Only Sister.

Stepmother looked worried.

Father took me aside and told me Stepmother had not been well. I knew she had missed having dinner three times that week, and Poh-Poh had had me take up to her in bed special teas and soups. He studied my puzzled look.

"Poh-Poh say you old enough now, so I tell you something."

"What?"

I felt my eyes widen with pleasure: I was old enough for another secret. Father unbuttoned his shirt collar.

"Gai-mou is expecting a baby."

"When?"

"Maybe February—maybe March."

"A baby boy!" I said, thinking of my growing boss status. "Poh-Poh will be happy!"

"Yes, that's so." But Father looked unsettled. "If Poh-Poh be right, of course."

The nervous way he yanked off his rimmed glasses and rubbed the bridge of his nose confused me. However, like Poh-Poh, I felt no doubt about the outcome. The birth of the baby boy would be a great joy. As Jung-Sum had started out with me all bones and weakness and had turned out to be tall and strong—with brain and brawn—and as baby Sekky seemed much better every day and was more and more active without too much wheezing, I would not mind having a third brother to train.

But Stepmother did not look happy. As she threw the fresh bedsheets over Liang's little bed, she suddenly clutched her stomach and sat down.

"We see Mr. Gu," Father said. "Maybe see doctor . . ."

Even Poh-Poh felt Stepmother's wan eyes and pale skin, her uneven breathing, were beyond Mrs. Lim's special recipes, even beyond her own blood-strengthening soups and herbal teas, and certainly beyond the mahjong ladies' hopeful chatter.

"New baby," Mrs. Leong said to me, her hand tugging at my sweater.

Poh-Poh accepted every best wish for the safe delivery of her fourth grandson.

Everyone said the baby would be a boy. Boys were often born around spring.

"Best time of year," Mrs. Chong said. "Cool and quiet time. Lots of *yin* current with fresh *yang* energy!"

Stepmother, perhaps, was discomforted thinking of those winter months before the baby's delivery; her smile was forced.

"Yes," she said. "Good time to have a son."

Mrs. Lim and Mrs. Wong thought so, too. Then the women began to fuss over Poh-Poh's new flowery dress. Mrs. Sui Leong had helped to pick it out for her. White and pink flowers decorated the fabric like ghosts.

Pink! Stepmother must have seen my face and guessed at my concern: *What if the baby was . . . a girl!*

A half whisper came towards me and stroked my ears. "It be a boy," the voice said. "No worry, Kiam-Kim."

One hot August day, with nothing better to do, Jung and I decided to return some library books. In lock-step like soldiers, Second Brother and I raced past Jenny Chong and a couple of her friends up the curving stairway of the Carnegie Library at Main and Hastings. Perhaps upset that we had ignored her, Jenny said, "There goes Kiam's shadow!"

"Ha, ha," I said, turning around to stare her down. She thought herself out of our hearing, standing on the sidewalk with her two twittering friends. She rolled her eyes at me. It made me think of her mother. Whenever Mrs. Chong wanted more tea or dumplings, or more attention, her dark eyes would roll up in the same way, and the pupils would narrow, pulling you into range so you had to say something. Anything.

"Jealous?" I said, remembering how I once had saved her from her mother's wrath.

"Yeah," she said, pointing at Second Brother, "I always wanted a dog."

For weeks, she had been begging her mother to buy her one of those lap dogs she had seen scampering about in a Shirley Temple movie. Poh-Poh told her dogs were dirty, but cleaned up, they were good for eating. Maybe she was thinking of that. Maybe she didn't realize how Jung would take the joke.

Before I could stop him, he jumped down the steps and booted her in the shin. She let out a screech, dropped her books, and hopped about. Her two girlfriends scooted behind one of the library pillars to peer warily at Jung. He stared back, his fists clenched.

I ran down the steps, threw my free arm over him, and started dragging him away. I barely hung on to the books in the crook of my other arm as he struggled against me, his thin limbs flailing in the air. An old man stopped to ask Jenny what was the matter, but she couldn't tell him for her hopping about and her crying.

"You're going to get it," I said as I pushed with my back against the heavy library door. But someone I hadn't seen was already opening the door, and with Jung still struggling against me, we twisted backwards into the air and fell sprawling into the main hall. A middle-aged white lady stood over us, eyes wide with surprise. I still had a grip on Little Brother and a tighter one on the three books. She was about to say something when she noticed Jung's eyes bulging like a cornered animal's. She quickly left.

"Sticks and stones will break your bones," I chanted, letting go and slapping dust off my pants, "but names will never hurt you."

Little Brother wasn't impressed. As I brushed his hair back, he took hold of my arm and squeezed it in frustration. I sensed he was near tears, but I started laughing at how we had fallen backwards and ended up sitting there on the cold floor like clowns. I laughed even harder remembering Jenny Chong's look of shock. The hall echoed with my laughter. A librarian in a pink dress came rushing out, bent down, and snatched away the three books. She pointed to the front doors.

"You can both come back," she said. "when you decide this isn't a playground."

Before Jung could figure out a way to kick her, I shoved him through the doors.

"Don't," he said. "I wasn't going to do anything."
His thin face turned serious. "That lady doesn't call
people names."

A warm breeze whirled candy wrappers and tissues
around the pillars.

We sat on the steps of the Carnegie, without a single word between us; after a while, Jung-Sum leaned
against me. I put my arm around his knobby shoulders.

"Did you have to kick Jenny?"

Second Brother whispered into my ear. "*Ngoh
m'hai—gow!*" he said. "I'm not—dog!"

Later that afternoon, of course, Mrs. Chong dropped
in for tea to complain to Poh-Poh and Stepmother
about the "brutal" kicking incident. They all agreed it
wasn't necessary to involve Father.

When I walked into the dining room to take my
place at the corner desk and spread out my Saturday
Chinese school homework, Mrs. Chong's voice was
already pitched high above Grandmother's calm.
Stepmother sat leaning into her chair, one sleeveless
arm resting across her belly. Her eyes were red.

I had just uncapped the bottle to dip the brush
when a familiar voice caught my attention. The Old
One was telling Mrs. Chong that Jenny had been
jealous.

Just as I had guessed, *grass green with jealousy.* Poh-Poh
turned her head. She looked directly at me. I ducked.

"Kiam-Kim stood by," she said. "Is that so?"

I pretended I didn't hear. Too late.

Mrs. Chong looked dejected. "Jen-Jen's leg all blue and sore."

"Blue and *green*," I muttered.

Grandmother saw my lips moving. Her voice was grave, her Sze-yup tones formal.

"Did Grandson see this happen?"

"Yes, Poh-Poh," I said, responding in dialect. "Jenny called Jung-Sum a dog—*my* dog. And Second Brother kicked before I could stop him."

"Did Jenny speak *lao-fang wah*, foreign words?"

"*Hi-lah*," I said. "She spoke English words."

Poh-Poh mulled over things. Mrs. Chong's raised eyebrow suggested she hadn't heard this version of the incident before.

"Jen-Jen just say her greetings," she said. "I'm sure you and Little Brother misheard her."

"*Lo-faan wah*," Stepmother said, "difficult to hear."

Grandmother agreed. The three women nodded in unison: English so easy to *mishear*.

"Is that not so, Grandson?"

"One sound like another," Mrs. Chong said. "Barbaric!"

I knew I was expected to agree. Dog. Log. Fog. Bog.

I nodded. I flipped open my copybook and began brushing my first page of Chinese script, fighting the urge to pitch the ink bottle at Mrs. Chong. Through the parlour doorway, I could see Jung-Sum busy playing Robin Hood with Only Sister on the linoleum floor, ignoring the talk from the dining room. He was rounding up Liang-Liang's population of cutout dolls to herd them deep into Sherwood Forest. Mrs. Chong raised her voice, determined to catch Jung's attention, but he played on, pushing paper figures under the sofa to shelter them from attack.

The Old One finally spoke aloud what she had been thinking all along.

"Your pretty Jen-Jen want to walk beside my grandson," Poh-Poh said. "So she be showing off to girlfriends."

"Think so?" Mrs. Chong said, her voice softening. "Jenny like to walk with Kiam-Kim?"

"Yes, so young, too," Poh-Poh said, tilting her head slightly. "How she get idea to walk with Kiam-Kim?"

For some mysterious reason, the two women wanted me to hear all this nonsense. I feigned deafness, my horsehair brush dashing strokes into characters.

"Of course, this not Old China way, this meeting of girl and boy," Poh-Poh continued. "This Canada way."

"Old way better." Mrs. Chong placed a teacup into Stepmother's hand. "Don't you think so, Chen Sim?"

Stepmother shrugged and smiled politely, as if her opinion could not matter one way or another. She sipped her tea while with the other hand she gently massaged her belly. She had come to us the Old China way.

"Old China way best," Mrs. Chong repeated, taking her eyes off Stepmother.

"I give you some ointment for your poor Jen-Jen," Grandmother said. She patted her open palm against the back of Mrs. Chong's wrist and continued in formal Cantonese. "So kind of you to allow me to know about this misunderstanding. I will certainly speak to Jung-Sum."

Things sounded as if they were being settled when I heard polite sniffing and looked up from my inky brush. I caught Mrs. Chong staring at me, her eyes softening.

"You good First Son," she said, her voice placating. "Jenny like you, Kiam-Kim." Maybe I shouldn't have smiled back. "Like you very much."

I glanced back at Jung-Sum playing in the parlour with Liang. I wondered if Second Brother understood he was in trouble. I cleared my throat; he and Liang raised their heads to see what I wanted. Just as I was going to make the sign of a slashed throat with my forefinger, for Jung to see, Father rushed through the front door, and Liang ran to him to be hugged.

Without taking his hat off, Father gently put Liang down and walked into the dining room. He pulled out of his coat pocket an inch-square velvety black box. It had a red phoenix seal embossed on the lid. Grandmother reached for the fist-sized container.

"This is the best medicine," Father said. "Cost eight dollars."

Grandmother pushed open the lid with her thumb. She picked out some dried leaves and a few knotted black things tied together with hemp grass.

"Everything soon be fine again, Chen Sim," Mrs. Chong said to Stepmother. "You very young. After Mr. Gu's herbal tea, you be strong again. No bleeding. Baby be okay."

Father cleared his throat. Time to change the

subject: big ears were listening. I didn't think of my own big ears; I thought of the two pairs on the two little heads that were now staring into the dining room, their senses alerted.

"Please come here, Jung-Sum," Poh-Poh said in her formal Canton manner. Second Brother hesitated, but the formal words meant he had little choice.

Poh-Poh stood looking down at him. "You kick Mrs. Chong's poor Jen-Jen?"

Jung just barely nodded. The Old One's frown slowly quashed him with condemnation. It was the same withering, anguished look the Old One gave me whenever she caught me disobeying Father. The high cheekbones lifted every scowling wrinkle on her old face; her ancient eyes penetrated your soul. Even I would have preferred to be whipped. Jung bowed his head. He knew I would be called as a witness if he said nothing.

"Yes. I kicked Jen-Jen."

Since the matter had been raised first between the women, Father kept quiet. The whole room waited for Poh-Poh's sentence. She shook her head. Perhaps she was overwhelmed by some shame for Jung's behaviour. Perhaps he now understood how he had shamed us all. As in the matter of a little stealing or a big stealing, boys do not kick girls.

"Go upstairs." Poh-Poh's voice chilled the room.

Second Brother bit his lip. He knew this meant he would have to wait for Poh-Poh's sentence. He might be locked in the closet all night, as Mrs. Leong had done to punish her third son; he might be deprived of supper for a whole month and have to find a way to eat double the lunch at school; certainly, Poh-Poh would use her knuckles once or twice, to knock some brains into him.

Father might add his punishment, too. There would be a stern lecture about proper behaviour. An assignment of twenty lines of Chinese writing. Half the lines committed to memory before bedtime. Perhaps a twenty-five-word essay to be written in English. Or, worse, he might be grounded for ten weekends and be assigned Sekky's dirty diapers to rinse and wash every day before bedtime. Jung-Sum would have to lie on his iron cot, count the minutes, the hours, until . . .

As Jung stomped up the stairs, Mrs. Chong sighed. All this time, Stepmother had been whispering to Father.

"Jung-Sum kicked Jenny!" Father said, appalled. He lifted off his glasses to think better. "Why?"

I spoke up. "Jenny said Second Brother's always following me around like a stupid dog."

Poh-Poh coughed loudly and waved her hand as if to expel the bad air: a warning for me to shut up. Her eyes shone. Seeing the intensity of those eyes, Mrs. Chong wanted to soften the Old One's tendency towards, perhaps, too much disappointment with her grandsons. She lifted a manicured hand to her forehead.

"My *mo yung* daughter! To speak too soon can be so thoughtless!"

"My *mo no* Second Son!" added Father, firmly putting back his glasses. "Acting before thinking!"

Between those two cries, a balance had been struck: neither family would lose face.

Stepmother shifted in her chair. She looked too tired to say anything. She was as slim as ever; her belly barely pushed against her dress, if it did at all. But thinking of how big her stomach would become, I couldn't help staring.

"Kiam-Kim," Poh-Poh said, "finish your school work."

"Have you not finished?" Father demanded.

As he drank his tea at the round table, Father watched me dip the brush and instructed me to hold my forefinger at a sharper angle against the bamboo stem. But I was distracted by my own thoughts. *To talk too soon . . . to act too quickly* must be unlucky forces.

Now Jung-Sum was going to get it.

"Why didn't you stop Jung-Sum?" Father said. "Don't overload your brush."

"He was too fast for me," I said.

"You be faster next time."

I knew what Father meant. As *Dai-goh,* I was supposed to protect Second Brother from himself, from his bad temper. I was to teach Jung-Sum how to be always patient. Set an example. I had not acted as a wise and all-seeing Big Brother for Jung-Sum. I had failed.

I listened for Jung's reactions to Poh-Poh's punishment, but except for the *daub-swish* of the brush as I dipped into the ink block, no sound came to my ears.

By the time I went to bed, I still hadn't found out what tough punishment the Old One had assigned to

Jung. In a slant of moonlight falling across the room, I could see the little guy fast asleep in his cot. I got up and shook him awake.

"*So?*" I said. "Did Poh-Poh speak to you?"

"Yes," came his sleepy voice.

"Well?"

"She told me . . ." It was as if he were thinking with difficulty, or falling back to sleep. Poor Jung, I thought. Poh-Poh probably force-fed him castor oil like Jack's mother once had done to him. She must have knuckled him. Twisted his ears. Pulled his nose. Made him swear he would never kick any female creature again—*never, never, never kick!*

"*Well?*" I said.

"Poh-Poh told me—" He yawned, shifting onto his side "—for the next time . . ."

I wanted to jolt him wide awake, punch my fist into his pillow as I used to do when we were younger, but remembered that I needed to set an example. To think before I acted.

"*Next time,*" I asked gently, "next time—*what?*"

"Next time, I to kick . . . *harder!*"

"You misheard her," I said.

But in the darkness, relentless old eyes penetrated my brain and left no doubt. *"Kick harder!"* Poh-Poh had said, and walked out of the bedroom, trailing her bitter anger to the end.

The Japanese were moving their armies down from the north into the Southern Provinces. China's divided armies needed the food to help them fight the growing war, not only against the Imperial Japanese but against each other, too. People were starving. No one was in control. By 1936, the news was always bad.

"New baby go hungry in Gold Mountain," Poh-Poh said to Stepmother.

We could buy good food that came from the Fraser Valley farmers, but the prices of anything like soy or oyster sauce, salted fish, rice, or thousand-year-old eggs, or any special herbs, or dried plums or oranges, if they were available at all, had all increased ten times over last season's prices. Shipping routes were mined by all sides. Fewer and fewer China goods arrived in Vancouver.

Father had to ask the Tong Association to lower the rent for our Keefer Street house. Stepmother, her belly growing ever larger, stayed home with Poh-Poh; the two of them worked together mending and altering second-hand shirts and pants to fit each of us. The Tong Association now paid half the fees for my Chinese school in exchange for Father's collecting their rents for them, and for Jung's and my washing the insides of the main office windows every three weeks. Without the variety of work Father now took on, Third Uncle told me, the Chen family would be in trouble: I would be out of school and know no Chinese and be ashamed and mocked as a "Gold Mountain dreamer"; finally, when all the family returned to China, even with Third Uncle, we would be just as poor as when we first arrived.

One rain-soaked day in February, Mrs. Lim and

Poh-Poh said that the baby would come very soon. While I did my school work, the two old friends sat stitching together old bedsheets to make fresh mattress covers. Stepmother was in the parlour, collapsed on the sofa. A towel-wrapped pillow had been put under her head. Her long hair was pinned up. She had asked to come downstairs to be with all of us, and did not seem to mind the family noise around her. Poh-Poh had put a blanket over her, though she seemed warmly dressed to me.

Sekky and Liang were playing house underneath Father's oak desk. Jung-Sum was studying for another test. And I sat wondering over my history book how I would feel next September when I would be in Grade 8, the highest grade at Strathcona. Then I heard the sobbing.

"Poh-Poh," I said, "Gai-mou is crying."

Tears ran freely down her pale cheeks.

Poh-Poh said, "Gai-mou not too well, Kiam-Kim. Father at Mr. Gu's store to pick up Tai Sim's medicine."

I knew Mrs. Tai. She always wore a bright kerchief and simple black dresses. She had come to our house one night, along with the midwife Mrs. Nellie Yip, a white lady who was almost as big as Mrs. Lim. The next morning, there was baby Liang-Liang suckling on Stepmother's breast. Mrs. Tai showed up again when Sekky was born.

I sat up. "Is Tai Sim coming to bring out the new baby?"

Jung was all ears. Liang hushed up Sekky to listen.

Stepmother looked flushed. Poh-Poh gently patted her knee. She reached deep into the sleeve of her quilted jacket and handed Stepmother a handkerchief.

"Tai Sim here?"

"No—not yet," Poh-Poh said. "*Soon.*"

"Kiam-Kim was not told—?" Mrs. Lim said.

"I maybe talk *too soon,*" Poh-Poh said. "Too sure and too soon!"

"Soon?" I said, confused again. "The new baby coming soon?"

"No, no," Poh-Poh said. "Not *this* time. Maybe too soon!"

She sounded confused herself. Stepmother groaned.

One hour later Tai Sim arrived and said she would sit with Stepmother, that we should go on with our usual business.

"I wait," I said.

But Stepmother's tears would not stop. Perhaps she had wanted a new boy sooner.

Father arrived home, took his hat and coat off, and went straight to Stepmother's side.

Tai Sim stepped back from the sofa. "Madame Nellie Yip come later tonight," the small woman announced to everyone in the parlour. She quickly knelt down, turned over Stepmother's wrist and tapped, then she studied Stepmother's tongue and the rims of her eyes. She rubbed the back of Stepmother's soaked neck and felt for tension. The towel under Stepmother was wet.

"Madame Yip know what to do," Tai Sim said.

Madame Nellie Yip had studied in Old China and knew as many dialects as any Chinatown resident, even more than Poh-Poh herself. She told one of her in-laws, in witty Cantonese, "You have perfect hips for having babies! Have a dozen!" Everyone wanted Nellie Yip to oversee their births: she knew both Western and Eastern ways. For years, she had fought to have sick Chinese people served properly in the city hospitals. In her adopted tongue, she was not "Mrs." but was highly regarded and called Madame.

Hearing that Madame Nellie Yip would be with her, working along with Tai Sim, Stepmother smiled confidently.

"You have the medicine for me?"

Father held up the black, velvety box. A crest of a red phoenix was embossed on its lid.

"Tai Sim thinks I might have the baby very soon."

"Everything go well," Father said. "No worry."

Tai Sim asked for the small box from Father.

"Give Chen Sim some warm soup," she said, "while I prepare phoenix medicine." She shook the velvet box. The contents made a soft pattering noise, like rolling BBs. I thought of the loud rattling pebbles coming from another, larger box. That one had had a golden dragon curved over the lid.

"Paid *many* dollars," Father said. "More than one week's salary!"

"Cost Gai-mou, too," the Old One said. Rain began pelting against the porch. "Very soon be over."

"Maybe too soon for me," said Stepmother. Her voice sounded strained.

"Maybe count wrong," Tai Sim said. "No worry."

A knock came from the front door. Shaking her umbrella, Mrs. Chong stepped into the parlour. With one glance she knew what was going on. Madame Yip had phoned her to bring over from her store a tiny tube of White Flower Essence, a bottle of Lysol, and thick cotton bundles of bandages. *In case.*

Jung-Sum took away her raincoat, I brought some chairs from the dining room. Everyone sat close to the sofa. Sekky and Liang brought out their toys to play at the foot of the big chesterfield. From her cane rocker, Poh-Poh nudged me to pour tea for our guests.

I poured Father's last. He looked first at Stepmother, then he stared helplessly at Mrs. Chong. Little sympathy reflected back from her. She sat in the sofa chair and reached into her purse for a cigarette. I took the Peter Pan Café matches she handed me. At one of the mahjong games, Mrs. Chong taught me how to be a gentleman with a match, to be like one of those picture-show stars she admired. I struck the match, and Mrs. Chong inhaled. The Sweet Caporal flared with fire and smoke. Then she exhaled and, with her pencilled eyebrows cresting elegantly, smiled at me. Her hand delicately fanned away the smoke. Across the room, Stepmother politely pointed out the ashtray on the end table. I set it on the arm of the sofa. It was the big ashtray Third Uncle used for his pipe.

"Everything fine now, Chen Suk," Mrs. Chong said to Father. "Chen Sim just have a little bad spell. Nothing more."

No one believed her.

We all watched Poh-Poh get up and press her palm against Stepmother's forehead. Tai Sim had taken the medicine box and all the packages into the kitchen. She told Father that the pills would have to be crushed and an assortment of herbs blended together with them. It would take an hour of steaming in a double-enclosed pot before the bitter liquid, distilled and cooled, would be ready for Stepmother.

"Sip when cramp push lower," Tai Sim had said with authority. "Strengthen muscle."

Hearing those words, Mrs. Chong grimaced and exchanged some nervous glances with Poh-Poh and big Mrs. Lim. My spine tightened. It was clear Stepmother did not want to move from the sofa. She did not want to move at all. Tai Sim had told her to stay put until she checked her signs again.

Father looked uncomfortable.

"Need more strength," Poh-Poh said gently to Stepmother.

"I make you very good soup," said Mrs. Lim. She folded her hands, as if in prayer. "I now go home to make."

During the wait for Tai Sim to reappear, Father drank his tea and hardly took his eyes away from Stepmother. I could see she was holding her knees together, as if she were in pain.

"Oh, Chen Sim," Mrs. Chong said, "you must go upstairs into your big bed."

Poh-Poh looked alarmed. "Not here. I bring you soup upstairs."

"Yes," Father said, "much more room in bed."

"And the children not be there," Tai Sim said, coming into the parlour. She felt Stepmother's forehead with the back of her small palm; patiently, with her forefinger she traced the vein that visibly throbbed beneath the ear. Tai Sim sighed. "Not for children to see. Much to be done." Tai Sim marched back into the kitchen, her body rigid with efficiency.

"Kiam-Kim," Poh-Poh commanded. "You and Father help Gai-mou upstairs."

Stepmother leaned against Father's arm. Then she put one hand on my shoulder and asked me to walk up the stairs first.

The Old One rushed back from the kitchen with a small lidded bowl. "I mix broth with honey," she said, climbing the staircase behind us. "Sweet and bitter balance heat and cold."

As we all shifted up the stairs, I glimpsed Liang through the bannister. She sat on the parlour floor, pushing a toy spoon of imaginary medicine into Raggedy Ann. With a tin horn, Sekky poked at its stomach.

At last, Stepmother lay down on the bed. Father began to undress her. Poh-Poh told me to run downstairs and help clear up the kitchen.

Mrs. Chong was slipping into her hooded raincoat. As she walked out of our house, the rain lashed against her umbrella.

I remember that Madame Nellie Yip arrived very late that night. Sekky, Liang, and Jung had all gone to bed hours before, and Father and I sat in the dining room, quiet and waiting.

Poh-Poh came downstairs to rinse and boil some more towels. She told Father that Stepmother had already taken half of the phoenix liquid.

"Go to bed, Kiam-Kim," Poh-Poh said. "This night for women only."

I went to bed, listening through the half-open door of the bedroom to the groans and troubling sounds coming from the room across the hall. I remember the stairs creaking as big Mrs. Lim made her way upstairs. Carrying a thermos of soup in one hand, she leaned against the doorway and peeked in, looking over at Jung-Sum. As I turned over, she said to me, "Go to sleep, First Son."

I sat up. "Will the new baby be okay?"

Mrs. Lim waved the container at me. "Good soup here," she said softly. "Not for you to worry."

"Father worries," I said. "He worries all the time."

"Yes, yes." In her Toishanese words there followed as blunt a truth as ever, as if one could not be defeated by even the inevitable. "Worry and die. Worry and die. What is the use of such a life? You go to sleep."

Mrs. Lim saw the sock I had jammed into the doorway so it would stay open. She tugged it out of the way, tossed it onto my bed, and shut the door tightly. There was nothing to do but listen to the rain, lie still, and be swallowed by the darkness.

I was wakened by a scream.

Jung-Sum sat up, too. I could hear Liang crying and jumped out of my bed to see what was the matter. In seconds, the three of us stood in the doorway and watched the last moments of the birthing. No one chased us away. Father was a few steps into the room, carrying a sleeping Sekky in his arms.

Bending over the bed, Madame Nellie Yip announced, "A boy," but there were no smiles on anyone's face.

The baby had been strangled by its cord.

I could hear Stepmother weeping softly, as if she were a child. I watched Madame Yip lift the small, glistening baby with the dangling cord into a tin pail at the foot of the bed. A folded bedsheet covered the galvanized bucket. Mrs. Lim bowed her head and walked to the other side of the bed, as if her weight might balance the cruel fate of birth and death.

Poh-Poh slowly took Jung-Sum to the bedside.

"This is why we were given Jung-Sum," she told Stepmother.

Then the Old One turned to me. "You hear, Kiam-Kim?"

Second Brother did not pull away. He stood tall and straight and held on to the Old One's hand.

Liang slipped into the room to be with her mother; then I stepped in, too. Then Father brought Sekky in his arms and stood behind Poh-Poh.

"Why cry?" she said. "Tomorrow we bury this one. We thank the temple gods that this grandson suffer only this night."

Father asked Madame Yip a complicated question I did not understand. The big woman bowed her head and looked solemnly down at Stepmother before she would answer. Stepmother's eyes were closed. The phoenix medicine must have done its work.

"No, no more," Madame Yip said.

The wet head lifted up from the pillow. Eyes opened wide. Stepmother smiled with relief.

"No," she repeated, "*no more . . . no more.*"

Father's hand gripped my shoulder.

~ *F I V E* ~

DURING THOSE WEEKS OF STEPMOTHER'S slow recovery, I wanted to do more work, to help out with things. Jack O'Connor already had a paper route for the *Morning Herald,* but Father didn't want me wandering the streets so early in the morning when the last drunks woke up looking for someone to beat up.

Third Uncle told Father that next year, when I looked older and stronger, and if business picked up, he would give me some real work to do. But just that week, he had had to lay off three of his best labourers, and it would be awkward, and shameful, to be seen bringing in a boy to do any of the men's work. The men would lose face, as well as lose hope.

"Let Kiam be lucky for a few more months," Uncle said. "Let him play like a rich man's boy."

But Father stared at the Free China poster hanging above Third Uncle's desk. It showed a sturdy young marching boy, dressed like a soldier, the flag of the Republic of China clutched in one hand, a donation can in the other. In the distance, coming down ancient hills, marching past schools and hospitals, hundreds of smiling young people were following, carrying blankets, farm implements, books, tin goods, warm clothing, and medicines . . . the good things that such donations would buy. Father saw me staring at the poster, too.

"You're thirteen," he said. "Would you like to take on more duties?"

Earlier that spring, Father had shown me some pictures of Chinese soldiers sleeping on snow-covered ground, their trousered legs hugging rifles. And pictures of starving children from all over China, their skeletal arms outstretched, eyes sunken with hunger.

"These soldiers will need winter blankets," he had said.

"These children need food," added Stepmother.

Father would take me with him when he went around Chinatown to ask for donations for the New China Relief Fund.

I thought now of the soldiers freezing in the cold, the children without even a grain of rice to eat. I nodded; I would do what was right.

First, I had to look my best. Father showed me how to polish my shoes with my own spit, as he had observed the Negro shoeshine man polishing boots and shoes at the CPR station. Stepmother pushed my arms through a freshly ironed and starched blue shirt and buttoned it up to my neck. Poh-Poh encouraged me to put on my best woollen pants with my new suspenders. I shivered as the tweed material prickled against my legs.

"Itchy make you stand up," she explained. "Make you taller."

"Kiam-Kim, hold still," Stepmother commanded. She rubbed her palms together with a dab of Father's emerald-coloured pomade, which one of his appreciative readers gave him as a gift and which came all the way from France. Then she ran her palms and fingers through my hair and neatly combed a part in the middle. By the time I stepped out of the house, my shoes and my hair shone and I smelled of fresh lemons. My first trial visit would be to the warehouse, and then I would go to the rooming-house district.

"Kiam-Kim," Third Uncle said, turning me around with a firm grip on my shoulders. "Let me see, front to back." He adjusted his silver-rimmed glasses along his nose. "Yes, yes, very good!"

Father looked pleased. Uncle went to a shelf of small cardboard boxes and picked one out.

"Hold like this," he said, showing me how my fingers should grip the box straight. The sides were covered with Chinese writing and official-looking paper stamps. At the top there was a slot. Third Uncle took some silver coins from his pocket and dropped them through the slot, one after another. He took my wrist and shook it. The coins jingled.

"That's all you do, Kiam-Kim."

Father waited a moment. "What do you say?"

"Thank you," I said. Father slipped some coins in. I shook the box and said, "Thank you."

"Yes, yes," Third Uncle said. "When box heavy enough, you or Father bring back here."

We walked down the long back staircase from Third Uncle's mezzanine office, the coins clinking with my every step. In the warehouse, I passed some of the men who were unpacking large China bowls.

"Go ahead," Father said. I walked up to the two men closest to me and shook the box. From the Saturdays helping with Father's paperwork, I knew them by their nicknames.

"A soldier for the cause," Father said. "My son, Chen Kiam-Kim."

"Yes, yes, Mr. Chen," Box Ears said, and dug in his pocket and put in some pennies. Long Arms, who could reach into the corners of any crate, quickly did the same thing, and I saw it was a nickel. I rattled the box and broke into a smile.

"Never forget to say—"

"Thank you, thank you!" I said, and ran down the back ramp of the warehouse and laughed to think how easy it was going to be to buy blankets for the soldiers and to feed the children of China.

After I'd spent five days going from shop to shop, door to door, shaking the New China donation box, Father told Stepmother that everyone seemed to enjoy giving me their attention. In fact, that was why the three-day assignment took us two extra days.

"People like his enthusiasm," Father reported to Third Uncle. "They like Kiam-Kim's cleverness."

"And people like to laugh," he told Box Ears.

It was true. Many times the elders and ladies would ask me what the money was for, and I would say in my excitement, "Blankets for rice!"

Father corrected me. I was to enunciate my short speech clearly, stand with my back straight, like a nationalist officer of the Kwomintang.

It wasn't easy. Cantonese tones were as complicated as the guttural Sze-yup dialects. Liang-Liang and Jung-Sum, after they stopped making faces, and Stepmother would sometimes sit on the sofa as my spectators. Poh-Poh ambled by the parlour during one of my final practices. I harrumphed, then began:

"Generous donations benefit our soldiers of Free China with blankets for winter. Spare coins fill the empty rice bowls of our starving countrymen. A New China will rise from the old. Every penny helps. Every dollar matters. Thank you, kind sir, kind lady."

And with my arms straight at my side, I bowed.

"Much better," the Old One said to Father on her way to the kitchen. "Sound like a smart parrot."

Father said I was ready to try again, and this time I would wear a new white shirt and double-polish my shoes.

After giving that short speech, I was to rattle the box—"not too loudly"—and Father would point to someone sympathetic I should head towards. Then I was on my own. Of course, I had to remember, if there were no ladies present, to stop the speech at "kind sir." I was also to take a breath after "countrymen," raise my voice on "dollar," and not rush myself.

"Think of the soldiers and those hungry boys and girls," Father said. "You speak for them."

We collected on the few blocks around our house where we knew Chinese families lived, and then we went into Chinatown to knock on doors in the rooming houses along Shanghai and Canton alleys. I hardly had to say my speech at all, because Father would just ask for a donation and I would rattle the box, and that was all it took. We stood in smelly hallways so dark that I could never make out whether pennies or dimes were being dropped into the box. If an old man came to the door, someone so obviously poor, his clothes ragged and patched, Father would say at once, "*Mh'koi, Senshaang!* Excuse, sir! Sorry, sir!—Looking for someone else." Father would push me aside before I could rattle the box.

Quite a few times a door would slam shut because we had disturbed someone's sleep. Or window blinds cut off Father's attempts to peek through the gloom. He couldn't figure out who was on shift-work sleep and who wasn't, who was hung over again and who was truly sick. But some opened their door a few inches and dropped coins into my donation box. A few lonely men begged us to visit with them, offering Father tea in stained cups, but he politely told them we were in a hurry.

I glimpsed entrances with stained walls and decaying litter piled under stairwells; stumbled in the murkiness past windowless chambers, tiny rooms with only soiled mattresses in the corner and wooden crates for tables or chairs. Wet clothes were hung across strings tied to nails. I heard coughing and hacking, the noise of shifting bodies and snoring. Most of the barely lit hallways stank like unflushed toilets.

After the third rooming hotel, Father, choking from the smells, said that from now on we would visit places where people were wide awake. As we walked down the steps into the bright sunlight, I noticed that my shoes were sticky. I hurried over to a patch of grass and rubbed the soles back and forth, back and forth. Coins rattled at my side. The poorest gave what they could.

"Did you say thank-you?"

Stung by the odours and by the sight of such poverty, I couldn't remember if I had said anything. It seemed to me Father hardly spoke himself but rather nodded as he pinched a handkerchief over his nose.

"Where do we go next, Father?"

"We go for more money," he said and signalled me to follow him. "March like a soldier, Kiam-Kim."

I thought of newsreel pictures, those grainy images of uniformed men trooping into jungles. I marched like a soldier.

Thereafter, Father and I spent all of our soliciting time at the all-day gambling houses, at the big and small family associations, the bachelor-men's clubs where the old men and the unemployed men wanted to hear from Father the latest news from China. In those places, I was always asked to recite my piece.

Someone was always willing to talk to me after my rattling.

"How many blankets will this one box buy?" Yim Sook the barber asked me in Toishan, in front of five old men waiting their turn to test his hand-operated clipper.

"Lots," I would answer back in dialect, "but none if you don't help."

"Gentlemen," Yim Sook announced, "free haircuts for your donations."

Money clinked into the box.

On my rounds, I shook some hands, smiled at everyone, and earned some pats on my back. Some people even gave me candy bars or Wrigley's gum, which I would take home for Jung-Sum to share with Liang and Sekky. At the B.C. Royal bakery, someone bought me a syrupy-sweet butterhorn and a tall glass of milk. Nickels, dimes, and quarters, even fifty-cent pieces, and two or three times silver dollars dropped into the New China donation box.

Everyone seemed to enjoy my cleverness.

"*Ho! Ho!*" they said "Good! Good!" and put in extra coins. I filled up five donation boxes, and Father signed up almost double his quota of pledges.

Father and Stepmother said I should teach Jung-Sum my little speech.

Only Poh-Poh resisted.

"You were born a clever boy, Kiam-Kim," she said. "But you not as smart as you think."

She was not happy with talk of a New Republic of China, not even of a New Reform People's China, as if the old Imperial China was beyond useless. Poh-Poh wanted me to respect the Old Ways, to believe in the forces of *feng shui,* the forces of wind and water, of luck and fate, and of Kitchen Gods and ghosts. She said that Father was a dreamer. But I wanted to be more like Father, who seemed to understand how, in Canada, everything was scientific and modern. Poh-Poh caught me scoffing once as she was telling one of her stories; after that, the Old One did not have much more to teach me.

The men of Chinatown became my teachers.

Third Uncle even encouraged the elders to show me how to fill a water pipe with tobacco, but not to smoke it. I just wanted to see how the thing worked. Others taught me how to pick up wood from the mills along False Creek and, with a paring knife, whittle them into small boats for Sekky to float in his bath. At MacLean Park, some of the younger men encouraged me to put up my dukes and box with them, show them every punch I had learned at the Hastings Gym.

And if my pals and I were playing soccer, someone like champion Quene Yip would step up and teach how to side-kick the ball, jockey the pursuing opponent to the left, feint a swift pass sharply to the right, change direction as elegantly as a gazelle, and kick straight ahead to score. Victoria, his beautiful lady, would cheer us on.

Some of the older men had not seen their own China families for five, ten, or twenty years. The lucky ones, the ones with enough money, started second families in Vancouver. But the men who indulged me must have longed for some semblance of family life. While Father went about his business of signing up pledges, some of the bachelor-men took me with them as if I were a favourite nephew into their gathering places, the community rooms in the gambling clubs, the narrow smoke shops, the pool-rooms and Tong Association reading rooms. They let me listen to their stories of Old China and gave me advice about growing up.

"You finish school," they said in Toishanese, their voices raised against the din. "Then you go back to China and help your own people."

"No, no," another would say, "Kiam-Kim marry a good Chinese girl first! Then go back!"

"No, no," another said with a laugh, showing off his Chinglish. "Kiam go China. Find goot Chinee gurlee there—my bessee daughter wait see you, Kiam-Kim!"

"Never mind who," Lau Sook, the pool hall owner, said, "as long as he marry Chinese!"

No one said anything. Everyone knew that Lau Sook had disowned his second son for marrying a white girl whose father was a church minister. "The pair went into the mountains. I think to Kamloops," I heard Mrs. Leong tell Stepmother. "Had to."

Lightning flashed and thunder shook the windows as I stood outside another store waiting for Father to finish some business. Old Wen urged me to take shelter with him inside the Hong Kong Café. We sat on stools that could swivel.

"I buy you tea and butterhorn," he said.

As we waited to be served, Mr. Wen stared a long while at me. The lights hanging over the counter flickered. Finally, the old man reached into his wallet and slid out a photograph.

"See, Kiam-Kim, my First Son. He be my only boy." Mr. Wen pointed to a grown-up man standing behind an old lady. "Last time I saw him, he be twelve or thirteen, just like you. Maybe taller. My boy liked to play ball, too."

People at the counter gathered around, squinting at the creased picture and commenting on how strong the man standing with the hoe looked. A thunderbolt rumbled across the sky and the lights flickered again. I studied the bent, worn picture and wondered if I would grow up as big, or even taller.

"Yes, yes," Old Wen said to everyone around him. "My own boy."

"This not a boy, Mr. Wen," I said. "He's *old* now."

"You lucky, Kiam-Kim." He pushed back his grey hair and stared at the photograph. "You have father and your Poh-Poh and Gai-mou."

Old Wen brushed the picture with his fingers, as if he might brush away all the years he had struggled in B.C. and sent home his money; brush away all the lost years while his boy grew into this frayed photo of a grown man.

Father came in and sat beside me. He took off his hat and wiped a few raindrops off his glasses.

Mr. Wen showed him the picture.

"My only boy," he said to Father, then carefully put it back in his worn wallet.

"He's *not* a little boy," I insisted.

"Very fine boy," Father said, pushing me aside. "Number One Boy!"

No one looked at me, and everyone was quiet. The April rain had just started to fall.

There was a big map of China at one of the Tong Association reading rooms. Men would gather around it when Father showed up. He used the glass magnifier hanging on a string to read the tiny print.

"My little village?" someone would ask. "Dog-shit Japs bomb there?"

Father pointed out where the enemy was located. Pointed out the village. Explained that Japanese planes could fly anywhere and drop their bombs at any time, just as they had done in Manchuria. There were now rumours of a road being built in Burma to supply the Nationalist military with food and munitions.

Father always asked if the person had received any news from their village district.

"No letters for six months," someone answered.

At the social clubs Father and I would visit with our collection boxes, Father would be confronted about his writings.

"Chen Sen-shaang, why don't you come right out and say 'Kill the bastard Communists'?" Mr. Lam, the Main Street herbalist, asked him. "You too soft."

"All the same dog shit to me," another would say.

Father refused to give up.

"Your village and all of China," he said, "need a stable government. Look how the Americans support Chiang Kai-shek. Why don't you donate a few coins, maybe even pledge a few dollars a month? Here, my son will recite the Three Principles of Dr. Sun for you."

And I would chant with thirteen-year-old confidence "*San Min Chu Yee . . . ,*" repeating three minutes of rhythmic sounds I had memorized, understanding the Principles about as much as I had understood every morning at Strathcona the ritual words I mouthed, "Our Father who art in Heaven, Harold be Thy name."

Loose change clinked into the donation box to save the homeland.

"Teach Kiam to read omens," an Elder would say. "Old sayings much better than new ones."

But as many times as some Elders would remind Father that forces such as Fortune and Fate influenced the future, Father politely and patiently spoke to them of economic forces, the Japanese invasion of Northern China, and the secret backing of the mighty United States for the New Republic of China. But every overseas political group said they loved China, it was explained to me, and that was why, in China itself, every Communist or Nationalist, Reformist or Socialist party had to destroy the other groups who also loved China.

And Father would tell me that killing was wrong, and worse, yes, that the Chinese in Old China were now killing each other, even blood brothers and same-village families. But soon everyone would focus on the real enemy, the Japanese, and China would be united again. No more Chinese killing Chinese.

"We all need to sit down and discuss these things," Father said. "Meanwhile, Kiam, we collect money for peace."

Third Uncle had promised Father that the money he was collecting was not for bullets or guns but for blankets, medical supplies, food for orphans—the *ho sum* things, the good-heart things. Other fundraising efforts were started, and those were for buying China bonds, for building planes and tanks, for guns and munitions to fight the Japanese menace.

"But we collect for the heart, Kiam-Kim," Father said. "We help all the people of China."

I was puzzled. "Even those who kill other Chinese?"

"Yes," Father said. "Of course."

"But never help the Japanese?"

"Never."

Father and I went to small businesses and larger ones, collecting a little sympathy if not always money. Everyone knew how sincere Father was, and perhaps how much a pain. We would go to corner stores, too, like Ben Chong's.

"Well, well," Mrs. Chong said, looking up from her cash register. "More politics? Talk to Ben."

Father nudged me to do the right thing.

Bowing slightly, I said to Mrs. Chong, "*Tso shan, Chong Sim*"—Good morning, Mrs. Chong—and quickly followed Father double-stepping up the stairs to Ben Chong's book-lined office.

The office had barely enough room for his desk and two visitors' chairs. Small glasses perched on his nose, Mr. Chong was bent over, fingering an abacus, working on invoices. He squinted over a pile of papers to look at us. I imagined a scribbler flapping down on his head, like the broadsheets flapping down over the counter of the *New Republic Daily*. He smiled and shook Father's hand. They talked business at once.

"The Old One agrees with everything?" Mr. Chong gave me a serious looking over. I was eyeing the candy bars, but I knew he was talking about Grandmother.

"If the two like each other, why not?" Father said. "She agrees."

It must have been private business between our two families. I had overheard Mrs. Chong asking about buying a piece of jade from Third Uncle and Grandmother was always consulted. It was only right that the eldest, especially Father's own mother, should approve any family concerns. Her blessing mattered: if she died unhappy, we would be cursed by her ghost. And Poh-Poh's curses, all of Chinatown knew, were fearsome. The butcher who tried to cheat her lost both his business and his health within three months.

The two men looked at me and laughed heartily. I hadn't caught the joke.

"Your father and I have to talk some more," Mr. Chong said. He handed me a box of Rosebuds. "Go to the other room and say hello to Jenny."

The box went into my shirt pocket for later.

"Get to know her better, Kiam-Kim," Father said.

"Yes, yes," Mr. Chong said. "You two always be good friends. We are all Chinese."

I looked down the narrow hallway.

"That way, Kiam-Kim." Mr. Chong pointed out the curtained doorway with his glasses. "At the end of the hall."

Someone started to play the piano. From behind the curtains, the notes stumbled. I pushed aside the curtain.

"Don't snoop, you Nosy Parker!"

Jenny was sitting on a bench at an old standup piano, pretending to concentrate. Her close-cropped hair made her look like a boy. The last time we had passed each other at school, she had given me a cold stare, as if I should say something first.

Half a dozen framed pictures of the Chong family back in China lined the top of the piano: seven round, serious faces stared out through a haze of burning incense sticks. Some oranges and silver paper ingots sat in a bowl. Jenny was hitting a run of notes, in no particular order.

She had on a pink sweater that was too big for her. It bunched up on her back. If she wasn't going to talk, I thought at least I might get back at her for always looking at me as if I was a nobody.

"So why didn't you say hello to me when I saw you at school?"

"Why should I?"

I stepped around the piano so she had to see me.

"Your mother told Poh-Poh you can't go back to that Catholic girls' school. That's why you were back at Strathcona."

"So what?"

"She said you can't because they found out you weren't Catholic."

I thought she was going to say something like "None of your beeswax!" or "Get lost!" Instead, she half turned to me, and the thin line of her mouth started to tremble.

"I'm going to . . . *to die,*" she said. "I'm going to end up *in Hell.* That's what Sister Marie told me!" Tears dribbled from her lashes. "I hate you!"

She turned back to the piano and started playing again. A big voice boomed down the hallway.

"Kiam!"

I stepped out and saw Father at the end of the hall shaking Mr. Chong's hand, thanking him for the finished business and for his donation.

"Let's go, Kiam."

As I hurried down the hall, the piano began a complex tune.

I caught the scent of incense trailing after me down the stairs. With each step, the donation box rattled in my hand like a tambourine. At the front counter, Father folded an official-looking paper into a large envelope and began humming the same melody that Jenny had been playing. He looked cheerful. Jenny had looked terrible. It was a successful visit.

At the cash register, Mrs. Chong stopped serving a customer to smile at Father. She could see everything had gone well.

"Bring Kiam to visit again soon," she said. "My worthless Jenny thinks the world of him."

Like shit, I thought.

I told Jack O'Connor about Jenny Chong not being Catholic and having to leave the girls' school.

"One of the sisters told her she was going to die and go to Hell."

"I hear that all the time," he said, brushing back his tightly combed hair. His broad forehead gleamed with hair oil; his blue eyes suddenly flashed with knowledge. "You have to be baptized by a priest and be a Catholic to get into Heaven."

"Yeah?" The information irked me. "Well, you have to be Chinese to get into *our* Heaven."

"That makes sense."

Jack had been lifting weights in the sun, shirtless, trying to build up his tan like those billboard ads. He said he wanted to look like Charles Atlas to attract the girls at school. I myself was getting dark brown, not at all like the ads; Jack's freckled back and chest mostly burned. But there was a hint of tan on his face, which made both Jung and Liang refer to him as the cowboy.

"My mom says all the nuns in her old school in Ireland used to warn her about going to Hell," he said. "Especially when she married my father. He's a sort-of Protestant. But my Father says, 'Not to worry about Hell. Probably more fun there.'"

"What does your mother say?"

"She just pokes my father and tells him he doesn't know what he's talking about. 'Frank,'" he mimicked, "'now don't be confusin' the boy!' But I looked up Hell in our *Books of Knowledge*. There was a fold-out copy of a painting of Hell. It looked pretty gruesome."

He sucked on a blade of grass. Jack knew Jenny. Like everyone in the neighbourhood, the O'Connors shopped at the Chongs' corner store. And the three of us had sat together a few times on our front porch when Jenny had visited with her mother. But Jack thought she looked too skinny to be a real girl. He said her legs were like toothpicks, and he didn't like her Catholic school chopped-up haircut. That's why he was happy he didn't have to go to a church school. All the boys there had the same crewcut. Jack noticed people's hair. He liked the way all the up-to-date girls had curls.

"She's a chatterbox," he said.

My eyes must have bugged out, but Jack didn't notice.

"Hell must be confusing for Miss Bones," he said. "Being Chinese and all."

"Great deduction, Sherlock!"

"I don't even think Chinese people go to Hell. There's some Chinese nuns at St. Joseph's."

I thought of Mrs. Chong in a nun's habit, with her fierce eyes and shrill voice, telling Jenny about Hell, the Chinese Hell that the foreman at Third Uncle's warehouse had told me about to warn me away from playing with any of the bad boys in Chinatown. Third Uncle said it was a far worse place than any Christian Hell. He said that evildoers were boiled alive in huge vats until their fingernails and toenails melted and their eyes popped out, only no one ever dies. He told me about the Temple of Horrors he visited in Canton when he was a boy. There, lit by glowing lanterns, life-sized statues depicted what could happen to evildoers in the Buddhist Hells. There were different Hells for different kinds of sins. And the more you sinned, the more levels you were thrown into. Each level exacted ten thousand years of pain. And being boiled alive for ten thousand years was one of the lighter punishments.

"Each level more painful than the next," Third Uncle concluded, shivering at the thought. "You can ask your Poh-Poh. She knows about that place in Canton."

Jack began to tell me about the picture of Hell he saw. Every kind of torture was depicted.

"Chinese Hell is even more horrible," I said, thinking how Jack would look with his eyeballs popped out. "They boil you until your fingernails melt off, but you never die."

"Well," Jack said, "that's one lucky strike for bein' shamrock-green."

Jack picked up his dumbbells and began doing some exercises. I took up a blade of grass and fell into thinking about what had happened the day before at the Good Luck Barbershop.

One of the elders was upset with something Father said about the civil war in China. He had challenged Father, asking him which "political gang" would kill and torture the least number of Chinese people.

I didn't understand much of their talk until the old man flipped open a *Life* magazine.

"Look," he said. "This be war. This be patriotism!"

He held up the double-page spread of pictures for everyone to see. Some of the men laughed nervously.

"Here, look, Son of Chen," the old man said. "You be old enough to see, too."

I stared at the black-and-white picture of weeping Chinese women and children, their faces twisted and dust stained. But what held my attention was the sagging corpses at their feet. One had no head. Another's stiff arm stuck into the air, palm opened and fingers stretched out as if to stop a sudden blow.

In the next picture, an old soldier grasped at his side the handle of a long sword. A few feet away, another Chinese soldier, his arms tightly bound behind him, knelt waiting his turn to meet the executioner's sword. His eyes were opened wide.

The third picture held my attention even longer. Another tied-up man waiting his turn, his eyes tightly shut, his lips frozen with fear. He looked like David Ang, the grocer's oldest son who always joked with Stepmother about which vegetables were fresher, which a better buy. A gust of wind had lifted up the front of his open army jacket. I could hear and feel that wind, the parting of the drab tunic like broken wings. When the soldier was a boy running freely down a hillside, he must have felt such a wind.

All at once, the sad and terrible stories I overheard the men tell of Old China seemed more real than anything I had imagined. My heart raced with a cold I had not felt before.

"This captured prisoner fights for China, too," the elder shouted.

"Yes," someone said, "but for what side?"

"Damn *what side!*" The elder threw the magazine on the floor. "Isn't he a patriot? Which side is *not* patriotic?"

"Of course," the barber agreed, "he wears a soldier's uniform."

"Well," someone else said, "they all wear some kind of uniform."

"Tell me," the elder said to Father, then turned to everyone in the barbershop, "how many *patriots* would the Reformers execute? How many will the Republicans kill? How many will Socialists dispatch? And the Communists?"

No one answered.

The old man turned back to Father and took out his thick gambler's wallet. "You tell me who kills no one—which side will not kill a single man, woman, or child . . ." Some bills fluttered in the air as he waved his bulging wallet. "Tell me which side and I donate two hundred dollars to their side. Right now!"

"No political change without sacrifice," Father said.

The elder laughed and put away his wallet. "Then I say hellfire on all of them!"

"Gentlemen," Father said. "We collect for blankets and food."

I forgot to say my speech.

Some of the men turned away from Father, refusing to debate with him; some gave reluctantly after I shook the donation box in front of them.

Sitting on the grass with Jack, thinking of all this, of Jenny crying in fear of ending up in Hell, of a young man, who looked like the grocer's son, waiting to be executed, of Chinese killing Chinese, suddenly I felt Hell was all too real.

Jack set down his weights and sat next to me. "I'm not afraid of Hell," he said. "Are you?"

"No," I said. "Just spooked."

Jack laughed. "My mom says all those loose women trolling the East End—they'll go to Hell for sure." He licked his lips. "If some of those really big-chested good-lookers were there, I wouldn't mind visiting Hell for just a look-see. How about you?"

"No Dogs, No Chinese Allowed," I said.

"Oh, yeah! Those White Labour Only signs."

"Don't forget, No Fuckin' Irish!"

"No Jews!"

We shouted out all the signs that both our fathers told us had once been stuck up on the front gates of big estates and on the doors of private clubs and theatres. If you went up to the British Properties or near the golf courses at Shaughnessy or Marine Drive, if you walked along Granville Street and looked into certain entrances, you could still run into those signs.

Would Hell be divided up, too?

For a while, the world around me seemed a swirl of dire news about the war and the famines in China, the Depression and the jobless in Gold Mountain, and Father's and Stepmother's struggles with meeting the rent and buying enough decent food. We weren't poor, thanks mainly to Third Uncle and a new loan Father got from the Tong Association, but we seemed to be broke.

Sitting at Father's desk early one evening, my

brain darting from a math problem to the world's problems and whether or not I would end up in Hell, I tossed aside my pencil and began fiddling with the Chinese brush. I dipped its soft tip into the soot-smelling ink pot. Delicate strands of the brush reminded me of the colour of Jenny's close-cropped hair, the way she turned her head away from me and how the blackness shone as if dipped in fresh ink. Or wildly lit by hellfire.

The desk lamp went off, then flashed on. A violent rumble shook the house.

Stepmother called out from the parlour. "Go upstairs and close the bedroom windows, Kiam."

In the parlour, Poh-Poh was sorting out her small collection of old silk shawls and dresses she had long ago salvaged from the two wives of Patriarch Chen's no-brain sons. The wives had decided to dress like Westerners, Poh-Poh had told me, so she took from their tossed-away habits the very best items. Stepmother held up a richly embroidered *cheongsam* against herself, and Poh-Poh's slave-trained hands began pinning where alterations were required. The blood-red silk shimmered with leaves and ornate blossoms.

I walked past Jung sprawled on the linoleum floor, trying to make something out of the leftover Meccano pieces from my original second-hand set. Sekky chattered away beside him.

Upstairs, I found Liang quietly dressing up three dolls at her small orange-crate table beside her pallet. My only sister, humming a nursery song about a tipping teapot, was far away from any thoughts of Hell.

In the front bedroom, I paused before the open window to look over at the Douglas fir across the street; the wind was stronger now, and its branches swayed, rattling the needles. Though the tree shook, its trunk remained strong, unmoving. I wondered if Father had taken his umbrella with him that morning, and if cool winds ever blew in Hell. I thought of the young soldier caught in a gust of wind, waiting for his death, how the wind threw open his jacket. I pushed the window shut. Rain fell.

I looked towards the outcrop of rockery where Mrs. Lim's wooden shack was perched on stilts. I wondered why widowed Mrs. Lim didn't panic, didn't worry that her house might be snatched up and blown away. I knew her windows were always shut, the shades drawn, to preserve the *che* forces, the spirit forces, of her home. I wondered if that was why she did not worry. I wondered at our bedroom window, which was now holding against the force of a slamming North Shore wind, probably with the same force that hit the soldier's face and forced him to shut his eyes.

I went downstairs. Everyone was still busy with the clothes. A delicate silk shawl now lifted into the air; embroidered butterflies caught the light.

"You think too much, Kiam-Kim," Poh-Poh said, gathering up the shawl. "Gai-mou agrees."

"I can't help it," I protested.

I wanted to explain to them how I puzzled over why things happened, what things meant. I wanted to understand what the elders told me about Old China, about which side was good, if any side was good at all.

I stared into space, thinking about my own life inside the borders of Chinatown, a life sometimes so far away from the Old China world they all still lived in.

I went to the parlour and picked up Sekky and swung him, giggling, into the air. I wanted to toss him higher than any Hell could ever reach him.

After weeks of moping about, worrying, and pestering everyone about the dark place called Hell, I began to brood over the fate of my siblings and Stepmother's Lost Baby.

"Did he go directly to Heaven?"

Maybe Father would have been less worried if I was more like Jack, whose fascination was with girls, or like Jeffrey Eng, who fretted endlessly over car engines. Instead, he and Third Uncle decided that I should attend a few Sunday school classes at the Good Mission Church on Keefer Street.

"Let Kiam-Kim learn as much as possible," Father said to Poh-Poh, who resisted. "He should hear about Heaven, too."

It turned out that Stepmother had a close friend in China named Chen Suling who, after she accepted Christ into her life, was thrown out of her family compound. Suling's father did not appreciate the fact that, like a barbarian, his useless daughter would drink the blood of Christ and eat his flesh.

Chen Suling found shelter at the Mission Church.

If church people were such good people as to save the lives of useless or orphaned girls like herself and Suling, Stepmother did not mind if I went to Sunday school. Quite a few Chinatown families belonged to the United Church.

"I don't want Kiam-Kim to eat flesh and blood," Poh-Poh warned. She had herself once witnessed Christians eating only wafers and drinking only wine, but someone warned her that the wafer and wine instantly turned into the actual flesh and blood of the Lord Jesus. Poh-Poh spat at the thought.

Third Uncle promised Poh-Poh that no possible harm would ever come to me at the Mission Church. I would be asked to swallow neither flesh nor blood. Instead, cakes and tea were often served. He would take me with him himself until my bowl was full of Light, or at least with enough wattage to chase away the darkness.

Third Uncle had some acquaintance with the Bible and with the minister at the church. Twenty-five years ago, he had attended English classes there taught by a Mrs. Simpson. She had introduced him to the Chinese Bible, and occasionally they still arranged to meet at community fundraisers. Third Uncle and the church people spoke together about my teenage fears, my obsession with Hell. The minister said that I should attend Mrs. Simpson's First Instructions class. We were to avoid the Baptists, the Jehovah's Witnesses, the Catholics, in fact all groups who believed everything was always about darkness and punishment, always about sin and Hell.

"Of course, Kiam-Kim, there is a Hell," Mrs. Simpson said matter-of-factly. "But good Christians and good people don't need to worry about that. We should all think about God's Heaven. That's where we truly belong."

Mrs. Simpson had tight curly hair, more white than brown, and she wore thick glasses through which grey eyes shone. She had a strong, motherly voice that suited her big-boned height. She wore a blue jacket with a cherub pin on the lapel.

I liked Mrs. Simpson. She had no fear of the Devil or of Hell; she would not even listen to the list of tortures that I had nightmares about. She was intent on teaching us her version of the Bible.

I knew that many Chinatown men and women went to these Church-sponsored classes, often because it was a safe place to socialize. Tea and cookies were served—and if they were hungry, no one looked if they pocketed some extra biscuits—and the classes required a donation only of a nickel, maybe a dime. Some basic English could be learned, and then, when you felt you had enough English words, you would simply not show up.

Some, like Mrs. Leong and Mrs. Wong, attended English night classes for other reasons. When the evening's language and Proverb lessons were done, these two women, souls refreshed, hats adjusted, coats tightly buttoned, walked blissfully in the moonlight the two blocks to Mrs. Lim's. Then the three of them would powder their noses and go and play mahjong at Betty Lee's. For them, salvation always came first, *in case.*

"Well," said Mrs. Chong about the three mahjong ladies, "why be saved for nothing?"

Poh-Poh laughed. "Too late for me."

Third Uncle told me he used to feel very lucky after some of those Bible lessons; he would rush off at once to the *fantan* tables, and often won quite a few dollars.

"Of course," he said, "I donate to the church."

Mrs. Simpson warmly welcomed us that first day, taking us from the minister's office to her Beginner's English and First Instructions class in a small meeting room at the back of the building. Also in the class were Mrs. Poon and her oldest daughter, Joanne, four years older than me, who came to continue their Bible lessons and to learn English; a white lady from Poland who hardly spoke any English but clutched a picture of Jesus and the Virgin Mary against her thick sweater; Miss Abbey, a Siwash Indian whom Mrs. Simpson had saved from a bad life and who seemed to only half listen as she pulled strands of her long, black hair between her fingers; two other kids around my age, Steven and Jess; and Third Uncle, who had brought me.

Mrs. Simpson could see from Third Uncle's rice-bowl loyalty (for he now came to classes only when he needed to understand certain English phrases related to business) that through Third Uncle's recommendations she could at least still increase the flock. He had sent her way a steady stream of sheep, old like Mrs. Poon and young like myself. Joanne and I could speak English and Toishanese, so we were asked to help translate for Mrs. Poon and for the two youngest in the class.

"Let the light guide you," Mrs. Simpson said, "not the darkness. Angels fear not the darkness." Mrs. Simpson smiled at the mix of adults and children before her. "The good people who love us are also like angels. They will help us fight demons and temptation. Be a good person and you will have wings to fly over God's Eternal Garden."

Joanne and I translated what we could. If Mrs. Simpson noticed any one of the eight of us struggling, she would walk straight to her special green felt board and illustrate her meaning. She stuck up an angel-shaped felt cutout and a thin red strip with a pointed yellow dot on top.

"Like angels, you will bring your light to this dark world."

After the first month, not everyone stayed. The Polish lady, tongue-tied, did not come back, and neither did Mrs. Poon, whose husband, Third Uncle told me, was angry at her for coming at all. Joanne Poon, however, signed up for more classes. She wept for joy that she might be an angel, since she was only a girl at home.

"She work harder than you, Kiam-Kim," said Third Uncle.

"She prays harder," I said, though I knew everyone in the family was concerned that my grades were slipping. I had too much to think about. I stayed in my room and sank deeper into a grim-faced melancholy. At night, Jung quietly slipped into his small cot and said nothing. I prayed for his soul.

Whenever I grew restless, on those Beginners'

mornings, Mrs. Simpson's steel eyes bored into me.

"If you remember to be patient, Kiam-Kim," she said, "as Jesus taught us to be patient, even under the lash, then Heaven will be your reward." Her stories held my attention. There was the tale of a man who helped another man who was beaten by crooks and left to die. A felt cutout of a man lay on a grey patch of felt road. "Other holy men passed him by, but a Samaritan, the kind of person thought to be the least respectable"—Mrs. Simpson looked at Miss Abbey— "this worthless outcast rescued the bleeding man. That good Samaritan has no fear of Hell. He is one of God's angels."

I thought of the blankets and food my Free China donation boxes were helping to buy, my efforts helping to guard soldiers against the cold, and orphans against hunger. For the next three Sundays, Mrs. Simpson told other Christian stories. She assured us of the promise of Heaven granted to all good people. She asked each one of us to think about our own goodness. There was a scarcity of goodness and mercy and charity in the world—but one had to choose to be good, to be merciful, to be charitable. That was God's gift to us, that choice.

"Free will," said Mrs. Simpson. "So choose wisely."

I thought of Jenny Chong banging away at the piano: she didn't seem to realize there was Heaven as well as Hell. And just as Hell had obsessed me, I began to see the Heavenly Light everywhere. I smiled like an idiot.

As quickly as the fires and demon visions had flooded my thoughts, they just as suddenly receded. One bright May Sunday morning I woke up, either saved by Jesus or surrendered by the Devil, and knew this would be my last visit to the Mission Church. I told Mrs. Simpson that I could see the light now, though I knew it was not exactly as she might have wished.

"As long as you believe this," she said, "then all will be fine, Kiam-Kim. Bless you."

I suppose if I was so concerned about Hell, I should have asked Third Uncle about Heaven as well. The Chinese Heaven was certain to be more splendid than the Christian one. And there were Chinese guardians, too, though I always felt unsure about them, like Poh-Poh's Kitchen God, and the Goddess of Mercy in our parlour, and the pictures of our distant dead cousins on the end table between the incense and the thick red candles. Chinatown was flooded with spiritual wealth. Most everyone we knew had a laughing Buddha sitting on top of their piano or on a plate shelf. Every Chinatown business had the fierce-faced God of Good Fortune standing on a temple-shaped platform, and almost every store sold incense and lucky envelopes.

I could see now that in Chinatown there was more Heaven than Hell.

Leaving the house for school one beautiful morning, with Liang and Jung tagging behind me, I said, out of the blue, "I'm lucky."

"Why?" Jung asked.

"Because we're a family," I said. "We have Poh-Poh and Father and Stepmother with us."

Jung-Sum smiled. "And they have me."

"Me, too," Liang piped up.

"And all those Chinese gods," I said, touching my forehead and crossing my heart just as Jack had taught me to do. *In case.*

~ *S I X* ~

JEFF ENG ALREADY WORKED AT his family's garage, learning a trade. Fat Wah Duk washed dishes and chopped vegetables like a real chef in the kitchen of his family's restaurant. At their market store, Joe Sing helped his parents, too, and not just with household chores or with rattling donation cans. Even Jenny Chong worked behind the counter at the corner store.

Father said we couldn't do fundraising as much any more. Third Uncle said everyone was too used to me now. New boys were rattling the cans, a few for rival charities and with different political names. Instead, I was to devote more time to my Chinese lessons.

But I did have one consistent job. Stepmother and Poh-Poh both said, "Take Jung-Sum with you."

"You be *dai-goh*," Father said. "That's your duty."

As Jung was now stronger and taller, I talked my pals into letting him play soccer with us. Whenever we were short of team members, Jung was appointed our goalie. At first, he didn't block that many goals. He grew increasingly frustrated, madly dashing to block the speeding ball with his feet and missing his target by a mile. But he soon figured out another tactic: he hurled his whole body at any human trunk charging towards the goal. He never missed, his feet kicking up dust before they flew into the air, his lean torso crashing like a battering ram into his opponent, sending legs and arms and head smearing into the ground.

"Your goalie's crazy," one white boy said to me, wiping at his bleeding lip. "He thinks nothing can kill him."

We each got our share of scrapes and cuts. Jung just got more than most. I told Poh-Poh he was crazy.

"Boy-fever," Poh-Poh said.

Stepmother shook her head in amazement: why would anyone choose to injure himself? Poh-Poh and Father, however, admired our warrior wounds. In China, Father said, we would make good soldiers. We could do anything.

Stepmother looked away. I remembered Poh-Poh telling me about Stepmother's tragic time. How her child's eyes once peeked out from beneath a stack of clothing, how they had witnessed bandit soldiers raising their swords; how Stepmother had heard and seen, unblinking, five blades hissing in the air to strike at her trembling family. One blow for each of them.

"Teach Jung-Sum how to kick and pass the ball," Father said to me. "Canada never need soldiers."

"Need soldiers in China," Poh-Poh said, slapping the last bandage on my arm. She poured her stinging homemade lotion on one of Jung's battle wounds. "Fight the warlords! Fight the Japanese!"

He barely flinched.

I felt a thrill to think that I might one day be a soldier in China, too. A good soldier fought in the battlefield, or sat bravely waiting for his execution, faithful to his country, not like one of those warrior-scholars from the Cantonese opera who wrote poems and fought or died for love.

Jung-Sum flexed his arm. The pain was nothing.

After every soccer game, we would break up, winging back to our own flock, chattering in Italian, Polish, Chinese, or whatever language we spoke at home. We took it for granted that every Vancouver family, in their own household language, had endlessly recited the same edict that Poh-Poh and everyone in Chinatown had repeated to me, *Stick to your own kind.* And for the most part I did.

However, Jack O'Connor and I remained best pals. But Poh-Poh tested our friendship.

One day, when we were out on the porch working through a Grade 8 history project together, the Old One came out with a plate of lunch for me. Jack grimaced at the Chinese sausages and red-bean-paste buns. Poh-Poh wafted a steamed bun under his nostrils. He curled his lips and pinched his nose.

"How can you eat that stuff?" he asked.

Another time, undeterred, the Old One pushed up the porch window and offered him a steamed black-bean sparerib. I wasn't surprised when Jack jumped back from the garlicky smell. His family lived on boiled meat and potatoes, beans and wieners and bologna sandwiches.

Poh-Poh shouted at him, "Demon boy no know-how! No sabby!"

"Kemo-sabe!" Jack shouted back. He looked at me in surprise. "She knows *The Lone Ranger*!"

I was impressed that Poh-Poh had tolerated all these years my barbarian playmate, even after she caught him mimicking her Chinese speech and threw a broom at him. Years ago, when we were first neighbours, she and Stepmother saw Jack with his mother beside him hanging out the laundry in the backyard, turning up their noses at the cooking smells drifting from our window. But our household had some judgments to make, too.

Against the white bedsheets, the bright sun made Jack and his mother seem even more chalky and wan. In their veins, Poh-Poh said, there ran no soy sauce, no hot sauce, *no sauce at all!*

"*Aaaiiyaah!*" Stepmother said, with some pity, "They so pale!"

"They die soon!" said Poh-Poh.

But from the beginning, Stepmother thought Jack's and my friendship was probably best for me: from my new friend I would pick up more English words. Father agreed.

Our two fathers got along reasonably well, and always greeted each other over the porch rails. When we were younger, we often spent time on each other's porch and our toys often lay scattered together where we left them, warriors and cowboys side by side.

Nevertheless, "Don't let the demon boy in the house," Poh-Poh warned me. "He not Chinese!"

And so the rule was set. Throughout Chinatown, in fact, it was rare to have any outsiders visit our homes. There didn't seem to be any good reason to have foreigners come into our places and have them judge what we ate or complain about how we lived or have them ask too many questions.

Although inside the O'Connor house I would listen to the radio or work on a project, Poh-Poh made it clear that Jack would not be welcome to step inside our door.

"Chinese air kill him," she said.

"But I've had hot dogs at his place," I protested. "Why can't you make hot dogs?"

"Hot dog, no head, no tail. Not real food," Poh-Poh said, rolling up her sleeve to tear the feathers off a freshly killed chicken. She lifted its sagging head. "*This* real food."

The beady eyes of the dead chicken stared me down. What would Jack say if he saw the chicken when it was finally cooked, with its head and beak lolling on the platter? Or what would he think if he heard the scratching noises coming from the crate under our sink? Uncle Dai Kew had brought Poh-Poh a live turtle to make them both a special soup for longevity. Even I had to shut my eyes as the cleaver fell and split apart the wiggling creature. And what if he came upon the dried-up sea horses, the clump of costly bird's nest, or the dehydrated black-bear paw?

Perhaps it was better that Jack never set foot in our house.

Stepmother was not so antagonistic towards the O'Connors. One day I had spilled some groceries on the sidewalk after a bully ran by and knocked me down. The eggs were smashed and the bags were torn, and goods lay strewn about me. Stepmother had fallen behind to gossip with Mrs. Leong. I could see her half a block away just as Mrs. O'Connor came down from her garden to help me pick up the groceries.

"Why, this is parsley," she said. "And it's all covered with egg."

She told me to wait. It wasn't long before she came back with some fresh parsley in her hand and some grocery bags. By then I'd gathered up as much as I could, and Mrs. O'Connor went back into her house.

Stepmother caught up with me and I told her what had happened.

"Jack's mother," Stepmother asked, "does she like anything Chinese?"

I told Stepmother that according to Jack the only thing the thin woman liked about Chinamen was China tea. That evening, Stepmother wrapped a small packet of tea and gave it to Jack to give to his mother.

"We say thank you," she said, which I translated for Jack, who bowed his head as if he were in a Charlie Chan picture.

Next day, Jack's mother sent over a folded handwritten note with flowers on one corner. I glanced over it and told Stepmother it was a thank-you note. But

Mrs. Chong took it from me and translated every word for her: "'Thank you for the peasant tea.'"

"Not *peasant* tea!" protested Stepmother. "First-class oolong!"

Doubting that Mrs. O'Connor would mean to insult her, Stepmother had Mrs. Leong's oldest daughter retranslate the sentence: *Thank you for the pleasant tea.*

Stepmother had often looked with envy at Mrs. O'Connor's small front yard crowded with flowers. There were no flowers on our side; Grandmother had planted rows of beans and vegetables to catch the long and late afternoon light.

One afternoon, after observing Stepmother staring again at her front yard of blooms, Mrs. O'Connor sent over some roses. Later that week, she told Jack to pick some daisies and snapdragons for me to take home.

I carried back packets of tea. The two women smiled at each other.

"I should give garlic bean paste," declared Poh-Poh. "Finish things up!"

"Leave them alone," Father said. "No one troubling you."

"No trouble," said the Old One. "No taste."

Jung-Sum and Liang, and now Sekky, too, got the same warning that I had been given.

"Stick to Chinese," Poh-Poh said to them, clipping Mrs. O'Connor's fresh pink roses to fit the vase Stepmother gave her. "Don't play too long over there."

Then she wrapped up some ordinary tea and sent Jung-Sum over the porch.

"Why did you send her *English* tea?" I asked. "They must have lots of that."

"Best for pale skin," Poh-Poh said. "No flavour."

Jung said Mrs. O'Connor told him she hadn't brewed that brand for a long time.

The Old One smiled. "She more Chinese now."

Although the O'Connors and the Chens had lived side by side for more than ten years, Jack and I took for granted that both our families were too familiar and too strange to explain. What mattered to us was that, as a team, fair or not, we bloodied the noses of Strathcona recess bullies and earned a reputation for sticking together.

Of course, having to attend Chinese classes meant that more and more I hung out with Chinese boys my age who went to the same school, or who wanted to play hooky as badly as I did. We learned by rote, attempting to follow the basic discipline of a thousand years of writing history. We needed to train our young eyes and inexperienced hands to coordinate our fingers, to make the ink-wet brush move into the dips and dashes of Chinese script. Reading lessons were shouted back and forth between teacher and students, repetitions of one boring edict after another, as if by repetition they would sink into our hearts if not our heads: *Respect the elders first. Always obey your parents. Study hard. Do your homework every day.* Because of the strict way everything was taught to us by the male teachers, with bamboo rods slamming down on tables or palms, we mimicked the lessons like trained seals. Chinese school was always heads down, concentrate, recite and copy, copy and recite. The more restless of us did everything to get out of going to classes; a few, like me, who sometimes earned some praise because all the teachers knew of Father's writings and saw in me a little potential, or the few whose merchant family connections were powerful and known, did nothing to shame our families. I came to see the serious need to focus and accept the discipline that had given Father his pride in his work, whether with accounts or with essays: Father had endured school himself, and his discipline with brush and pen helped him to earn a living in Chinatown. When he had time, I would read him back the week's lessons, and Father would illustrate an aphorism with a story he himself had learned in his school days.

"Yes, yes, study hard!" he would begin, then tell me the story of the young student—"a boy like you"—who kept a jar of fireflies so that their collective fire would allow him to study through the night to pass the Imperial Exams. But two weeks later, the Chinese words would fade from my brain, and the order of dips and dashes would be lost to my brush, and I would be left wondering, *What do fireflies eat to keep them burning so bright against the night?* Father complained about my constant slippage with my Chinese writing and reading, though I was an excellent writer and enthusiastic reader at English school.

"Not enough time for both," Third Uncle told Father. "Too much English school."

"Let Kiam-Kim learn what he can," argued Stepmother. "Impossible to do much more."

"Keep my grandson Chinese," Poh-Poh urged one of my teachers at the school, and Teacher Sing smiled politely to ease her concerns. But for the majority of us Gold Mountain children, it was a smile against futility.

I went to Chinese school every weekday, and on Saturday mornings until half past noon. I spent a lot more time with my studies than Jack ever did. And Jack himself, free from the extra burden of memorizing and deciphering dips and dashes, soon fell into happy companionship with a roving gang of blue-eyed, red-headed Irish boys. Then, as the years claimed our days, though our proximity to each other as neighbours assured that we remained best friends, I fell into step with a Chinatown crowd and Jack moved from one gang to another, but mostly with those like himself, white-skinned and sports-minded. Each to his own kind.

"I get the best deal," Jack told me one day when I rushed past him with my leather case filled with copybooks, texts, ink, and writing brushes. "I don't have to go to any Chink, Jew, or Wop school like all you other guys."

Sometimes in the hour between the end of English school and the start of Chinese school, Jack, Jeff Eng, and I met behind the sheltered bathrooms at MacLean Park. In that dank, echoing chamber, next to a row of stained urinals, we inhaled, along with the flavour of stale piss and ammonia, the Player's or Exports we had cadged from older boys.

Once, one of Jack's pals turned up with an almost full bottle of hard liquor, filched from a wedding. We dared each other to take a swig. Jack tossed his head back like the pirates in the picture shows we saw; we each threw our head back, coughed and gagged at the burning alcohol, and wiped our eyes without shame. After another dare or two, a big second gulp followed.

"The bottle's not finished," Jack said. "Anyone game for more?"

"Maybe after Chinese school," Jeff said. "I'm for it."

The two looked over to see what I had in mind.

"Count me in," I said. "We'll all meet here right after school."

Jeff slapped me on the back.

"It's a deal," Jack said.

Jeff's mother and sister had come to the house to warn us about the strange illness that made Jeff so late coming home from Chinese school. And how odd, Mrs. Eng noted, that her son's breath smelled so freshly of a thick wad of Wrigley's spearmint. When I stumbled into the house much later, everyone but Father, who had yet to return from work, was standing waiting. Liang hid behind Stepmother's dress.

Without a word, Poh-Poh touched my head, squeezed my cheeks so that my mouth opened wide. She sniffed my breath and looked at my tongue. She watched me try to follow her finger with my crossed eyes, then she sent me right to bed.

Moments later, or so it seemed, half out of my clothes, I heard Father arrive home. He asked Jung-Sum why he was bringing me dinner on a tray.

"Dai-goh sick," I heard Second Brother answer. Poh-Poh called Father into the kitchen.

"No one's telling Father anything yet," Jung told me. "Just that you have a fever." He put down the tray and helped me yank off my pants. "Poh-Poh told Stepmother you probably have boy-fever. You get over it soon."

"Where's Stepmother?"

"She's in the bedroom. Sekky is playing with his tanks in the pantry. Only Sister is with Poh-Poh."

"I know," I snapped, threading my legs through my pyjama bottoms.

I started to eat, to show Jung how stupid talk of boy-fever was. After two big swallows, with the food halfway down, I pushed the greasy plate aside; my eyes began to bulge, my stomach lurched. Of its own accord, the plate of food floated above the tray. Jung grabbed everything from me. I raced downstairs and pounded on the bathroom door for whoever was inside to hurry the hell up. I pushed my way in just as Father was buttoning up his fly and yanking the chain. He was as red with surprise as I was green with bile.

I bent over and puked my boy-fever into the swirling waters.

Father smelled the sour air. He sniffed again, recognized the sharp odour. Without a word, he knuckled me. He grabbed my hair and yanked me to my feet. A mistake. I spewed more bile onto the floor and side of the tub.

"Useless boy!" Father twisted my ear. "Drunken dead boy!"

I felt a sharp kick on my rear end, and the linoleum floor and the white sink and the tin-plate ceiling spun around and around. I heard Stepmother calling my name from upstairs, telling Father to stop.

"Send him upstairs."

Father took a deep breath. "Go," he said. "I kill you later."

Sekky dashed out of the pantry and disappeared behind the sofa in the parlour. Liang was standing beside Poh-Poh by the stove, holding her breath, waiting for my early death.

I walked by Jung-Sum, who was standing by the front doorway. When I made it safely up the first three steps, Second Brother went into the parlour to comfort Sekky. The two of them huddled together beside the sofa to watch their big brother's progress.

Clinging to the bannister, thinking as clearly as I could manage, I paused a moment to consider what would happen next: Stepmother would deliver a stern lecture and set down some rules for me; of course, I would lose some freedom . . . but I felt oddly content. I started to say something, to set a good example, but a sudden queasiness oiled the back of my throat. I bent over and clutched at the railing. My ribs ached. The pungent smells on my shirt and hands made me gag.

Before I knew what was happening, Jung-Sum was at my side, trying to lift my arm back onto the bannister. Sekky was clapping his encouragement, as if he were watching a performance.

I heard Poh-Poh cleaning up the bathroom, the mop banging against the tub, and Jook-Liang in her little voice saying, "Dai-goh so sick!"

"*Good* sick," the Old One was saying. "This sick is *good* sign. He send out bad stuff."

I shoved Second Brother aside. I thought that it was my duty to set a manly example.

But as he fell back, something in Jung's eyes made me want to reach out and pull him back towards me; when I didn't do anything but wait for him to regain his footing, he must have realized, in that instant, that I could never be trusted.

I shut my eyes, pulled myself slowly up the stairs.

The bedroom door was shut. I knocked.

"Kiam-Kim? Come."

Stepmother was rummaging through the trunk. When she found what she was looking for, she told me to sit down on the chair before her dressing table. In her hand was my mother's picture.

"You remember this?"

"Yes."

I tried to focus my eyes to see the small woman in the frame. The dresser mirror reflected back the image.

"After Liang was born, your father showed me your mother's picture. He told me no one could ever replace her."

"Yes," I said.

"You are the son of your father and First Wife?"

"Yes."

"Can anyone replace you?"

This was a game, but I thought it was best to play along.

"Only I can be First Son."

"Poh-Poh tell everyone your mother spoke to you before she died. Do you remember that?"

"No," I said, "but Poh-Poh says so."

"Your poor mother's final breath was used to speak to you, Kiam-Kim. You were the last one. Poh-Poh told me you even answered her. That was what the maid witnessed."

"Yes," I said.

Stepmother's words echoed in my head. What everyone said had happened, I had been too young to remember. But I was now old enough to know that the maid must have been mistaken, and that Poh-Poh had always imagined such things to be true.

"Gai-mou, what are you going to say to me?"

"Nothing. I am not your mother."

In the mysterious quiet that settled between us, Stepmother's eyes seemed to swallow me up. As I looked away, the image in the dresser mirror wavered. In the back of my mind, someone else's despairing eyes drifted towards me, and I longed to fall into their darkness. Stepmother's fierce gaze drew me back to her, made me focus through my drunken haze and pay attention.

A firm voice broke through the silence.

"When you go back to your room," the voice said, "call back your mother, Kiam-Kim. Tonight, before you sleep, think what she would say to you about your behaviour."

Gai-mou touched my forehead; she traced the wetness on my palm and studied me a moment. She got up and put away the picture.

"Stand up, Kiam-Kim."

She put her arm around my shoulder and guided me to my bed. I felt like a child again. She folded down the blanket, even lifted my foot to help me slip under the sheets, her every gesture as gentle as I imagined my mother's would have been. Stepmother's warmth made me want to lean against her, as if she mattered more to me than anyone else.

"What would your mother say to you, Kiam-Kim?"

I closed my eyes. The nausea began to settle. The round face in the picture floated towards me.

I lost track of time and did not hear Jung-Sum come into the room to go to bed.

"Dai-goh," he said. "Are you dead?"

Silence.

"Dai-goh?" he persisted. "Are you awake?"

I nodded, but did not open my eyes. Later, Jung told me he had asked if I still wanted him as a brother. I said that he would always be my brother. But I remembered none of this.

The next day, Poh-Poh came to my room first.

"Father downstairs. He wait for you."

I sat up, rubbing my eyes, put on my kimono, and carefully navigated my way down the stairs. I dragged myself along the hall into the dining room, where Father pointed to the empty chair. With my blood pounding in my ears, I sat across from Father at his desk. Slowly he set his glasses down and pinched the bridge of his nose.

"I'm sorry, Father," I said.

A teapot sat before him, steeping.

He looked at me carefully. I lifted the lid and absent-mindedly tapped it twice on the side of the pot. Then I poured a cup for him. Something made me bow my head. I had no more words to say. I was too ashamed to look up.

We sat in silence. After a sip of tea, Father told me that Third Uncle wanted me to do some real work at the warehouse that weekend. A shipment of pottery had come in from Hong Kong.

"You will be on time?"

"Yes," I said. "Right after Chinese school, I will go to the warehouse."

"Bring some tea to Stepmother. She is upstairs with Sekky waiting for you."

I poured a cup and took it to her. Sekky was pushing the extra pillows together to make a mountain for his fighter plane to fly over.

"Well, Kiam-Kim?"

"Mother came to me," I said, "but no words were spoken. I think I only dreamed she was with me. I—I was very sick."

Sekky's fighter plane zoomed between us and almost caused the tea to spill. Stepmother put her hand out to subdue him.

That afternoon Poh-Poh asked me, "Where Father kicked you, any bruise?"

To change the subject, I told her the good news, that I was going to work at Third Uncle's warehouse.

Poh-Poh ignored me. "When you tapped the teapot, your father almost wept that he had hurt you in such anger. Your mother used to do that every morning, Kiam-Kim."

"Do what?"

"Tap the lid of the teapot."

"Why would she do that?"

"She said that was how she woke up both you and your father."

After I had barely recovered from my hangover and after my protest against Poh-Poh, who, with her own hands, insisted on putting some of her lotion on my backside, Mrs. Chong came over with some egg tarts.

I should have guessed she would show up. The night before, Poh-Poh had felt the need to walk over with Liang to the Chongs' corner store to get me some aspirin. No doubt Jeff's mother had already told Mrs. Chong a few details. The mahjong ladies were a tight group.

"Heard you still recovering, Kiam-Kim," said Mrs. Chong slyly as she stepped into our front hall. She was wearing a new hat with tiny feathers. "Your father told Third Uncle he feels terrible about what happened." To let me know how much was known, Mrs. Chong, her tongue clucking away, pointed at my rear end.

I led her into the kitchen and put some water on for tea so she could sit and gossip with Stepmother and Poh-Poh. I turned down the offer of an egg tart.

"Later I make you some delicious soup, Kiam-Kim," Mrs. Chong said. "Settle your tummy." She went on about the imbalances in my hot-cold *che*. She was right: there was a lingering acid taste in the back of my mouth.

"Only boy-fever," Poh-Poh said. "All over now."

Later that afternoon, Jenny Chong appeared with some of her mother's promised soup. I hadn't seen her for months and noticed right away that her hair had grown in, thick and dark, which distracted me.

"How hard did your father kick you?"

I ignored her and went straight to the kitchen. I kept myself busy unlocking the tin container of soup. She took another tack.

"Why didn't you tell them the whole story?"

"What story?"

"Why didn't you tell your father that Jack was involved, too?" She sounded breathless. "Jack's been boasting to Shelly Larkin about getting drunk at MacLean Park. Shelly's mother says Jack's just like his father."

"Why should I tell anything?"

Jenny took a bowl from the shelf and poured me out some soup. No doubt following her mother's careful instructions.

"Try some."

It tasted good, like a plain beef broth but with a tangy flavour I couldn't identify. Jenny pulled up a chair and sat down next to me, her eyes wide open with digging prospects.

"Well?"

"Good soup," I said.

"Mother said you got kicked. How hard?"

The two words shot out like a real dare.

I did not want a girl like Jenny to think of me as a second-rate sufferer. I put down my spoon and waved her to follow me through the screen door. I made sure no one was walking in the alleyway and the O'Connors' backyard was empty. I stepped away from Jenny.

"Don't move."

I turned my back, and with one thumb hooked under both my pants and underwear, I yanked them down. The breeze felt cool. I looked back over my shoulder, and I could see behind her the climbing beanstalks and the bamboo staves.

I had studied the bruise in Father's bedroom mirror. Running down my left side was a dark, blood-clotted beauty stained with Poh-Poh's lotion. A first-class bruise.

"Go ahead," I said, holding on to my pants. "Touch it."

Jenny's warm hand hesitated a moment, waiting to see if I would draw back. Her fingers were surprisingly delicate, and I thought of the small feathers on her mother's new hat. Her palm rubbed the broken skin and glided across the bluish streak where the heel of Father's shoe had landed.

Jenny lifted her forefinger, caught my eye, and jabbed at the sorest spot.

I flinched.

"Must really hurt," she said. I thought she sounded impressed. Her palm lingered.

A tap gurgled in the kitchen. I straightened up. The trousers' rough edges made me flinch again. The tap went silent. I heard the unmistakable sound of the Old One's feet rushing out of the kitchen. Though my pants were buckled up again and my shirt neatly tucked back in, I felt oddly exposed, as if I were even more naked than before.

Jenny's eyes rested upon me. Her high cheekbones reminded me of Stepmother's postcard picture, the one taken beneath a moon gate when she was a young girl standing beside her friend. Jenny's eyes narrowed. She glanced left, then right, and then stared back at me. I hadn't noticed before how her small lips could pulse and tense up, turning a wetter pink. When at last she spoke, it was like a soft release of both our breath. I hadn't realized that I had stopped breathing.

"Look," she said. Her long piano fingers reached under a flap of lace and began to unbutton her blouse. The light material spread wide apart like two delicate curtains. Her skin glowed in the summery air. "See?"

It was my turn to stare.

Two rising mounds greeted my eyes. I wanted to touch them. I did. I bent down to smell them. Talcum. I stuck out my tongue to lick the tip.

Jenny pushed me away. The flaps of her blouse closed as quickly as they had opened. Her fingers raced through the tiny pearl-shell buttons.

"Don't tell," she said, as if I didn't know better. "Just between us." She took my hand and laid my palm flat and burning against her chest. My other hand rose on its own, a little shaky, and took its fiery place. "What do you think?"

She knocked my hands away.

"Pretty," I said, stumbling. "Real . . . *nice*."

I clung to the sweet smell of talcum, my palms thrust behind me, pulsing fresh from the incredible touch and push. If I wanted more, I shouldn't say too much, so I said, catching my breath, "What about my bruise?"

She giggled and shoved me aside. She bounded down the steps and into the backyard. I regained my balance. My eyes longed to see her skirt fly higher between the rows of tangled vines in the garden. At the back gate beside our shed, she paused. Her right hand rested over her heart; with her other hand, she brushed back her dark hair. She was making up her mind about something. She turned, and I thought she smiled. I waved.

"Don't tell!" she shouted, waving back.

I shook my head. *Never!*

She was gone.

When I turned to the screen door I could see someone standing at the sink, looking back at me, satisfied.

"Take Liang-Liang to playground," Poh-Poh said. "Push her on swing. Good exercise for your sore bum."

"No more lotion," I said. I did not want my bruise exposed again, or to be touched there by Poh-Poh.

"Finish this soup," Poh-Poh ordered.

Liang stood waiting for me, grinning.

I wasn't allowed out for two weeks, not even to go to any weekend events or picture shows.

That night while Jung was telling me about the soccer game I had not been able to attend, I lay in bed and couldn't get out of my head the feel of Jenny's palm on my backside.

"You didn't miss much," Jung said. But he was anxious to know something else. "Did Father say anything to you about . . . getting . . . sloshed?"

"No," I said. "Nothing more. Except to go to bed early and get some rest."

"Father looked really sad that he kicked you, you know."

"I know."

"Poh-Poh told Gai-mou that Jenny Chong came over."

"Oh?" I turned myself over, careful to avoid the tender spot.

"Why did she come?"

"Her mother sent her with some soup just for me."

For a long moment, there was no response.

"I still don't like Jenny very much." The voice sounded firm. "I still want to kick her."

"Go ahead," I said. "And go to sleep."

Shadows thrown by the bright moonlight played across the drawn shade. I closed my eyes tight and pretended I was a million miles away. The day's events began to tumble through my brain. I put my hand deep under my pillow.

The outside world was changing again.

I could hear Jung-Sum breathing rhythmically. He had always fallen asleep quickly, as if sleep were a hideaway from all his old memories. But now he often fell asleep as much completely exhausted from the day's rough play with a gang of his friends as from habit.

A cat screeched. A garbage can toppled over.

I pushed off the sheets and walked to the window to see what there was to see. Nothing. The street lamp made a buzzing sound, like the drone of an insect. A sudden and deeper quiet came over me. My fingertips brushed the sheer curtains. Their delicate roughness reminded me of something, and a smell, like talcum, came over me. I put my hand on my groin. Staggered back to bed.

Like me, Jack had been forbidden to go out because of the drinking. Two weeks passed before we were free to meet again, and we sat on a patch of grass in his backyard. The turf smelled fresh and the air was cool.

I slipped down one side of my pants and showed him the now-faded bruise.

"Looks like your father's boot was on target."

"And you?"

"Got whacked a few times across the head."

No worse, I thought, than Poh-Poh's knuckling my head. We didn't want to think what might have happened at Jeff Eng's house. His father was known for his strictness. Jack yanked some long blades of grass and handed me one to chew on.

"Damn," he said cheerfully, "you and Jeff got to lose your cherry."

"What do you mean?"

"Getting really drunk," he said. "That's like losing your cherry with a girl. That's what every Irish guy has to do. Puke his guts out a few times."

"Well," I said, "once is good enough for a Chinaman."

We slapped four palms in agreement, as if we were Harpo and Chico. We leaned back on our elbows and watched birds in the blue sky. Some cats began yowling in the back alley.

Over and over in my mind, I felt Jenny's hand on my skin, relived the moment when she let me bend down and smell her; how she took my hand and let me touch her afterwards. But did she really like me? Or was she making fun of me, testing me? I spat out some chewed-up grass like a baseball player. Jack still chewed his blade. He looked so sure of himself: he would have known what to do if he had been on that back porch. I didn't want him to know how confused I was and how much I wished for Jenny to lie beside me now.

I didn't want anyone to know anything.

Almost fifteen, I knew that by not saying too much, or by saying only half of whatever I knew, I could keep things simple. I could be with Jack just the way I always was, as his best pal; with Jenny, there was another world growing in my head. I had to be careful not to expose any qualms, as if I couldn't trust either of them, as if they might appreciate me less or even mock me. Instinct told me that these separate bonds I shared with each of them should never cross; somehow, in my silence, I could belong.

The back door slammed shut. The Old One came out with Liang to hang up some laundry. Jack waved to them. Liang giggled to see her golden boy sitting on the grass with Big Brother. The laundry line squawked as Poh-Poh pulled it towards her. In seconds, billowing sheets hid them both from view. I threw away the grass and picked up some clover to suck out the drops of nectar.

Poh-Poh and all the rest of the mahjong ladies, especially Mrs. Chong, would make such a fuss over what happened between Jenny and me. And if Jack found out what had happened on the back porch, he would laugh his head off: "Why didn't you make a move, Kiam!" No, I didn't want anything to spoil the secret world Jenny and I had opened up to each other. If she weren't taunting me, if she liked me in some real way, like the way I thought she meant when she looked back and smiled at me, then what had happened was only between the two of us.

Enough thinking! I fell back and looked up at the sky. White clouds scudded over us.

"Restless?"

"No," I said. "I'm okay."

"Let's hunt up some ball players."

Jack jumped up and gave a Tarzan yell. I was in mid-yell when Poh-Poh yanked back one of the sheets and shot me a no-nonsense look. I choked, as if I had only meant to cough.

Jack grinned at Poh-Poh. I called out to Liang to throw me my catcher's mitt hanging on a hook by the screen door. Giggling, she threw it right to Jack. He caught the thick mitt and jumped over the back fence and into the alleyway. I made it over, and we raced down the narrow lane.

I took a deep breath and sprinted as fast as I could. When I caught up with Jack, I spat out the last bits of clover, savouring the keen, sweet taste.

Jack and I had hoped for a game of baseball that day but found ourselves with nothing to do after an hour of bat-and-ball with a couple of other guys. We were too short of players to challenge another gang. And then Kenny Cheng had taken his prized bat and left for home.

Jack said, "They got new wheels at Haskins this week."

We headed down West Hastings to Haskins & Elliott. It was midsummer, afternoon, the sun shining so bright between the drifting clouds that you could look up at the North Shore mountains and see a dozen shades of green; a perfect day to daydream in front of some rare Raleigh ten-speeds, shiny wheels neither of us could afford.

Then we ran into an East Hastings gang.

Everyone knew their reputation. They called themselves the Mafia Boys. Three Italian hoods in their twenties, tough-talking, block-your-way, leaning-against-the-wind pomaded-hair guys, had just stepped out of Mario's Barbershop.

Jack and I, about fifty feet apart, were playing fly ball. Being the smartass, I was tossing my big mitt sky-high when the leader of the Mafia Boys shoved me aside. My leather glove spun, flipped, and plopped down like an oversized plate onto his freshly trimmed head. Instantly, three black suede jackets were sprayed with a fine sooty grit from the impact.

The tallest guy spun around and hauled me up with his thick-knuckled fists, my feet dangling two feet from the ground. I tried to speak, to apologize, but my yanked-up collar gagged me so tightly that all I could do was sputter.

Drops and drips of my saliva dotted the veil of grey dust now covering his midnight jacket. He shook me hard, then let go.

I dropped like a dead weight.

The three surrounded me. They swore in Italian, then one after the other they stepped away from me. Each one brushed himself off, rubbed his knuckles in ritual glee, and glanced at his pals as if to say, *Let me at the little bastard!*

My right foot felt as if it had withered; my left foot went lame. I looked down: I was standing with one running-shoed foot stuck in my offending mitt.

No one laughed.

Jack had missed the last fly and had gone chasing after the ball. When he was ready to throw me one, he must have waited for me to catch my tossed mitt, only to witness it thump down to grave consequences.

Barely breathing, I realized that each second of my life was driving me closer to my end.

The shortest one of the three, thick chested and mean-looking, started slamming me with the heel of his palm, jolting me backwards. The one behind me, his fedora half off his head, shoved me forward. The tallest guy, smelling of aftershave, grabbed my shoulder. I wished I had worn long sleeves. My skinny elbows shook below my short sleeves.

"Whatcha doin' here, *Chink!*"

His other hand slipped slowly inside his jacket. He stepped graciously back, as if to invite me to leave the party. I could see the sidewalk opening up between the two of us. His hand was still inside his jacket.

Smiling weakly back at him, I discreetly tried to yank my stuck foot out of the mitt—the better to run away as quickly as possible—but I stumbled backwards.

"Hey! We got a chickenshit China-boy here!"

The shouter stomped on my foot. I yelped. The tall guy swung his long face down towards mine and his forehead cracked into my skull with a sharp and sudden pain. In a daze, I hoped that Jack had escaped. There was nothing even ten fighting Irish boys could do against these three men. These weren't ordinary bullies.

The three tightly closed their ranks; they were too close together for me to duck and run. They were breathing hard and hovering above me; their eyes shone like demons'. I heard a soft click.

I stood still, gasping, waiting for the next blow.

"Hey!" a familiar voice called. "What's that Chink doing in Wop-land!"

It was Jack, moving in. He was just a few inches taller than me, and still about a head shorter than any of the Mafia guys. He shoved his way between two of them, clutching the baseball as if it were a grenade. The two guys pushed back, then they moved like lightning. Jack ducked, and his hand, tightly gripping the softball, deflected something hard.

The ball snapped back up with a loud *thwack!*

Jack held on to the thing, wildly pivoting to bash in a head or two. A fist glanced off his jaw, and a bigger fist plowed into his chest. A half-blocked kick landed in my groin, and I doubled over onto the sidewalk. I saw a heavy black boot rising above my head, ready to stomp.

A rattling like machine-gun fire grew louder and louder. The faces froze high above me.

Between someone's pant legs I saw Mario the barber tapping furiously on his front window with a pair of scissors. Italian words thundered through the plate glass. The three guys slowly dropped their fists.

"Okay, Papa!" one of them said. "*Si, si,* Papa!" He gestured his two friends away. "Let's go! The Chink and his pal got the lesson."

The tall guy lingered, still pissed off. He slipped his hand back into his jacket. Napoleon retreating.

"Don't waste your time, Gabby!"

Gabby swore, spat on my face. Then the three marched away. I pushed myself up on my elbows. My chest and neck hurt. Jack felt his jaw for broken bones.

"Got out of that pretty easy," he said, wheezing. "That other guy almost killed me."

"Well," I said, catching my own breath, "I think I got the shit kicked out of me."

"Kick nothing," Jack said firmly. "The guy was aiming to *kill* you, Kiam."

Jack pointed to Gabby, several feet away. The man held out a long switchblade and stabbed it neatly into the telephone pole. The blade sliced off a sliver of a poster. Then, in a frenzy, another slash and another, until the poster hung in shreds like torn flesh. The knife snapped shut, and Gabby's hand went back into his jacket. His friends pulled him away.

"Definitely *killed* both of us!"

My mouth dropped open. "You knew that guy had the knife?"

"For sure," Jack said, and laughed like a fool. "He was swinging the blade towards your gut just when I shoved against the other two to get at him."

"I was trying to get my shoe out of my mitt," I said. "I didn't see the knife at all."

"Didn't you hear it?"

I shut my eyes. That odd clicking sound came back to me. I nodded.

Jack held up the ball.

"Look."

The covering had been slashed. The point must have landed just between Jack's fingers.

"No bleeding, eh?" I said, and forgot about my own pain.

He showed me his hand. He wasn't cut.

"You okay, Kiam? We could've been killed."

"He missed," I said. "The knife didn't get near me."

At the thought of that possibility—*thwack!*—I took a deep breath and lifted my skinny arms into the air. We both examined my arms: scratched and dirty, but not a single cut. Jack looked over the grimy front of my shirt. Nothing, except for a missing button just below the collar.

My legs began to shake.

"Wipe your face, Kiam. Use my sleeve."

It just came upon me, the crying.

Jack handed me my mitt. We sat on the edge of the sidewalk. My shirt was a mess; my pants covered with dirt. We had only been fooling around, playing catch, lusting after shiny new bikes in Haskins' window . . . I hurt all over, and Jack's eye was swelling up.

Mario banged on the window and waved us to move on.

"You shouldn't have been such a hero," I said, limping slowly, feeling as if my groin were on fire. "Cripes, what were you going to do with that stupid baseball?"

Jack laughed. He had enjoyed the adventure.

"I'm going to have a shiner," he said.

"Fuck you," I said.

When I finally got home, I was the centre of shocked attention. But the Old One and Stepmother only shook their heads. Father would need to deal with First Son.

Poh-Poh wanted to knuckle me for my dirty clothes; instead, Stepmother went to the kitchen pantry and gave me some lotion for my bruised arm. "You tell Father what happened, Kiam-Kim," Stepmother said.

I explained everything when Father returned home that night. Stepmother sent me up to bed. I thought I had gotten away easily.

"You die soon," Poh-Poh said behind me as she guided me up the stairs. I flinched. The kick had left its mark.

It wasn't until Jung-Sum came up and helped me pull off my dirt-encrusted pants that I felt lucky.

He said, "Dai-goh, there's a big rip here," and poked three fingers through the Irish tweed.

A few inches below the crotch of my baggy pants, he wiggled his fingers and laughed.

Then I remembered O'Connor had butted his way between the two bullies and had caused one of the guys to knock me sideways, full tilt. Reliving the pandemonium before that kick to my groin sent me sprawling, I felt, as in a nightmare, a glancing coldness along my thigh: it was the sliding chill of a steel blade.

I had some claim to toughness once word got out that the notorious Mafia Boys had picked on Jack and me and that we had lived to tell of our deadly encounter. My reputation only grew after one of them was arrested a week later and charged with the attempted murder of a rival gang member.

Jack sported his black eye proudly and retold the story of our death-defying escape more times than I could count. When he related details that were not exactly as I had remembered them, I nodded agreeably: Jack was the true hero as far as I was concerned. And he had the wounded baseball to prove to any skeptic how close I—we—had come to being knifed to death.

In all the telling, Jack never deserted the core of our friendship: he shared the glory with me. I had somehow slipped on my mitt, knocked my elbow against the knife and managed to save him, too. Not as spectacularly, of course, but there was enough in his version to earn me a share of real respect.

In Poh-Poh's version, told to Mrs. Lim and the mahjong ladies, stark references were made to every bruise that showed up on my legs and back, my arms and neck. Jung proudly included the detail of the razor-sharp blade that ripped through my trousers, nearly slicing off the family jewels. Each time he heard Jung's version, Sekky grabbed himself at the crotch and fell down dead. Then I would pick him up and throw him in the air and bring him caterwauling back to life.

Liang was more interested in Jack's black eye, since it ruined his good looks for weeks, and she wanted his cowboy handsomeness back. When his puffy eye got better and the blue-black stain disappeared, she got up her nerve to ask Jen to get her father's boxy Kodak camera and take a shot of her beside Jack's spotless good looks. Of course, I had to ask Jack if he would mind. He didn't at all. He lifted Liang onto the porch rail and sat with his arm around her.

Jenny presented a framed copy of the picture to Liang on her tenth birthday. Jack even signed an extra copy for Jenny; he wrote, "Your hero," and included a row of X's, just as he had done on Liang's copy.

Other pictures were taken that day. Jack and me with our arms around each other's shoulders. "Forever pals," we wrote on each other's copy and signed our names. Liang took one of Jenny standing between the two of us. But she didn't hold the camera steady, so the shot was blurred and half of Jack's head was cut off.

Father spoke little about the Mafia Boys incident; he saw the whole episode as senseless. Third Uncle said that I was lucky that Jack was around that day. Stepmother didn't think I should hang out with Jack so much, if only to appease Jack's parents, who rightly thought that I was to blame for not watching where I was going. Stepmother reiterated that I spend more time with good Chinese sons.

Joe Sing, Jeff Eng, Fat Wah Duk, and I would hang around in the alleyway under the rows of bachelor-room rentals behind the Chinese school, just at the back of the W.K. Restaurant. Our favourite spot lay below half-opened windows, beneath the criss-crossing shadows of a plunging fire escape. We were pumped up that day, Joe and I shoving each other around, dragging on cigarettes from our communal package of Exports. We clamped the fags between our lips like Hollywood gangsters, while Jeff and Wah Duk tapped the latest beat on some garbage cans. We pretended we were in the Benny Goodman band.

The racket roused someone from a troubled sleep. A God-like voice boomed above us: "Shut the fuck up!"

We looked up at the strip of sky caught between the alleyway buildings. One floor above us, an angry face stuck out between swirls of stir-fry vapours hissing from restaurant vents. The whites of two dragon eyes nailed us to the ground. The thick hair protruded like horns. The dark-tanned face twisted with rage, spewing out ancestral curses in Chinese, in broken Italian, in what we eventually came to be told was fractured Hebrew and Hindu, punctuated with

some Indian phrases and highlighted with cries of
Goddamn! Damn! Damn!

Our hearts pounded.

Right above the iron cage of the swing-down fire
escape, the words were coming out of the cursing
mouth of Chinatown's Number One black sheep. All
of Chinatown knew that sneer, that angular face per-
petually black eyed and bruised. Respectable mothers
and fathers made sure we knew that the nineteen-year-
old menace was the single most notorious demon in
Chinatown history.

When the menace once staggered by us at Pender
and Carrall, Grandmother sang out to him, "Drunk at
noon, die soon." And he turned his gaunt face, his
thin lips contorting, and spat at her feet. Poh-Poh
threw back some colourful curses, which made him
shake with laughter; he tipped his hat to her, as if each
of her curses were a blessing in disguise.

Jeff and Joe traded nervous glances, hoping the
other might make the first move. But we were rooted by
a deep and attractive dread: no one wanted to be the
first to run. No one wanted to miss what would happen
next. We swallowed the stale alleyway air, our lit Exports
burning inert, stuck to our dry lips.

The dark head disappeared. Above the pounding
of our hearts, we heard shuffling noises. Wah Duk and
I chewed on our half-smoked butts; Jeff and Joe sucked
away defiantly. *What next?*

A door slammed. Before any of us could mount a
four-way split, a body came vaulting down the echoing
stairwell.

"Whadda we have here?"

The voice caught us off guard: it was breathless, but calm. The quiet before the kill. The menace tilted forward from the third step and jammed his fists against the lintil to tower over us, daring us to make the next move.

Those long legs could outrun a fox. His dark jacket was half hooked over bare muscled shoulders, his lean torso veined with sinew. I smelled a brute ready to pounce.

Jeff Eng gulped. My eyes widened. Joe Sing looked as if he could wet his pants. We tried to look away. It was no use. We were doomed. The killer finished buttoning his fly, then casually jumped the three steps and landed in front of us. The black leather jacket, a match for his pants, shifted like a cape.

Wah Duk took one step back, knocked against a half-empty garbage can. He stuttered the dreaded killer's name: "F-f-frank Yuen."

A clanging bell echoed in our heads. *Round one.*

Frank Yuen spat on my school bag, shoved Jeff, and snapped his fingers at Joe. Joe stumbled backwards.

"What have you boys got to say?"

He rested a hand on my shoulder and squeezed hard, enjoying the fear written over my face.

"S-s-sorry," Jeff managed.

Frank smirked, taking time to study the four fledglings cringing before him. We could see the legendary scars on his chest. Jeff Eng let out his breath. Maybe Jeff knew as much as I did.

Frank's oldest scars were from the belt beatings he received at the hand of Old Yuen. Frank's mother had tried to escape with her son three times, but Chinatown dictated that she should return. *Who will feed you and your boy?* Finally, unable to endure any more abuse, she left with Frank for good and did the most menial jobs to survive. She cleaned out the spittoons and bedpans in rooming hotels, cleaned up the rooms after bachelor-men had died there of old age or illness, until she herself died of TB, coughing blood until she choked to death. Then Frank's father fell ill and became too weak to beat his son, and Frank moved back. At fifteen, Frank took charge of his father's rent, his food, and medicine. The old man was still alive, and Frank was still taking care of him.

Father had sent me to collect the rent from Old Yuen a few times. I saw a man only ten years older than Father, a man too worn down to live but too stubborn to die. When I took the envelope of money Frank had left behind, I wondered why he did not walk out on Yuen, especially after all of his father's abuse and the loss of his mother.

Father said to me, "Nothing to think about, Kiam-Kim. Frank is First Son, Only Son."

Instead of defeating him, everything bad, even unlucky, just toughened up Frank Yuen. Grandmother told her mahjong ladies how she liked his tiger spirit. She called him "a good demon-boy." Whenever Frank Yuen was sober, she would greet him with a grin; he would hold his palm out to her as if begging for coins. Once, she plunked down into his bandaged hand a bottle of her homemade cure-all lotion.

"For fast healing," she said. "Not for drinking!"

Frank laughed, spun the slim bottle in the air.

"Yes, yes," Poh-Poh shouted after him. "Shake before use!"

If he stumbled by in a drunken state, she would chant, "Frank Yuen die soon."

But today, confronting us in the laneway, he was very much alive, albeit hung over, leaning against the brick wall, still trying to focus. Drunk, he would have been deadly.

"Get rid of those shitty-tasting butts," he ordered.

Four smokes hit the ground.

"Good going, men," he said. "Always obey your superiors."

Joe Sing snapped to. "Yes, sir!"

Frank laughed. It was a genuine, persuasive laugh.

The restaurant vents began to hiss again, sending out greasy aromas; someone above us was snoring, coughing; and in the fading light, shadows melted.

I stepped on the butt burning at my feet. Jeff stepped on his, too. For something to do. Frank watched us. He reached into his inside breast pocket. I expected to see the gleam of a switchblade, or even a handgun. But the face didn't register any killer's instinct. I stepped closer, just to look. We all did.

With a steady, practised hand, Frank slipped out a thick cigar. Then, as if he had considered everything about us, and liked whatever he had considered, he gave us a smile, his demon eyes suddenly human.

"Try this Cuban," he said.

The voice sounded easygoing, an amiable spirit willing to take us in. Our anxiety almost vanished. We had become an exclusive mob, a gathering, a club. We were desperate to be taken in. We looked at each other, our fears sinking away, our sense of adventure surging. Jeff Eng broke into his first smile. I relaxed, too. We all grinned. Frank Yuen didn't seem so bad, up close, with his tousled hair. Fat Wah Duk had boasted before how Frank the Hood always tipped his mother well at their restaurant. Maybe there was a good Frank, a generous Frank, a kind Frank for mothers and boys. We let out a collective sigh.

Frank began to roll the thumb-thick cigar between his palms. It crinkled in its brown-and-gold wrapper. The warmth of his hands teased out the delicious aroma. He passed the six-inch Cuban under each of our noses.

"I'd like to try," Joe Sing said.

"Yeah?" Frank said. "And you two punks?"

We nodded.

He tore off the paper ring with its embossed gold crest, slowly unwrapped the stogie like an elder unwrapping a rare ginseng root.

"Any objections to this torpedo?"

No one objected.

Frank licked the sides of the cigar until it gleamed, then bit off one end, spat it out, and smartly, struck a wooden match. Gently, puffing softly, easily, he lit the thing. The tip glowed, and a quarter inch of pure white ash curled into life.

I thought of the thick red candles Father lit before the gods in our family tong temple, the candles burning in the two Chinese theatres in Chinatown. How the candlelight glowed and the porcelain faces of the

Smiling Buddha, the Gods of Good Fortune and Luck, and the fierce God of Theatre flickered with life. In the growing alleyway darkness, our boyish faces gained new life.

Frank twirled the thick cigar in his manly fingers. He took one last drag. Phantom smoke hung above our heads. It smelled as sweet as the first taste of rum I ever had, just the few seconds before the alcohol burned up my insides and snapped off my head.

"Ready?"

We nodded.

"Take three deep breaths," Frank said, handing the cigar first to Jeff, "then inhale deeply—one, two, *three* times—*without* exhaling. Hold the smoke in your guts as long as you can. Do it."

Our fingers itched to take a turn.

Jeff Eng put his school case down, held the cigar in as manly a way as he could and stuck it in his mouth, inhaled *one*, deeply, *two*, deeply, *three*.

"Hold it in, champ," Frank said. "Next. Hurry up, guys."

One after another, we took three deep breaths and held. Then, as the sickly-sweet smoke threatened to implode and eat away our semi-virgin lungs, Frank said, "Let go!"

We exhaled. Jeff gagged and spilled out his guts. Wah Duk spewed the Oh Henry bar he'd eaten ten minutes before. I grabbed Joe, and we both doubled over and retched, but nothing came out except trails of smoke. When we doubled up with spasms, Frank doubled up with laughter.

I don't know how many minutes went past, but when I looked up, three of us were splayed against the wall; Wah Duk was still heaving into the garbage can. Frank surveyed the disaster.

"Never inhale cigar smoke. Only suck-ass kids with something to prove inhale cigar smoke."

Jeff groaned. "You should have told us."

"Why?" Frank said. "So I can save you the trouble of learning something? You don't learn this shit in school books."

"*Learning*—?" I asked, fighting my nausea.

"Learning that you don't have to grow up so fast." Frank slammed a fist into a garbage lid and sent it flying down the alley. "Not everything has to be learned first-hand. *Catch?*"

Oddly, I didn't feel tricked. My stomach churned; my mouth tasted like a sewer.

"By the way, gentlemen," Frank said, "did any one of you little fuckers *know* that you don't inhale cigar smoke?"

Jeff weakly raised his hand.

"Then why the hell did you do it? Why didn't you warn your buddies?"

He looked down at the ground.

Wah Duk stood up straight at last and started to walk home. Joe Sing followed him. Jeff wiped his mouth on his sleeve and tugged at my arm to go. I wanted to stay, to hear more. But Frank slapped me on the back, as if to say, *Get going, there's nothing more.*

"Tell your Poh-Poh I need some more lotion. Got in a bad fight yesterday."

He showed off his fists. The knuckles were bruised.

After that evening with the cigar, Frank Yuen didn't seem to mind that Jeff and I liked to hang around him. Whenever we heard he was back from the lumber camps, we called up to his rooming-house window and waited to see if he would come down to join us. Sometimes he told us to fuck off, he had had a hard night; most evenings, though, he came down in his best clothes, scented with aftershave, ready to embark on a visit to a favourite sweetheart or to meet his friends at the Jazz Hut, an all-night hangout.

He would spend twenty or thirty minutes with Jeff and me, telling us stories about fights at the camps when someone called him a Chink, about his three near-death accidents with shingle-mill saws, or about the time when the two tractor pull-chains swung towards his head in the sawdust air.

He lifted his shirt and pointed out his scars, tracing the deep cuts where a ripsaw had torn past his sleeve and grazed his shoulder; where a fight with a knife ended with a slash across his back; where, on his left arm, he'd been splashed when his father had thrown boiling water at his mother while she held young Frank, trying to comfort his crying in the night. About some scars Jeff or I pointed to, he had nothing to say. Only remembered waking up in the first-aid shed cut up badly.

"Yeah," he said, "I lose a few, too."

I thought of my life at home, how easy everything was. Father would never throw boiling water at any of us. After our first taste of alcohol, Jeff Eng's father had beaten him with a razor strop, but even Jeff knew that he had pushed his father too far that night.

Poh-Poh asked me if I had taken the medicine to Frank.

"Yes," I said. "He wants to know how much for the bottle."

Instead of answering me, Poh-Poh said, "Tell Frank Yuen I say war come soon."

For weeks she had listened silently to Father and the elders debate the war news from China. The Imperial Japanese troops were amassing, aiming to march southward into central China.

"Poh-Poh, how much for the tonic?"

"Frank teach my Kiam-Kim everything. That the cost for Frank Yuen."

No one in the family said anything to me about Frank. Poh-Poh told Stepmother not to worry, to leave me alone. "Frank Yuen," the Old One said, "*good* demon-boy, not *bad* demon-boy."

Jeff Eng's father didn't like his son hanging out with a boy like Frank Yuen, but Jeff snuck away to join up with me and the demon hood.

One night Frank wrestled away Jeff's and my pack of Player's and crushed it in his fist.

"You two look like you're sucking on a tit," he said.

We boasted about our third round of drinking. He spat.

"Try growing up first," he said. "That's the tough part."

If he was suspicious, he would smell our breath for a whiff of tobacco or alcohol. We were slapped for our efforts to cover up with bits of licorice Sen-Sen. I didn't mind. Being seen with Frank Yuen made us feel like big shots. We expected him to slap us around to smarten us up. To make his point, he stopped smoking in front of us.

One evening, Frank's father, drunk again, stumbled down the rooming-house steps and pushed his way through the gang of us.

"Frank, tell them everything," he said in Toishanese. "Just like I tell you." He was on his way to one of Chinatown's gambling dens. "You be their *dai-goh*."

"Yeah, sure," Frank said. "Make sure they get into trouble."

"First Son," the old man said, "tell them everything."

Jack had been working on the docks on weekends, piling goods onto lifts, shift-work that his father's union boss got him to keep him out of trouble. That was okay with Jack: the extra money impressed the girls. I wanted him to meet Frank Yuen.

"He's as tough as those Mafia guys," I said. "Got more scars on him than a road map has streets."

"Is he the guy that hangs out at the Jazz Hut? Has this scar just below his lip?"

"How'd you know!"

"Look," said Jack, "anyone who can give a ten-spot to the guy at the door gets in. Inside, everyone thinks I'm one of the busboys."

I was impressed.

"You should meet him," I said.

"Already have. He asked me to clean up his table."

"Did you?"

"What choice did I have?"

When I told Frank that he had made my best friend clean up his table, he laughed. He liked a kid who would show up at the Jazz Hut just to be there. The music was hot. The girls were hotter. Frank remembered O'Connor.

"Looks like a choirboy," he said. "Did he like my tip?"

"Didn't say."

"Bastard!"

I arranged for the two to meet again one Saturday at the Blue Eagle. Jack rushed over from the docks during his lunch hour. I made it out of Chinese school with an hour to spare before I had to go to the warehouse. And Frank had said he would be nursing a hangover at the back table.

Jack was already there, turning his blond head to grin at me.

"Been listening to stories," he said.

There were a few scummy Irishmen labouring in those work camps, Frank had told him, and they looked like Jack. They had the best swear words, in a language you could hardly bear to listen to, but when they sang, everyone stopped. Frank had O'Connor sing one of the old songs his parents taught him. But he sang in English, which disappointed Frank.

"Where's your blood language gone? Why sing in Limey talk? Who the hell are you?"

Jack swore in the choice Chinese words Jeff and I had taught him, blistering phrases the elders used about smelly women's parts and loose-limbed mothers. He even repeated one of Poh-Poh's curses.

"Goddamned Chink," Frank said, slapping him across the head. "You're a fuckin' Irish Chink!"

Three tables away, people were laughing.

The more we hung around Frank, the more we came under his care. He concluded that we Chinatown boys, including Jack whenever he was with us, shouldn't grow up ignorant about *real* life; he said he was going to give us an education, and he began by taking us around to his favourite hangouts. Sometimes he opened the door of a bar to let us peer inside. We ducked our heads in, looked at the long row of chairs and tables, at men laughing or swearing, slugging back beer. Through the doors marked "Ladies and Escorts," we could never get a proper look.

Whenever he grew tired of his three or four do-nothing boys, he tossed back his thick locks, brushed his tailored cuffed pants, and said, "Piss off."

We did.

Some of our lessons with Frank were far more interesting. He would bend a discarded coat hanger and draw anatomical pictures in the alleyway dirt, thrust his hip back and forth, laugh to see some of us amazed.

"That's how babies are made," he said. "You knew that, didn't you, Kiam?"

I nodded, in my head comparing the wealth of details and guesses that O'Connor and I had thrown each other's way: Father and Stepmother, and her swelling belly.

"You boys get *hard*, don't you?"

With everyone else, I blushed. I couldn't help it: I thought of Jenny, of my two hands rubbing against her, of the smell of talcum and the feel of her breasts.

"Right," he said, looking directly at me. "You do." His face darkened.

Frank said we shouldn't play with our dicks or we'd be totally useless where women were concerned. He told us what desperate men did; he warned us we were always in danger of becoming pansies. Like some of those bachelor-men who went crazy or queer, stuck in wretched run-down rooming houses, worse than the one he and his father shared; those elders torn apart from their wives in China for far too many years, their "bachelor" tag, their madness following them into their graves.

"I want you guys to grow up properly," he said. "That's my job. So I'm going to tell you everything. You sure you know about sex?"

Frank said it was better to pay for good sex than to stay pure for a woman you weren't going to see for years. Men who kept to themselves like that gambled everything away, clutched at other men in the night, drank themselves to death.

Frank said, "A woman's juices keep a man sane.

And a woman needs a man's juice, too."

It was female *yin* and male *yang*, he said. Balance. Harmony.

One summer evening, walking with Jeff and me, Frank stopped in front of the Jazz Hut, where he said he took certain girls, danced with his sweetheart of the night, warmed her up for later. This was a certain class of girl, he said, not your regular three-buck whores.

"Tell that to your Irish pal," Frank said. "Tell him to wear a rubber."

We toured the back rooms of the Hastings Gym where he worked out and where even boys like us could buy emergency Frenchies for a quarter from the towel boy, who was a Ukrainian man as old, I thought, as Poh-Poh. Frank boasted about the sweethearts he visited upstairs in the East Hastings Hotel. Sometimes Jeff and I gulped some of Frank's beer on the alleyway steps, eyes wide, catching every detail of his grown-up world. He drank in clubs where only twenty-one-year-olds could order a drink. After hours, like at the Jazz Hut, it cost underage Frank a wink of the eye and extra folding money pushed into the right palm to get in. I thought of O'Connor, tall enough, like Frank far ahead of me, getting whatever he wanted before I even knew such wanting existed.

Although none of us boys could understand everything Frank said, we would exchange knowing looks. Then one day, Wah Duk, who was the youngest among us, boldly announced, "I can shoot *juice* now."

And Frank said, "Hey, schmuck, I told you not to

play with yourself!" He looked at each one of us. "Anybody else going to go crazy? Anyone else turn into a pansy?"

Our eyes shied away from his chuckling, piercing scrutiny.

When Frank wasn't around, the gang of us stood in front of Ben Chong's corner store on Princess Street, drinking pop or talking baseball scores, often repeating the sexy things Frank told us about girls, over and over again, as if talking was just like doing it, the bulge in our pants proud proof of our manhood. Desperate, playful, we grabbed each other, bashing each other with our school bags, laughing like clowns, then holding back, looking as innocent as we could, if we spotted a dress sauntering haughtily past. One day, Mrs. Chong stepped out of the store.

"You boys be good!"

We looked around, as if she meant some other boys.

"Kiam-Kim," she said, "you come in, please."

The others scattered. I walked into the store.

"Jenny need more help with her school work. Maybe you help a few minutes every day?"

Taught to comply with the requests of family friends, I nodded. Jenny was at the back shelving some tins. I could see her back stiffen.

"Maybe start today?"

Upstairs, Jenny and I settled in chairs facing each other across a small table. Her sweater fit her perfectly. She opened a textbook and looked up at me as if she had a serious question to ask. I picked up a pencil.

"Are you," she began, "going to the roller-skating party?"

"If I get away from the warehouse," I said. "You going?"

"A bunch of us are showing up around four."

And so Jenny and I skated together, bumping into other couples who whirled past with confidence. After, she took me into a narrow hallway behind the benches. It was a narrow hallway that seemed to go nowhere. We pushed against each other and kissed. She let me lift her sweater, and my palms eased over her breasts. She could feel my hardness against her and she responded by pressing her thighs together. Then someone started coming down the hall and we broke apart.

"You make my mother happy, Kiam," she said. "I want to know what she sees in you."

Mrs. Chong and Poh-Poh wanted to see us together. I didn't mind. We could conveniently play along, let the blind hope of our families see whatever it wanted to see. Maybe one day I would love Jenny and she would love me. For now, I knew only that my hands, my body, felt a need that responded to Jenny's hands, Jenny's body.

"Be free," Jack always said. "Cop a feel when you can get it. Dip your dink in."

When we joined the others back at the rink, some of the guys smiled at me in an expectant way. Jenny had a reputation. She caught their looks.

"Forget it," she said. "With your equipment, you guys can't even get to first base."

Some of the girls broke into wild laughter. The slim figure skated away.

My heart began to race.

Most of the time, Chinatown girls were kept busy looking after their younger siblings, kept busy with mending, cooking, washing diapers or minding their elders as Liang was being taught to do, busy with the endless housework and homework. And with their girlish daydreaming, I imagined, reading moving-picture magazines, catching up on the latest starlets and their blue-eyed boyfriends, scouring the pages of sewing magazines, wondering how many quarters to save for the latest mail-order dress patterns. Jenny was a little crazy about clothes. Maybe she was a little crazy for me, too.

Jenny giggled and passed notes to her friends in class. After school, they mocked the boys, brazen with their Grade 9 lips, lips shiny from a shared tube of lipstick. From far corners, the quiet girls smiled or looked away if you approached them. They didn't interest me.

But every Chinese girl, with few exceptions, was the concern of her Chinatown family. After our fifteenth birthdays, unless we were properly dressed up in a clean shirt and good pants and accompanied by someone much older—like an annoyed brother or perhaps a compliant sister—I noticed that boys were hardly allowed near any Chinese girls of a similar age. After a girl turned fifteen or sixteen, an older escort was always present with a dating couple, or the pair was encouraged to go out with a group headed to a bowling alley, say.

"Safety in numbers," Mrs. Pan Wong always said.

Chaperoned double- or triple-dating among "good" families, I realized much later, was Chinatown's idea of birth control.

Our numbers could protect us from many dangers as we wandered together into areas where we didn't really belong. When we went to a Granville Street movie house, or to theatres like the Orpheum and Capitol, we were usually expected by the management to sit in the very front rows or at the very back. There was less tension if Jack O'Connor happened to have joined up with us.

"What's the problem?" he would bellow, his Irish blood rising with the beam of light that skirted back and forth across our faces.

"No problem, buddy."

"You sure?" Jack would say.

And the once-authoritative usher would click off his flashlight and leave us alone. Then we would watch some British politician on the screen calling on all free countries to prepare for war against German aggression.

Jack nudged me. "I'm joining up."

Beside me, Jenny bent forward to stare across at him. "We're not at war yet."

I put my two cents in: "Wait for it."

"Yeah? Well, you Chinks are at war. How come you aren't over there fighting the Japs?"

"Because he's not stupid," Jenny said.

I laughed agreeably. Jenny pulled her hand away from mine, as if she were suddenly shy. Perhaps she didn't want Jack to know too much about us, though I had told him nothing myself. Jenny and I were a now-and-again necking couple, but nothing more. And if nothing really happened, there was nothing to tell.

As for going to fight in China, I had never seriously considered the idea, though the elders always said that one day every Chinese would go back to their home village. And many *had* gone back. But where would I go, with barely any memory of the old country? And where would my two brothers and sister go? Or Jeff and Jenny, who had also been born here? What world did any of us belong to? What world would we fight for?

~ *S E V E N* ~

DURING THAT FIRST SUNDAY of September 1939—
that Sunday when England declared war on Germany—
all of Chinatown waited for word from Ottawa.

In the days after the declaration, Father went to the
Chinese Times office after each shift at the warehouse to
track the conflict. Stepmother instructed me to go to
the office after Chinese school to tell Father to at least
come home for supper, as he had promised to do the
day before.

"Too busy," he said, but he invited me to stay a
moment so he could show me where the Nazi *Blitzkrieg*
had struck. Father and two of the newspapermen had
been comparing Chinese maps with the maps printed
in *Time Magazine* and in the late-arriving journals from
the States and overseas. Together the men drew arrows
and carefully pencilled in new borders on fold-out
maps of Europe. They compiled a master list of the

correct English spellings of towns and cities and wrote in their Chinese equivalents. The air smelled of fresh newsprint rolls and chemicals. Heavy black presses, greased and ready to run, stood silent behind the long counter; before layers of shelving loaded with printers' trays, three typesetters wearing inky aprons stood waiting for their instructions.

"Here blood is spilled," Father said to me at the large layout desk. The point of his pencil touched inside the borders of Poland. Arrows pointed towards a large circle. "The territory between here and here like China's countryside. Towns one third the size of Nanking totally destroyed. Here the bombs fell day and night."

"Shameful," one of the editors said. He was the one Father called Grey Head, the one who had always considered Europeans the most civilized people in the world. As a young man, he had studied in England and travelled through Germany with a companion. "German music and art far superior to the Chinese," he had once declared to me, pushing away my Chinese school book. Now he shook his greying head and shouted over and over again, "No better than anyone else—barbarians!"

Father circled a name on the map. "Kiam-Kim, look at this."

I looked: W A R S A W.

"Listen."

I wasn't sure what Father meant. Grey Head turned up the volume on the shortwave radio sitting on his desk, and music burst into the newsroom. The martial notes sounded through the static like bold but desperate calls.

"They play Chopin's *Polonaises*," Grey Head explained to me, "to let the whole world know that the citizens of Warsaw remain the defenders of Poland."

"Not for long," one of the printers said. He pointed his thumb down.

A BBC announcer interrupted, and then the king's soft-spoken message to the Empire was rebroadcast: "In this grave hour, perhaps the most fateful in our history, I send to every household of my peoples, both at home and overseas, this message, as if I were able to cross your threshold and speak to you myself . . . We are at war."

The idea that Chinatown was within the "household of my peoples" made me smile, yet everyone around me saw nothing funny about it. They were waiting for Canada to make an announcement of its own: we in Gold Mountain would soon be at war.

"Run home, Kiam-Kim," Father said. "Tell Poh-Poh and Stepmother I'll be working late. Maybe sleep over at Third Uncle's again."

As I walked out into the early-evening light, past the lineup of men reading the latest news posted on the office windows, the stirring strains of Chopin had their effect on me. I pictured myself as a soldier tearing through the streets of Warsaw while bombs exploded around me. Instead of the sky streaked with trails of chimney smoke from the False Creek refineries, I saw anti-aircraft guns fired into the sky at Nazi bombers. It was a vicarious thrill, but one that a growing number of boys and young men were beginning to manifest in their brave talk and open resolve to fight for England, for Canada.

Chinatown veterans of the last war merely shook their heads and coughed into their hands. They eked out their wounded days and nights sitting in the Hastings Street coffee shops and lived in those tiny rooms around Water Street, just below Victory Square, burdened with their painful memories. The men were forgotten already, but stories of that war's great battles were now being retold in the English-language newspapers, told as adventures that had turned inexperienced boys into fighting men.

But all the articles featured white faces and white names. Jack especially was thrilled to read about those veterans, to imagine himself taking back a hill from the Germans. His own father had been in that war but said nothing except, "If you have to, you fight for your country."

Like a bushfire, patriotism raged across Gold Mountain. The JOIN UP posters that began to show up on buildings and in hallways stiffened my resolve to see beyond those cheerless faces around Victory Square.

I thought of the thick packages with all our birth documents and travel certificates. On those documents I was designated "Resident Alien." The rumour was that because of our alien status, our yellow skin, and our slanty eyes, the young men of Chinatown would be discouraged from signing up.

"Won't be home for supper," I shouted as I entered our front door and threw my school things into the corner.

Stepmother was in the parlour showing Liang how to finish her knitting project. They looked disappointed to see me alone but got up and went into the dining room.

Jung-Sum was showing Sekky how to set up the oak table for dinner. As the two of them helped me to pull the round table away from the wall—but not too close to Father's corner desk—Stepmother and Liang straightened out the plates and bamboo mats on the table. Neither Father nor big Mrs. Lim would be joining us tonight, so I set up five chairs. Poh-Poh hollered for us to watch out and slowly brought in the soup tureen; Stepmother and Liang followed with rice bowls and savoury dishes. I carried in the last plate of stir-fried greens and beef. I thought of all the fathers in Warsaw and wondered whether they, or their sons, would ever again sit together to eat dinner at the family table.

Sekky hopped onto the chair between Poh-Poh and me and hooked his feet behind the wooden legs.

All that week we waited for the news from Ottawa that would commit Canada to the war in Europe. Bombs fell elsewhere in the world. Each day brought more newspaper and magazine pictures of the battles in China and of the carnage in Poland. In the school hallways, we talked about those pictures, and our teachers pinned them up on boards. A great darkness began to close in on our Gold Mountain world.

One evening when Father did make it home for supper, Poh-Poh filled each of our bowls with his favourite soup.

Father began humming a fragment of one of Chopin's *Polonaises* as he picked up a choice piece of leafy greens and put it on Stepmother's plate. He stood up, reached over and added a crisp stem of bok choy to Poh-Poh's rice bowl, and then Liang decided to share a slim piece of stir-fried beef with Sekky. I pushed a chunk of pork into Jung-Sum's bowl. I wanted somehow to make a gesture of gratitude for this family meal. Instead, I told Sekky to stop kicking the legs of his chair.

"Listen to your *dai-goh*," Father said to him.

Father's words made me suddenly feel that I mattered, that in some ancient way, order prevailed amid the growing darkness.

On the morning of September 11, I put on my kimono and sat down with Father as the radio tubes buzzed and hissed into life. A solemn CBC voice repeated the announcement from England: His Majesty the King had officially accepted that Canada was now at war.

"Difficult time," Father said.

"Yes," I said, but I thought of the dinner we had had a few nights before, though bombs fell around the world. Everything this morning looked as ordinary as any other day. The sun shone through the front windows, and above us, I could hear the family stirring awake.

Father adjusted his pyjama top and began to hum.

Poh-Poh was stricken with a nagging cough at the beginning of the Easter holidays in 1940. The phlegm she showed Stepmother, what little there was caught on a patch of paper napkin, was always clear, with no sign of mucus or, worse, of blood; no unusual heat radiated from her wrinkled brow, no sweatiness, no wet palm, nor any sign of a debilitating exhaustion ever appeared; the Old One's eyes remained clear, bright; her limbs and joints felt only the usual minor aches of a woman in her eighties.

"Throat too dry," she would tell Mrs. Lim. "Spring air too heavy."

But drinking cups of tea or sipping glasses of hot water did not put an end to Poh-Poh's daily hacking. Finally, Father insisted she get some medical attention.

In Dr. Chu's office in the Holden Building on Hastings, Father told me, the doctor had Poh-Poh raise both her arms high above her head so that her outer- and underclothing rose and gave him some access to her thin frame. It was a trick he used with all the old village women; their modesty sometimes left them vulnerable to certain womanly diseases allowed to progress undetected until they proved fatal.

"In China," Father explained to me, "a sick woman would point to a porcelain doll to indicate the location of her pains and symptoms. Of course, Dr. Chu was referring to women of the upper classes, those with bound feet who were cocooned by their great wealth and trained to do nothing important and know even less. Unable to run away from the Japanese, Kiam-Kim, they have been raped and slaughtered by the tens of thousands."

Dr. Chu peered over his glasses and agreed with the Old One when she mumbled that her lungs were wearing out. When the doctor pushed against her chest, she had cried out, "*Ho git sum.*"

The Old One's heart, Father told me, was cramped up with decades of bitter history and unspeakable frustrations. That was what she, as a matter of course, told the doctor herself.

"For your age, Chen-mou, I have great respect," responded Dr. Chu. "But there are no cures for either old age or a cramped-up heart."

They both laughed, and Dr. Chu began to fish for more information. "Some like your friend Mrs. Lim and certain tong elders might say otherwise."

Father said Poh-Poh nodded in agreement, hiding the fact that she was among those who always thought otherwise. Perhaps she remembered Mrs. Lim's rueful comment about Dr. Chu's Westernized ways: "Why shout truths at a stone ear?" And Poh-Poh would say, knocking her palm flat against her forehead, "Stone ear, stone brain!"

For the Old One's coughing fits, there was at least some relief. Dr. Chu gave her a bottle of a greenish liquid: one tablespoon to be swallowed three times a day. *Yes, of course*, she might also try whatever Chinese herbs were still available; that is, if Father could afford them. The price for the best ginseng root from Korea, the kind Dr. Chu himself preferred, had increased more than twenty times since the war began. He heard that the rich merchant families had been buying up every single root left in Chinatown.

We were all relieved when Dr. Chu said that the Old One's coughing was definitely not contagious. Samples of her phlegm had been tested in a laboratory and had come back negative. Papers were signed by the doctor and mailed to the school board declaring that no family member had any suspicious signs of TB.

"Only a nuisance for now," Dr. Chu cautioned Father, "but if it persists, this dry hacking, it might weaken the Old One's ability to fight off colds and flus later in the fall season."

He told Father that the Old One needed to rest, to finish the medicine and stay at home until the coughing stopped.

But Stepmother had been offered work sewing in a factory that made uniforms; they were actually hiring Chinese women to take on some of the work left behind by the men and women who had gone to fight in Europe, or gone to Ontario to earn higher wages. Grandmother and Little Brother would have to be left by themselves. Stepmother suggested she might reject the offer of work, but Poh-Poh wondered aloud how the family would survive without the money. She counted on her fingers the Western medicine for herself, Sekky's two regular pills and vitamins, his monthly visits to the specialist, and her last visits to Dr. Chu. And all the children were growing up so fast, there were more shoes and clothes to buy—everything cost so much money. Stepmother must keep working. Even Liang would soon need to look for some part-time work. Jung had already done a few hours at the warehouse and was also a volunteer "villager" being trained by Master Ying of the Sing Kew Opera Company to perform a new sword dance for the latest Free China drive.

"No more worry," said Poh-Poh with a stubborn shake of her head. "Grandson and I get stronger. We rest at home."

Sekky grinned. Though he himself was forbidden to attend public school because of his own lingering cough, Little Brother now felt himself to be in charge of Poh-Poh's welfare.

"We'll be okay," he assured all of us.

But to Poh-Poh, he fretted. "What will we do all day?"

"Maybe take short walk. Maybe stay home and I talk-story. You help me make *jook*. We make Old China toys. I teach you."

"Teach him what?" Father said when he heard of the Old One's plans.

Poh-Poh laughed. "Teach everything. Teach Old China ways. Teach Sek-Lung lots and lots of things."

Father looked alarmed. Stepmother whispered in my ear, "*Things* not always good."

Late that evening, when everyone else had gone off to bed, the two of them sat me down. Stepmother was knitting a dark blue sweater for Poh-Poh.

Father started at once.

"Think of those women back in Old China, Kiam-Kim. Look what happened when they became diseased. Or worse, what happened to them when the war came. Gold Mountain is not Old China. You watch out for Sekky."

Would Sekky listen to me if I challenged the Old One? *Stone ears, stone brain!* The knitting needles click-clicked with life.

"Kiam-Kim," Stepmother began, her fingers working swiftly. "Make sure Sek-Lung not believe everything the Old One tell him."

Father let out a heavy sigh, perhaps thinking of his own growing up. "Very awkward. Too many ghost stories! Sek-Lung has no Strathcona School to teach him Canada ways."

"Sekky listen to you." *Click-click!* "Need to balance old with new, Kiam-Kim."

"New better," said Father, and looked hard at both of us to make sure his was the final word. With a quick adjustment of his glasses, he snapped open the *Chinese Times*.

Stepmother stared at me as if she did not mind. And neither did I. Her eyes told me more than the back of the *Times* ever did.

Instead of staying home or just going out for short walks as she promised, Poh-Poh started an odd routine of putting on her favourite quilted jacket and taking Sekky out on lengthy excursions to collect junk from alleyway trash bins.

Strengthened by the herbal teas and soups made for her by concerned Mrs. Lim and Jenny's mother, and by Stepmother's special stews left simmering half the day, the Old One felt steadier than ever. Most days, if she remembered to take the full dose of Dr. Chu's medicine, she rarely coughed. Each additional tablespoon seemed to give her more and more hours of relief, though she complained about fighting off drowsiness. If she fell asleep, she told Stepmother, how would she keep her eye on Sekky? No, sleep was for others. At the end of life, she joked, there would be more than enough sleep.

She felt herself strong enough that she had Third Uncle deliver to her an unused old table from the warehouse. She asked Father to buy her two dozen sets of bamboo chopsticks and told Stepmother to pick up some spools of the strongest thread from Gee Sook at American Steam Cleaners. No use to argue that she should be resting. She had already paid for the thread. She even boiled together a special recipe to make pots of glue.

Her bedroom door would be shut to all of us except Sekky. After supper, if we pressed our ears against the door, we could hear them tinkering away. Every morning around ten, when we had all safely gone to school or to work, she would bundle up Sekky and herself to start their late-morning tour of the back lanes.

We soon discovered that she and Sekky were collecting coloured glass, fragments of dime-store jewelry and pieces of broken mirror. Anything that reflected light was wrapped in small bundles of old flour and rice sacks and stored in cardboard boxes under her bed. Eventually, all these materials were to be shaped with a glass cutter, then glued and crafted into toy windchimes.

Grandmother patiently taught Sekky how to handle the shards so that he never suffered a single cut. She told him that each raw piece, rescued from the trash, was now more precious than any fiery diamond or glowing emerald, more priceless even than thin slates of Imperial jade that might easily shatter.

"That was why I never hurt myself," Sekky told us in the parlour one evening. Poh-Poh sat in her rocking chair watching over him carefully. Liang and Jung were on the floor waiting for the show to begin. Father and Stepmother sat on the sofa and watched as Sekky held two fingers in the air, dipped them down, and pretended to lift up a fragile fragment from a pile. Then he very gently laid it on the ground. He picked up a shard, wrapping up the piece, as Poh-Poh had shown him, "like the wing of a butterfly." He stared at me to see if I could tell he would never, *ever* crush its delicate wings.

Poh-Poh smiled at all of us. "Smart grandson," she said. Then, remembering that the gods might strike, "*Aaaiiyaah!* Not too smart."

Father applauded the demonstration, and we all joined in. Since the activity seemed to be well taught, and there seemed to be no excessive dangers involved, none of us could have any objections.

"When do we see these windchimes?" Stepmother asked. "What do they sound like?"

"Do they really work, Sekky?" Liang wanted to be impressed. "If they're really pretty, can I give one to my teacher? And Kiam can give one to Jenny, too."

Using the pantomime skills Master Ying had taught him at the Sing Kew Theatre, Jung-Sum mimed lifting himself to his feet with two fingers by gripping a tuft of his own hair: a loose-limbed human windchime. He stood a moment, swayed as if a wind had hit him, shook all over, and made rattling noises.

"Sound like that, Sekky?"

"Be patient," Poh-Poh said, and she laughed to see how fine a reception her youngest grandson had been given.

"The chimes are really beautiful," said Sekky. "Takes hours and hours just to make one small one. We show you soon!"

Poh-Poh nodded. It was time for her and Sekky to return to their work table upstairs and to shut the door against the world.

"No harm," Stepmother said, but Father gave us all his worried look. Acquaintances, neighbours, all sorts of people had spied the Old One with Sekky rummaging through bins of waste in the alleyways, shaking out discarded purses and opening up promising shoe boxes. Friends and strangers wondered at her sanity. Word got around. Jenny warned me that among the Chinese students at King Edward High School, the two scavengers were a hot topic.

When I complained to Father, Stepmother interrupted me.

"No harm done, Kiam-Kim. I speak to the Old One."

Whatever Gai-mou said to her had some result. Poh-Poh now insisted she was only taking Sekky out for short walks. Letting her grandson take in some fresh air. Exercise her creaking joints. "And ease my cramping heart," she claimed. Nothing more.

Then she and Sekky would disappear into her

bedroom and shut the door. We knew they would be bent over her large table, working away with the day's accumulation of junk. I came home early one afternoon and found the two of them washing their small haul in boiling water. Both of them wore flour-sack aprons.

"Cleaning up," Sekky said. "We always clean up."

Poh-Poh threw in a kitchen towel to help absorb the bits of scum floating to the surface and to settle the dancing few inches of debris. The towel sank into the mix. The kitchen smelled of sweet lye and melting Bakelite.

"Safer to be clean," I said. "You don't want to catch any germs."

"Poh-Poh says I'm getting stronger." He flexed his short-sleeved arm to show off a tiny bump of muscle.

"You bet. I can see that."

Poh-Poh laughed, then began to double up with coughing. She had forgotten to take her medicine. I stepped forward, but she waved her hand at me to stand back.

Sekky said, "And I'm not coughing so much." He grabbed the Old One's waving hand and held on tightly. "And neither does Poh-Poh."

With the strain showing in her stooped back and half-shut eyes, the Old One willed herself to stop hacking. The large veins at the side of her neck protruded from her effort. In those scant seconds, Little Brother looked at her with such haunted eyes that my own need to do something fell away.

The pot rattled for attention.

Grandmother shook off Sekky's grip and wiped her hands on her apron. She opened the bottle and tossed back the medicine. It was more than a tablespoon, but there was nothing I could say. Colour settled into her cheeks. She was breathing easily again.

"See?" Sekky said. "Nothing wrong!"

Poh-Poh pointed to the kitchen tongs on the table. Before I could reach over, Sekky grabbed them.

"Dai-goh! Watch me! I get to pull out the biggest pieces."

As he pulled over a chair to stand on, Poh-Poh gave him a big smile. But the strain on her face was too obvious, even to Little Brother. As if he hadn't noticed this, Sekky—using both hands—dipped the long metal tongs into the pot. He pushed aside the soaking towel and he twisted and gripped the tongs to fasten on to the biggest piece. It looked so simple, but I knew that he had to balance the object's size and weight, had to judge exactly the tension he would require to pull the piece away from the dancing clutter, to yank it firmly from the metal sides of the pot, to do all this with the skill of an engineer, without the piece cracking or shattering.

I smiled at Sekky's skill. After he set the piece down on a towel spread on the kitchen table, he grinned back at me.

As the war advanced, and events grew even more complex, one of my monthly duties was to help Father shift or add pin-tags on the large maps of China and

Europe hanging at the Chinese Benevolent Association Reading Room on Columbia Street. The tags were little flags, with symbols or words representing the Allies and Axis powers. It was Father's idea that every citizen should understand clearly what was happening in the world conflict. After all, the war was coming closer to our doorstep.

"The truth will make us strong," he said to me. "We pin down truth."

For the many citizens of Chinatown who could not read at all, the colourful flags created a vivid, shifting picture.

"China knock out soon!" an old man said to me in his best Chinglish, shaking his white head at the enemy flags eclipsing more and more chunks of Chinese and Southeast Asian territories.

As Father and I stood on three-legged footstools, I could see how the swastika also darkened whole parts of Central and Eastern Europe, all of the Netherlands, Denmark, and Norway. On a blank tag, Father wrote "Russia" in Chinese and jabbed it into Finland.

With much head-shaking, Mr. Sung, who had been observing Father and me working away, explained to his audience of six old men that the great Allied armies were now retreating to a beach called Dunkirk. Mr. Sung compared Dunkirk to the stretch of sand at English Bay.

"Imagine ten thousand German bombs dropping there! Killing all the sunbathers!"

Later, Father explained to me that Mr. Sung had translated the word *retreat* in his own way and compared

Dunkirk to Chiang Kai-shek's brave soldiers *regrouping* in Chungking.

Mr. Sung put on a more positive front for those who could not read. But there was worse news to come. Mr. Kang, the Chinese school principal, told Father he was fearful of the negotiations between Washington and Japan.

"Americans promise to stay out of the war," he said in formal Cantonese, "and the Japanese buy up six million tons of scrap metal since the Rape of Nanking." The big man cuffed his bald head in frustration. "Buy up Ford machinery!" *Slap!* "Buy up oil and coal!" *Slap!*

"To fuel the slaughter of the Chinese," Mr. Sung commented. "How can the Americans not know?"

Father, a champion of American democracy, had no ready answer. I picked up the Free China donation box sitting on the table and slipped in some loose change, rattling the box to distract the two men. To my surprise, bald Mr. Kang dug in his pocket and dropped in some coins. Loud thunder suddenly shook the walls, and lightning flashed. A downpour slashed at the storefront windows. Liquid shadows streaked across the maps. Someone switched on the main light.

Stepmother, with Liang and Sekky, who had been shopping in Market Alley when the shower burst over them, dashed in, shaking the rain off themselves. Other men and women came running in for shelter. From habit, I shook the donation box.

A toothless man looked away from the map of China and said, "We lose." He spoke with a thick Hakka accent. "I keep my money."

"Be strong, Mr. Lew," said Father, putting away some leftover pins. "We win soon."

Mr. Lew spat. To the disgust of the women shoppers, he missed the spittoon.

From across the room, Mrs. Leong greeted Stepmother with a hearty shout. "*Mmh tauh-hohng!* Never surrender!"

Liang and Sekky smiled at the startled faces on the bench. That any woman would be quoting a British politician caused a few others to giggle. Mrs. Leong, undaunted by the disapproving looks of the men, made a show of reaching across the table for the donation box. She smiled at me and stuffed in a dollar.

"Mr. Lew," she said, "some coins for a Free China?"

Mr. Lew unfolded a strip of old newspaper before my face. The paper crackled with age. He translated the English headline for Mrs. Leong and everyone to hear. His rough Hakka accent made the *Vancouver Sun* headline seem even more ominous: "DEATH STALKS THE CHINESE." The rain lessened. There was quiet in the room.

People shook their heads at the bad sign. I knew if Poh-Poh had been there she would have snatched the evil words and torn them up and burned every scrap, and lit incense. I went to get the donation box and overheard Mrs. Leong tell one of the ladies that she was relieved to see Sekky with Stepmother. She half whispered that it was best for the boy to have a break from his grandmother. "The Old One behaving so strangely," she said. "Saw her with young Sekky looking into garbage cans." She tsk-tsked to the others, who all looked sympathetically towards me.

Father ignored the whispering. "Gloom-collector Mr. Lew!" He gave a little laugh, politely, so that Mr. Lew would not lose face. "Read out the date on that newspaper, Kiam-Kim."

I read, first in English, and then translated in Chinese, "Nineteen thirty-seven."

The yellowing paper was three years old.

"China not dead yet," announced Father. "And you will soon see America fight with China." He pointed to the large maps on the side wall. "Soon these evil flags will be defeated!"

"Soon? America!" A few of the elders on the bench laughed. "American soldiers! How soon?"

With a *slap, slap, slap* to his bald head, Mr. Kang shouted, "When *no-more-profit* soon!"

Father and I had only been the messengers in the Reading Room, shifting the pin-tags according to the most recent news. Stepmother signalled with a discreet nod that it was a good time for the family to leave, but Father did not make any move.

An elder hawked, drew everyone's eyes to his queasy act, and spat a bull's eye of slime directly into a corner spittoon. Father winced.

"This for your dog-shit writing!" the elder said.

Another said, "Good man, Mr. Chen! Write more!"

After an awkward pause, someone said, "Look!" and pointed to the two maps. "So many enemy flags! Look!"

The newcomers rushed to the wall. Necks craned. Stepmother held back Sekky and Liang. Father had given her a frown, as if he knew something was going to go terribly wrong. But he would not follow her eyes to the door and take the chance to exit.

Around the table the anxious murmuring began to escalate. People pushed forward and began to study the map of China. Whenever someone asked about their home village, Mr. Kang, carefully perched on the footstool, expertly pointed to provinces and counties, being careful not to dislodge any of the pins.

"Your village located here," he would say like the schoolteacher he was. "By this river section."

There were gasps. Mr. Kang's finger rested right beside a deadly Rising Sun.

The names of other towns and villages were shouted out. A woman in a quilted jacket felt faint and had to be guided to a chair. I looked with confusion at Father. Truth had brought only gloom and despair to the whole room.

Stepmother looked over at the sullen men in their shirtsleeves sitting on the long bench by the windows. For a long moment, her eyes lingered on the woman in the quilted jacket whose soft, round face had frozen when Mr. Kang pointed out the Rising Sun, the pin like a bayonet pierced into the heart of her town district.

"My son and daughter—*still there!*" she said, and dissolved into tears.

The way the big woman shook, no one could doubt that the horrors of Nanking had flooded her mind.

Stepmother must have felt Father's sudden loss of face before Mr. Kang and Mr. Lew and felt, too, the contempt of that old hawker. Even Mrs. Leong stared at the map, open-mouthed. An enemy pin was stuck right next to her birth city of Canton. No one even noticed when the sunlight swept across the tear-stained windows.

Stepmother surveyed the rays of dust-speckled gloom around her. All at once, she straightened up. Her eyes shone. She waved her knitted grocery bag, almost like a flag, to catch the eye of Mrs. Leong at the far end of the table. The bench-sitters turned their heads.

"Leong Sim!" Stepmother's voice boomed across the long reading table. Leong Sim turned her attention from the map. Stunned by the sudden interruption, Mr. Kang's polished head shot up. Everyone stared at the guilty party.

"Leong Sim!" Stepmother's voice grew even louder. "The Old One now at American Steam Cleaners"—and louder still—"Poh-Poh and Gee Sook to alter the greatcoat of Mr. Yuen! To pin up the great-coat for Jung-Sum!"

Mrs. Leong frantically fanned her palms, as if to say, "Chen Sim, I'm not deaf!" Mr. Kang frowned at Stepmother's poor attempt to speak formal Cantonese.

But the eyes of all the elders on the bench were riveted on Stepmother. And the last face, wiping away tears, turned away from the map of China to focus on her, too. Everyone wondered what was wrong with the slim woman with the two children, speaking so wilfully about fixing up a greatcoat. *So mad! So unbecoming!* Father furrowed his brow, suggesting Stepmother lower her voice, but she—bristling—faced Mr. Lew, the brittle *Sun* headline still dangling from his hand.

"Our boy just thirteen, Mr. Lew!"

Abruptly, Stepmother's volume dropped. I heard a familiar gentle tone; her softly spoken words began to fill the stillness of the room. "But my young man in that tailored coat . . . *oh, such a coat . . .*" Her voice fell almost to a whisper. People tilted their heads to catch her words. "*Our Jung-Sum stand like a soldier . . .*"

Father quickly caught on; after a moment, I, too, understood Stepmother's motives. Jung-Sum's name meant "Loyalty," "To Remain Loyal," "To Remain Faithful." Still keeping her voice low, Stepmother let her final words rise to a ringing clarity.

"Our Jung-Sum, he stand like a soldier!" She stared directly at the round-faced woman who had been crying. "Never to surrender! Never!"

Someone applauded. It was bald Mr. Kang. Mr. Lew tore up the strip of newspaper headline he had saved for three years. Others began to applaud. The old men on the bench broke into toothless smiles. Mrs. Leong looked at the women about her and sternly pointed at the donation tin. Purses snapped opened, and I heard coins clinking down. In the hubbub that followed, Father rushed his family out the Reading Room doors. My feet hit the wet pavement last.

The afternoon sun skated over pools of gold. Stepmother took some quick steps ahead of us so she could shake out her shawl and jiggle loose her knitted grocery bag. Each of us took a long, deep breath. The air tasted of salt.

"We buy a fresh chicken," Father said to the slim figure walking ahead of us. "Third Uncle give me a raise today."

Sekky shouted, "Gum cards!"

"I'll buy you some," I said, and remembered too late that all my spare change had gone into the donation box back at the Reading Room.

"Don't spoil that little brat." Liang pulled at my shirt and latched on to my warehouse-calloused hand. With a proud authority, Only Sister shook her Shirley Temple curls at Little Brother. "He only wants, wants, *wants.*"

"*Do not!*" Sekky said and pushed her aside.

Father gently knuckled him and took him by the hand before Sekky could swing his fist at Liang.

With Stepmother leading the way, we headed east to Sing's Poultry, where Father said that Sekky could help him pick out the fattest bird. Liang skipped ahead of everyone. She stopped and waited to take her mother's hand, which she had not done for a long time. As the two walked before us, deftly avoiding the puddles, damp flowery patterns clung to Stepmother's shoulders.

"I learned something today," Father said to me.

"What's that?"

"*Pins.*"

Father smiled to himself. A dozen questions crowded into my head, but we walked on in silence, content to follow the prancing edges of a shawl.

Father was right. The war was at our doorstep.

At King Eddy, more and more of the senior boys discussed enlisting. Over their boxed lunches, some declared that right after graduation, they would join the Royal Canadian Air Force; others said they wanted the navy life. I noticed that, like me, most of the boys from Chinatown, and some of the Japanese guys from Powell Street, were silent.

Our classroom bulletin board was crowded with clippings about the men and women from Vancouver who were fighting in Europe. Thumbtacked under THINGS TO DO were reminders to collect tins of lard and pieces of scrap iron and to bundle up newspapers. Another sheet reminded us of the proper procedures to follow in case of an air-raid exercise. I was responsible for seeing that all the lights were turned off, and Jeff Eng that the plug of Mr. Waites's fish tank was pulled out.

Announcements about food drives, victory dances, volunteer work with the Red Cross all became a part of our weekly assembly. At the end of each month, the names of former staff and students missing or killed were read out to us. During the two minutes of silent prayer, we bowed our heads in Christian fashion. Throughout the world in many other school assemblies, there must have been longer lists of names being read aloud, like the list Robert Donat read in *Goodbye, Mr. Chips*. I wondered how many boys had whispered to their best pal—as Jack had whispered to me in the theatre and in the school auditorium—*"No guts, no glory!"*

From the stage, Principal Sanderson tapped his knuckles on the microphone and waited for us to settle into quiet. The flowers on the stage and his black armband reminded everyone that today was another solemn occasion.

"At this time of war," he began, "the world has no use for a quitter, another name for the fellow who feels sorry for himself. A teacher familiar to all of you has asked that he be allowed to commemorate two names this month. I am sure you are aware of his own loss."

Moustached Mr. Fry took the stage. His hands clenched the lectern. As he related a funny incident involving Mr. Thompson, his delivery was flawless. Some of us even laughed.

"That is why we will fondly remember Mr. Robert Thompson," he concluded, "who was a friend to so many and a respected member of the Science Department. And last . . . my son, Collin Jonathan Fry."

We all sat up.

The gravel voice carried on. "Six years ago, Collin graduated from King Edward. My colleagues might well recall how proud I was that he was chosen to be his class valedictorian. But I remember how much more proud Collin was to have played offensive tackle on the senior football team. May God grant them both His merciful and eternal peace."

"Amen" echoed up and down the rows of bowed heads. Mr. Fry adjusted his glasses and sat down.

This time, Jack did not poke my side: the war was too real and too threatening. Or was it that we had glimpsed another kind of glory, another kind of guts?

On the home front, Chinatown citizens were kept too busy to dwell on disastrous retreats and sad departures. By the summer of 1940, the fighting had brought a wartime boom to Third Uncle's warehouse and to Chinatown itself.

Under the Georgia Viaduct, the factories and mills were humming twenty-four hours a day, attempting to fill quotas for finished lumber, for fuel and military goods, and no one dared to complain about the smells or the noise. Chinatown restaurants began to feed hundreds of workers and off-duty servicemen looking for a cheap meal or a night on the town at the W.K. to dine and dance, or just to listen to a live band. Tailor shops were selling fancy pants and suits again, though most materials were restricted. Downtown weekly-rental hotels and rooming houses rarely had vacancies. Every excuse for a basement suite had a lineup of young couples willing to move in.

"No room to die in," grumbled one of the elders.

Third Uncle hired more men, and Father worked overlapping shifts to track the goods and supplies coming into and out of storage.

One Saturday, after working at the warehouse moving stock, I took a quick shower, dressed, and picked up Jenny at the Chongs' store to bring her home for supper. I promised her parents that afterwards I would help her prepare for her new math class, set to start in September. Father would not let Ben Chong pay me any money.

"We all Chinese," he said. "We like family in Gold Mountain. Kiam be happy to help your Jenny!"

And so I was. We met most evenings upstairs at the corner store, in that room with the stand-up piano. I borrowed Jack's math book for the summer. Most Chinese girls took that class, just so they could enter commercial school with an extra credit and take a

four-month course in secretarial and accounting skills.
Ambitious Chinese girls dreamed of office jobs in the
sugar refinery or insurance and accounting firms.
These large companies took on Chinese girls, at even
lower wages than were paid to those they had replaced,
to work not at the reception or front offices but in the
back rooms, filing and bookkeeping. If any of the other
workers complained, they were told that the war
necessitated "this kind of hiring" and "cheap labour"
permitted the company to pay the others a better wage.
With a commercial-school certificate, a Chinese girl
had a better chance of getting one of those positions,
advertised as "Grade 10 starting position in large
office. Now hiring."

"Wear best clothes," Mrs. Chong told Jenny.

Most Chinese girls and their families considered
any office job outside Chinatown a *real* job, prestige
employment that meant you were educated and more
refined.

"Be together like family," Mrs. Chong called out as
we left the store. "Enjoy special dish!"

Outside, I asked, "What was that all about? 'Be like
family'? 'Special dish'?"

"Father sent over a whole chicken to your house
this morning. My mother has designs. Watch out."

When we settled into the dining room, Poh-Poh
insisted that Jenny sit right next to me. Liang sat
across, and stared at Jenny, as she had told me she
intended to do.

"Will she get dolled up for supper with us? What
kind of makeup does she buy?"

I didn't blame Liang for her interest in Jenny. When she got dressed up for any weddings our two families attended, she was very pretty. She would curl her long hair in that fancy way, and she had her mother's taste for wearing the right dress. Jeff Eng said he could go for Jenny. I tried not to think too much about what I felt for her, but there were times when we sat together doing her math lessons that a hint of her perfume caught me off guard. Whenever my eyes drifted away from her pencilled notes to linger on the soft curves now pushing against her sweater, my throat would go dry, my palms a little wet. Even Jack noticed how Jenny had transformed from a bit of a stick to a real looker.

"Do you ever sit beside her and get a hard-on?" he asked me. "How can you stand it?"

"I focus on math," I said. But Jack grinned. "Well, I do most of the time," I added.

"That's all?"

"We go out with the gang."

Jenny and I hadn't been on an official date together. An official date required the permission of the lucky girl's guardians and that the two families burn incense to the ancestors and sacrifice three chickens—well, almost. You were at least expected to bring a gift to the parents, buy a corsage for the girl, and suit up in your best slacks, wear a starched shirt and fancy tie. It wasn't my style.

Liang had told me that Jenny had been on her first "official" date with Al Sen, the son of rich merchant Sen Kwok. I knew about that date: it was a kind of business obligation on the Chongs' part. The chaperoned date was just a social courtesy—at least that was what Mrs. Chong told Stepmother and Poh-Poh. Al was reluctant to go to the party welcoming his father's new companion from San Francisco—"a lady of a certain age," as Mrs. Chong put it, who had once danced in the chorus line at the old Pantages vaudeville house—so the Chongs volunteered their Jenny, who, nevertheless, was dying to go to the W.K. to dance with a full orchestra playing and all the women and girls in formal gowns. The two dined and danced, and Liang—who stated bluntly, "Al Sen is nothing to look at"—was impressed that Jenny had on a long black dress and her mother's pearls.

"Like a real princess," Liang said. "I'm going to ask to see the dress. Will she let me try it on?"

"When you grow up," I said.

At the dinner table, I could see that Liang was disappointed that Jenny wasn't wearing a corsage and had on only a touch of lipstick, but she was happy to see Jenny with me. It would make for some good gossip with her girlfriends: "Guess who sat *real close* beside my brother at dinner on Saturday?"

Jung carried in the soup tureen. He didn't have much interest in girls. At thirteen, he was focussed on sports and building a reputation with a growing gang of his own. He set the bowl down and shouted for Father to come to the table. Poh-Poh and Stepmother came out of the kitchen, and everyone sat. Mrs. Chong's words came into my head: "Be like family."

Even though Father happily greeted Jenny, he turned at once to a subject that had been troubling him.

"The war very much now in Chinatown," he said. "You think about that, Kiam-Kim."

Father reached for a fine piece of chicken and lifted it onto Jenny's plate. She waved her hands at the generosity.

"We thank your *fuh mouh*, your parents," Poh-Poh said. "Tell them Number One bird. Fat and tender."

The Old One filled her soup bowl with a ladle of bean curd and broth, and Stepmother scooped some steaming rice into her other bowl. Poh-Poh urged Jung to pass some greens into Sekky's bowl. Sekky made a face.

"Be aware," said Father to the two boys. "Every day so many young men fight in the war. People soon wonder where are the Chinatown boys? Why your *dai-goh* not in there? Tell them very soon we all be there."

"When?" asked Sekky.

"Not yet," Father said. "Chinese not yet needed."

"Not *wanted*." I couldn't let Father be misunderstood. He and I both knew that some of the older Chinatown boys who attempted to join up had been turned away. "There's a big difference—isn't there, Father?" I said, carefully adding the question so Father would not lose face "—between being not wanted and being not needed."

Father thought a moment. His authority would be the final word on the matter. "Yes, Kiam-Kim, as I was saying, the Chinese are *not wanted*."

"Yes," Stepmother said, but her eyes twinkled, "that's what Father said."

Sekky didn't quite get the point. He sailed his palm in the air. Number One Fighter Pilot. "When can I go?"

"Not yet," I said. He bit his lip. "We go together when you are as tall as I am. How's that?"

"A pilot, Dai-goh!"

I had told him the story of Robert Shun Wong, who had hand-built his own single-seat Pietenpol airplane in his family's upstairs apartment overlooking Market Alley. Three years ago he had gone east to sign up with a flight school. Maybe he was in the sky now, flying over Nazi territory. Sekky said he was going to build an even bigger plane. Our house, he insisted, had to be bigger than any apartment in Market Alley.

"Can we both be pilots and fly over the Burma Road?"

"If we win this war," Father said, "anyone here can be anything they want."

"End of school next year," Stepmother broke in. "What do you want to be, Jenny?"

"I think I want to be with Kiam-Kim," she said, breaking into a giggle. "Would you mind?"

Liang gave me a quick look. I winked at her.

"Sure," I said. "We'll make it official."

"Yes, yes—when?" Poh-Poh said, coughing a little but joining in the laughter with everyone else, except Sekky, who looked up scornfully, annoyed that he might have to give up his co-pilot.

Liang reached for some soup and pointed out that Jenny's lace blouse was tied at the collar with a pink ribbon, just like her own.

"We're in style," Jenny said. "We girls know how to dress."

Liang beamed. Hers was actually an old blouse from the Mission House Bazaar that Poh-Poh had altered. Father said the two of them looked liked sisters. Of course, Liang looked little like Jenny. My sister had Father's round face, Poh-Poh's small eyes. But her lips were like Jenny's: perfect.

When I turned to give Jenny a choice piece of chicken, I saw that she had a profile like Kwan Ying, the Goddess of Mercy. Like the familiar statue sitting on Stepmother's dresser, Jenny was actually beautiful. The food was exceptional that night: the dining table was rich with savoury dishes.

"Maybe Ben talked to you about this already," Father said to Jenny, and he explained that the Chinatown boys, supported by men like Jenny's father, were holding meetings to encourage others to enlist.

"What for you fight a white man's war?" some of the elders challenged the younger men. The old men reminded everyone not to forget the 1911 demonstrations along Hastings against the Chinese vegetable sellers. Then there was the famous strike by the white waitresses after the city council said it would not permit them to work in Chinese-owned restaurants. Any restaurant owner would be fined and lose his licence if he hired a white woman.

"And what about the goddamn city council?" demanded someone else. "They pass a motion to tell Ottawa not to offer the vote to Orientals. We fight. We die for nothing!"

I thought of the boy-soldier who knelt on the ground with his hands tied, waiting for the executioner's sword, the torn flaps of his jacket lifting in the wind like broken wings.

"Go back to China," the elders said to the Canada-borns who wanted to join the Canadian forces. "Fight for China. You Chinese! Look in the mirror!"

Father sniffed. "What's that smell?" A sudden taint of chemicals had fumed the dining-room air.

"It's"—and with seven-year-old dramatics, holding his nose and covering his mouth, Sekky squealed "—yes . . . eww . . . it's a *fart!*"

"False Creek," I said. "The wind must have shifted."

As if to listen for the changing current, everyone grew silent: a slight popping and a rattling-tin sound came from the back of the house.

"Go check, Kiam-Kim," Stepmother said. "Sit down, Sekky."

I got up and shut the small window by Father's desk and went to the kitchen to make sure everything was shut there, too. The back door was open. Through the screen, I could see Jack holding a pellet rifle, aiming at a row of tin cans set up in front of their shed. The tins went flying, one after another. With beer in hand, Mr. O'Connor stood on their back porch watching quietly.

Jack had joined the Rifle Club at King Ed. As he reset the cans on his makeshift platform—two old saw-horses with a pair of flashlights tied from the shed to shine down on them—I wondered about his father, standing stock-still. Mr. O'Connor had spent two years in the Great War, but it was a war he spoke very little about. When I switched on the dangling porch light, his shadow quivered in the bluish dusk.

I called out to Jack, asked him what he was doing later that evening. As he turned, his blond hair danced against the growing dark of the yard. I thought, *What an easy target.*

"Have a date with Moira," he called back, holding his gun as though he were Hemingway. Then he whipped himself around, and the final tin bolted into the air.

I realized that the sulphurous smell of gunpowder could not have come from Jack's target practice alone. It was definitely blowing in from False Creek. The huge refineries there had been cooking up new chemicals for the military. Bright yellow warning signs were now posted on chain-link gates under the Georgia Viaduct: DANGER—NO ENTRY. Armed guards kept watch in one-man booths. The *Province* and the *News-Herald* had reported that some Victory Gardens in backyards a few blocks away from the viaduct underpass grew thick vines that suddenly withered and died. The day before, a brownish fog had saturated the area. People still complained of brown spots ruining their clothes and bedsheets. Gasping lungs and short breath marked lives lodged too near the viaduct. The summer breeze smelled of deadly secrets.

When I returned to the table, Father was still talking.

"Maybe," he was saying, "even go back to China to fight."

"*Aaaiiyaah!* More fighting!" said Poh-Poh, raising her eyebrows. "Everyone die."

Jenny started to protest but caught my look. Playing host, I lifted some snow peas onto her plate. Poh-Poh coughed again. With concern creasing his brow, Father asked the Old One, "Did you take your medicine?"

Poh-Poh nodded—*Of course! Of course!*—but Father exchanged doubtful looks with Stepmother and me. The rest of us kept quiet while Poh-Poh went on about the dire news arriving every day from all fronts.

The war news had been so discouraging, old village people like Poh-Poh became the *lao naauh,* the Old Scold, to heckle and mock away the curse of bad news. In threatening times, the elderly of Chinatown would blurt out the worst thing they feared could ever happen—*All soon die in China! All die!*—then a lightning-swift smirk would cross their lips. To be sure to disarm ill fortune, they shouted out the worst.

"I join! I go fight!" Sekky's palm sliced into the air like a bomber, skimming over Jenny's soup bowl.

Poh-Poh knuckled him. "You dead boy!"

"I fight!" said Jung and threw some shadow-box punches in the air to exasperate Poh-Poh, who couldn't reach him with her knuckle.

At the Hastings Gym, the trainer, Max, had been teaching Second Brother how to box like Joe Louis, how to fake a left and deliver a smashing right hook. For a few nights, Poh-Poh insisted on dabbing her special lotion on Jung's bruised knuckles. "Dr. Chu chop them off!" she threatened, looking up at the fierce Kitchen God.

That weekend, the Old One served a steaming dish of knuckle-like oxtails to strengthen the joints of her pugnacious grandson.

My two brothers were no different from all the other Chinatown kids who knew nothing of politics but played at war with a fierce and dedicated craving. MacLean Park was crowded with boys of all ages shooting at each other with toy weapons, the older ones rumbling in jerry-built tanks nailed together out of wooden crates and cardboard flaps. Boys like Sekky even wore war-surplus goggles and dented helmets, ran amok with tin-pressed planes held high in the air ready to drop their bombs. His lungs were getting stronger, and his roaring about was proof enough of that. He had taken his medication, rested when any of us told him to; he swore to Father he would become a pilot and go "kill the Japs to death."

"Dai-goh," Liang began, picking up a piece of bok choy, "what're you going to do if the Japs invade B.C.? Are you going to join up?"

"Of course he is," said Sekky, rolling his eyes. "Jung and me, too!"

"For sure Dai-goh will fight," Father said. "We all fight."

"Eat more," Poh-Poh said to Jenny. "Kiam-Kim, fill her soup bowl."

Stepmother said she had heard that some Canada-borns had been applying for permission to join the American armed forces.

"Yes," Jenny joined in. "That's what Frank Yuen plans to do."

Frank had been discouraged from volunteering with the Canadian army at Little Mountain headquarters; others, too, like Allan Wong, were told by the Naval Office that if they insisted on signing up, they would be assigned only a shore job like cook's assistant. Others were told they would be given orders to dress fresh meat to be flash-frozen and loaded onto ships direct from the slaughterhouse. "Lots of guts," Allan told a bunch of us at the Blue Eagle, "but no glory."

Father said the three Chinese-language papers had already reported on those frustrated attempts to enlist. *The Chinese New Republic* headlined the story, "UNWANTED CHINESE GHOSTS," and the reporter wrote, "The loyal gentlemen of B.C. Chinatowns are as undesirable as the dead if they want to fight for this country."

"For now," Father confirmed, "Ottawa say no Chinese."

"But if there be more bad news," said Poh-Poh, "they take even me. And I bring my chopper! Chop Japs to death!"

Everyone laughed at the thought of the Old One in a helmet, swinging at the hapless enemy. Sekky clapped his hands. "Kill them all, Poh-Poh!" Father lifted his chopsticks and awarded Poh-Poh the prized chicken head.

Gradually, as we feasted on delicious meats and greens and contentedly swallowed clear broth, we spoke of other things besides the war. Jenny gossiped with my sister about movie stars, told her how she could pin her hair back like Ginger Rogers so it wouldn't fly into her eyes when she tap danced. I admired the way Jenny raised her smooth, bare arms, her fingers pointing at her head to show Liang where hairpins might go.

Jung-Sum finished his third bowl of rice and started telling Sekky about the last matinee he had seen at the Rex, *Stagecoach*. "John Wayne fights these bad guys, and the horses . . ."

But I noticed Poh-Poh was paying no attention to the chatter around her. I thought she had raised her hand to stop herself from coughing again; instead, she held her palm halfway between the table and her mouth. She stared past the table, right over me, as if someone, or *something* were standing directly behind my chair. I deliberately moved my head to distract her, but her dark pupils stared, unmoving. Perhaps she was seeing ghosts, as she sometimes confided to Mrs. Lim and Stepmother that she had. Poh-Poh dropped her hand and nodded, just slightly, as if whoever was standing behind me were demanding her attention.

The Old One's chopsticks slipped from her fingers and clattered onto her plate.

"Ma-mah!" Father said. "Are you all right?"

Everyone stopped talking.

Stepmother took the Old One's hand.

"You're shaking, Poh-Poh," she said. "Tell me what's wrong."

Grandmother snatched her hand away. "Just thinking," she snapped. "Thinking Old China times."

I looked behind me. There was nothing there, of course. Nothing but the small, shut window and the wall. And Father's oak desk. Sekky sat up and looked, too.

"I know, Dai-goh," he said. He panicked. "*Don't look there!*"

All at once, Sekky threw his head back and fell into a choking fit; his heavy rasping made him clutch at his throat.

Stepmother rushed to the pantry to get the breathing salts. Father ran around the table and began pushing with both palms on Sekky's chest while Liang held the back of Sekky's head.

"We know what to do," I assured Jenny. "Just sit quietly." I rushed to the kitchen and grabbed a towel in case he threw up.

But Poh-Poh did nothing. She was usually the first to be with Sekky, slapping his wrists and pinching his pale cheeks between her thumb and forefinger. This time she stayed in her chair, still staring straight ahead. Jenny followed the Old One's eyes. Jung looked, too. Behind my chair. Between the window and Father's desk. Stepmother and Liang looked.

Nothing there.

I looked again.

Nothing.

"No, no . . . not yet," Poh-Poh said quietly. "Not yet."

Her old head dipped slightly; she shook herself. A moment went by. She smiled down at Sekky.

"You be all right, Sek-Lung," she said. "You live long time."

Father stopped pushing. Sekky was breathing regularly again. Stepmother had just unscrewed the smelling salts. "Not needed," said Father.

A sharp tap of a soup spoon made us all look at Poh-Poh. She sat firmly in her chair, her authority in full force.

"Everybody go back to eat," she said, as if nothing had happened. Her old eyes surveyed the table. "Give your guest more chicken, Kiam-Kim. What's wrong with you? The Chongs will think we have *mo li*."

I put the towel over the back of my chair, sat down, and picked up a piece of bok choy for Jenny. Stepmother and Father, too, sat down. Poh-Poh and Sekky were already eating away, Sekky lifting his bowl of soup, the Old One choosing a piece of pork from the hot sauce. Father gave each of us a quick glance: *Eat. Everything be fine now.*

Jenny nudged me under the table. I took her hand and squeezed it.

Sekky said, "When the team of horses broke away, what did the cowboy do?"

Second Brother took a deep breath. "He held on to their reins and was yanked into the air . . ."

Jenny fell into step and started telling Liang where she had purchased her blouse. The room happily buzzed with our voices. I asked Poh-Poh if I should put the water on for after-dinner tea.

"No," she said. "You and Jen-Jen study first, then you take her home. I make tea for everyone."

I felt a sudden chill. The hairs on the back of my neck stood up. Perhaps the wind had shifted again. It shook the small window behind me.

"So drafty these days!" Stepmother said. She had goosebumps on her arms.

"Why not?" said Poh-Poh. "Soon be winter."

Much later, when I was alone with Father at his desk, he assured me, "Only a draft, Kiam. I felt it, too. Vancouver is not a village in Old China."

After dinner, I set up the card table in the parlour. Jenny opened up the math book, and I tossed down some loose-leaf pages and two pencils. Father called to me from his desk in the corner of the dining room that he had the title for the new editorial, "Gold Mountain Says No Chinese Soldiers Wanted."

Poh-Poh shouted out from the crowded kitchen, "Write down, 'No one fight, no one die. Everyone fight, then everyone die!'"

"No, no, not everyone," Stepmother protested. Dishes were being stacked. "Not everyone dies."

The Old One's voice lost its timbre, and she shrieked above the noise of the kitchen: "Yes! Oh, yes! *Very soon! I to die! Very soon!*"

Everyone in the kitchen stopped what they were doing. Jenny held her pencil in the air. The house was still. How did we all know—for even Sekky had stopped playing—that this time the Old One's words were not merely *lao naauh*?

I could hear Stepmother speaking a few words, gently, sweetly. But Poh-Poh answered very clearly: "Gai-mou, you know as I know what the Great Buddha himself say: 'The only cure for old age . . . is to die.'"

Poh-Poh broke into laughter; her sharp cooking tools clattered into the sink to be washed.

"She will die, you know," whispered Jenny. "At dinner tonight, I think she was having a stroke or something. She's in her eighties, isn't she?"

I could hear Father returning to work at his desk. Jenny took my hand. We heard him crying.

The noise of cleaning up filled the kitchen again, and we heard Poh-Poh begin a nursery song. Someone turned on the faucet, and the voices of Sekky and Liang and Jung joined the din of dishes and pots being shuffled along the metal trough of the old sink.

Sekky came out to the parlour to say that tea would be ready after everything was finished in the kitchen. "Poh-Poh says so."

"How long?" I asked.

He looked at Jenny. "Whenever your pretty girl-friend wants it."

Jenny smiled. "How about in an hour?" she asked. "Will that be okay?"

"Okay," he answered. "Do you want the English or Chinese kind?"

Jenny pretended to mull this over. I could see she was checking Sekky out.

"Chinese would be nice."

"Okay," he said, "but I'll check with Father. He gets first choice."

"That puts me in my place," said Jenny after Sekky dashed away. "But 'they also serve who also'—how does that go?"

"'Who only stand and wait.'"

Jenny and I finished the math in just under an hour. She hadn't done badly. But she could sense my brain was now buzzing with other thoughts.

"What will you do if they start needing Chinese boys? Will you join up?

"I guess. But I need to know if we'll always be Resident Aliens."

Poh-Poh moseyed into the parlour. She looked the same as ever.

"Oolong tea now being served," she said.

Oolong tea was saved for only special occasions, since there was hardly any left in Chinatown because of the war. She wiped her hands on her untied apron and proposed the impossible to Jenny.

"If he fight," said Poh-Poh, "Kiam-Kim go back to China with me!"

"Better to be with Jenny," I said and made an Eddie Cantor wild-eyed face.

Poh-Poh fanned her apron in the air. "Too much hot air in here. You two finish tea outside."

Liang and Sekky wanted to go outside with us, but the Old One shushed them. "We keep Gai-mou good company. She show you how to knit. After that, I tell you all ghost story."

Poh-Poh directed Jenny and me outside, and the front door locked behind us. Voices trailed away back into the kitchen. Two cups of steaming tea had been placed on the porch railing for us. No doubt Poh-Poh had sent Jung and Liang sneaking around from the back. The cups were our special guest cups, too. Peonies curved around their rims. Jenny stretched her arms up into the air.

WAYSON CHOY

The night air was cool, and the North Shore winds had chased away the tainted breezes from False Creek. The street lamps would be turned on tonight for an extra hour; the radio reported that the whole Pacific coast was free of any enemy planes flying towards us. Though bombs terrorized England every night, the king and queen refused to leave, setting an example. In Vancouver, people wanted to live as if the war, the recent curfews, the blackout curtains were merely a nuisance, just as the Royals had implied by staying home. And so tonight, in a defiant spirit, the city street lamps were to be left on for an extra hour.

Jenny nudged me. "Jeff Eng's thinking of enlisting in one of those towns like Kamloops."

"Why there?"

"Father told me the recruitment offices in the Interior will fill their quota with any breathing body they can get."

"Why so desperate?" I asked. A shooting star crossed the sky, but we didn't pause to make any wishes. Jenny didn't notice. Her attention was caught by a car driving by, its headlights taped over except for a sliver of light.

"His sister tells me he needs to get away from his father. He hates working in the garage."

"O'Connor does, too. I mean, wants get away from his parents."

"Don't you?"

"Not really," I said. "No reason to."

"Funny," Jenny said, and bit her bottom lip. "I want to get away from Mother."

She rested her head against my shoulder. The sky

~ 326 ~

was darkening rapidly; a full moon looked down on us.

Behind the parlour window, I heard the muffled voice of Poh-Poh dramatically finishing her ghost story, Sekky calling out for more, and Liang racing Jung to use the bathroom first. Then I knew the two would take turns helping Sekky with his home studies. Stepmother would sit and knit and watch over them, making sure that they also did their own school work—quietly—while Father continued to write. The ordinary made the brutal wars in Asia and Europe seem remote.

Jenny and I leaned into each other. The porch steps were hard, but I didn't mind at all.

"If you go, Kiam," she began in a voice that I had never heard her use before, with an emphasis I sensed she had not known herself: "I'll—*I'll miss you*."

I shifted my rear so that my back pressed firmly against the porch column. Jenny shifted, too, and leaned her whole weight against me. I pressed my cheek against the top of her head and closed my eyes. Her drowsy weight slipped onto my chest, and her small hand crept between two buttons of my shirt and slid across my undershirt and came to rest over my heart. Strands of her hair played in the night breeze and brushed against my face. She smelled faintly of perfume. A comforting instinct led me to think I could slip a hand under the back of her blouse, too, just to rest my palm against her warmth.

"Kiam?" she said. "Could you really kill someone?"

The question surprised me. She gave a little shiver. The air was getting chilly.

"Would you, Kiam?"

"If I had to? Yes . . . I could."

Another little shiver ran up her back. I had no other answer, except to remove my warehouse-rough hand and make a show of taking off my school sweater and draping it around her. I wanted to keep her secure and encircled within my arms, safe from the war, from all the things that would divide us from this night. Her smooth fingers wove into mine; her other hand rested on my arm. I might have once felt just as deeply attached to another—surely, as a baby in my mother's arms—but those were phantom memories. Then, I was protected and held on to; now, my arms reached out to hold on to someone of my own, shielding whatever it was that seemed so suddenly fragile.

"I have to get home," Jenny said, lazily pushing me away. "My mother will be anxious."

The street lamps switched on, and Jack's long, whistling shadow came into view on the sidewalk below us. He had on a white shirt under his school cardigan, and his hair was combed back in that lady-killer style of Gary Cooper's. He had also perfected the Coop's lanky cowboy swagger that all the girls pretended not to notice. Jenny was always curt with Jack, once pushing his hand off her briefcase. "I'll carry my own books, thanks," she had told him and hurried to my side. That gave me a chance to return Jack's noble gesture. I had given him a brush-off salute.

"Had to try," he told me later.

When Jack spotted Jenny and me on the porch, he opened wide his arms as if to catch the moon and stars and throw them back into place again.

"All this," he laughed, whirling like Fred Astaire, "these stars and this paper moon, just for you two love-birds."

"How come you're not with Moira?"

"Left Moira Williams steaming at her front door," he said. "Here I have a willing dick, she has the greatest tits, but we're going to end nowhere."

He paused, waiting for an outraged reaction from Jenny. She only stiffened a little. Perhaps the wind again. I put my arm around her and she leaned back. Her indifference was like a red flag being waved before a bull. Jack marched up and sat two steps below us. Jenny pushed closer against me.

"You and Jenny look perfect together, Kiam. Am I intruding?"

Jenny put her chin down on her knees, as if she hadn't heard him. Jack must have followed her eyes, for he turned his head slightly to look up behind him. Because of his blond hair and pale skin, the glow from the streetlamp reflected back from our front windows heightened his good looks.

The night was beautiful. The moon seemed closer and the North Shore mountains were topped with new-fallen snow. The starry air was momentarily still. I thought even Jack must have been held captive by the quiet. And then he glanced at me uneasily, as if he didn't know whether to get up and leave or stay seated. As he turned awkwardly, he bumped the two of us, and Jenny and I shifted ourselves to make some more room for him on the lower step; she didn't seem to mind that his left side was now half leaning against her, just as she leaned back against me. And for some reason, I didn't mind either. For so many years, we had known each other: our being together like this on a beautiful night seemed inevitable.

After some minutes, I felt the urge to rub the back of Jenny's neck. She felt tight.

"Kiam tells me you're going to leave B.C."

Jack's life held no secrets. He was proud of that. Ask him anything and he would tell you.

"Are you really going, Jack?" Jenny asked, and gently pushed away my hand. She straightened up, pulled at her skirt so it hugged even tighter below her knees. The wind was rising. He brushed back a shock of hair.

"Have to, Jenny," he said at last. "My dad's been drinking again—and so have I, for that matter—and my mother's been falling back into her black moods worrying about my soul." He snapped his fingers. "Got to get as far away as I can and—"

"And?"

"—and save myself."

"From what?" I asked.

"Everything."

Jenny again broke the silence.

"Why?" she asked.

"Because no one else can save me."

Jenny folded her hands beneath her knees. My sweater slipped off her shoulders.

Jack looked steadily at her. "I could just run away from everything tonight."

He waited for a response, but clearly not from me. I felt as if I were not right there beside the two of them.

I reached up and began to rub Jenny's back; she didn't seem to mind, but she could not look away from Jack.

"Whatever you do," she half whispered to him, "just don't . . . get . . . killed."

"Why not? Everything would be over with."

Jack leaned unsteadily forward; he put his hand on Jenny's knee. His downcast look was genuine. He had had a few beers too many.

"Too many great-looking girls will miss you, Jack," I said, too casually.

He didn't react at all, didn't even smile at the joke. "Think of poor Moira Williams and her big tits," I said.

I expected Jack to rag me, Jenny to rip away my pitiful remark and put me in my place, but neither said anything. Instead, their silence caused me to hold my breath and close my eyes. My clumsy attempt at a joke had trampled over a scary possibility: like any other soldier, Jack could be shot and killed, or blown to bits and erased from the planet. When I opened my eyes, Jack's hand was still lingering on Jenny's knee, as if he could not let go.

The catch in Jenny's voice had unexpectedly grazed something in me, awakened some deeper meaning; and it had also touched something in Jack. That's why not one of us had moved; not my palm warmly against her back, nor his hand on her knee, nor Jenny's eyes from his.

I meant to speak up, to break the spell with an apology for not stating my own fears for his safety, when Jack lifted his big hand away from Jenny's knee and bounced it roughly onto my leg, as if his hand lingering so long on her knee had somehow been a carefree moment, or even a joke. But it was neither, I knew.

Jack jumped up. He regained his familiar gruffness.

"Keep her warm, buddy," he said. "I hear it could rain later tonight."

He stepped over Jenny and me. And the porch creaked with his sudden weight. He bent down to slap my shoulder and bump my head with the heel of his palm, the way he did when we played soccer and I had taken a pass and scored. A few more steps and he leaped over our porch rail. I heard his keys rattle and the door shut.

Jenny picked up my sweater and wrapped it around herself.

"Walk me home now," she said. "It's late."

Under the same night sky, Jenny and I hardly spoke more than a few sentences. Small talk, empty words to keep the quiet from growing between us. She huddled in my sweater to stay warm. Sudden gusts of wind were already edged with the smell of the early snow falling on the distant peaks. We started to walk faster.

In the Chongs' back-door alcove, lit by the moonlight, Jenny removed my sweater and put her key in the lock. Then she turned and fell crushing against me. My back hit the wall. She threw my sweater around my neck and firmly, gently, pulled me against her. She lifted her blouse. Under the thin fabric her fingers guided mine to caress the tips of her nipples. We kissed. Jenny forced her wet tongue between my lips, and I gasped at the thick, moist sensation of flesh. My tongue eagerly pressed back, licked and curled and longed for more. Someone started to clump down the back steps. Breathless, Jenny turned the key in the lock, and left me, abruptly, wounded beneath the stars.

When I was in bed that night, something more than passion began to entangle me. Subdue me. Defeat me. Earlier, I thought I had heard Father crying at his desk. Now I wondered at my own tears.

By the end of July, the show Sekky and Poh-Poh had promised us was ready. Everyone in the family was invited to come up and see the finished chimes.

A spray of colours greeted my eyes: a wall-to-wall length of windchimes hung from a sturdy rope stretched taut and high across Poh-Poh's double bed. I stared at the array of glass glittering before me.

Working meticulously, the Old One had neatly cut the pieces so that half a dozen or more of these pane-weighted threads, each perfectly balanced, swayed and dangled from a cross of thin bamboo.

Happily stretched out on the bed in his short pants, Sekky was staring up at their shifting stillness. With just enough of a draft, each strand would strike a single note. But Little Brother, barely able to hold in his excitement, wanted me to experience something more spectacular.

"Dai-goh," he proudly commanded, "pull the rope."

I did. The dangling fragments of cheap jewellery and glass bits wildly spun and hit, and sang. Finally, with a pinging echo, the last note was struck, and like fragments of prayer, like those messages Poh-Poh still set afire to the Kitchen God, the smoky colours on the wall wavered in the stillness. *First the chaos*, I thought, *and then the stillness before questions can be asked*. Sekky called me back to earth.

"Did you like that?"

I rubbed his tousled head in answer and lifted him up so he could give the rope a jerk. Then I sank back on the bed alongside him. Lying there, looking up, I mused over what had been created from discards and scraps. When the last note was struck, I listened to Sekky breathing beside me and closed my eyes. Stepmother was right: there was no harm done.

Jenny came over with some soup her mother had made for the Old One, and she gushed over the display. Sekky and Poh-Poh gave her a windchime of her choice.

"I'll hang it next to my bed," she said.

Lucky chimes, I thought.

I asked Father how Poh-Poh could have learned such a skill, and he told me she had been taught when she was just a young girl in Old China, before she was sold during the famine to a rich family.

"She told this story to you before," Father said. "That's how she got that small piece of jade she never tires of showing Sekky."

I remembered. The jade was unusual for its colour, and a peony was carved on its quarter-sized face. Poh-Poh had told the story to me when I was even younger than Sekky: the pinkish jade was exactly the colour of the eyes of her first love. He himself was a magician of sorts, a performer of street magic, who stayed some time on her father's farm. In her words, "he was as pale as a ghost," which alone would have fed a lifetime of her fantasies about him. Of course, I now realized that he was an albino.

Poh-Poh fell in love with this much older man, and he became, to her, a kind of phantom lover, a young girl's first infatuation. He avoided sunlight, she told me, and did his magic only in the half-light of dusk. But the magician went away and never came back, though he left in her care the jade peony and promised that he would return for her.

As a boy, I had no mind to remember such tales of unrequited love, nor did I think too much of wind-chimes and jade carvings when I most longed for swords and guns and for stories of the Monkey King and the River Dragon. But to Sekky, who had spent so much time alone with her, and who always listened, enchanted, the story of her past returned.

It was only to be expected that Poh-Poh was now making chimes to bring back all the details of that fairy-tale prince. Like many of the elders I had observed, she was returning to her youth, a time now more vivid to her than the coming end.

~ *E I G H T* ~

I GOT PERMISSION FROM Third Uncle to leave the warehouse at three o'clock, instead of four, to meet Jenny and walk with her to the Carnegie Library, carrying with us our Senior English books.

When Jenny and I walked into the Carnegie that Indian summer Saturday, there were no wheelchair veterans promoting Victory Bonds, there were no community volunteer displays blocking our way to the study tables. Most people were already doing their share. Even the mahjong ladies were holding knitting parties and spending hours wrapping up cotton bandages for the War Relief Campaign.

In our classrooms, we were urged to become involved, to study hard, to exercise every day, to be fit and prepared to use both our brains and our brawn to fight the enemy. There were stories of spies lurking among the Japanese fishermen making their living along the B.C. coast, and even darker suspicions fell upon the owners of the Little Tokyo shops and those living in the three-storey hotels along Powell. To avoid the growing racial harassment of anyone who looked Japanese, and to stop the bullying of Chinese kids too young to defend themselves, Chinatown elders were talking about making up buttons that would read "I AM CHINESE."

People with German-sounding names and anyone with an Eastern European accent was highly suspect. Volunteers, among them Jack and his father, recorded the shape and formation of planes flying overhead, ready to report by phone any suspicious silhouettes. Even Sekky put away my old clippings of *Mandrake the Magician* and *Prince Valiant* for the more serious fun of collecting candy and cigarette cards that taught him the names of weapons and tanks, that illustrated the uniforms and the flags of dozens of countries. He taped his airplane cards in flight formation above his cot. All of us were growing aware that on sea or on land, and always in the sky, enemies were ready to attack.

I had given up a late-afternoon soccer practice to do some serious studying for Mr. Eades's first English test. There were plenty of others like us, books opened, eyes focussed. Jenny pointed to the seat across from hers, and her eyes said, *No fooling around!*

As she pushed my books across the table, I thought that she and I should have, two months ago, declared ourselves an official couple, especially after our fifth double date together. But Jenny didn't want that.

"Too showy," she had told me. "Maybe after we graduate. Next year."

She folded both our school sweaters together and neatly draped them over one of the empty chairs.

It felt good to be sitting across from Jenny. After reading a few thousand words of *Pride and Prejudice*, I nudged off one of my shoes, stretched out one leg, and rubbed against her ankle. Like a tomcat, I began to purr.

She rapped her pencil on the table like a librarian. "Read," she said. Her foot gently pushed mine aside.

A few chapters after the Netherfield Ball, my eyelids began to feel the weight of serious literature. The book suddenly slipped from my hand, or it was pulled away. Jenny was staring right at me.

"What?" I shook my head, wide-eyed, suddenly alert. "What is it?"

"Time for a break." She kept her voice low. "Are you interested in Meiying?"

Meiying was Mrs. Lim's adopted daughter, a girl the same age as we were. She kept to herself and went to Britannia High and was mostly a mystery to me. Beautiful to look at, for sure, with her long hair and long legs, shapely like a runner's; but she never paid too much attention to me.

"What does Meiying have to do with anything?"

Jenny pointed to her novel. "Something Austen says about life made me think of Meiying. About Mrs. Lim, too. About couples."

I straightened up.

"Kiam, do you like her?"

I played along, half whispering my words, using Meiying's English name.

"Well . . . I guess May's lovely to look at."

"Yes. Very. Mother tells me—" her tongue made a quick swipe and her bottom lip suddenly shone like the skin of a wet apple "—that Meiying's been going over to your place a lot. Does she?"

I thought of the slim figure standing in our doorway, asking me if Stepmother was home; the slim figure stepping into our house as Stepmother greeted her. Meiying's silk scarves would flutter as the door closed behind her. She was always polite, polite enough to ignore me standing in front of her. But Stepmother's firm manner of welcoming Meiying, quickly taking her raincoat from my hand, told me that their meeting was none of my business. Meiying had a flawless face, a face that turned heads like Jack's and mine. But she was like one of those beautiful Hindu girls at King Edward, the three who stood together during the sock dance at lunchtime because no boy dared to approach them. Surely they belonged to a more exotic world than the roped-off gym, with the Glenn Miller record playing crazily over the static-plagued sound system. Surely they would laugh at us for thinking we had any chance at all to take their bracelet-jangling hands and waltz away. And you could tell they didn't feel they belonged there, either. Meiying seemed like one of those lonely, distant girls to me.

"May's out of my league."

Jenny's eyebrows lifted: "And I'm not?"

"I mean that she's a little stuck up." *Pride and Prejudice* dropped from her fingers; an open-mouthed smile flashed back at me. I slouched down in my chair, pushed off my other shoe, and shifted both feet against hers. Jenny smiled.

"May doesn't say more than ten words to me. She only comes over to talk with Stepmother."

"About what?" Jenny's shoeless feet rested nicely on top of mine.

"A mystery," I said. "Whenever I'm home early, they always disappear up the stairs." I smirked a bit too soon. "You aren't jealous, are you?"

She ignored the question. "Since Meiying's been back with Mrs. Lim this summer, have you noticed anything different about her?"

I knew Meiying attended schools in Victoria, where she stayed with her mother's old opera ladies. For years, she came home to Mrs. Lim's only during the summer holidays. Third Uncle once saw her at one of Victoria's Chinatown fundraisers; she was giving a short speech in Mandarin and in formal Cantonese. He told Poh-Poh, "Lim Meiying is someone to admire, even from the back of a hall."

"Like opera star," said Poh-Poh, reminding him that Meiying's mother was Mabel Lim, the actress who drank too much and ran away to Toronto with Tommy Fong, a big-time gambler who didn't want any tag-along children.

"Why do you think Meiying decided to go to Britannia for her final year?"

I shrugged.

"What do she and your Stepmother talk about?"

"Told you, don't know."

Jenny tapped her fingers on the table. No one at the other tables was paying any attention to us. If they had looked up to see our bent heads and tangled fingers, they might have assumed we were a couple.

"Have you ever run into her when she's come downstairs?"

"Once." A cartoon flashbulb went off in my head. "I smelled Three Flowers on her."

Jenny knew that I was a sucker for perfume. On recent double-dates to the Jazz Hut, whenever we danced together, Jenny's trace of Chanel had me leaning in and breathing deeply against the nape of her neck.

"Three Flowers perfume?"

I nodded.

"Honestly, Kiam, you know the name of May's perfume!"

"Stepmother uses Three Flowers. I walk May to the door sometimes and—"

Now she seemed caught between being playful and being serious with me. She hesitated. "Should I be telling *you* anything at all?"

Before I could answer, a binder-sized sketchbook came sliding down the long table. With a drawing pencil tucked behind his ear, Jeff Eng watched with satisfaction as the large pages fluttered shut at Jenny's elbow.

"Tell Kiam everything, Jenny."

Jeff slumped into the chair beside me. Whenever he could excuse himself from his father's garage, Jeff would end up in the third-floor museum finishing painstaking drawings for his portfolio. Even after he changed his clothes, he smelled of grease or gasoline, but the staff didn't seem to mind. A few of the librarians even asked to keep some of his drawings.

"Tell Kiam everything you know about Meiying," Jeff repeated.

"Mind your own beeswax," Jenny said, looking down at her notes.

Jeff took in my feigned attempt to keep going with Austen. "Can you stand reading her, Kiam?"

"Have to," I said. "One more year to go."

"When they finally let us Chinatown boys fight this war, I'm joining up to make some real money."

"First," Jenny said, without looking up from her book, "come back alive."

"Yeah . . . and after that. I'll take painting and illustration at Central Tech."

Jeff flicked his sketchbook open. Jenny took one look at the open page and shrank away. I almost turned away, too.

Staring up at us was the unravelled head of an Egyptian mummy. On one whole page, Jeff had drawn the decayed features of the mummy as if it were alive and raging against its shrivelled condition. The sockets were so expertly drawn, so sombre and darkly toned, that their deep emptiness seemed to stare at us with ghostly eyes. The mummy's rags, cut away from the parched face, lay squirming on the page.

"Looks like a case of bad laundry," I said.

Jeff frowned. "A die-hard Chinaman like you would know about laundry."

Jenny kicked. Jeff let out a mock yelp.

"Are you going to let your girl kick your best friend like that?"

"You're on your own, pal," I said.

"Hey, why not kick our local honky? Jack came here with me." He looked around. "He must still be down in the stacks. My sister and Martha are there too."

"Let me see the drawing," Jen said. "Seriously."

Jeff obliged.

Flashing through my mind was a picture of Jack and me at the Rex when we were just kids, how we almost pissed in our pants screaming "Watch out! Watch out!" as Karloff shuffled down the castle hall.

"Someday," Jeff said, "all three of us are going to look like that."

"Yeah," I said. "But we'll have better laundry."

A swift kick.

"You behave," Jenny said. "We won't be doing laundry or waiting on tables if we get an education."

"Or if we join up," Jeff said. "The government has to give us some kind of recognition. We'll be able to work in good jobs like everyone else. And whatever my father thinks, I'll still be an artist."

Everything would be solved, I thought, laughing to myself.

"I'm going to see if I can find Martha and Susan," Jenny said. "The library closes in less than an hour."

She had heard Jeff go on about his hopes for the future too many times. I should have left with her and let Jeff bleed over his drawing, but it wasn't the time to leave him alone. Jeff had already come to blows with his father for spending his father's money on art supplies instead of on the mechanic's tools he was supposed to have bought for himself.

For what seemed forever, I stared down at that drawing of his, listened to him commenting on shading and cross-hatching and how tricky it was to create the shadows in the eye sockets *just so.* I couldn't sit still any longer.

"I'm going downstairs," I said. "Can you guard all this stuff for us?"

"Definitely. Oh, if you want to say hello to Jack, you should try the morgue. You know where it is, don't you?"

"*Morgue?*"

Jeff smirked. "That's what they call the room where they keep the dead newspapers and magazines. It's way in the back, behind the two tallest shelves. You go down this deep ramp. There's a big double door. Can't miss it."

I just wanted Jenny to walk home with me. And, if he was ready, for Jack to walk with us, too.

I found myself standing in a space between the tall shelves, at the far end of an enormous and mostly deserted basement, standing on a steep ramp and looking down through the slightly opened double doors. Beyond some more shelves, lit by an overhanging lamp in a crisscross of light and shadow, I could see him leaning against her, his big back facing me.

The shelves surrounding them, standing at all angles, must have made them feel that no one could see them. Jack's hand was under the familiar blouse. Jenny was squirming, kissing him, her hand rubbing the back of his head, and he was pushing hard, back and forth.

Back and forth.

Jeff was still working intently on his drawing. I opened *Pride and Prejudice* and pretended to read. I would wait for her. I would wait. I wondered if she would walk up by herself. Or would they come back together? I would smile when she saw me, as if I had seen nothing. I would not say too much; I would not know too much.

Jeff closed his sketchbook and started putting away his pencils.

"Stop daydreaming, Kiam."

I looked up. Jenny was coming towards us.

I gathered up my things.

"We've got to go," said Jenny and grabbed her books and my arm.

As we stepped out of the building, the fresh air hit us. Jenny took a deep breath.

"Let's not talk," she said.

By the third week of September, the lingering warmth of summer was replaced by a layer of cold air that sank into the Lower Mainland and overnight silvered the city landscape. This was a record-breaking frost, arriving months before such conditions would have been expected. A sudden early snowfall had blanketed the highest peaks of the North Shore mountains, and people began to dress in their fall coats and jackets.

The freak cold created inversions, so that fog and mists clung to the ground, and leaves, still green with summer, fell. On her high porch, two rickety staircases up, Mrs. Lim's yellow roses dropped their petals and floated down to the street. Mrs. O'Connor's garden began to fade. Leaves and petals swirled into tiny mounds against the curb and settled into the corners of our front porch. People were saying that the war must have changed the conditions in the upper atmosphere, the blast and heat of all those bombs altering the weather. No one could recall such an early cold.

During that first day of frost, Poh-Poh stayed home with Sekky, who had been told once again he was not strong enough to start school. A new set of home-study readers and blank exercise books were sent over to our house, and Little Brother didn't seem to mind too much. But the situation worried Father, who wondered aloud to Stepmother and me if the Old One was not having too much influence on Sekky.

"Old ways," said Father, "not Gold Mountain ways."

To add to his burden of concerns, Poh-Poh told Father that her time was near: the frost was the first of the signs that she had been expecting. It was time to complete her final windchime, the one she told Sekky she had longed to finish from the very beginning of their laneway adventures. She cautioned him that it would be the one that would be raised only after she had died.

"Why?" Sekky had asked.

"So my ghost can hear its music and come back to you."

Sekky later told me that this made perfect sense to him. And it made more sense when Poh-Poh whispered into his ear that this final, most glorious windchime was a Number One Secret, and that although he had been helping her with its construction all these months, helping her to slide the unwieldy parts under her bed, only she could finish it.

Another sign appeared. A new janitor had lit the large furnace in the Chinese Presbyterian Church to warm up the building. In the middle of the night, hours after the man had gone home, the whole building burnt down.

"How sad all beautiful windows lost," big Mrs. Lim told Poh-Poh at the kitchen table while Sekky slurped up his morning bowl of *jook*. "How lucky church be empty."

Poh-Poh smiled at the news. Sekky smiled too.

Right after Mrs. Lim left our house that morning, Sekky and Poh-Poh put on extra sweaters under their coats and went to scout the smoking site. They picked up fragments of half-faced men and angels, portions of raised hands in blessing, and eyes opened wide with bliss. Poh-Poh was ready to complete her work.

I was in the locker room at school when six-foot Spencer Langley said he had spotted Sekky and Poh-Poh rummaging in the ruins, and he said in his show-off Latin that Grandmother was *non compos mentis*. I started sputtering some response when Jack rushed up from behind me, set to punch Spence out. I grabbed his shoulder and told him to lay off.

"Just joking," Spence said, backing off into the shower.

"You okay?" Jack asked me.

"Fine," I said. "Thanks." I grabbed my stuff, flashed my textbook at him, and walked away as if I were late for chemistry.

When I sat down in the lab, my heart was still pounding. I had told myself not to remember. Jenny loved me, surely, as much as she could ever love someone like Jack. Everyone knew he could have a hundred or more girls. She must have known that he would betray her as easily as he betrayed all the girls he dated. Moira had been the fifth in a line.

Across the aisle, seats were filling up. Mr. Ainsley put on his lab coat and started to take supplies from the storage cabinet.

I tried to focus, but my mind would not rest: Jack was just a guy who might never settle down, who could never be faithful. He and Jenny had acted impulsively. Nothing had been planned between them. And if I believed that nothing had really changed between Jenny and me, if I remained steady and didn't rock the boat, it would be the last time they would be alone together like that. What had happened would never happen again. I was the one who loved Jenny and would always be faithful. She knew that.

"Mr. Chen?"

"Yes, sir?"

"We're waiting for you to open your textbook . . ."

I told myself, when I calmed down, when I remembered how much Jack also meant to me, that I could still think of him as my best friend. He thought he was coming to my defence with Spence. I should drop over to his house, catch up on his news, and thank him. I opened my book.

As it turned out, I didn't get over to Jack's that evening. Instead, Jenny came by to warn me that a couple had come to her store to buy some film. They'd asked her if she knew about this old Chinese lady and the little boy. What time might the two show up at the ruins?

Just the night before, Father and Stepmother had asked me to speak to Sekky. When they'd left for work, I'd shaken my young brother awake.

"Father told me to tell you to stay home and do your school work. Too dangerous out at the church. Don't go there any more."

"Why not?"

"Poh-Poh or you could slip and fall. The frost makes everything icy."

"That's okay," he said. "Grandmama says she got everything she needed. I even found a piece of an angel's wing for her."

I heard sighing. It was me.

"Don't do that," Sekky said.

"Do what?"

"Sound like Father."

I did not protest. How could I not sound like Father? I was more Gold Mountain than Old China. Father appreciated that I, First Son, would do my duty to teach my siblings what was true and what mattered.

"Don't worry so much about Sekky and the Old One," Jenny said. "When you think too much, you get so quiet. You scare me. Stop it."

"What's wrong with thinking?"

"Gets you nowhere."

A light kiss landed on my forehead as if I were as simple as my little brother.

I pulled Jenny against me, felt how real she was, the smell and colour of her hair, the way her one leg moved between mine, the laughter in her eyes, and the way she was smiling, the way my hand cushioned the back of her head and our foreheads bumped, her lips leaned towards my own, and her eyes reflected the lamplight, and all this realness made me want to hold her forever, exactly as I was, entangled and lost, silent and hard. Back and forth.

The fall winds were harsh, and winter was coming. Father and Stepmother were worried that the Old One might leave the house for more treks through alleyways and ruins and endanger both her life and Sek-Lung's. Father decided it was time to speak up.

After the three youngest ones were in bed, Stepmother and I watched as Poh-Poh sat silently in her rocking chair while Father carefully explained the untenable situation to her.

After a long pause, she said, "Yes, yes, I stay home. I wait for the last sign."

"Which sign?" I asked her as patiently as I could.

"A sign that my friend the magician has come back for me."

"But—"

"I have everything now," the Old One said, gently cutting me off. "I have three grandsons. Good family. Plenty food. I rest and wait. I have long life already."

I saw Father take out his handkerchief. Stepmother took Poh-Poh's arm, and they went upstairs.

Father said to me, "First Son, the Old One is going to leave us very soon." He stayed as calm as he could manage, and waited for my questions.

I had none. Jenny and I had spoken about Poh-Poh's leaving, about her death. I found myself resisting the thought.

"Everyone dies, Kiam," Jenny had said to me when I spoke of Poh-Poh's shaking hands and slowed steps. "Everything ends."

"It can't be that simple," I said, though I felt she was right. "Things never are that simple."

"The other day," Father said, "the Old One asked me how you and Jenny are doing. She say Jenny so much like herself."

"We're okay," I said.

"I know she like you, Kiam-Kim." For emphasis, Father tapped his glasses with his forefinger. "Her mother tell Poh-Poh Jenny think about you all night and all day. Just you."

A lie, I thought, and the painful truth of that assessment made me flinch. My silence gave me away.

"Be careful, Kiam-Kim," Father continued, with a small laugh. "Love too much, and love make you suffer." He removed his glasses and pinched his nose, a gesture he always made when there was something too important or too personal to share. "Gai-mou and I," he began, "we . . . *like* each other. Very much, of course."

"Liking each other, is that enough?"

"Yes, all these years, that has been enough."

"But you loved my mother?"

Stepmother came into the parlour. Father and I had not even heard her coming down the stairs. She sat down on the sofa close to Father and picked up her knitting from a basket at her feet. Poh-Poh's blue sweater was almost finished. Father had stopped talking, as if he were wondering how much she had heard, though I didn't think that he had said anything that was not true. He had assessed his twelve years with Stepmother, seen her raise the two children that were her own, watched her care for the Old One, and liked how she stood by him. When Stepmother began to talk, it became apparent that she had heard his every word.

"Yes, Kiam-Kim," she said, "your father *like* me. Like me very much. That is true."

Stepmother stared at the two of us, as if to decide whether to say more. She herself must have thought a long time about her own situation, accepted things as they were. She was Father's helpmate; she was our *gai-mou*. The knitting needles began click-clicking. Her beautiful eyes focussed on her work; her long fingers moved rapidly, confidently, as if from those hands the voice would take strength, at last, to speak out.

"Your father love only First Wife, Kiam-Kim," she said. Her head bent lower. "Some nights your father, half asleep, he call me by your mother's name."

And her tears fell.

Father gently reached for Stepmother's hand. The blue sweater collapsed in a heap in her lap.

There was nothing I could have said that would have changed the situation. I left them alone and climbed the stairs to my room.

By some miracle, just before supper the next day we were all at home at the same time. Everyone was busy. Sewing supplies for uniforms and knapsacks were held up by shortages, so Stepmother was sent home from work that afternoon and was pinning up Liang's school dress for her. Father was at his desk writing furiously to meet another deadline; the wastebasket was filled with his crumpled efforts. And I was home interrupting Father to show off my latest 90 in the weekly math test.

Father held the paper up for Jung to see.

"I got an *Excellent* last week!" he said, shadow-boxing with the lamp on the floor to help outline every imaginary blow. He bounced on the balls of his feet like his hero, Joe Louis. Sekky was in the parlour cutting out some newspaper pictures of tanks and planes to paste into his scrapbook. Poh-Poh was busy in the kitchen.

Liang said how she wanted her dress hemmed closer to her knees.

"Not possible," Stepmother said. She was rushing to finish so that they both could join the Old One in the kitchen and help prepare dinner.

I looked up from my math book and watched everyone and imagined how Jenny would fit in, and how, one day, she would have a big family with me. We had joked about having six kids, if I was capable.

The crash of garbage cans from the back porch startled us. An alley cat screeched, its cry almost half-human, and then another crash struck our ears as one of the galvanized cans fell over, spilling its contents, its lid, and store of empty tin cans clattering down the porch steps.

Father looked at me sternly, as if I had forgotten to set the cans up properly. More screeches. Father threw his papers down.

"Those damn cats!"

I sighed. Someone had forgotten again to lay the heavy plank over the two pails so the four-legged pests would not knock them over. I started to get up when I was hit by Poh-Poh's intense cry: "*Aaaiiyaah!*"

Father ran past me. I rushed into the kitchen after him.

The Old One stood at the threshold of the back door, holding her head in her hands, her shoulders shaking.

"He's come back!" she said. "I saw him!"

"*Hai bin-goh?*" Father asked. "Saw who?"

"Him," she said, her Toishan words cracking with remorse. "He came staring at me with his eyes . . . and I cursed him!"

I pushed aside the curtains and peered out the back window and saw through the murky evening light the shape of a large white tomcat—the biggest one I had ever seen—crouched halfway down the steep steps, looking up at me. A foggy mist swirled at the bottom of the steps. The wily creature licked its lips, its hollow-looking eyes glowing like fire.

"It's just that new alley cat," I explained. "It's been hanging around for days."

I did nothing more. I would have shouted at the animal to scat, tossed the other lid crashing down the stairs to scare the scavenger off, but the way Poh-Poh looked past the half-opened door, the way she shook her head slowly, sadly, left me unable to move. She patted her wrinkled forehead as if she wanted desperately to erase some memory. When the white tom bounded off the steps, meowing, Poh-Poh looked frantic: her dark eyes had seen more than a cat. She stumbled over to Father and put her small hand on his arm.

"Too late," she said to him, her words quaking in her throat. "Too . . . too late . . ."

Father held her close and said, gently but firmly, "Tell me what you saw."

Poh-Poh looked up at him. "I saw . . ." Her eyes were wet. She whispered to him, as if she were a child, "It had . . . pink eyes."

The eyes of the pure white tomcat came back to me. Their glow was odd. *Albino*, I thought.

"Please clean up the mess, Kiam," Stepmother said. "And close the door. Too cold for Poh-Poh."

I looked down to the bottom step. Garbage was strewn everywhere. The cat had snuck back. When I bent to pick up one of the lids, it crept away and vanished into the mist.

The back door squeaked open, then shut. Stepmother had sent Jung-Sum out to help me. I pointed to the shiny lid at the bottom of the steps. He started down the first step, then turned around, as if he wanted to talk.

"What?" I said, impatient.

"Dai-goh, why did Poh-Poh look so scared?"

I shrugged. "Just a cat," I said. "The size of the thing must have rattled her old bones." Jung raised his eyebrows in disbelief. "Poh-Poh's just a little confused," I said.

"Kiam, she just told Father she's going to die."

"Oh, *again?*" I smiled. "It's just her old way of talking."

"Dai-goh." His murmuring grabbed my attention. "This time it's true."

"Why do you say that?"

"Father believes her this time."

"Go pick up the lid," I said.

Peering through the window into the kitchen, I saw Father and Stepmother holding on to the Old One. Father was wiping his eyes with his sleeve. I pressed my ear against the back door: Poh-Poh was saying over and over again the same words, shaking her head—*pink eyes, the cat, pink eyes*. She pushed away and went to the sink and began rinsing out some greens. The crisis was suddenly over. Stepmother hesitated, then picked up the rice pot and went into the pantry. Father paused a moment, too, making sure that the Old One had settled down. When he saw the greens hit the colander, he went back to his desk as if nothing was wrong.

I picked up some tins and newspaper bundles full of food scraps and stuffed them back into the cans. I didn't want to think about Grandmother's breakdown.

When the dinner dishes were finally put away, and Poh-Poh had taken Sekky up to her room, closing the door behind them, I looked up from my Chinese brush work.

"Poh-Poh saw a ghost?" I asked Father, getting straight to the point.

"The Old One thinks she did." He shuffled uneasily at his corner desk. "You know how it is with old people."

"Jung-Sum heard her say she was going to die."

"Yes . . . that's what she says."

"Do you think so?"

"Poh-Poh thinks that person she loved—that magician—has come back for her."

I remembered his last words to her. *When you are ready, I come back for you.*

"She thinks the white cat—?"

"Yes." Father put down his fountain pen. "The problem, Kiam-Kim, is that she cursed that cat and thinks she has cursed her own fate by chasing it away."

"What kind of curse?"

"A very wicked Toishan curse to send it away."

"How wicked?"

"The powerful kind she claims killed—you remember?—Mistress Mean-Mouth. She didn't want the garbage spilled again."

"It's not logical, Father."

"These things never are, Kiam-Kim, but they have power over Poh-Poh."

Two glowing eyes pierced through the dark caves of my brain. I thought of Poh-Poh and Sekky upstairs behind the closed door. I took in a deep, deep breath and asked "Should Sekky be helping Poh-Poh with her last windchime?"

"It's good for Sek-Lung to know about death, don't you think?"

I thought of the times Stepmother, with two fingers, had held Baby Sekky's mouth open when he could barely breathe; and Poh-Poh bent over the crib and with her own mouth forced air into his twelve-month-old lungs. I thought of the hours the two women cradled him and rocked him back to life, again and again. I thought of all the talk-stories Poh-Poh breathed into each one of her grandchildren, as if they were the air she herself depended upon. And I thought of that day when I turned fifteen and scorned to be at her side to listen to one more silly story.

"You listen again one day, Kiam-Kim," Poh-Poh had said to me. "I no be here then."

When I went upstairs, I could hear the sharp crunch of pieces of glass being cut in the Old One's room.

Poh-Poh began coughing badly, worse than when it had started six or seven months before. But this time she refused any medicine from Dr. Chu. "No use," she said. Even Mrs. Lim could not persuade her to swallow the special herbal tea she had concocted. The mahjong ladies came and saw how hopeless things were. They patted Father's hand, and Mrs. Chong urged him to send Grandmother to the Catholic Home for Chinese on Campbell Avenue. But Poh-Poh refused to leave her bedroom, and Sekky, who sat by her bed every night, refused to let her go. Father asked Third Uncle what else could be done.

"I ask Sister Fung," he said.

Teresa Fung was one of the nuns who operated a dispensary and home for the Chinese on Pender Street. Sister Teresa often went around to the local gambling houses and stores, shaking a tin can and asking for donations. Once, Father and I ran into her at the Lucky Fortune Club when I was doing the same thing for the Free China effort.

"Wherever help is needed," Sister Teresa said to me in excellent Cantonese, "that is where good people must go."

One afternoon, I found the small woman in her nun's black habit sitting beside the Old One. Before she arrived, Sekky had been sent over to Mrs. Lim's house to fetch some herbal soup. The nun, nodding her caped head, and Poh-Poh, sitting against her pillows, spoke quietly and thoughtfully with each other, in a dialect that I did not understand.

Sister Teresa handed me a piece of paper with

Chinese and English writing and, rubber-stamped in English, "Please Admit to St. Paul's." Then she prayed for a few minutes over the Old One. Poh-Poh shut her eyes and said nothing more. Sister made the sign of the cross and smiled at me. I watched her go soundlessly down the stairs, where Father opened the front door for her. The elders thought of nuns as crows or black ghosts. As she stepped out, she lifted her habit and seemed, quickly, to fly away.

When Father came upstairs, I handed him the sister's note. Stepmother asked what it said.

"There's no room left at the Catholic Home," Father explained. "This note will allow us to take Poh-Poh to the basement shelter at St. Paul's Hospital. They have a doctor there."

Sekky arrived back with the soup and asked the Old One what was going on.

"Not much," Poh-Poh told him. Father raised her pillow so she could talk more clearly. Sekky held the soup spoon inches from her mouth until she relented.

"A good spirit in the dress of a black crow came to pray for me," she told him.

"What happened, Grandmama?"

"We talked, Little One, then I sent her away."

Sekky looked up at me.

"Dai-goh, did you see a black crow?"

Against my better judgment, I nodded.

Neither Father nor Stepmother could make a difference. Jenny told me her mother said it was probably hopeless. No one could dissuade someone from dying if the person believed the time had come. Jenny brought the Old One some candy and kissed her forehead and held her hand.

Poh-Poh's wrinkled complexion grew paler, her hacking and coughing at night more violent. Third Uncle sent over a herbalist, who told Father the illness was pneumonia. She had caught some very bad *feng shui*, he explained, and the house was too drafty. "Best to go to St. Paul's," the herbalist instructed.

Around two that morning, Father, with Sister Teresa's note clutched in his hand, woke me up to help him carry Poh-Poh down the steps and into a taxi. I put on my kimono. Between us, her small body swayed on our crossed arms like a bundled sack. She was so light, so small in stature, I thought we were carrying only a wisp of her spirit.

"You tall as Father, Kiam-Kim."

Sticking out from a shroud of blankets, strands of the Old One's white hair lifted in the night wind. She was not coughing any more; with each descending step, she wheezed, half-in, half-out. Before the taxi pulled away, her trembling hand touched my arm. I wondered what she was thinking about. I had been thinking of Jenny, wishing she was here with me. A light turned on at the O'Connors'. I could see Jack's silhouette in the upstairs window. I had forgotten to thank his mother for the vase of flowers she had sent over. I waved at the shadow looking down at me; the shadow waved back.

☙ ❧

Father, Stepmother, and I took turns staying with Poh-Poh in the basement clinic of St. Paul's. She lay in one of the emergency cots, in a segregated area with three other women, separated from the men's side by drawn grey curtains. The fold-away sat directly under a long rectangle of window. Indians and blacks, Asians of every variety—all those who were not permitted entry into regular hospitals—ended up, if there were any spaces available, at the segregated Home for Chinese, or at St. Joseph's Oriental Hospital, or in the grey-painted basement of St. Paul's.

In the October light, pouring down from a bank of basement windows, the tall trees growing along the side-walk threw fragments of shadow across the cement floor. After I relieved Father, my nose quickly adjusted to the antiseptic smell—a chlorine smell like the chemistry lab at school—and my ears soon grew deaf to the loud hacking and constant coughing throughout the ward.

On the second day, Poh-Poh told Father that Stepmother and I must go to her. "It is time," she said.

I sat in the wooden chair with my homework on my lap. Hoping for the best, I called, not too loudly, "I'm here by your side, Poh-Poh."

She stirred. One of the nuns came over to me.

"Rub her hands, son. Get her blood circulating."

I did, gently.

Just when I had almost given up believing that she had enough energy to stay awake on my shift, the Old One opened her eyes. Her hand felt so fragile and bony, but the smile was familiar, encouraging. I smoothed the wrinkles on her brow.

"That cat with the pink eyes came back to the house, Poh-Poh."

"How so?"

"He came back three times. Sekky even told the cat you were at the hospital."

"Not . . . not possible."

"Third Uncle said he saw it, too, when he came to find out how you were doing."

I wasn't making it up. Third Uncle had seen the cat hop off our front porch and run down Keefer Street. I knew Poh-Poh was thinking of the curses she had spewed in rage upon the white cat. Foul curses she knew she could not take back. I kept telling her how clearly I, too, had seen its pink eyes.

"My juggler . . .," she said.

"Perhaps your curses do not work in Gold Mountain."

"Perhaps . . .," she said, as if she did not hear the lightness in my tone, "perhaps for me, Kiam-Kim, *he has come back* . . ."

A wetness brightened her eyes. Her head seemed to lift from the pillow, then slowly fall back. I had not the heart to tell her how foolish she was to think about such things. She caught my doubting look.

"You wait," she said, and her voice sounded stronger. She pointed at my textbook. "Work," she said and closed her eyes to nap.

I rustled the pages of my biology book and loudly shuffled my notes so Poh-Poh could hear how hard I was working as she fell asleep. After a few minutes, when I happened to catch the shadows dancing from the window above us, a white cat pushed its face against the pane. Of course, I said nothing. Its eyes were clearly not pink.

After an hour, Stepmother showed up, wearing her factory smock. An oversized envelope stuck out of her handbag. My mind went back to the time she arrived to be with us and pulled out a similar envelope to hand over to the Old One. I recalled the tiny silver butterfly she had given me that day. Stepmother still looked the same to me, her delicate features unblemished by the years.

Poh-Poh gestured for Stepmother to help her sit up. I pushed the cot close to the wall and placed the Old One's pillow at an angle so she could lean against me as well. The grey hospital gown heightened the lack of colour in her cheeks, but I was happy to see her effort and the way the cloudiness in her eyes seemed to diminish.

"Let First Son see," Poh-Poh said.

Stepmother hesitated. I wondered what was going on. Reluctantly, Stepmother slipped out from the large envelope a photograph I had never seen before. Stepmother held it up. It was a formal picture of a middle-aged man dressed in a mandarin coat. The picture was cracked with age, but every feature was clear. Stepmother handed me the photograph.

"Look at that face," Poh-Poh said.

The man looked like Father, but was not him.

"Who is this?"

Stepmother said, "Your grandfather."

I laughed. Impossible. The full-length portrait showed a wealthy man dressed in a fine robe embroidered with dragons, with carved jade pendants hanging from his neck. He sat posed in front of a carved ebony screen. Even in the black-and-white photo one could see that the panels of painted flying cranes were inlaid with ivory and gold. The elegant long nails on his hands suggested he had never had to work a day in his life.

"Who is he really?"

"Look again at the face."

The high forehead, the wide nostrils and broad cheeks . . . the way the hair beneath the mandarin cap seemed to slightly curl . . . I was looking at Father's twin. The rich clothing had distracted me.

"Patriarch Chen," Poh-Poh said. She leaned back to study my expression. "I was a grown woman in his service when he forced himself on me." She sensed my disbelief. "Do you understand?"

Stepmother quietly said, "That was how things were in Old China, Kiam-Kim."

"Then Patriarch found Lord Jesus," Poh-Poh said. "Or Lord Jesus found him."

Stepmother tried to help me make sense of things: "Kiam-Kim, how do you think Poh-Poh come to Gold Mountain with you? Old and poor house-servants like her do not leave China."

The Old One smiled. "Your father a smarter boy

than the Patriarch's two ox-brained sons. He send your father to school. But the family of Patriarch Chen," Poh-Poh said, "his two sons and three daughters, his two wives and his concubine, they all hate us, Kiam-Kim. Heart-bitter that slave woman and her bastard son favoured by the Patriarch. They say his new Christian ways make him crazy. They say it is madness to treat a slave and her bastard as if they deserved kindness."

Poh-Poh half shut her eyes. Stepmother urged her to rest, but the Old One persisted, the front of her grey gown rising and falling with the effort.

"And so, when Third Uncle ask for a family, for peace in his own household, Master Chen send us all away to Gold Mountain."

The Old One's tone revealed neither regret nor sorrow, but her voice grew raspy, her energy a low tide slipping away: "Such things I tell . . . Now, no more talk."

The words had been abrupt. The odd silence that followed was unfathomable; secrets were not always necessary to explain. Enough had been said. This much I should know and no more.

I thought of the tiny shoes that Poh-Poh kept in her trunk that were once worn by my mother. I thought of the Old One as a small woman cornered by Patriarch Chen. The portrait felt heavy. I could not erase Father's exact features staring back at me. Stepmother gently unclenched my fingers and took the photo from my hand. Someone coughed, hacked, and antiseptic burned my tongue. Poh-Poh, her eyes now completely closed and her cheeks collapsed, looked exhausted but at peace. I knew I was only to listen and not speak; to observe and, somehow, accept.

I thought how I had never called the Old One anything but Poh-Poh, as if she were my mother's mother, and not, properly, Nai-Nai, my father's mother. Years ago, when I asked about this, I was told all the immigration ghost papers, the *gai-gee*, all those false documents made it so. For me, as a child, to slip up and call the Old One Nai-Nai would have caused the demon customs officers to scrutinize our papers and ship all three of us back to Old China. Documents also made Liang and Sekky, and even Jung-Sum, my blood family. We have lived only as a family, I told myself. How could all this matter?

Why did I need to know at all?

Poh-Poh began to breathe with difficulty. I looked at Stepmother to guess her thoughts, but she was busy helping Poh-Poh to lie back down on the cot. I removed the pillow and placed it under the small head. The Old One smiled, contented.

"Does Father know all this?"

"Yes," Stepmother said. "And so does Third Uncle."

"Then it doesn't change anything," I said. "Nothing has changed."

"You know now that your father endured many humiliations in China. That has changed."

Something else did, too, but I hadn't noticed it at the time. My love for each of them deepened and grew. But I was thinking of the Old One when she was a young girl,

and I thought of Patriarch Chen and how he must have
. . . I wanted to rip up and burn the photograph.
Stepmother saw how my eyes must have turned hard.

"Poh-Poh has forgiven the Patriarch," she said.
"Everything has turned out for the better."

"How is that possible?"

"You, Kiam-Kim, are here and . . ."

"And?"

"And Poh-Poh told me that you will marry Jenny."

A thick knot began to unravel. Its tightness had
been there inside my gut ever since that afternoon in
the library basement. I thought that time would
smooth things over, push away my knowledge of what I
had seen, but I knew now that what I had seen beyond
those half-closed library doors in those few seconds
would be with me forever. Yet Poh-Poh had not only
experienced the worst, she had survived, had even forgiven the abuses committed against her, and had taken
her life to be her own. The bitterness of the past never
left her, but her strength was to see that her survival
would mean something more to those she loved than
it would mean to her. She had gone further than I
thought I ever could, or wanted to. I hadn't forgiven
the two closest friends in my life: I had accommodated
them. Instead of resignation, or feeling any sense of
weakness, a strange relief came over me. I had been
doing my best.

I sighed.

Poh-Poh's eyelids lifted up, and her pupils grew
large and bright. Her voice was clear, triumphant, and
she stared beyond the grey ceiling of St. Paul's.

"Patriarch Chen had only two *say-no doi*—two dead-brained sons—but I have three grandsons!

"Have sons, Kiam-Kim," she said to me. "Have many tiger sons with Jenny."

I smiled; then, at her look of joy and irrepressible triumph, I broke into laughter. How was it possible that Poh-Poh could ever leave us?

The next day, Father came home unexpectedly early. Stepmother met him at the front door and took his hat and coat. They spoke at once in hushed tones. Sekky stood at the top of the stairs, a toy tank in his hand. His mouth dropped open. I ran up to him and picked him up.

"It had to be," I told him. "Poh-Poh was very, very tired."

Father came upstairs and into the Old One's room. With Sekky in my arms, we watched father from the doorway. He slipped out from under her bed a large, flat carton, the kind that ceremonial Chinese robes were once packed in. He drew aside the lace curtains in the window and lifted from the box Poh-Poh's windchime. In the sullen universe of her small room, the glass pieces spun and sang.

A few weeks later, over cups of tea around the kitchen table, Mrs. Lim pointed out how the white cat had never been seen again.

"Very powerful curse," she said. "Very powerful."

Father bowed his head. Stepmother said nothing but began to sort out the root vegetables Mrs. Lim had generously brought over from her garden. Yes, she would be very happy to stay for dinner with the family. Stepmother put on a familiar apron. Out of the corner of my eye I glimpsed the tattered Kitchen God tacked on the wall above the stove.

~ *N I N E* ~

ALL THE YEARS THAT FATHER and Poh-Poh lived their lives together in Old China, they had survived through unspeakable hardships and borne the burden of secrets. And when the three of us arrived in Gold Mountain, the two of them lived their lives in front of me as if nothing were out of place. Even when Stepmother came to join us, I grew up protected by the comfort of their silence. Whole families and all of Chinatown grew used to such silences. And when finally it was time to tell me some of the truths from the past, I was ready to listen, ready to accept my share of silence. In all the ways they lived their lives, survivors like Poh-Poh and Stepmother, Third Uncle and Father, and those elders who hacked their breath away, they were all saying, *Sail, paddle, swim, but push forward to shore. Do not drown in the past.*

At the Armstrong & Company Funeral Home on Dunlevy, during the Old One's service, I watched Jenny nod to acknowledge Jack, but when he approached the two of us, she turned her back on him and said something to Mrs. Leong about the beautiful flowers arranged around the casket. When I next had a chance to look for the only blond head in the crowded room, Jack was standing near the far door, offering his handkerchief to Liang and touching Jung-Sum's arm. Then he jostled through the crowd and disappeared.

Looking at Jenny with her high cheekbones and wilful eyes, I wanted to have the tiger sons Poh-Poh had urged upon her and me. What I had witnessed in the basement of the Carnegie Library was in the past, and would stay in the past. We would live on. And our mutual silence would comfort not only ourselves but those tiger sons of ours.

My youngest brother, though, was struggling to put old ghosts to rest.

"Sekky thinks he sees Poh-Poh," I explained to Jenny.

"No one should be surprised," she said. "I'm not."

We were walking home after seeing *Rebecca*, by coincidence a tale of a haunting, and Jeff and his date had dropped us off a block from Jenny's place so we could have some time by ourselves. Because of the blackout restrictions, the street lamps were soon to be turned off, but there was little to worry about. A bright harvest moon hung above us. The grey mist skirting Keefer Street and curling away from the Strathcona school buildings made me think of the fog-shrouded Cornish coast and of the haunted characters who could not let go of the dead Rebecca. Like Sekky, haunted by the Old One.

"Because the Old One promised to come back to him, Sekky's imagining that he sees her," I said. "Don't you think so?"

There was only the sound of our footsteps slowing down on the pavement. The damp night air tasted of salt.

Jenny let go of my hand and threaded her arm through mine. It was a comfortable fit.

"So poor Sekky sees Poh-Poh," she began again.

"I don't mean he actually sees her."

"Why not?"

"Sekky *believes* that he sees her, but it's all in his imagination."

"Under stress," Jenny countered, "people see things."

I took a deep breath. "I think it's because Poh-Poh told him too many ghost stories."

"And you?"

"Yes, she passed them along to me, too, except Father taught me to be more sensible about what I heard from her."

"Sensible?" said Jenny, as if she didn't care for my answer.

"Something the matter with 'sensible'?"

"Yes . . . and no."

There was nothing more to say. We were young and slowly pacing our steps, arm in arm, and the moon was bright. She looked splendid in her long red coat. The air was damp, chilly, but we didn't mind.

But something sinister stirred to life in me, and I blurted out that Jack and I had bumped into each other in front of our houses that morning and that he and Moira Williams seemed to have moved past any misunderstandings they may have had.

"Good," Jenny said too quickly.

"I'm happy for Jack," I said. "Moira and he look great together—they make a perfect couple. Can't you see them married one day?"

"You're his best friend," Jenny said. "You should know."

Her grip on my arm tightened. I thought it best to change direction.

"What should I do about Sekky's ghost sightings?" I said.

"Nothing," she said. "Leave him alone."

"You think so?"

"He needs to work things out his own way. Everyone needs to do that. I bet you've already tried to reason with him."

I did tell Sekky that I understood how hard it was to miss Poh-Poh so much, and had explained to him, as gently as possible, how there was no scientific evidence for ghosts. Not even for the ghost of Poh-Poh. I described to Jenny how Sekky had sat on his bed, crossed-legged, and listened intently to my every word.

But the very next day he told me he had seen her again, in the blue jacket we had buried her in, standing by the kitchen stove. Of course, as in any good folk tale, she vanished when he approached her.

The mist was thickening into layers of lamplit fog.

"Let Sekky have his way," Jenny said, taking her keys out. "It won't last."

We had just stopped at the front entrance of the store. I had hoped we would head for the back alcove where we might have lingered a few minutes, as we had done the last few weekends, and we would have kissed, I would have held her against me.

The door was stuck. I reached out for the handle.

"Leave Sekky alone," she went on. "Why do you have to be so sure that reason is always the answer? It isn't."

A nervous laugh escaped from me—a stupid titter that mocked me, not her. Jenny shoved my hand away. Under the light of the street lamp I could see her eyes narrowing. Her nostrils flared.

"You're so goddamn sure!"

The door shut behind her. A Drink Orange Crush sign swung haphazardly in front of my face: CLOSED, PLEASE COME AGAIN.

Talk of Sekky seeing Poh-Poh must have started the impulse that pushed Jenny away from me. She was, after all, haunted by her own ghost. And I had mentioned her ghost by name, again and again, deliberately.

On Monday, I approached Jenny at school during our lunch period. Before I could even greet her, she said, "I'm sorry, Kiam. I was rude to leave you like that."

"It was pretty damp," I said, "and cold. I don't blame you. I wasn't laughing at you. Just nervous, I guess."

"It was cold," she agreed, "and the movie left me a bit spooked."

Like two lost souls on a sinking boat, our words kept paddling towards the safety of some distant, familiar shore.

"By the way," Jenny said, as we were getting ready to go off to our separate classes, "your little brother's situation isn't one that reason will solve. As my mother says, 'Ghosts are ghosts. *Aaaiiyaah!* Doesn't Kiam-Kim know that simple truth?'"

Jenny left me laughing at the realization that Mrs. Chong, as usual, had had the last word.

But the two were right about ghosts being ghosts. I could not just reason away Sekky's sighting of Poh-Poh. And big Mrs. Lim swore she saw Poh-Poh's ghostly figure in the upstairs window.

Sitting at his oak desk, Father slapped his newspaper down and complained to Third Uncle that Sekky's ghost stories were fuelling gossip, tarnishing his reputation in Chinatown.

"People are saying he must have done something to offend Poh-Poh's spirit," Liang had told me, delighted to report to me every detail of a grown-up conversation she had been allowed to overhear.

"People talk," Third Uncle said. "What can you do? Sek-Lung and Mrs. Lim, they tell everyone they see the Old One."

People in the newsroom said Father must have failed to do the correct filial ceremonies for her. But Father had done as much as he could afford to, with Stepmother's and Third Uncle's approval, spending a lot of money on the Old One's eight-table memorial dinner, on piles of funeral "cash" and on symbolic paper ingots of gold and silver, all to be burned for the Old One's use in her afterlife, and on her polished coffin.

"The Old One very stubborn," Third Uncle commented. "Maybe need something more."

And then, as if aware of Father's loss of face, of the pressures he was creating in our household, Sekky stopped talking about Poh-Poh's ghost.

Arrangements had been made to cut down on Stepmother's sewing shifts so she could watch over Sekky in the daytime. And Jung and Liang each took a turn rushing home from school to be with him when Stepmother left for her shift. I assigned him his take-home school work, telling him that Poh-Poh would have wanted me to check only his best efforts, that she always wanted him to go to school. He agreed, and his work was faithfully done every day, ready for me to check over the pages with him at night. Stepmother took him shopping and visited the mahjong ladies at their houses and Gee Sook at American Cleaners, and he gave her no trouble. His behaviour was as Poh-Poh herself would have wished it to be.

Of course, when things go too well, the gods strike. Poh-Poh had often have warned us about that.

It was Christmas Day, and Sekky had not even opened his presents when he confronted Father and Stepmother. He wanted them to take down the picture of the Kitchen God and burn it, as Poh-Poh always did as the New Year approached.

"We'll see," Father said, and afterwards consulted me.

"What harm will it do?" Stepmother said.

"We're not back in Old China," I protested.

"Sekky still thinks Poh-Poh is with him," Stepmother said. "So does Mrs. Lim. She tells the mahjong ladies."

What harm could it do to burn a cartoon picture? But still, I felt stuck. I told Father that I agreed with Stepmother. We should burn the picture of the Kitchen God at least, this last time, for the sake of peace in the house.

During the six days between Christmas and the New Year, Sekky began mumbling about seeing Poh-Poh again. And Liang, who was now staying in the Old One's bedroom, said she was feeling uneasy—and kept the door open so that Father or Stepmother could check in on the room at all hours. When Father brought his last editorial of the year to his colleagues at the newspaper office, he told them that his youngest was seeing a ghost again. He had hoped his Gold Mountain workmates would enjoy the joke.

"I wondered," Grey Head said, with not even a smile crossing his lips, "when you would be ready to hear the truth."

The other reporters nodded, as if to agree.

"Talk to your old mother's spirit," Mr. Wen at the *Daily Republic* told him. "Tell her that you respect her old ways. Then she'll leave your little boy alone."

On New Year's morning, my head still pounding from celebrations with Jenny and our Chinatown friends the night before, I woke up thinking that the pounding had grown even louder. Then I heard Father run out of his bedroom and Stepmother calling me.

I struggled out of my tangled sheets, grabbed my kimono and, in spite of my headache, found myself standing at the top of the steps watching pint-sized Sekky dragging and bouncing a big urn down the staircase. It thumped with each step he negotiated. It was the special urn, of porcelain and brass fittings, that Poh-Poh would have had Father or me carry down for her to set on the back porch. I would fill it with some dirt and Poh-Poh would stick in some incense.

"You go help him," Father said to me, shaking his head. There was no going back. We were going to do what Sek-Lung wanted us to do. We would watch the Kitchen God, Tsao Chung, rise in the smoke to journey to the Gates of Heaven.

I lifted the heavy urn and carried it down the rest of the stairs. Sekky followed me to the back porch. He had dressed in his best shirt and new pants, and he wore the Buster Brown shoes he got for Christmas. Jung and Liang, in their pyjamas, rushed down to watch the event unfold. Stepmother ordered us all to put on our winter coats.

I went into the soggy garden and brought up a shovelful of loose dirt for the urn. Stepmother, curlers in her hair, found some sticks of incense in the pantry, lit them, and let Sekky push them into the urn. Father unstuck the picture of the Kitchen God and was ready to strike a match.

"No! No! Not yet!" Sekky grabbed Father's hand. "We have to do everything right! You forgot the honey!"

That was true. Poh-Poh always smeared some honey on Tsao Chung's lips so that he would report sweet things about our family to the Jade Emperor.

Stepmother came back with a honeyed spoon, and the task was done.

Father lit one corner of the picture. Liang and Jung stood back. The flames licked up the side of the colourful poster, which was made of a special paper so it would burn slowly and produce the greatest amount of smoke. Sekky watched the cartoon picture drop into the urn. We all watched as it curled gradually into fuming ashes, the white smoke mingling with the sandalwood incense. Father and Stepmother could not help smiling at the bright eyes following the trail of smoke as it rose and dispersed into the morning air. Everything seemed to have gone well. I had even momentarily forgotten the thumping in my head.

Then Jung-Sum said, "Shouldn't we have waited until Chinese New Year?"

"Yes," Liang said. "Poh-Poh only did this on Chinese New Year."

Stepmother tried to shush them up.

I held my breath, counted each terrible second that went by.

The small head shook. Every vein and muscle on the slim neck strained to hold back the wetness now rimming his eyes, until the tide of heartbreak all at once sent him shuddering into tears. Father, distraught, picked him up and carried him into the house. Liang and Jung ran after him, trying to take back what they had said. But it was too late for Sekky, howling in the kitchen.

Stepmother held me back to whisper in my ear. "Very bad sign. Very bad, Kiam-Kim."

"No harm done," I said, with too little conviction even to convince myself.

"Yes, no harm," Stepmother repeated with the same uncertainty, but looked hopefully towards the empty sky.

By March of that year, 1941, pressured by so many of the elders in Chinatown for the family to have a proper ceremony to exorcise Poh-Poh's ghost, and deeply troubled by Sekky's continued sightings of the Old One, Father relented. On the auspicious day selected by the exorcist, Father, Jung, and I moved Liang's bed and things into the hallway.

With a bald-headed monk attending in the empty bedroom that had been the Old One's, the *bai sen* ritual, the three-times bowing ritual, took place before the Old One's portrait, an oversized enlargement that the Yucho Chow Photo Studios had prepared for Father. We dutifully lit some incense, and each of us, including Third Uncle and weeping Mrs. Lim, took our turns bowing before the Old One. The robed monk and his helper, a stringy-haired geomancer, had made sure the *feng shui* were in harmony. The curtainless windows were opened. Two large bowls burned with incense. The monk chanted blessings to set Poh-Poh's spirit free. The smoke rose into the air, and the smell of jasmine permeated the room.

Sekky was impressed to see me fall on my knees and say a few words to Poh-Poh's portrait. I thought of Jack O'Connor, who went to church even when, as we both knew, he didn't put much credence in all that ritual, in the wafer and wine, the ten thousand miracles of the saints. But he did go at Christmas and Easter, and to mass, and even confession, when his mother wore him down, because he felt he had to for her sake.

It made sense to me. Poh-Poh had taught me, as she had instilled in Father himself, that duty to those we love must come first, before our need to please ourselves. And so I knelt before Poh-Poh's stern eyes and barely smiling lips.

Shortly after that day, though both Sekky and Mrs. Lim swore to everyone that a stubborn old spirit had come back two or three more times, to say that things were fine, Poh-Poh finally left them alone.

"The Old One has gone," Mrs. Lim reported to Stepmother. "Poh-Poh say a good ceremony, a good leave-taking."

When Stepmother asked Sekky about this, he solemnly nodded. "Poh-Poh just said goodbye to me in the kitchen." And then, matter-of-factly, "She just left."

Late one night, restless from too full a day of playing war with his playground pals, Sekky came to my room and woke me up. He whispered that the Old One said she would never leave him. But she had.

He held in his hand the pinkish jade amulet that Poh-Poh had slipped into his pants pocket before she was taken to St. Paul's.

"Would you like to give this to Jenny?" he said, in a hushed voice.

"No," I said as calmly as I could. "You keep it safe."

He looked doubtful.

"Poh-Poh gave it to you for safekeeping," I reassured him. "She loved you very, very much."

His small fingers clutched the carved peony. He climbed into my bed for warmth and quickly fell asleep against me.

I don't know if Sekky believed that Poh-Poh was gone, but he did not mention her ghost again, at least, not to me. And that night, exhausted from a full day at the warehouse, I dreamed of the jade peony falling from the night sky into Jenny's palm.

It was just a dream, like any other.

The war never left us, and through the spring of 1941, the newsreels would break up the Hollywood dream sequences that starred Astaire and Rogers, Rooney and Garland, Carmen Miranda, Hope, Lamour and Crosby with scenes of bombs dropping, of soldiers firing machine guns, of refugees fleeing and ships blown apart, jolts of reality that reminded us all that we had a duty to serve King and Country. But our talk was more about whether we could afford the latest tightly cuffed pants or the new shoes or buy the right suit for the graduation prom two months away.

Then, one April afternoon, Jack sat astride our porch rail, waiting for me to come home.

"Need to talk," he said. He lifted his leg and swung himself around to face me. "Got some news."

To keep my eyes from squinting at the sunlight behind him, I leaned against the wall of the house and fell back into the shade thrown by the porch roof. At first he glanced away from me, as if to check whether anyone might overhear our conversation.

"What's the news, Jack?"

"You're the first to know, Kiam," he said. "Then I have to figure out how to let my mother know."

He hesitated. I could tell the news must be serious, and that made me pull him off the rail to stand with me.

"Go ahead," I said. "Is there anything I can do for you?"

"I've done it," he said, stepping into the shadow with me. "Told the school that I was dropping out today, and next week I'm headed for Manitoba."

"You got a job?"

"No. I'm leaving town in five days for Winnipeg. Joining up with the Grenadiers. Nice outfit. I checked out their history. Sign up. Go fight for the good guys. No matter what, it'll take me as far away from my parents as I can afford. Got the bus ticket in my pocket."

"Jeez, Jack, you've just got two more months till graduation. Look, I'll help you with your chemistry. Everything will be fine. Get your diploma first."

"I can't concentrate too much these days, Kiam.

Besides, the government's going to call me up any day, and this way I can make my own choice."

"But why leave so suddenly? I know guys that went to—"

"Not the same for me, Kiam." He turned away from me and slammed his fists on the porch rail. "I have to let you know something."

"We can study together, Jack, you'll ace the finals and—"

"Kiam!" He spun back to face me. "Jenny saw you in the library basement that day she and I— *You saw us*, goddamn you! An hour ago I went to tell her that I love her but she shut me down with these words: 'Kiam was there.' All this time you've let on that there was nothing wrong between you and me."

I couldn't fake that I hadn't known. The same knife was stuck inside each of us, and the honed blade began twisting inside our guts.

"Best friends, eh? All this time, it's been killing me, Kiam. I wanted to tell you, but I couldn't. And you, you bastard, you could have said something to me! Made it easier for me!"

I thought I had safely put away that day, put what I'd seen in some memory box that I could avoid, if not forget. I felt pushed against the wall by his guilt. I hadn't thought that what happened with him and Jenny was of any consequence to him. But now I pushed back. How was I supposed to make things easier for him?

"How far did you get with Jenny?"

I could see him trying to figure out what to say. He didn't have too many choices.

"Doesn't matter, Kiam," he said finally. "We stopped when she pushed me away a second after she must have seen you going up the ramp."

"And that was the end of it?"

"You want to know what happened next?"

I shoved him against the rail. Jack jumped in front of me and blocked my way into the house.

"Hang on," he said. "Goddamn it, Kiam, you've got to listen to me!"

I tried to push him aside. "Listen to all that bullshit? No, thanks!" I drew back my fist. My knuckles landed hard on his chin, stinging. Jack stumbled and fell onto the deck. Anyone with half his smarts could have seen my fist coming a mile away and blocked the blow. And Jack knew how to fight. But he had done nothing to stop me.

Liang's face appeared at the front window. She must have heard him falling. She waved to me, and I signalled her to stay inside, smiled like an idiot Big Brother and made it seem that Jack had somehow tripped, tumbled, an accident. She frowned, suspicious. I put out my hand and Jack gave her his idiot's grin, too, and we both gripped, and I yanked. He got up, putting his weight on my arm before he recovered his balance. We were leaning against each other like two drunks. Liang laughed and turned away from the window, went on with whatever she had been doing.

"I want to kill you," I said. "It was your turn not to tell me anything, goddamn it. You tell me this now, and you're fuckin' leaving for the army! And you'll get fuckin' killed! Great! What does that solve?"

"Whatever happens to me, wherever I go, I want you to know, you're the only friend I count on. And I . . . I . . ."

He roughly felt his chin. As far as I was concerned, I hadn't drilled him half as hard as I had wanted to. I wanted him just to piss off and leave me alone, but I couldn't say anything like that. And I could sense he wanted to leave, too, but hung on. Like a couple of stunned fighters at rest, we both sat down on the porch steps.

We avoided looking at each other and stared across the street at Mrs. Lim's old shack. She was outside, shaking out a large floor rug. She waved to us. I waved back. Meiying came out and took one end of the heavy rug and shook it with Mrs. Lim.

"Love is funny, isn't it?" Jack started to say. "Meiying is thrown away by her real mother and some-one crazy like Mrs. Lim takes her in. Remember when you told me her story, how I laughed and said that was stupid? I think we were ten years old then, and I thought only her real mother could love Meiying. Then you told me about Jung-Sum coming into your family. 'We take care of our own kind,' you said. I think your stepmother told you that. Remember? I thought about that for weeks."

The April afternoon was warm, and everything was green and blooming and Jack kept talking. "She came to find me down in the morgue that afternoon. I don't think she planned to take me on like that, believe me. And I was easy. Didn't mind one bit. She said she was curious about making love with me. Something she had fantasized about. 'A white boy,' she said. Just once. Like that was the only reason. She didn't want anything else from me."

"Then I showed up."

"You showed up, it turns out, and that's when Jenny pushed me away. That shove jolted me. Then something inside me made me think of you—you were my only and best friend, Kiam. We grew up together. I thought of what I was doing with your girl, and I felt sick."

"And Jenny?"

"She fixed her dress. Asked me if her hair was messed up, and she left."

I swallowed. It was a bitter taste, like the tea that Poh-Poh and Mrs. Lim used to share. "Bitter life, bitter tea," they would say. But something told me Jack was telling me everything as he understood it.

"The thing is, after Jenny left, I wanted her so badly. No, not just the way you're thinking. All the times we ever met, she was the only girl that got me interested in talking and battling back with her. But I know now that whatever may have started is over. And so here I am, talking to you. Then I go home and tell my mother I'm leaving her. Unfinished business."

"Wait until graduation. That's all they want you to do. Just wait."

"Waste of time. I've got to go, Kiam. Everything's getting to me. I'm going to let the army tell me what to do. When to eat. When to sleep. When to march and when to shit."

"Look, Jack, I'm— No, I—"

We both smiled at my stumbling. All the talk had been about the truth, and it had mattered.

"Don't say anything, Kiam. This is just the way things are. Jenny loves you. You're the only one for her."

"Does Jenny know you're leaving?"

"I'm counting on you to give her the news. Will you?"

We hadn't noticed that Meiying was standing below on the sidewalk, waiting to get our attention.

"Can you help us put a rug down?" she said. "We're having trouble."

Jack and I looked at each other. The bastard's jaw was turning a little purple. We got up, brushed off our pants and went with Meiying into Mrs. Lim's cramped front room. The few pieces of furniture were outside on the porch. The rug was a heavy one, but she wanted it to lie flat on the floor, even though it was too big. And it had been too big all the years she had it.

She handed Jack a knife. "Cut, please," she said.

Meiying explained to us what Mrs. Lim wanted done. Jack stabbed the blade into one end of the oversized rug. I held it up at an angle so he could slice as cleanly and as straight as possible. When the job was finished, the rug fell down flat. Perfectly. Mrs. Lim pointed to the boiling pot and a platter of savouries she had been making. Jack made a face, the same face he always made when he smelled Poh-Poh's garlicky cooking coming through our windows. He suddenly looked like the kid I grew up with, all tousled blond hair and blue eyes. I was waiting for him to tell me how Chinese people eat all kinds of things that crawl.

"They do, you know," he once said to me. "I read it in a book. And my mother says so."

Mrs. Lim could see that Jack would not be touching any of her wonderful cooking. The black-bean sauce and the fermented soybean cakes were already causing him to wrinkle up his nose. He clearly just wanted to get out of there. We both laughed.

"Tea," Mrs. Lim said to Jack. "Drink goot tea."

And we were gone.

That night, in Third Uncle's warehouse office, I phoned Jenny.

"Jack's leaving in a few days. He's quit school and he's going to Winnipeg to join up. He wants to do his share."

"I know. Moira told me in the store tonight. She'd just seen Jack and her eyes were red."

I looked at the piles of account books on the desk, and then out the huge windows overlooking False Creek. The trains were pulling in long lines of freight cars, and they seemed like those fabled creatures Poh-Poh used to tell me about.

"Jack told me everything, Jenny." I let that sink in a moment. I needed time to reflect. Yet I wanted desperately to know that something was sure, beyond illusion. After a long pause, I could hear Jenny crying.

"I want to be with you, Kiam. Only you. Please understand."

I did. But it wasn't in me to let her know that I understood.

"Look," I said, "someone wants to use the phone. I'll see you on the weekend."

I hung up.

I thought of a story I'd read, a Greek myth about a warrior who raised his knife in the air to kill this woman for revenge, and the woman, whom he had never met, looked up at him, and their eyes met, and in that second, the murderer fell in love. When the two were in the library, who was the murderer, and who the victim? I could not guess, but I felt as if I were the knife plunging down, and they looked at each other, and love happened.

I wanted things to be as they had been. What truths were being told between us, what I could understand of them, I did not think should take away everything that I found impossible to surrender. No, I did not want to surrender what was still good and decent among us. However unfair and unjustified things might appear to a stranger who was only skimming the surface of our lives, even the lives of strangers, I felt, should never be quickly judged. And not one of us were strangers.

When I got home, Liang handed me a note from Jack.

"Did you hit him?" she asked. "He looked like somebody really socked him one."

The note was brief and was headlined with a sombre title: "LAST REQUEST."

He said was leaving on the weekend, but just this once, he wondered if I would ask him over for dinner with my family.

"My mother's fed you plenty of hot dogs at my place, pal," he wrote. "Let me know. Just me and your family. Okay? I want to make sure I have the guts to swallow anything thrown at me before I go off to wrestle some Nazis with my bare hands in a shit-hole trench. Like my father did in the last war."

"But he hates Chinese food," Stepmother said, her Chinese words snapping to life. "Poh-Poh used to say, 'The brat make pig noise, puking and farting noise.'"

"Are you kidding?" Jung said. He laughed at the idea that O'Connor would even sit near our everyday food.

"Will he really puke?" Sekky asked, excitement in his eyes.

I explained that he was only a boy then. And Jack didn't think he would be coming back to Vancouver after the war was over. Plus, he was my friend.

Stepmother sat back in her chair. She had been studying me. "I make something only for Jack to eat," she said. "I know what he like."

Father objected. "He eat what we eat."

"Yes," said Stepmother. "But I make for him special dish."

The next day, Jack knocked at the door, right on time. And with a bunch of his mother's flowers in his hand.

For the first time in the almost fifteen years we had lived as neighbours, he walked into our front hall. I noticed all our coats were neatly hung up. I led Jack through the parlour, which Liang and Jung had swept and tidied up. Stepmother arranged the long-stemmed flowers in one of Poh-Poh's favourite vases, the one with the dragon crest. I put the vase on a corner of Father's desk.

The table was set. A red tablecloth, for luck, covered the round oak surface. Two dishes were set out already, steaming. But others were waiting to arrive.

Stepmother said, "Sit here."

Jung pulled out Jack's chair. His place at the table was obvious. A metal soup spoon, a metal knife, and a metal fork surrounded a large empty plate, just like in a western-style restaurant. Finally, one after another, the dishes arrived. But the special dish that Stepmother had promised to make for Jack would, of course, come last.

Sekky grabbed his chopsticks, and Jack asked if he could try them. He did, expertly. He had obviously been practising.

"Kiam, would you ask if I could have some chopsticks, too?"

I translated the request. Stepmother looked disconcerted, but Father said, "Of course, of course," and quickly the metal "weapons" were removed and a set of chopsticks was laid across Jack's plate. They were Poh-Poh's special ones, carved from ivory.

"Good friend," Stepmother said with a smile. "Get best."

Then she went out to the kitchen and we all waited for the special dish for Jack. We listened to the quick chopping rhythm of the cleaver. Finally, Stepmother proudly carried in the special dish and set it down before Jack.

The whites of his eyes widened.

A complete whole-wheat peanut butter sandwich sat majestically in front of him. It was perfectly sliced into bite-sized cubes, for the use of chopsticks. Two hot dogs tucked in bread rolls had also been chopped into two-inch segments, each part held together with toothpicks. The thick pieces rolled against each other.

"No, no," said Stepmother. "One wait!"

She came back. A new bottle of Heinz ketchup was presented to our guest of honour.

"Oh," Jack said. "You really shouldn't have."

"Eat," Father said.

"Father." I smiled. "Perhaps Jack wants to say a prayer first. That's what he does at his house."

Jack gave me a look. "No, that's okay."

"Pray! Pray!" Sekky said. "That's good luck!"

Everyone stared at the guest. The cornered look that those blue eyes gave me began to melt away. He bowed his head, but the words he spoke for those few seconds we could not hear. Then we heard, "Amen."

Liang and Jung said, "All Men," as they did at morning prayer at Strathcona.

Jack picked up his chopsticks and offered Liang the first piece of hot dog. He saw my look of surprise.

"Moira," he said. "She knows about Chinese etiquette."

I lifted up the best piece of steamed chicken and offered it to Jack. Stepmother began spooning the golden chicken broth into his soup bowl. Father told me to bring Jack his own rice bowl and a porcelain Chinese spoon.

"You come back safe," Father said to Jack, carefully enunciating his best English.

Jung-Sum handed me the note that Mr. O'Connor had left for me.

> *On October 27 Jack will be coming by train to Vancouver. Winnipeg Grenadiers and Royal Rifles are headed for the front some place in Asia. Can you and Jenny meet him that day?*

The Grenadiers came into Vancouver to board the reinforced freighter *Awateau,* and Jack managed to slip away from the station and taxi home to say goodbye to his mother and father.

There was a loud rap on our front door. Liang got there first. She waited for Jenny and me to stand behind her before she would open it. Jung and Sekky came halfway down the stairs and stopped for their bird's-eye view. Sekky had one of his tanks in his hand, ready to storm down the wooden rail and attack. I nodded for Liang to open the door.

It was noon, there were clouds in the October sky, but the light was bright enough to silhouette the tall, gallant figure standing on our porch.

"The Chen family, I presume, and the lovely Miss Jenny Chong," said Jack, and gave a heel-snapping salute.

"You look," I said, "like you belong in that outfit, Jack."

Sekky raced down the stairs with his tank. "Jack, do you get to drive one of these?"

"Not yet," said Jack. He raised his fists at Jung. "But I get to box a round or two, how about that?"

"Show me!" Sekky said. Jack kept his dukes up. Sekky attacked with his metal tank.

"Hey," I called, "how about you all leaving Jenny and Jack and me by ourselves for a few minutes?"

The three resisted for a moment, wanting to take in the shiny boots, the thick lapels, the brass buttons . . . and the man that was now the Winnipeg Grenadier Jack. Then one by one, they left us alone.

We sat ourselves down in the parlour.

"So how are things?" I asked. "The training go well?"

"Fast and furious, Kiam. But there's been more damn marching than shooting."

Jenny asked him how he was, and I watched him answer her as if nothing had ever gone on between them. With his blond hair shorn, he looked older than his eighteen years. I had just turned eighteen myself, was attending Western Commerce, preparing for my future. But unlike the soldier in front of me, I still wondered where my duty lay.

"Should I be there too, Jack?"

"No, don't even bother signing up," he said. "I'll be back by Christmas. You won't even get your turn."

But Jack had been too ready with his answers. He looked at his watch. "The taxi's waiting outside."

Jenny said, "What aren't you telling us, Jack?"

He sat up, pushed back his shoulders. "Not enough training for the most recent ones of us that joined up." His jocular manner had disappeared. "We're being pushed into this fight without enough thinking from the top. At stops during the night, some of the guys just hop off the train and disappear." He slammed his fist into his palm. "*Gone!* Just like that. I counted at least a dozen of them. But I believe in defending King and Country. And I haven't got any excuse not to be in this uniform."

I wasn't sure if he was making a dig at my situation, but there was no malice in his tone. In fact, something in me envied Jack, that much I knew.

"I'm shipping out to Hong Kong. Looks like I'll end up being more Chinese than Irish after all." He looked at his watch again. "One thing I came back to say to you two was to wish you well. And I'm glad to know we're still friends." The words were rushed, but it was clear he had thought about them.

When we stepped outside, his mother and father were waiting on the sidewalk, their autumn coats tightly buttoned against the cold. It was a brisk day, and leaves rustled as they gathered in piles against the curb.

"Keep my place on the soccer team, Kiam."

In the rising wind, Mrs. O'Connor adjusted her kerchief and pressed her thin lips to stop the tears. Jack held the car door open for her and respectfully saluted as she got in.

The car coughed, and then it began to move forward, crunching the leaves as the driver slowly, slowly, pulled away from us. Jack stuck his head out the window and shouted back, "Ulysses gotta go look-see!" ·

Jenny said softly, "Come home."

The North Shore mountains glistened with snow. Not knowing any better, I imagined it would be hot where Jack was going. Sekky started roaring about with his tank, shoving it against a pile of leaves in front of us. I began to talk nonsense.

"It's semi-tropical where he's headed. Jack's lucky to get his chance to fight. He's—"

Jenny bent over Sekky and snatched the toy tank from his hand. She threw it, bouncing, into a patch of dead grass. Jung quietly went over and picked it up, and Liang took her little brother by the hand, and the three of them climbed back up the stairs and went into the house.

I thought of a poem Jack and I had committed to memory when we were in Grade 7. We had played some clubhouse game in the back shed and had promised each other we would live by those words spoken by Tennyson's Ulysses: "to strive, to seek, to find . . . and not to yield."

In the fall of 1941, Little Brother was discovering his freedom, and was proving a discipline problem. Left by himself after school, he began to play with matches and hang out with the rowdy Han twins, tearing up and down the street playing war games, hopping into neighbours' backyards and gardens. Jung or I would have to race down to MacLean Park and drag him home, muddy and wet and late for his supper.

After some discussion, Mrs. Lim agreed that she and Meiying would take on the task of looking after him. She had thought it over and decided that Meiying could also use some help herself. She wanted Meiying to be more like the other young women of Chinatown. There was way too much talk, she thought, about "the perfect Meiying."

"What to do?" Big Mrs. Lim said in dismay. "Meiying read all the time. Can't even boil rice! I keep her home this year. Teach her important womanly ways. You help me, Chen Sim."

"Or the gods will punish her." I heard Poh-Poh's voice in hers.

"Meiying too smart and too beautiful," Mrs. Chong told Stepmother at the mahjong table. "Better be smart and plain like me."

The Chinatown ladies who came from the old villages as mail-order brides or wait-on-table "hostesses" saw no future for such a bright girl. What Chinese boy would want her if she outsmarted him in every way and was so restless?

"Better she stay home for now" was the conclusion of all the mahjong ladies. "Make her good wife material."

"Meiying should have been a boy," said Mrs. Chang, the butcher's wife, who waved her straw fan to chase the flying insects away from the meat. "What a waste!"

Since returning from Victoria, Meiying had regularly stopped in to visit with Stepmother. Seeded by these earlier, more casual meetings, their companionship now grew into something more. Stepmother taught her young friend the household skills that she had had to learn before she was sent over to become Father's helpmate.

Mrs. Lim was happy to see some of the results of Meiying's "education." In her tiny shack the bedsheets were folded down at night and tucked in neatly in the morning. Pillows were fluffed. Small savoury dishes, dainties, were added to the coarse recipes that Mrs. Lim always made. Meiying paid attention to Mrs. Lim's hair, helped her to wash her back in the iron tub, added special soaps to the water and perfumed the air with Three Flowers. She began to fuss over her guardian as if she were a rich lady.

By the second day of his first week with Meiying, Sekky stayed up late to tell me the news: "May knows the flying range of all the bombers!"

It turned out that Meiying knew more about Zeros, Spitfires, and Messerschmitts than she did about laundry and cooking. She had written a paper on the Great War for her history class in Victoria, had delved into the subject of old and new planes and their advantages in modern warfare. Part of her essay was even published in the *Colonist* newspaper. All the Chinese papers reported on her success.

Within days, half Sekky's tanks and toys were at Mrs. Lim's house. Father was reassured by Mrs. Lim that everything was going to be fine. The beautiful Meiying might even inspire his son to study harder. I noticed Sekky straining to make out the long words in the *Life* articles that Meiying had cut out for his scrapbook.

Sekky had found someone to fill the space left by his Poh-Poh. He loved stories, and stories were told. He wanted to learn a song that Meiying was humming, and he came home singing the folk song that Meiying's mother had once taught her. They went out on crisp days to get some fresh air, to run through MacLean Park, Little Brother pretending that he could shoot down her enemy planes. She ran from Sekky with arms outstretched so that her silk shawls floated like wings.

"Beautiful to see," Mrs. Leong told me. "People stop at the edge of the park to watch the two of them."

About the perfect Meiying, who stayed away from the usual Chinatown gang, speculation grew.

"Maybe she's going to be one of those volunteer spotters," Jenny argued, "learning all that stuff about Jap planes."

We were at the Blue Eagle, and I was trying to get Sonny to hurry up with my double-decker clubhouse special. We were with Susan and Cindy and their boyfriends, who had disappeared into a back booth to play a round of poker with some China-borns.

"Interesting you should say that," Susan Eng said. "Does Kiam know where Meiying and Sekky have been seen together?"

I didn't like the tone.

"Yeah," I said. "At MacLean Park, if they go out."

"Really?" Susan was playing coy, as usual. "They've been seen near the Powell Grounds, you know, that park in Little Tokyo."

"So? Probably watching baseball. That Jap team is made up of championship players."

"Well, it seems that one of those younger players is a close friend of your Miss Meiying."

"Get to the point, Susan!" Jenny said. "We're not our mothers dragging out the news over a mahjong game."

Susan smiled. "Kiam? Ask your little brother where he goes with Meiying sometimes."

"Why don't people just stick to their own places and be happy? Stick to their own kind," said Cindy. "Japs stay in Japan. Indians stay in India. Chinese stay in— never mind."

"Stay in the Powell Grounds," said Susan, laughing. "My boyfriend, Alex, works at the docks and he walks by there to get to work. People always mistake him for a Jap, can you imagine? He's sure he's seen Meiying down there a few times."

Jenny said, "That's exactly what Meiying told me."

Cindy looked surprised. She began tapping her spoon on the saucer.

"You talk to her?"

"She comes into our store. And I like her," Jenny said. "So does Kiam. She says she likes to watch baseball. Maybe she likes to watch your gorgeous Alex walk by, too. So what's the problem?"

Susan gave up. Her little bit of news was not going anywhere. I knew that Sekky had been told never to cross Hastings Street. And never to go down to Little Tokyo. Gangs were picking fights with anyone they thought was Japanese. But he was with Meiying. What could go wrong?

But if the rumours were true, everything could go wrong.

In Chinatown, those whose families had been murdered by the forces of the Rising Sun, and people like Father and Third Uncle and the elders who knew the extended history of Japanese aggression in China, people like these long believed that anyone too friendly with a Japanese person was consorting with the enemy. By the winter months of 1941, British and Commonwealth soldiers were fighting Japanese intrusions in India, Malaya, and Burma. And losing. All along the West Coast, Japanese people were being viewed as dangerous and potentially traitorous citizens.

So the growing talk about Sekky and Meiying being seen at the Powell Grounds worried me. During exam week, in mid-November, I finished early and took the Hastings streetcar to Jackson. The Powell Grounds were just one block north. The streets were overrun with small kids getting out of school, rushing past me in waves.

My walk took me right down Powell Street. Some elderly people stared at me, and I wondered if they could tell whether I was Japanese or Chinese.

The stores were cleaner and neater along this street than most of our cluttered Chinatown stores. Window displays were so unlike the haphazard piles I was used to seeing on Pender. A single flower in a vase stood on a pedestal in one shop selling cloth. And the bolts of cloth were arranged like a huge fan of many colours. In Chinatown, you could barely see an inch of any bolt, except their stock ends peeking out of piles rising from sewing table to ceiling. Another window displayed some exotic fish in a large glass bowl. A single pair of chopsticks leaned against the glass. It was a pleasure to see one window after another treating housewares and ordinary goods like art pieces.

I wondered how the Japanese scurrying by me would feel in Chinatown, with our loud chatter, the hawking on the streets to get rid of bad waters, our rough village ways, and the insistent jostling.

A reflection caught my attention. In the tilt of a window, a young boy who resembled Sekky was walking towards me. When I turned around, he was gone.

That night, Sekky showed me his scrapbook. It was a storybook that he and Meiying had created. The pages were blocked in comic-strip fashion, and Sekky and Meiying had cut out magazine pictures to tell a story of a young boy who fell into a magical land and had to fight monsters to save the people. The cutouts were shaped to resemble the monsters. Parts of tanks with fish heads lumbered over green landscapes.

"Do you do this all the time with Meiying?"

"Only when it rains."

"What else do you do?"

"We go to MacLean to play." Sekky gave me a look that suggested he had been through this third-degree before. Father or Stepmother must have queried him.

"Do you ever go to the Powell Grounds?"

"No."

"Are you sure, Sekky?"

"Maybe sure."

"And that means?"

"Dai-goh," he said, his tone changing, "Meiying says we all have alliances. Friends. We have to keep secrets if we're friends."

"When you go to Powell Street, what do you do there?"

"Nothing."

"So you go there?"

"No."

Sekky knew he had been tricked. His bottom lip started to tremble. I didn't want to push things too far. I just wanted to know what was happening. The rumour that Meiying had a Japanese boyfriend was difficult to digest. Mrs. Lim would kill her. Father would cut her off from Sekky if he knew they went down to Little Tokyo. And Stepmother would be forced to end her friendship.

"I got to go," Sekky said.

"You be careful. That's all I want to say."

He ran upstairs.

I should have been paying more attention to Father, who was tracking the news from China. But each time he swore against the Japanese atrocities and the "dog-turd Japs," I shut my mind. There were all kinds of poisons in the world, all kinds of wars to be fought. It seemed we were all caught up in village gossip and in village hatreds. In a country as vast as Canada, people living in a few city blocks were divided from others inhabiting those same streets; divided by their colour and fears, their language and beliefs.

And then the news came one Sunday morning before any of us were awake. There was a pounding on our door. I threw on my kimono and ran to see who was there. Third Uncle pushed his way in to get to the radio.

"Open it," he said. "Open it!"

I turned the dial and waited for the voice to come in clearly. There was some static, and then: "Pearl Harbor has been bombed . . . President Roosevelt has announced . . ."

Third Uncle jumped up from the sofa and grabbed Father's hand. They danced about.

"America now on our side!" Father sang. "I told them so! I told everyone! Soon America fight, too!"

Catching their fever, Jung-Sum started to punch into the air for a knockout, and Liang hugged Stepmother. Sekky hopped up and down.

"Allies!" he said. "Alliances!"

Stepmother was holding on to Liang, but she looked at Sekky in the same way I did. We looked at him together and wondered. He caught my eye and turned away.

Secrets.

"Be happy, Kiam," Father said to me. "Soon the war be over! America bring more men and more weapons to kill the dog-turd turnip-heads."

I put my ear down to the radio. My heart began breaking out of my chest. What was happening in Hong Kong?

It happened on Christmas Day. The radio reported on a fierce battle. Outnumbered and outgunned, the

Hong Kong defence collapsed. A list of Canadian soldiers reported killed or captured or missing was published the next day in the *Sun*.

Father had received an expensive tin of English toffee as a gift from one of the merchants in Chinatown, in appreciation of his editorial faith that the American forces one day would be fighting for China. Everyone agreed that Father should take the unopened box to the O'Connors.

At the door, Father and I spoke a few words with Jack's father. I mentioned that Jack had vowed he would come home for sure. That his name was on the "Missing" list only proved that possibility. But when our brief visit was over, all I could remember was that Mrs. O'Connor never smiled once. And as we left the porch and started down the stairs, I saw her pulling shut the blackout curtains.

That first week of January, everything came to a head.

"Meiying sick too much with flu," Mrs. Lim told Sekky when he went to show her his new storybooks. He wanted her to help print out the dialogue he had in mind. But Mrs. Lim stood fast. "Best for her to stay alone. You go play, Sek-Lung."

Stepmother sent over some special teas from Poh-Poh's pantry to help cool Meiying's fever.

The next day, at Third Uncle's, after working a hard midnight shift in the warehouse replacing someone who was sick, I sat in the small office, trying to catch up on the accounting entries that had piled up since the holidays, but I was making all kinds of stupid mistakes.

"Go home to sleep, Kiam-Kim." Third Uncle passed along some extra money for my next semester. As he walked out to join a meeting in the larger office down the hall, he gave a little laugh. "You too young to work to death."

When I finished correcting my last entries, I put on my coat and walked down the hallway to leave by the shaft elevator. Some of the merchants were in the big room loudly talking about the camps being set up to intern all of British Columbia's Japanese people. I stood by the doorway and listened. Since Pearl Harbor, there had been demands that all citizens of Japanese heritage be moved away from the coast. Partisan posters were showing up all over the city. LOCK THEM ALL UP, read one; GOOD-BYE JAPS! And a cartoon buck-toothed Japanese soldier was depicted burning up the forests of B.C. The rumour was that the properties of all Japanese, whether Canadian citizens or not—their houses and stores, all their goods, their farms and fishing boats, everything— were to be seized and sold off at auction. Mr. Wong suggested that all the tongs, the wealthier family associations, should be asked to put up some money to invest in the properties along Powell Street.

"Everyone at city hall debating these matters now," Mr. Wong said. His political connections kept him well informed. "We need to invest wisely."

Third Uncle looked up to respond, no doubt favourably, when he spotted me. He got up to shut the door.

"Go home, Kiam-Kim."

At home, I rushed in and interrupted Father talking to Stepmother to tell him what I had overheard at the office. He said he knew about all this, and he was just now writing something to support the merchants' grasp of the financial potential. At the other side of the dining room, Stepmother sat knitting in her chair and said nothing. But her tight lips warned me that I should not have interrupted them.

"I write three articles, Kiam-Kim," Father concluded, "to be published in a series."

He spoke so specifically in Stepmother's village dialect that I knew it was all said for her benefit. But she kept knitting, as if she were deaf.

"Look at all the land the Japanese have taken from China! Now it is our turn, don't you understand?"

"We don't want any of it," cried Stepmother.

Father glared at her. The atmosphere between them was explosive. The argument I had interrupted was obviously a heated one. I expected that she had held her ground.

They each retreated to work. Father tore up sheet after sheet and angrily threw the crumpled balls into the wastebasket. Stepmother kept knitting in a fury, the needles clicking loudly. Jung slowly came down the stairs, testing the quiet. But perhaps sensing the storm gathering in the calm, he stopped midway and turned around. Liang sat down at the table with Stepmother and pretended to read her library book. Sekky began to play quietly on the floor at the foot of Father's big desk.

I fiddled with one of Father's brushes. I wanted to take my head away from the crush of tension in the air. Stepmother's abrupt dismissal of the idea that Powell Street should be taken over by Chinatown must have boiled inside Father. As if men like him could afford to turn their backs on such an opportunity.

"You should have chosen a damn rich man!"

The needles went silent. Stepmother's face reddened with pain. I remembered the night Father had told me he liked Gai-mou but that he loved my mother. Though she wept that night, I assumed that Stepmother had accepted her position, accepted that she belonged to the family in the only way that was possible. But her whole being protested.

"I *chose*? I was *bought!* Even my own two children call me *Step*mother!"

Both Liang and Sekky averted their eyes. They must have sensed that their mother was battling against invisible and entangled ways. Against their ancient powers, she was as helpless and defenceless as I was.

"The Old One decided," cried Father. "*You* accepted!"

I saw now that Father had taken for granted the Old China ways without realizing how Stepmother had been pushing against them. Stepmother's eyes flashed in the same way that Jenny's did whenever she felt cornered. I thought of Stepmother's Three Flowers perfume, which I smelled on Meiying when I happened to bump into her coming down our stairs, rushing away from our house to go *where*? To meet *whom*? Did Stepmother dab some perfume on Meiying and say, "Go meet the boy tonight"?

And what had they been talking about under the ruse that Stepmother was teaching Meiying her household skills, helping Mrs. Lim's adopted daughter to become *sensible*? And did Meiying push her Gold Mountain way into Stepmother's thinking? Sensibly, did Meiying ask, "Why do your own two birth-children call you *Step*mother?"

I thought of Poh-Poh's old story about the tyrannical mistress who had whipped her, how even a lowly servant girl could fight back against all those days and nights of injustice. But Stepmother needed no magic combs to turn into river dragons; she had her silence. This time, I could see, she would not weep a single tear.

Father must have known he could not simply reach out and take her hand as if nothing had changed. He looked around the room and sought to re-establish his place.

"One of you, make some tea," he said. "Should be making lunch by now."

Everyone, including Father, held their breath. Her knitting needles clicking away, Stepmother refused to move. I knew what I had to do. I got up and went to the kitchen. Father went on writing, as if it were not unusual for First Son to make him his tea. He would not lose face.

After filling the kettle, I turned my head as Poh-Poh might have and looked for the Kitchen God. But Father and Stepmother had decided not to remind

Sekky of last year's ritual burning. The Kitchen God would not come into this house again.

While waiting for the kettle to boil, I stood at the back door and looked out at the wooden fence dividing the O'Connors' backyard from ours. If I shut my eyes, I could go back many years and see Jack playing there that first winter in this house, when we were just getting to know each other. He had seen me on the back porch and waved his mittened hand and pointed at the half-made snowman.

Tall Mr. O'Connor, who came out from their small shed with two pieces of coal, was waving at me, too, to come down and join Jack.

"Snow not good for you," Poh-Poh said, calling me to come in. I had already been coated and sweatered up for the cold, ready to go out with Stepmother and Poh-Poh to shop at Market Alley. The snow and building a snow creature was too tempting. I had seen the snow pile up that winter and envied the other boys playing outside, building forts and snowmen with coal eyes and carrot noses, which they knocked down with glee. I broke away from the Old One and ran out the back door, plodded through the foot of snow and attempted to climb over the fence. Mr. O'Connor lifted me up out of the deep snow and put me down beside Jack.

Poh-Poh told Stepmother to call me back, but Father and Third Uncle, meeting over business, must have been watching from the dining-room window.

Later, Stepmother said Father had told her and Poh-Poh to leave me alone. Third Uncle said to them, "In Gold Mountain, First Son must learn other ways."

Jack and I babbled at each other as if we were using the same language. We finished the snowman, and with Mr. O'Connor guiding us with shovelfuls of snow, we constructed a fort. Finally, Mr. O'Connor lifted Jack and me back over to our yard, where the snow lay pristine, unbroken except for the trail I had left behind. He directed Jack with a torrent of words, and I watched as Jack fell backwards into the bank of snow. Then the tall man pointed at me. I threw myself onto the deep snow, and pushed my arms up and back along my side. Then Jack carefully stood up to see what impression he had made. I did the same thing. My eyes widened at the wonderful sight. Butterfly creatures were pressed into the snow. Mr. O'Connor flapped his arms as if they were wings and called out, "Angels."

Stepmother clapped her hands at the snowy creations, and Father laughed with delight, but the Old One shook her head.

"Soon all gone," she said.

"No matter, Kiam-Kim," Third Uncle commented. "Still beautiful."

The kettle rattled me back to the present. A different winter now stared at me from the backyard—dead vines tied up with string, brown stalks of dead plants and grass, patches of bare earth, and the leaning slab fence. I picked up the pot holder in one hand, and with the other I lifted the teapot from the warming shelf and shook in some tea leaves from the old caddy.

Just as I was reaching for the boiling kettle, there came a loud banging on the front door. Father quickly unlocked the door. Mrs. Lim barged through, shouting to Stepmother.

"Chen Sim! Chen Sim! *Aaaiiyaah!* Lim Meiying! Meiying!"

Mrs. Lim did not have her winter coat on. Father led the big woman into the parlour. She was almost incoherent. Then, with chilling effect, she screamed to Stepmother, *"In her room! Meiying in her room!"*

Father and I looked at each other.

"You and Jung take Liang and Sekky to Third Uncle's," Father said, "and wait for me to come for you."

I grabbed their coats, but Sekky was gone.

Looking past the open door, I saw him across the street, chasing after Stepmother, climbing up the two rickety flights of stairs as fast as he could to catch up with her. As we rushed to Third Uncle's, I could not shut out Mrs. Lim's cries: *"Aaaiiyaah! Lim Meiying! Meiying!"*

Overnight, the news ran through Chinatown. Perfect Meiying had given herself to a Japanese boy. She had to do something and failed terribly. She had bled to death. Two ambulance men arrived, and a crowd gathered to watch them take away the bundled body. Word had been sent to Meiying's mother in Toronto. And a Buddhist monk arrived right away to chant and perform special rituals to expunge the bad luck such a death would surely leave behind. Yes, yes, a terrible, terrible loss.

The third day after Meiying's death, and the day before the private burial, Jenny agreed to see me. I had tried twice before, but whenever there was a visitor for her, whether her other friends or me, Mrs. Chong said she would lock herself in her bedroom.

"I never see her like this before, Kiam-Kim," she said. "Her heart so broken over Meiying."

But this time Mrs. Chong noticed the door unlock, and she led me upstairs and knocked gently.

Jenny's eyes were swollen from crying, and she could barely speak. Her throat was parched. We were alone in her small bedroom upstairs, and she seemed unable to sit up.

She looked at me, her eyes dark with pain.

"First Jack . . . then poor Meiying. They're both gone now."

I guessed at Jenny's thoughts. She and Meiying had both crossed the line with someone not of their own kind. "No, not both gone," I said. "Someone missing is not dead."

I picked up the glass of water on her bedside table, lifted her head, and encouraged her to drink.

She swallowed, and sat up against her pillows. "Don't stay with me, Kiam," she began. As I held the glass, she took another sip of water. Then another, until the glass was empty. "Break off with me, Kiam."

I answered the only way I knew how.

"Marry me," I said.

She grabbed the glass from my hand and smashed it against the wall.

Mrs. Chong came running up the stairs.

"What is happening, Kiam-Kim?" she cried, wiping her hands on her blue smock. "What's wrong, Jenny?"

"Nothing, Mother," Jenny said. "Kiam just asked me to marry him."

Mrs. Chong jumped. "And how did you answer him? What did you say to Kiam-Kim?"

Jenny looked at me as if she had thought of this moment many times before.

"*Aaaiiyaah*," said Mrs. Chong. "*What did you answer him?*"

Jenny's eyes did not move from mine. "Why not?" she said. "My heart answered him, 'Why not?'"

"Yes, you mean *yes!*" Mrs. Chong leaned against the doorway. Jenny and I turned to see triumph gleaming in her eyes. "Kiam-Kim, your Poh-Poh will have many great grandsons!" She took a deep breath and began shouting, "Ben! I have news for you!" She disappeared down the stairs.

Jenny held my hand. In the haunted quiet between us, I surveyed the fragments of glass reflecting the sunlight.

~ *E N D I N G S* ~

WAITING ON THE RAISED station platform, impatient for the arrival of the Red Cross train, I looked at my watch and said, as much to myself as to Jenny, "He'll be here soon."

I followed a flight of gulls as they swooped over the dark waters of Burrard Inlet and soared over the Second Narrows Bridge, and felt lost. Jenny, too, seemed disoriented. She leaned against my shoulder, her arms resting on her swollen belly; it was 1947, and our first-born was due in less than a month. But for now, with the taste of soot on my tongue, we waited anxiously for another arrival: Jack was coming home.

Families wandered about us, smiling bravely. People clutched each other for support. Volunteers and Red Cross nurses in dark capes paced attentively. The temperature felt mild for December, and the air smelled of wet hay.

We were all waiting next to a fenced-in yard with chutes usually used for transferring prize livestock to the Exhibition grounds. The long platform built alongside the tracks next to the station office had been swept clean, and wide wooden ramps were lined up, ready to be lifted into place. Severely wounded veterans— amputees, paraplegics, burn victims—were returning to their homes in Vancouver. High above the flat roof, a flag flew for King and Country. There were no news photographers or politicians.

I had been meditating on what had brought us to this station platform. Deep in thought herself, Jenny did not mind my seeming indifference. Invisible forces, like luck or fate, and like the ghosts of Old Chinatown, had come back into our lives, if they had left us at all. Jack, too, must have had such hauntings.

Mr. O'Connor had not been told how his son had escaped the Japanese. Jack himself recalled nothing. The official report stated that during the defence of Hong Kong, Jack had been trapped in a firestorm of burning buildings, and it was only the fragments of his uniform—labels stuck to his skin— that enabled the Chinese underground to identify him as an Allied soldier and smuggle him onto an American ship. Months later, he woke up in Winnipeg, in the burn ward at Deer Park Veterans' Hospital, with his arms tied to a special bed. And then after years of intensive care, refusing to see any visitors, after his massive wounds had healed into scars and his memory had slowly returned, he asked to be transferred home. His father was too sick to leave the house, and so his mother had come to our apartment one evening.

"Jack asked if you and Jenny would bring him home," she said. "Just the two of you. No one else."

"Yes," I said, as simple as that. Jenny, unable to speak, took Mrs. O'Connor in her arms, and the two women embraced as if they were companions in loss.

"Don't you mind if my boy looks so terrible?" Mrs. O'Connor kept saying, over and over. "Don't you mind?"

If Jenny minded, she said nothing. And while we waited for Jack's train, she said even less. A cloud passed over us, melting away the shadow of the bridge, and a light rain began to fall. Jenny lifted her shawl into a makeshift hood. Her eyes were sad, but in the sombre light she looked even lovelier.

"Jack won't know me," she said. "I'm a different person."

A horn shook the air, followed by a clanging bell.

"Ladies and gentlemen," announced a man wearing a CPR cap, "please stand back from the tracks."

A small crowd rushed to the farthest end of the platform to wait for the engine to round the bend. Some openly wept.

The young nurses passed among us to explain how the arrivals might be expected to disembark. Ramp A was for veterans who would be arriving strapped in rigged cots, and B and D, fitted with extra handrails, were for those using crutches. Ramp C, the longest ramp, was for those using wheelchairs. Each passenger car would display a designated letter.

An old man standing near us glanced at his watch and made a face, as if to say to everyone, *Get ready*.

A short blast sent flocks of gulls into the sky. The train's clanging bell echoed under the bridge and re-echoed between the inlet shores. Jenny and I headed towards ramp C.

Voices rose and fell.

"Tell me, Kiam . . ."

We stopped. There was no rush.

"Tell you what, Jenny?"

Another blast sounded. Attendants shouted instructions. The heavy wooden ramps were being lifted and dragged, leaving behind claw marks.

"Tell me, Kiam, why you and I can't let him go."

The train thundered forward and drowned all our voices. Puffs of white smoke billowed under the bridge. I held my breath. A long time ago, I had seen such clouds of steam rising from a great distance. With an ear-wrenching screech, like the cry of a dragon, the train halted. Soon we would be home. I put my hand on Jenny's shoulder. We watched as ramp C was locked into place.

~ *N O T E* ~

The "dark time" in the Dedication refers to the year 2001 when my life was interrupted by medical emergencies. This book is dedicated to the excellent medical and rehabilitation teams, the doctors and nurses, and the vital volunteers, of Toronto's St. Michael's Hospital and Bridgepoint Hospital.

The book is further dedicated to the friends and family members who stood by me and rallied my spirit and to the communities of Humber College and the Humber School for Writers who kept in touch during those four months—all of you contributed to my eventual recovery. Many should be named, but I resist for fear that I might, inadvertently, leave out someone who mattered.

And, not least, this book is dedicated to Wayson Michael Lowe, to Quinn Roy and Tessa Hill, to Kathryn Schweishelm, to Tosh and Gary Noseworthy, and to their loyal and affectionate families.

Please know that your love and generous actions have deepened the moral fabric and themes of *All That Matters.*

~ *A C K N O W L E D G E M E N T S* ~

Regarding this work, the following contributed to my knowledge of the period—aside from those already acknowledged in my novel, *The Jade Peony,* and in my memoir, *Paper Shadows*—the books are: Brereton Greenhous, *A Canadian Catastrophe, 1941-1945* (Dundurn/Canadian War Museum); Margery Wolf and Roxane Witke, ed., *Women in Chinese Society* (Stanford University Press); Ono Kazuko, *Chinese Women in a Century of Revolution, 1850-1950* J. A. Fogel, ed., (Stanford University Press); Thomas Tsu-wee Tan, *Your Chinese Roots, The Overseas Chinese Story* (Times Books International); Bill McNeil, *Voices of a War Remembered* (Doubleday Canada); Michael Kluckner, *Vancouver, The Way It Was* (Whitecap Books); Wing Chung Ng, *The Chinese in Vancouver, 1945-80* (UBC Press); E. G. Perrault, *Tong, The Story of Tong Louie, Vancouver's Quiet Titan* (Harbour Publishing); Faith Moonsang, *First Son, Portraits by C.D. Hoy* (Arsenal Pulp Press); the writings of Roy Mah, Larry Wong, and Paul Yee. Extensive interviews, photos and relevant clippings, school annuals and catalogues were generously shared by King Lee, Robert Yip, Fred Jong, members of the David Lee family, Alex Louie, Norman Wong, David Smith, Marie Yip, Larry Wong, Helen McQuade, Wesley Lowe, Sister Marie-Vie Chua; and in Hong Kong, Watt Chow, Crystal Tang, Allen and Brenda Wong, Donna Mah; and countless others.

The dedicated professionals at the Vancouver Public and Metro Toronto libraries, particularly those members in the reference and archival departments, were an immense help. I must single out John Smith of Toronto who went searching the War Museum and Ottawa archives for a single detail. Personal help was given by Michael Glassbourg and team members Elisa, Michele, Laura and Tanya.

Of course, for the purposes of a fictional work, I am responsible for my characters' insights and for their limited and sometimes distorted knowledge of the world they inhabit. I have simplified the various ways to reproduce Chinese dialects, choosing my readers' comfort over any academic correctness. For the same reason, I have simplified traditional references to family and friendship relations (for which there can be over one hundred possible words in Chinese).

My early and most recent readers deserve thanks for their astute suggestions, including Charis Wahl, Antanas Sileika, Joe Kertes, Ken Dyba, Karl Schweishelm, Betty Thiessen, Janet Somerville, 'Esco', Angela Fina, and my indomitable agent, Denise Bukowski. Jacob and Alice Zilber, Kit Wilson-Pote and Mary Jo Morris read the material many times over with a verve for details, as did Judy Fong Bates and Michael Bates. I also thank copy editor Shaun Oakey and proofreader Alison Reid for their professional work.

For their unbending faith that this book would be completed, and as my publisher and editorial advisor, I especially thank Maya Mavjee and Martha Kanya-Forstner.

Finally, the blessings of a community of friends and readers have supported my writing and kept me going. Ten thousand thanks to everyone.

know your
SETTERS
AND POINTERS
raising, care and field training

by William F. Brown
Editor: The American Field Publishing Co.
Chicago, Illinois

Earl Schneider, editor

THE PET LIBRARY LTD

THE PET LIBRARY LTD

The Pet Library Ltd, 50 Cooper Square, New York, N.Y. Exclusive Canadian Distributor: Hartz Mountain Pet Supplies Limited, 1125 Talbot Street, St. Thomas, Ontario, Canada.

Exclusive United Kingdom Distributors the Pet Library (London) Ltd, 30 Borough High Street, London S.E.1.

No portion of the text or illustrations of this book may be copied or reproduced in any manner whatsoever, in whole or in part, without express written authorization in advance from the proprietor. THE PET LIBRARY LTD.

PRINTED IN THE NETHERLANDS

Copyright in all countries subscribing to the Berne Convention.

1 2 3 4 5 6 7 8 9 10

CONTENTS

1 Foreword

There is no greater thrill than hunting upland game birds with pointing dogs. The vibrancy, grace, animation, the speed, desire, determination and courage of the dogs in questing for game, the instinctive wisdom, climaxed by a statuesque point, embodying age-old urges, excites the sportsman as no other recreational activity can do. Indeed, the stimulation of the quest transcends the taking of game . . . and what greater testimonial can be given to a pointing dog as an invaluable accessory not only to the pleasure of the sportsman, but to the cause of conservation!

The sporting breeds have been in favor for centuries. New breeds have been developed and recognized for specialized uses. Among the pointing dogs, Pointers and English Setters have been the most popular, and their breed excellence and individual proficiency have kept them in the front rank. But other recognized pointing breeds, like the Brittany Spaniel and the German Short-haired Pointer, to name only two, have also demonstrated their effectiveness.

Pointers and Setters have sustained their popularity over a long term of years . . . and with good reason. Their effectiveness and value in the hunting field provide unmatched recreation in both shooting and in field trials.

2 The quality bird dog

The quality bird dog is a wonderful animal. It is generally conceded that pure-bred Setters and Pointers are best fitted for the performance of bird finding, a capacity handed down to them through generations, each intensifying desirable characteristics through astute selection and careful breeding. Pointers and Setters have inherited instincts which give

SALLY ANNE THOMPSON

Pointers and Setters are usually kennel dogs but can be fine house companions as well. Keeping a hunting dog in the house doesn't ruin him as some may claim. Indeed Mississippi Zev, the immortal Setter, winner of the 1946 National Championship and four titles in all, was "babied" by May Bufkin, the wife of his handler, Earl Bufkin.

SALLY ANNE THOMPSON

The English Setter is a great and glorious breed with a brilliant history. His affectionate disposition and loyal devotion, together with beauty, grace, intelligence and aristocratic appearance, have endeared him to sportsmen.

them a particular aptitude for bird handling. Verily, "the experience of centuries is a priceless heritage."

Consider the high-class bird dog. The animal is, first of all, a gentleman of the species—of affectionate disposition, tolerant, and with an unmistakable charm. There is grace in his manner of movement, love in the soft depth of his eyes, withal a fineness of spirit that embraces ambition, courage and loyalty. The quality bird dog never fails you. He is constantly at your service, eager to give his best, with the will to keep trying when the going is roughest.

3 Setters

There are three popular breeds of Setters—English, Irish and Gordon. All have many similar characteristics, and 75 years ago the principal difference was in color of coat.

Bernard Waters, an early American authority on pure-bred dogs, said in effect that the origin of the Setter, like nearly all breeds, was obscure. However, many modern authorities accept that the "Setting Spaniel" was the forerunner of today's Setter. The Setter breeds were developed principally in Great Britain, and Edward Laverack, one of the outstanding breeders of the 1800s, described the English Setter as "a Spaniel improved."

English Setters

The English Setter is a great and glorious breed with a brilliant history. His affectionate disposition and loyal devotion, together with beauty, grace, intelligence and aristocratic appearance, have endeared the breed to sportsmen.

Principal credit for the development of the modern English Setter must go to Edward Laverack, author of *The Setter*, a resident of Whitchurch, Shropshire, England, who, through inbreeding, perfected the type that became not only the standard of excellence in his time (1815-1900), but that upon which the present-day English Setter was built.

Students of the history of the breed know that the famed Llewellyn strain was founded on the Laverack Setters with Duke-Kate-Rhoebe, three celebrated progenitors of the Llewellyn Setters. The latter is not a distinct breed, but only a strain of English Setters.

The Llewellyns enjoyed their greatest vogue in the 1890s and early 1900s. When imported to this country, the dogs virtually revolutionized performance standards. Straight-bred Llewellyns dominated American field trials for a span of a quarter-century, and even today there is a high percentage of Llewellyn blood in the successful so-called "grade" Setters.

The late R. Ll. Purcell Llewellyn of Pembrokeshire, South Wales, another famous British breeder, used the Laverack blood principally in the development of his strain. In England, during the period from 1915–60, the late William Humphrey, Esq., of Shropshire, carried on the Llewellyn strain. Indeed, Mr Humphrey brought back from the United States to England a number of straight-bred Llewellyns which he used in his matings.

The English Setter—although some, like James C. Foster, Jr, prefer the designation American Setter for dogs in the US—was the outstanding bird dog breed for several decades. Based on major field trial competitions in this country since, say, 1920, the Pointer has usurped the English Setter's former pinnacle. Yet the English Setter remains the favorite of countless hunters and field trailers.

The English Setter is a handsome animal, but its engaging warmth of personality and fine character transcend its physical beauty. The dog is parti-colored, white predominating generally, with black, tan-orange and chestnut the other principal colors. There are some fanciers who breed only the so-called tri-colors—white, black, tan and ticked. Height at shoulder ranges from 22 to 25 inches. Weight varies from

SALLY ANNE THOMPSON

Show Champion Silbury Soanes of Madavale. This fine-looking, English-bred, show English Setter was supreme Champion at Crufts, the largest and most prestigious dog show in the world. The show English Setter is somewhat different from the English Setter used in field trials. It is a larger, bulkier dog with heavier coat and more feathering.

30 pounds to 60 pounds, conditioned for field work. The average setter of today is of slightly smaller stature than the typical specimen of 60 years ago. This has no reference to bench show English Setters, which are more cumbersome specimens, lack the litheness, the grace, energy and hunting savvy of Setters bred principally for the fields.

Briefly, the standard for the English Setter: A long skull with well-defined stop and long, fairly square muzzle, straight and not dished. Moderate length ears, carried close, and set well back and low. Chest, of good depth and the back straight and strong. Legs, strong and dense bone, not porous. Feet, closely set and with tough pads. Coat, moderately long and flat, thin feathering on the legs. In motion, the English Setter shows ease of action, grace of movement, and smoothness indicative of endurance.

The English Setter with its longer coat is better able to withstand lower temperatures than the Pointer, although this characteristic will vary with individuals. By the same token, the smooth or the short-coated Pointer is preferred in the South, although the Setter is the favorite grouse dog in northern latitudes. The Setter's longer coat also affords protection against punishing cover, although here again there is a wide variance in individual dogs of different breeds.

Irish Setters

Of the three varieties of Setters, the Irish Setter is second in popularity. There was a time when the red dog commanded

There is no denying the eye-catching qualities of the Irish Setter. His beautiful red coat commands attention at once. SALLY ANNE THOMPSON

admiration for his excellence in the hunting field alone, but the beauty of his coat, his handsome conformation and attractive appearance persuaded fanciers to breed him almost entirely for exhibition purposes, and the fame the Irish Setter gained as a bench dog militated against his goodness in the shooting field. Since about 1900 the Irish Setter has not been used so much as a hunting dog, not nearly as much as his English cousin.

Some contend that the Irish Setter was established as a breed prior to the English and Gordon. It is known that the Irish Setter was bred and used early in the eighteenth century. His reputation broadened from his native Ireland to the rest of the British Isles, to Europe and to these shores.

There is no denying the eye-catching qualities of the Irish Setter. His beautiful red coat (a rich golden chestnut or mahogany red) commands attention at once. Small white markings on chest, throat or toes are permissible. It might be interpolated that in Ireland, where the earliest ancestors were principally red and white, there are some today where white still predominates over the red. But in this country inconspicuous white markings are acceptable.

Because the Irish Setter was bred principally for beauty of conformation and coat, and for show purposes rather than for field work, the breed's popularity with gunners suffered. However, around 1940, some Irish Setter fans, intent on restoring the hunting qualifications of the breed, developed what became popularly known as the "Red Setter." The characteristics of the three Setter breeds are such that the *Field Dog Stud Book*, the authoritative all-breed registry conducted by the American Field Publishing Company of Chicago, Illinois, permitted interbreeding and the progeny could be registered as Cross-Breed Setters. Then, if such offspring were bred back to pure-breeds of a single parent's breed for three generations, the puppies could be registered under that breed, possessed of all its characteristics.

The Irish Setter fanciers made an infusion of English Setter blood and then bred the resultant progeny back to straight-bred Irish Setters with field qualifications, designating these as "Red Setters" until the three complete generations of pure Irish Setter ancestry had again been established.

There is no question that this increased interest in the Red Setter as a hunting and field trial dog, and there has been an upsurge of interest in the red dogs both for gunning purposes and for field trial competition.

The Irish Setter is not as fast in the field as his English cousin, does not range as boldly, and is, on the average, a larger and heavier dog. If gifted with a good nose, the Irish Setter can be developed and trained into a desirable and highly useful gun dog.

Gordon Setters

The Gordon Setter is rarer than the English Setter or the Irish Setter. But this black-and-tan performer has a hard core of sincere fans. The Gordon originated in Scotland, its name implying that it came into existence at the Castle Kennels of the Duke of Gordon. Perhaps it was being developed earlier,

Gordon Setter Champion Downside Bonnie of Serlway. Gordon Setter admirers claim that for close shooting in cover where the dog's range must be restricted, a Gordon is at his best.

SALLY ANNE THOMPSON

but it is known that His Grace was partial to the black-and-tan Setters. The variety was bred at his kennels during the latter part of the eighteenth century but other wealthy Scots sportsmen were doing the same thing.

The Gordon Setter is very similar to the English Setter and the Irish Setter. He is pretty much the same in stature, in general appearance, perhaps not so racy in build, but he is rugged in the field, sound in his searching, and can do a workmanlike job.

The Gordon's color has affected his popularity as a field performer, because the black-and-tan markings do not contrast with surrounding foliage and make him difficult to see in certain types of cover. The English Setter, with those that are nearly white preferred, is more conspicuous in the field than either the red Irish Setter or the black-and-tan Gordon. There are those who say that this in a measure is why the English Setter has been bred more extensively.

Gordon Setter admirers claim that for close shooting in cover where a dog's range must be restricted, the Gordon is at his best. He lacks the blinding speed of major trial English Setters but covers the ground thoroughly. The Gordon Setter gives the impression of being sturdily constructed, blessed with adequate bone, a shade lower at the shoulder than the Irish, and is perhaps a few pounds heavier than the average English Setter. Although there have been instances of all tan Gordons, the *FDSB* has black and tan the only permissible colors, the tan markings being on the legs and underparts, the border lines between the black and tan colors defined clearly.

Although the Gordon Setter has never enjoyed the popularity of the other two varieties in the United States, there were periods when he attained considerable prominence. Charles T. Inglee of New York and his Gordons became nationally known; and concerted effort on the part of several field trial clubs to promote the Gordon in recent years, particularly in the north-eastern area, has brought increased prestige for the breed.

SALLY ANNE THOMPSON

Pointing is an instinctive act. The trainer simply reinforces the dog's stance and makes him steady.

4 Pointers

The proper designation of the breed is English Pointer. However, some authorities in this country, where the dog has been bred so extensively, insist that it would be more correct to use the term American Pointer. There is no denying that the Pointer in America is a distinctive as well as a distinguished bird dog.

Authorities differ on whether the Pointer came originally from Spain or Portugal. And there are others who insist that the breed was familiar in England before the importation of the Spanish Pointer. Nevertheless, it seems fair to concede that the Pointer, as the breed is known today, derived from

Pointer varieties in Spain, Germany, France, Italy and England.

The Pointer got his name from the fact that he was the first dog to stand—or point—game in the precise sense that the term is used today. The Setter ordinarily dropped or "charged" when indicating the presence of game, and it was more common for the Pointer to remain standing, although Pointers were also trained in early years to drop at wing and shot, or just before the birds were flushed.

The Pointer descended from hound types, or at least infusions of Foxhound, Greyhound and Bloodhound were used in the evolution of the breed, with the "Setting Spaniel" having a role in the development of the Pointer with which we are now familiar.

Pointers were known in England about 1650. The dog was used chiefly for the purpose of finding game; subsequently, his all-round qualifications as a top gun dog were developed.

The heavily-built, strongly-made Spanish Pointer was unquestionably a principal progenitor of the modern English or American Pointer. It is believed that fanciers used Foxhound and Setter crosses to produce a faster dog, and selective breeding contributed to the superior qualities of the present-day Pointer.

Pointers indubitably influenced the way of working for Setters and all the pointing breeds. The dogs became celebrated for their effectiveness in hunting upland game birds by body scent. While it is true that the great game-finders may resort to ground or foot scent at times, they use body scent for quick and accurate location of their game.

The standard of performance demands that a dog locate its game swiftly and exactly. When it approaches near enough, the dog stiffens into a stanch and stylish point and holds a rigid position until the hunter arrives and flushes the birds. The broken dog will remain steady to wing and shot. The inclination to stand motionless on scenting game is a heritage of many animals that hunt by scent, but this proud heritage of the Pointer has been developed to a high peak of excellence through years of careful breeding and training.

Importations of pedigreed English Pointers to America from England were made just about a century ago. It may be said that Edward Dexter with his Charlottesville Field Trial Kennels did most for the breed in this country, and the modern American Pointer is descended from Price's Ch. Bank, Mainspring and King of Kent, plus Rip Rap, a son of King of Kent, and Jingo, who was a son of Mainspring.

The Pointer's coat is short, predominantly white, and the principal colors are liver, black, orange and lemon. There are tones of these colors, even to a tan. It used to be that white and black Pointers were called "Rip Rap" Pointers because many fanciers thought that because the great Rip Rap was a white and black dog, all his descendants were of similar color. Actually there are more white and liver Pointers. A student of color inheritance and the chemistry of pigmentation finds the Pointer a splendid example to use.

Pointer technique in hunting parallels that of the English Setter. But authorities find a considerable variance in the disposition and temperament characteristic of the two breeds. Both are endowed with high speed, the desire and ambition to range out widely, both have excellent noses and possess remarkable endurance. Professional trainers of hunting dogs say that the Pointer develops more quickly than the Setter and that the Pointer will accept discipline that the Setter may resent. Judging the results of working and training thousands and thousands of Pointers and Setters, it is generally accepted that the Setter ordinarily needs more time in his training and extra attention in his education. Setter men say that the Pointer does the job because he was simply bred for the work, whereas a Setter is more of a companion and does it not only as a natural inheritance but because of his devotion to his master.

The modern Pointer is about the same size as the English Setter—perhaps averaging a bit more in weight and height

SALLY ANNE THOMPSON

The German Short-haired Pointer is truly an all-around dog. In his native land the Shorthair was used not only for game birds but on many kinds of animals and wild fowl as well.

—a symmetrical dog with a short coat that fits him to hunt in the South and gives him an advantage where burrs are plentiful, although, as mentioned, the Setter's long hair favors his use in northern latitudes and punishing briary coverts. Both the Pointer and the Setter are symbols of elegance in the hunting field; they are classy movers, merry in action, lofty in carriage.

German Short-haired Pointers

The German Short-haired Pointer, more familiarly referred to as the German Shorthair, hails from Germany as its breed name implies, and was exploited in this country as an "every-use" dog. In his native land the Shorthair was used not only for game birds but for practically all kinds of game animals and wildfowl as well. His development came about

SALLY ANNE THOMPSON

The Weimaraner is said to have an extraordinarily fine nose, tracing to its Bloodhound ancestry. Its fast, silent method of hunting has caused it to be dubbed the "Grey Ghost."

after Germany became the home of a number of Spanish Pointers. They were entirely satisfactory as pointing bird dogs, but German sportsmen felt that what was needed was a hunting dog for every use—one that would point birds and furred creatures during the day and could be used to trail game animals at night. It is said the Spanish Pointer was crossed with the Bloodhound, resulting in a heavy, short-haired dog that could be used for upland game in the day-time and as a trailing dog after dark. Breeders gradually refined the cross to the German Short-haired Pointer as now known, although in Germany there are many diversified tests of finding, trailing and tracking in rating the excellence of individual dogs.

The German Shorthair came to notice in this country during the 1920s, and toward the end of that decade some of them were appearing in field trials here. The breed was slower and closer working than were Pointers and Setters, but in certain environments, and for a particular type of work, they demonstrated desirable qualities.

Important strides have been made by breeders in the last forty years. There is no doubt that use was made of agile American Pointers, but it must be said that the German Short-haired Pointer of the 1960s is far better adapted to American hunting conditions than were his forebears with an "all-purpose" dog tag.

Liver is the only acceptable color with white, and when a black Shorthair appears it is indisputable evidence that an outcross was used.

The popularity of the German Short-haired Pointer has made giant strides in the last fifteen years, and fanciers have engaged in more and more field trial competitions.

Brittany Spaniels

The Brittany Spaniel, the only Spaniel which points its game, or is supposed to, is an even more recent addition to the Pointing Dogs of America than the Shorthair. A popular gun dog in France, the first importations to the United States were made in 1931 by the late Louis A. Thebaud, who had a similar role in introducing the Wire-haired Pointing Griffon many decades earlier.

Some American hunters describe the Brittany as a small Setter. It is approximately twenty inches at the shoulder, its ears are set higher than the Setter's, its muzzle is not so long or square, although in the Brittany, as in other pointing breeds, a snipy nose is not desired. The Brittany's coat is not as dense or heavy as the Springer Spaniel's, nor is its body as heavy. Its principal colors are white and orange and white and liver, with shades of mahogany, chestnut, lemon, etc.

The Brittany had a naturally short tail. Tailless Brittanys are occasionally bred. History records that the first tailless ancestor appeared in about 1830, at Pontou, a modest town situated in the Valley of Douron. Nowadays most Brittany tails are docked.

SALLY ANNE THOMPSON

Brittany Spaniel: Pamalie of Autron. While most Spaniels are used only for retrieving, the Brittany Spaniel is used both as a Pointer and Retriever. Some American hunters describe the Brittany as a small Setter.

The Brittany, because of its size and hunting habits, has found favor with a large section of the American sporting public. Field trials for Brittanys have also increased, almost phenomenally, and notable advances have been achieved in the dogs' qualifications.

Weimaraners

No breed of hunting dog was ever introduced to this country with greater fanfare than the "Gray Ghost." Howard Knight, of Providence, R.I., brought a pair to the United States in 1929, although the breed had been developed and used in Germany for more than a hundred years before that. It was supposedly established at the German

SALLY ANNE THOMPSON

The Hungarian or Magyar Vizsla, one of the newest hunting breeds in the United States, attained its present popularity following World War II.

court in Weimar about 1825, and was intended as an all-purpose hunting dog, one which would instinctively point game, would retrieve expertly from land and water, and would trail big game. In its capabilities it paralleled the German Shorthair, but Weimaraners were even more closely controlled, for no breeding operations could be carried on without specific approval of the parent club.

The Weimaraner is distinctive in coat and color. It is

smooth-haired with a dense woolly undercoat which enables the breed to withstand cold and wet; it is principally gray, the color varying from silver-gray to silver-taupe; blue Weimaraners are taboo. The tail is docked to about one-third its length, its eyes are amber, giving a brassy appearance. Weight varies from 55 to 80 pounds, and height at the withers from 22 to 26 inches.

It is an upstanding breed, has a moderate speed and range compared with Pointers and Setters, and is said to have an extraordinarily fine nose, tracing to its bloodhound ancestry, for the red Schweissehunde was a progenitor.

Bloodhound. Both the English Pointer and the German Shorthaired Pointer owe a great deal of their keenness of scent to the infusion of Bloodhound into their ancestry.

SALLY ANNE THOMPSON

Vizslas

The Hungarian or Magyar Vizsla attained its present popularity when introduced to the United States after World War II; in fact, it was in the 1950s that the first Vizslas were flown to Kansas City, Missouri, and the effort made to establish the breed in this country.

Like others of the so-called German Pointing Breeds, the Vizsla has a long history, reportedly being used by Magyar tribes which lived in the Carpathian Basin as far back as the eighth or ninth century. No less than the Weimaraner, the breed was carefully guarded. In fact, because of the Russian occupation subsequent to 1945, the true Vizsla almost disappeared. Breeding records were lost or destroyed. Fortunately, dedicated Hungarian sportsfolk "saved" seed stock, and with the importation of some Vizslas to the US, the breed's popularity has grown.

The Vizsla is not as large as the Weimaraner; it has a distinctive golden rust color, a smooth coat, and is of symmetrical proportions for its weight of 50-70 pounds and its height at the shoulders of 21 to 24 inches.

The *Field Dog Stud Book* of Chicago, Ill., after considerable research, was the first registry in the United States to recognize the breed. As in the case of the Brittany, the German Shorthair, Drahthaar and Weimaraner, there are also field trials exclusively for the Vizsla.

Other Pointing Breeds

The German Drahthaar (Wire-Hair) is similar to the Shorthair in many respects, except for its distinctive coat. It is a rugged, fine performer.

The Wire-Haired Pointing Griffon had its heyday in this country following its introduction in 1901. Louis A. Thebaud, who was later to be prominently identified with the establishment of the Brittany Spaniel in the United States, was the first to bring the Griffon to these shores.

E. K. Korthals of Holland was said to have developed the breed about 1875, and its harsh wire coat was a distinguishing feature. The Griffon was used chiefly by gunners in heavy coverts where the dog's coat afforded protection against punishing cover. A close-working dog, thorough in its search, of moderate speed, the breed never attained much popularity, but there are good specimens still bred in America.

The Spinoni, the Italian pointing breed, has a wiry, straggly coat, is a bit higher on the leg than the Griffon, but only a few were ever brought to this country and never bred extensively.

5 Selecting the puppy

If you are a novice, the best way is to have an experienced dog man help you choose your puppy. While there is a great deal of guesswork in picking out the best puppy in a litter, the successful breeder can distinguish certain qualities that usually ensure that a puppy will develop along proper lines.

If there is no one with such qualifications among your acquaintances, be sure that you go to a reputable breeder whose kennels are known for reliability. Check on the bloodlines, ascertain that "papers" are available, which means simply that the dog is eligible for registration, in either the *Field Dog Stud Book* or the AKC, for the former registers by many thousands the greater number of Pointers and Setters, which are bred for hunting and for field trials. If you refer to the advertising columns of the *American Field* of Chicago, a publication wherein a majority of Pointers and Setters are offered for sale, you are assured that an effort has been made to check on the seller, and if there is any misrepresentation the publication will assist you in a satisfactory adjustment.

SALLY ANNE THOMPSON

In order to train a dog, you must have clearly in mind precisely what you want him to do.

Granted that picking out the best puppy in a litter is largely a guess, you can select one that appeals to you. Your eye is taken by one of the youngsters. You like his looks, you like his behavior, you think he has *it*. That's the one for you to select. Simply keep strongly in mind not to pick a

SALLY ANNE THOMPSON

This is a Choke-Chain, or Slip collar. The leash is attached to the ring at the free end and jerked when the dog misbehaves or ignores a command. This causes the collar to tighten, but the tension is released as soon as the lead is slackened.

"Coming when called." Call the puppy to you. If he does not come promptly and willingly, enforce the command by hauling him in to you but then make a fuss over him.

SALLY ANNE THOMPSON

pup that is shy, timid, or physically unsound. Don't select an oversize puppy or a runt. Get one that has the physical appearance and color markings that are attractive to you.

6   Important natural qualities

The mission in life of the Pointer or Setter is to hunt upland game birds. Here are the natural qualities that a bird dog puppy should possess so that he may be developed and trained into an excellent field performer:

1. Instinct to hunt.
2. Good nose.
3. Instinct to point.
4. Intelligence.
5. Good constitution.
6. Nervous energy.
7. Good eyesight and hearing.
8. Tractable disposition.
9. Courage.
10. Good conformation, style and appearance.

A puppy possessed of these natural qualities may be expected to mature into a competent bird dog, for proper development of these will result in:

1. An intense desire to find birds for his handler.
2. A nose keen to detect the presence of game, and to locate it accurately and quickly.
3. Stanchness on point, without false pointing or blinking.
4. Bird wisdom, intelligent ground work, and the pace and range most effective for the work in hand.
5. Stamina—the endurance to see a job through.
6. Speed, industry and independence at work and intensity in searching.
7. Quickness in locating his handler, and in seeing and hearing his commands.

8. Kind handling and good manners, including steadiness to wing and shot, and backing his bracemate's point, and, if desired, prompt, tender retrieving of game.

9. Boldness on game and willingness to face unflinchingly heavy cover, briars, or other obstacles or handicaps.

10. Style of carriage and grace of movement, searching the wind with high head and merry tail, and standing up well on point with head aloft and tail level or elevated in the modern manner.

7   Training of bird dogs

You have acquired your puppy and believe him to have the natural qualities enumerated. Where do you begin his education?

There is no set formula endorsed by all authorities on training. In the case of hunting dogs and field trial performers, there are some who prefer to school the puppy in obedience, putting him through the yard training routine preliminary to field excursions. But most professionals, particularly the handlers charged with the development of wide-ranging major circuit field trial performers, believe that the prime essential is to excite the dog's interest in hunting and that outings in actual game environments are the proper way to get the youngster started. In fact, many six-month-old puppies are given the freedom of the prairies in the provinces of Saskatchewan, Manitoba and Alberta as a prelude to their development, training and campaigning.

Because it is of the utmost significance that you get a line on the dog's natural qualities, you give him the freedom of the field, allow him to get out and run, to find, flush and chase birds, and to have a rollicking time as his hereditary predispositions come into flower.

In those preliminary outings do not distract him with orders or attempt to curb his natural tendencies, but capitalize on your chance to study his manner of moving, his carriage, observe whatever may be helpful to you in his subsequent education. Try to analyse his character, note any peculiarities of his temperament, determine what you consider his strong points and do not overlook any shortcomings.

In former times trainers thought that it was a waste of time to begin the education of a dog before it was eight or nine months of age. No less than with babies, it is now accepted that almost from birth the youngster is capable of absorbing knowledge. So don't fret about how soon you should start the pup's tuition. You can teach him elementary things like his name, a common command like "No," and to lead. The more time and attention you can give him the better, although serious field work and obedience lessons as such can be deferred until the dog is ten months of age. Don't be misled by that old saw "you can't teach an old dog new tricks" for to some extent a dog's capacity for learning is based on the excellence of his teacher.

"Down." The modern method is to have pointing dogs remain standing. Trainers nowadays do not teach "Down" unless it is necessary with certain pupils to achieve a desired result.

SALLY ANNE THOMPSON

SALLY ANNE THOMPSON

"Stay." This is a prolongation of "Sit." The dog must retain his "Sit" position while you move away from him, and "Stay" until you release him.

There are precocious puppies just as there are child prodigies. Not all these mature into world-beaters. But it is mighty fetching to see a six- eight- or ten-week-old puppy pointing. The pup is simply doing something that comes naturally. Perhaps here would be a good place to consider the pointing instinct.

8 The pointing instinct

The instinct to point as expressed by Pointers, Setters and other recognized pointing breeds is an ancestral action handed down by heredity. Other animals show the same inclination, but pointing dogs have particularly well-defined hereditary characteristics. It is more than a predisposition, it is instinctive for them to point game and to stand motionless facing the scent to show the location of game birds.

When the dog strikes the scent of game, he points, and because he appears transfixed by the smell, some claim he is hypnotized, but it is simply suddenly suspended motion, the *pause before springing* that is characteristic of many wild animals that hunt their prey by scent and even of some that are sight-hunters.

When the dog finds game and points he is in full possession of his faculties; it is not a cataleptic phenomenon, though he may stand like a statue, with eyes dilated, jaws open (or perhaps champing), a slobber string drooling from his mouth, and flanks twitching. He realizes that his quarry is directly in front, and the careful breeding and training of generations of his ancestors, plus his own education, rivet him to the position. There he stands stanchly while his master flushes the game he has found.

At first, the point of a young dog, though stylish and intense, is likely to be of the "flash" type; there is scarcely a pause before, impelled by deep-seated desires, he will jump in, flush and chase. Such experiences heighten his passion for hunting and provide the wise trainer the opportunity to develop his prospect.

There are some who write about "teaching a dog to point." But pointing is an instinctive act; the trainer simply reinforces the dog's stanchness and makes him steady. However, the pointing instinct, as manifested by a Pointer or Setter, is not a single impulse, but a combination of several hereditary traits. All these instincts must work together to realize the excellence of the ultimate point. For example, when a dog's keen nose smells game nearby, the will to stop or point asserts itself, and all the innate senses that go into this action must co-ordinate simultaneously. If any psychical or physical part fails to respond immediately, the act may be marred. Each part must respond properly, culminating in the instantaneous action witnessed in the point.

There is a lot of difference in the way individual dogs go to their game and establish their points. Some disdain "making game," forego any feathering in the proximity of birds, but simply, with breath-taking speed, literally jump into point. Other dogs will get excited and busy when they strike foot scent or get in the vicinity of game, and will work feverishly and enthusiastically to locate it before pointing. In addition, the attitudes—expression, character, style, loftiness, intensity, rigidity—are widely divergent.

In the development of the pointing dog, the best method is to wait until the dog points naturally. Forget about artificial means to educate him. The day will come when the dog's natural manifestation of the pointing instinct will tell you plainly that he is ready for breaking.

9 Training the pointing dog

No writer on bird dog training would remain in good standing if he did not, at the very outset, say: "In order to train a dog, you must know more than the dog." It would be better to say that in order to train a dog you must have clearly in mind precisely what you wish to teach him. Then you devise an effective means of getting him to understand. "Rapport" is the way some put it. And, indeed, the training of a pointing dog does depend on finding a means of communicating to him what you want him to do.

Patience and perseverance are most important in the art of dog training. Bear in mind, too, that the health, diet, care and condition of your dog are also of great significance. Regular and careful feeding, clean drinking water, daily grooming, plenty of exercise, friendly companionship—these build an atmosphere of contentment, and the dog

SALLY ANNE THOMPSON

"Heel." A pointing dog should be taught to heel, both from foot and from horseback. Heeling means that the dog walks by your side, or just to your rear, and does not barge to the front.

eagerly gives the best that is in him. Too much stress cannot be laid on keeping your dog comfortable and physically fit. Regular veterinary care is recommended. Give him attention during the "off" season and see that there is a preparatory period prior to any actual hunting expeditions. Baseball players, pugilists, race-horses, athletes and animals in competition have "spring training." Don't expect a pointing dog, after a long warm-weather layoff, to be able to go out and hunt all day. Prepare him for the shooting or field trial season by short workouts.

Rewards and punishments are basic in any effective system of training. The usual way to teach a puppy his name is through his stomach. Pronounce his name as you call him to you and reward him with a morsel. Select a short, distinctive name. Dogs go by sound, not spelling. They're phoneticians, not orthographers. They may not understand many words to which they respond; they react to the inflection of the voice, the intonation. A trainer can use a different word that sounds the same, using a similar inflection and mannerism, and the dog will respond as if the original word of command had been uttered.

A puppy learns his name quickly. Assume a squatting position, call the dog's name and he will come willingly and cheerfully. Repeat this. It will be gratifying to see how soon the youngster knows his name. Then be sure to use the name whenever you have the opportunity. Remember the tidbit.

The command "Come" can be associated with the dog's name. Simply say "Come" or "Come here," and add the

Introducing the firearm. The introduction should be with the dog at some distance from the shooter. Try to cause the detonation under such conditions that the puppy is unafraid. If the dog shows uneasiness, don't try to reassure him, but simply act unconcerned.

SALLY ANNE THOMPSON

puppy's name when calling him to be fed. The prospect of getting a reward in the way of food prompts quick response and familiarity with the command.

A word of caution. Do not use several words for the same command. When you have chosen a particular word of command, use it and stick to it. A dog may be confused if you use different words or a series of commands for the same act.

During the early lessons, use your normal voice. Preferably use single words: the shorter and more distinctive the sound, the better. Give commands naturally. No matter what happens, do not lose your poise. Do not start to shout, stay calm and confident, and keep your tone friendly though firm.

Do not hesitate to add words to your puppy's vocabulary that will be helpful in controlling his actions.

All this can be fun, exhilarating, gratifying. It gives opportunity for the exercise of patience and perseverance. Persistence is essential to success.

Be sure that all lessons are short. You can make the dog's education fun in many ways, but never prolong any session until it becomes boring. True, later in exacting steadiness to wing and shot from the dog, you may, in certain circumstances, have to persist, but shorter lessons are desirable in teaching the fundamentals of yard training and obedience.

10   Yard training

This embraces the early lessons of basic obedience. You are into the yard training routine when you have taught your dog his name, in having him come when called, and when he understands and responds to simple orders like "Kennel Up."

Equipment

The good mechanic knows the importance of proper tools for a particular purpose. Among the implements of training are a collar, a plain flat leather one will do, with a ring to which a leash, five feet in length, may be easily attached with snap and swivel. Purchase a "check cord," lightweight rope, and it can be helpful if you have two of these, one 15 or 18 feet long, the other perhaps 30 or 40 feet long, for use in the hunting field. Get a good dog whistle, of metal or bakelite, the type with the "pea" or cork ball inside. You can, if you wish, get a so-called "silent" whistle, the high-pitched, scarcely audible kind, because the canine ear is able to hear vibrations up to six times the maximum for man.

Subsequently, if you give your dog a course in force retrieving, you will need a stripped corn-cob, a sawbuck or retrieving dumbbell, a pistol, a whip, force or spike collar, a small piece of wood covered with nails, a cushion pad and a dummy hare.

As the education of your pointing dog progresses and you train for refinements, you will want to supplement your equipment. Fishing rods, bird wings, releasers and call birds, not to mention horses, etc., if you are also developing for field trial competition.

Collar and leash: Put a collar on the puppy and let him become accustomed to it. Don't worry if he frets at first. When you attach a leash, he may have other thoughts about leading, but hold your ground, let him jump around, and when he is ready to go with you, take him for a companionable walk. Getting the puppy accustomed to collar and leash is preliminary to other elementary training.

Housebreaking: Pointers and Setters are usually kennel dogs, but can be fine house companions as well. Keeping a hunting dog in the house doesn't ruin him, as some may claim. Indeed, Mississippi Zev, the immortal setter, winner

of the 1946 National Championship and four titles in all, was "babied" by May Bufkin, the wife of his handler, Earl Bufkin.

If you want to housebreak your puppy, begin at an early age, just as soon as you get him, preferably when he is eight or ten weeks old. Regularity is the key. Remember that the puppy will want to relieve himself soon after eating, so about ten minutes after each feeding, take him outdoors for a walk, let him find a spot where he will do his duty, and on future strolls let him return to the same place. Praise him when he goes promptly. If he commits an error in the house, make him understand. Shame him, show him, convey your displeasure and immediately take him out-of-doors. If you can keep him out until he relieves himself, all the better. In the early stages you must take him out as frequently as is necessary. If you do your part it will be gratifying to see how quickly the puppy gets the message.

Coming when called: Actually, with most dogs you will have accomplished this while the puppy is learning his name. There may be some problems, however, when the youngster is out, enjoying his freedom, and does not want this interfered with even by a master he adores. So, attach a check cord to the collar. Call the puppy to you. If he does not come promptly and willingly, enforce the command by hauling him in to you, then make a fuss over him. This is repeated until response is automatic to the command. A few *short* lessons will be sufficient.

Sit: Teaching the dog to sit is a simple matter. But for this lesson, like all others, select a quiet place, free from distractions. Have the dog positioned in front of you. Take hold of his hide under the neck, holding his head up, pull him toward you slightly, then push him back. He will go to his haunches. You hold him in this position and praise him. With this method you do not have to press on his back or hindquarters.

However, most trainers make the dog sit by having the lead held high, then tapping the hindquarters gently with a switch or whip. The light touch causes the dog to assume a sitting position as his forequarters are held up by the trainer. Pressure is applied if needed. Again, praise the pupil. Repeat the routine until the puppy will sit at once on command, and then you can substitute a sign or whistle signal for the word "Sit." The tap on the rump is no longer required.

Stay: A prolongation of "Sit." You merely have the dog retain his sit position while you move away from him. At first he will probably follow you, but return him firmly and order "Stay." He must remain in the "Stay" position until you release him from it.

Down: The old-timer used the command "Charge" when he wanted his dog to drop. But the modern method is to have pointing dogs remain standing. While dogs may occasionally drop of their own volition in particular situations, trainers nowadays do not teach "Down" unless it is necessary with certain pupils to achieve a desired result.

Heel: A pointing dog should be taught to heel, both from foot and from horseback. Heeling means that the dog walks by your side or just to your rear, but does not barge to the front. With a suitably long lead attached to the collar, call the dog to your side, order "Heel" and begin to walk. If the pupil tries to run in front, restrain him. An easy way is to swing the loose end of the lead in front of you, retaining a hold on the dog, so that as the circular swish is maintained, it serves as a barrier. Some handlers simply use a switch and lightly tap the dog's nose if he endeavors to get too far forward. You may have the dog heel on either side. Many gunners want the dog on the opposite side from the one they carry the shotgun. The same procedure is used when having a dog heel from horseback.

SALLY ANNE THOMPSON

During the training period, don't fire over the dog's points until you know that he is not shy of game or fearful of the gun report. In fact, the first time a bird is dropped for the dog, it is better to stand a little distance from the dog's point when firing.

SALLY ANNE THOMPSON

Pointers and Setters can do excellent work as retrievers. In regular stages train your dog to go a distance when the command is "Go-Fetch" and retrieve the article. Here a furred dummy is being used.

"Whoa!"—an important command: Able professional trainers insist that *Whoa* should take precedence over all other commands. You can understand how important it is that you are able to stop your dog *when* you want and *where* you want. Teaching a Pointer or Setter to "Whoa" can begin at feeding time.

Place the dog's pan of food some distance in front of him, hold him from it, voice the command "Whoa," and stroke him gently as you restrain him. Keep him standing motionless. At first a few seconds are enough, and a cheerful "Go on" permits the dog to charge the feed pan.

Gradually increase the time you keep the dog waiting and get across the meaning of "Whoa." Then attach his collar and a check cord and use the same procedure, allowing the dog to start for the feed pan, then pulling him up a distance from the food.

When the dog stops and stays at the order "Whoa," you are ready to have him obey the command in the field. Stand in front of him, raise an arm, command "Whoa." When he stops on the command and remains standing motionless, you begin to move about in front of him. If he moves, put him back in his original position. Do so firmly. Repeat it as often as necessary.

11   Introducing the firearm

If the gun is introduced properly, there will be no problem with gun-shyness which is an acquired trait. Say that some highly nervous dogs are predisposed to it, if you wish, but veterans tell you that fear of the gun is not hereditary.

The firearm may be introduced at feeding time or while the dog is in the field, but when it is done the dog must be preoccupied with something other than the report of the gun, and consider it merely incidental. Try to cause the detonation under such conditions that the puppy is unafraid. If the youngster is hurrying about in the field chasing small birds, fire a small pistol loaded with blank ammunition. Pretend to be wholly unconscious of the report, and the puppy will take his cue from your behavior. If the dog is definitely uneasy, don't try to reassure him, but simply act unconcerned.

Under favorable circumstances, you will continue to shoot the pistol, gradually lessening the distance you are away from the dog. In due course the youngster will be ready for the shotgun, although there is never any need to hurry this. Let the dog become accustomed to the sight and sound of the gun under as pleasurable conditions as possible. Don't fire over his points until you know that he is not shy of game or afraid of the gun report. In fact, the first time a bird is dropped for the dog, it is desirable to stand a little distance from his point when firing.

A gun-shy hunting dog is worthless in the shooting field. Gun-shyness can be cured; there are trainer specialists who accomplish it in good time, but unless you want to take on a tough job, let the experts handle the gun-shys.

12   Retrieving lessons

Many hunters no longer want their pointing dogs to retrieve. In field trials for Pointers and Setters, it is no longer a requirement. Some shooters take Spaniels and the regular Retriever breeds along to recover game killed over pointing dogs.

Pointers and Setters, however, can do excellent work as retrievers. Many can be taught through the play method, but the only reliable retriever is one that is force-broken to retrieve. Force is applied—by collar, hand or other method—to make the dog do your bidding.

Lessons in retrieving should be short. The initial lesson is to teach the dog to open his mouth so you can put an object in it. The next is to have him hold the object, and then to carry it. You get him to accept the object from your hand, then to pick it up from the ground. Your next accomplishment is when the dog will go a distance and get it, and eventually will retrieve it to your hand.

These acts are steps in teaching a dog to retrieve, and each must be forced separately in sequence. A small, quiet room, barn or a secluded yard, where you are unlikely to be interrupted, should be used.

Have the dog sit; with a force collar or your hand over lips and mouth, get him to open his mouth, and slip the article between his teeth as you command "Fetch." Hold one end and try to keep the article in the dog's mouth. If he drops it, replace it. Use the order "Hold" when he is retaining the article in his mouth. He will soon be glad to hold

SALLY ANNE THOMPSON

The hunting dog is taught to return with the quarry and sit in front of the hunter, holding it in his mouth waiting for the next command.

and carry it. When you want him to release it, merely command "Let go." If his jaws are clamped tight, use force to make him open his mouth, just as you did originally.

By regular stages you get him to reach out and take the article from your hand, which is gradually lowered to the ground, then go to a distance where the command is "Go fetch." By degrees you instruct him in carrying it and in due time teach him to "mark" in the field.

13 The handling of pointing dogs afield

When a Pointer or Setter puppy is selected, the assumption is that it has the necessary qualifications to become a proficient performer in the hunting field. It is also taken for granted that the hunter going afield with a pointing dog is adept at handling the dog in the field.

It is true that the experienced Pointer or Setter has the instincts and judgment to hunt promising bird objectives in logical sequence, plus the know-how of handling game when it is found. But the hunter or handler can help the dog's game-finding efforts by piloting him to spots that may have been missed or overlooked, places that have gone unsearched but are promising concealments of game. A dog can be directed or encouraged to hunt places where hidden game may have sought refuge and which would probably be by-passed without a thorough search.

At the command "Let go" the retrieved object is dropped, usually into the hunter's hand. SALLY ANNE THOMPSON

In the hunting field or in field trial competition, the best results are obtained by the bird dog and gunner who know their business . . . and know it well. A pair that work harmoniously, quietly, as a team—without need for a constant flow of commands from hunter to dog.

Hunting technique

An experienced bird hunter can size up a countryside and quickly spot the more likely places for birds to be. The same goes for a seasoned bird dog, for his bird sense has been enriched by experience and training. The "bird wisdom" of the dog is evident as he "looks over" the country or area to be hunted, the manner in which he goes to objectives that are likely to produce game, and the technique he adopts in searching these places. The wise dog adjusts his work to weather conditions, time of day, and knowledge of the habits of the game birds being sought. The type of terrain and character of cover may be patterned according to the game birds being hunted, whether, for instance, they are bob-white quail, ringnecked pheasants, ruffed grouse, or prairie chickens (sharp-tailed or square-tailed grouse), etc.

Generally speaking, the greatest feeding activity of game birds is in the late afternoon. But when rigorous conditions are in prospect birds may feed feverishly to fill their crops before the impending storm.

Scenting conditions have much to do with the success of a dog's efforts. A dog has the best opportunity to find birds when the game is moving about and scent is strong. But you never know for sure about scent . . . until the dog proves the case for you. Nevertheless, because a dog can have an off-day, many seasoned hunters work a brace of dogs at a time, and this gives a check on each of them.

Any hunter's skill can be increased by watching an intelligent Pointer or Setter at work. Watch the way he patterns the country, the wisdom, desire and determination with which he casts to objectives, and the manner in which he locates and points his game. A smart dog expresses a great deal that enables a hunter to diagnose a situation quickly and accurately. A positive point, with high style and thrilling intensity, conveys that the birds are located exactly. When a dog's tail is waving and his demeanor irresolute, it shows uncertainty and lack of positive location, or it may mean that the birds are moving. A seasoned hunter who knows his dog and his expressions understands at once.

Refinements of training

Steadiness to wing and shot is indispensable for polished performance by a Pointer or Setter in the shooting field. Stopping to flush and/or shot is also necessary.

Confirming a dog in his stanchness on point and remaining steady to wing and shot is facilitated by his obedience to the command "Whoa." This also applies in teaching him that proper behavior is to stop at an accidental or wild flush or to shot.

Backing—honoring the stand or point of a bracemate— is another essential. A dog "backs" when he sees another dog on point, even though the dog which backs has not seen or scented game; many do it instinctively, but others are reluctant to do so voluntarily or even at command. Backing a bracemate's point is not only a pretty sight, but is useful as well, for it prevents one dog from coming into the vicinity and flushing, unwittingly or jealously, the birds a bracemate is pointing. Can you imagine a more beautiful sight than that of a bird dog pointing stylishly with one or more other dogs backing proudly?

14   Bad manners and serious faults

Undesirable habits may develop, but these can be corrected with intelligent tuition. An inclination of a dog to potter should be discouraged. The trainer must urge the dog to hunt at a smart clip, be quick to send him on at the slightest suggestion of lingering on ground scent, get the dog to seek for body scent, hunting with a high head, rather than prowling and nosing on foot scent.

Trailing: The act of following a bracemate or staying in its company denotes a lack of independence, initiative and confidence. Work the dog alone until he relies on his own abilities, or put him down with a dog so slow that he won't tag along but will decide to step out on his own. Conventional trailing is consistently following behind a bracemate, but there is the "head trailer" that stays ahead, either because he depends on his bracemate to find game or because he simply enjoys the sociability and is not honestly searching for birds. Overcome any tendency to trail by instilling independence in the dog, establish his confidence in his own ability to find game, and stimulate his desire and determination by killing birds over *his* points.

False pointing: This is a most annoying fault. It may be due to faulty training or a dog's tendency to point the slightest scent encountered. The cure? Simply ignore the dog's points. Don't pay the slightest attention when he stacks up. Get him to understand that you are only interested when he establishes a stand with game birds smack in front.

Blinking: The cardinal sin. A dog, aware of the presence of game, deliberately leaves or abandons the point. Or he may smell birds but refuse to indicate their presence by pointing: he avoids the game and continues on. A dog with this fault poses too great a problem and requires too much work for the average amateur trainer.

Rabbit chasing: Usually a phase in bird dog development. The use of the check cord and the whip will suffice for a cure.

SALLY ANNE THOMPSON

In the hunting field or in field trial competition, the best results are obtained by the bird dog and hunter who know their business, and know it well. A pair that work harmoniously and quietly as a team do not need a constant flow of commands from hunter to dog.

Never kill a rabbit when hunting with your pointing dog. Actually, most dogs will quit pointing fur or chasing rabbits when only birds are shot over their points.

Flushing birds: Playing with birds, lack of stanchness on point, unsteadiness to wing and breaking to shot will happen but need not be tolerated after the dog has been trained. Here the command "Whoa!" repays all the time spent making the dog give immediate response to the order.

Bolting: An expression of the dog's preference for hunting by himself rather than in the interest of the gun. Self-hunting fosters this. Once a dog is well into the training routine, many handlers do not permit any self-hunting. Bolting has been cured by hard-working professionals, but it isn't easy.

15   Proper conditioning

As summer wanes and the hay fever season subsides, the average sportsman begins to whet his appetite for some fall shooting or a resumption of field trial competition. He inspects his guns, checks on ammunition, examines shooting apparel, boots and other gear, looks over his stable tack and makes sure that all the paraphernalia dear to the heart of the hunter is ready for the new season.

There may be no doubt in his mind that his dogs will be ready. But he is in for an awakening. It is unreasonable to expect a dog, cooped up most of the time between hunting seasons, with a resultant softening of his muscles and thinning of the epithelium of the foot pads, to go into the field over all kinds of stony and sandy terrain, studded with stubble, thorns, burrs and briars, and have his pads and muscles stand the strain of the long hours of work demanded by his enthusiastic master. Nature seems to prepare the tissues of the body gradually to stand a reasonable amount of work, but when more work is given than nature has fortified the tissues to stand, various systems—muscular, bony, nervous, vascular, etc.—suffer to a greater or lesser degree.

Under proper conditions, slow and gradually increasing use of the pads causes a proliferation of cells, an increase in the number of cell layers, with a consequent thickening and hardening of the epidermis, the top layer of the skin. This is nature's protection against excessive wear and is exemplified in the thick, horny cuticle on the blacksmith's palms or on the feet of those who have gone barefoot for some time. This horny integument is not produced quickly, even under optimum conditions, and when rapid wear of thin tender skin reduces cells faster than they are repaired or produced, or when violent friction causes blisters, soreness results. Much more time will be required to heal the abrasion and bring the new epidermis to working condition than would be if care had been exercised to prevent such occurrence.

To toughen the pads, muscles, tendons and ligaments of your unconditioned bird dog, remove him from a damp kennel yard to a dry place two months before the field trial or hunting season opens, as dryness is one of the essentials in producing tough, hard horn. Soft, moist epithelium is quickly worn down. Start the conditioning process with a half-hour of walking, roading or slow running for a few days to build up the dog's tissues gradually and to reduce excess weight, and then increase the amount and strenuousness of the exercise gradually.

There are some kinds of topography over which the best conditioned dog cannot continue for very long without injury to his pads. In such a situation, judgment must be exercised to prevent wearing of pads.

Should your hunting dog become footsore at the beginning of the season, keep him in a clean, dry place, wash the feet occasionally with soap and water, and allow him to rest long enough for the worn pads to grow a new layer of

SALLY ANNE THOMPSON

Backing (honoring the stand or point of a bracemate) is another essential. A dog "backs" when he sees another dog on point, even though he himself has neither seen nor scented game.

cells on the thin places before working him again. It is helpful to place the pad of each foot, as often as is necessary to keep them covered, in slightly warmed roofing pitch, the kind that is brittle when cold, and to put a little cold water over the warm pitch that adheres to the pad before the foot is set on the floor. This will set the pitch on the pad and it will not be thinned out too much when the dog takes the first few steps after its application. Be sure not to heat the pitch so that it burns the pads, but just enough to soften it. The foot should be perfectly dry when the pitch is applied and any that happens to get between the toes should be removed as soon as it hardens. Remember that this treatment is for an emergency. It is only palliative and will not take the place of systematic conditioning.

Boots, properly fitted and applied, are most useful in protecting the sound pad when the dog is hunted over topography having an exceptional abrasive action, as well as in helping a worn or injured pad to heal.

But a dog's legs, feet and pads are not all that should be given attention in a conditioning program. Nutrition and parasitism should be investigated long before the hunting or field trial season opens. Nutrition contributes tremendously to the dog's health and vitality and his vigor and staying qualities depend upon it to a large extent.

Nutrition

Good nutrition is attained when the energies of the animal are not being dispersed faster than they can be renewed.

If diet deficiency is responsible for the dog's lack of staying qualities it can be overcome by proper feeding, a diet consisting of good grade protein, both animal and vegetable, as well as carbohydrates, fats, vitamins, minerals, etc., in sufficient amounts to repair and replace worn tissues and supply needed energy and heat.

It takes considerable reserve in the tissues to maintain stamina. The reserve is found principally in the glycogen in the liver and muscles and the dextrose in the bloodstream. Dogs should not be fasted too long before being given hard work. Ordinarily a dog that is to be hunted hard, if not fed generously for six or eight hours, should be given a little glucose in a few ounces of milk before he is released. Veteran trainers who are expert in conditioning dogs for long, strenuous heats in championship field trials realize the effectiveness of such sustenance during the arduous work.

Dogs that are hunted for many hours should have some nourishment during the day or toward the end.

Can you imagine a more beautiful sight than that of a bird dog pointing stylishly?

SALLY ANNE THOMPSON

16   Field trials

A field trial is simply a test of hunting dogs under actual or simulated shooting conditions.

The first formal field trial was held in England in 1866. The initial grand field trial in the United States took place on October 8, 1874, near Memphis, Tennessee. H.C. Pritchett's black Setter, Knight, won. In subsequent years the growth of the game was slow but steady until it surged to remarkable popularity during the last quarter century.

In 1966 there were more than 800 formal field trials held on the American continent for pointing breeds. Field trials have been fittingly described as the fastest growing recreational activity in the United States.

Field trials were not instituted for the purpose of developing a class of dogs suited to the needs of the average shooter, but to bring to public notice the performers best equipped to perpetuate the most desirable qualities possessed by the high-class field dog. Thus, field trials are regarded as (1) a spectacular form of sport; and (2) a basis for data on which to conduct breeding operations.

Field trials are held in all parts of the country—from the prairie provinces of Canada to the savannahs of the South, from Maine's rock-ribbed coast to the sunny slopes of California. There is competition for both the amateur and professional, but amateur status applies only to the handler.

There are three age classifications—Puppy, Derby and All-Age. As with race horses, January 1 is the universal birthday for Pointers and Setters which compete in trials. Puppies range up to about fifteen months; Derbies up to thirty months; and in All-Age competition, as implied, a dog of any age may compete.

A Championship title is won in sanctioned Championship competition. The *American Field* approves all Open Championship stakes; the Amateur Field Trial Clubs of America, parent organization of some 300 individual member clubs, licenses Amateur Championship events.

What does a Pointer or Setter have to do to win in trials? To put it succinctly, the All-Age dog must:

(1) Show class; i.e., bird sense, speed, range and stamina. (2) Hunt to the course. (3) Search upwind for body scent. (4) Locate and point quickly and accurately. (5) Be stanch. (6) Back his bracemate on sight. (7) Be steady to wing and shot.

He must not: (1) Get out of hand. (2) Bolt. (3) Cut in. (4) Cut back. (5) Hunt foot scent. (6) Blink. (7) Trail his bracemate.

Field trials are conceded by those who know anything at all about the pastime to be the cleanest of sports. Not the slightest breath of scandal has ever debased bird dog competitions. There are intense rivalries, but the standard of ethics is of the highest. Gambling is taboo.

Cash purses and trophies are offered as prizes. Purses may range from $100 to $6,000, as in the case of the American Field Quail Futurity. Entry fees also have a wide range, from a few dollars to $125.00 per dog in the National Championship.

The American Field Publishing Company, 222 West Adams Street, Chicago, Illinois, 60606, has kept complete records of all recognized trials since the first one in 1874. For any person interested in getting full information about the sport, it is suggested that the *American Field* be contacted.

17   Good breeding

In selecting the dams of the future generations of your dogs, after having obtained the bloodlines which it is wished to perpetuate, considerable investigation should be made to determine if there are any grievous hereditary defects in the ancestry, such as deafness, blindness, ectropion, entropion, hair lip, cleft palate, poor conformation, hip dysplasia, or other defects that it is not desirable to have passed on to the progeny. This refers not only to the dam, but to the sire as

SALLY ANNE THOMPSON

The ears of a dog should be cleaned regularly. Use a cotton swab dipped in light oil or a good canine ear cleanser. Never probe deeper than you can see.

well; both parents share in the good or bad traits that are inherited by the offspring after the combining of certain genes of the germ cells that control physique, character, intelligence, bird sense, etc., in the puppy, and which are contributed equally by both parents.

Too frequently the hereditary traits of the dam are given but little consideration because it is expected that an outstanding sire will overcome any defects the dam might pass on, that the sire will stamp the puppies with his own good qualities, no matter what the qualifications of the dam. *This is not true.* The dam is just as responsible for the good or bad qualities of the progeny as is the sire, and for this reason even greater consideration should be exercised in her selection.

Let us assume that the puppy you have selected to be a future brood bitch, because of desirable traits found in her ancestry, is between six and fifteen months old. During this time, depending on breed and nutrition of the puppy, the first oestrual (heat) period makes its appearance. If the puppy you have selected shows signs of her first oestrum at nine or ten months, the usual time, our advice is not to breed at this age, in order to give her more time in which to mature completely. It is best not to breed a bitch until her second oestrum which, in the normal female, occurs when she is about fifteen months old. By this time she is fully developed and pregnancy is not an added load to the developing tissues of her body.

See that she is well fed, not only in quantity but in quality as well. See that she receives sufficient exercise to keep up her muscle tone and that her health is promoted in every way possible. About one month before the beginning of her

A Hunting Dog must find his way through all sorts of cover. It is not unusual for him to pick up ticks, burrs, and other foreign matter in his coat. He should be brushed as often as necessary to prevent matting and to keep his fur free from disorders, as well as to maintain his proud appearance. SALLY ANNE THOMPSON

second oestrual period, some thought should be given to the presence of external and internal parasites. If a microscopical fecal examination discloses that treatment for any particular kind of intestinal worm is necessary, especially for hookworm, treatment should be given before the female is bred. Examine her skin thoroughly to be sure that she is free from skin disease of any kind. Too much emphasis cannot be put on the importance of a blood examination for *dirofilaria immitis* before breeding time, because infection from heartworms is always a possibility and a mighty serious handicap to both the pregnant bitch and her puppies. The filaria-infected bitch should not be bred.

The duration of the average oestrual period is about three weeks. Experience has taught that the opportune time to breed, in order to insure the greatest percentage of pregnancies, especially when only one service is allowed, is usually between the 12th and 15th day after the beginning of menstruation, or about the time the color has just disappeared from the menstrual discharge and at the stage when the vulva is softening.

Ovulation in the bitch takes place, on the average, about the 13th or 14th day after the beginning of menstruation, and as the ovum can be fertilized for only about a day or so, it is necessary that sperm be in the tubes or around the ovaries sometime during the life of the ova.

The oestrual period may be very much shorter or longer than is usual, and one has to be guided somewhat by the actions of the female toward the male as to the best time to breed. Usually only one service is necessary, provided service takes place at about time of ovulation. However, because of possible variations in the maturation time of the ova or the death of the sperm in the uterus or the tubes, or other possibilities that might hinder the meeting of the sperm and the ova at the proper time, it is best to allow two services, with one day intervening between each service, to insure the bitch becoming pregnant and to obtain the largest number of puppies.

During the period of gestation, which varies usually from 56 to 68 days, with an average of 61 to 63 days, the pregnant bitch should be kept in a clean, worm-larva or worm-egg free enclosure, not in a run or kennel that has been housing worm-infected dogs. She should be amply fed a good, mixed diet to which should be added cod-liver oil and dry yeast daily, as well as a liberal allowance of fat. She should have fresh, clean milk to drink daily; condensed milk has also proved effective. The bitch should have a supply of fresh water and also clean, cooked bones to gnaw upon for needed calcium and phosphorus. She not only needs calcium and phosphorus and other minerals for her own tissues, but also needs them to build the bony structure of the developing embryos and for numerous other reasons concerned with normal tissue growth and function. The vitamin D in cod-liver oil in the food, and the rays of the sun on the skin, all help the tissue to utilize calcium and phosphorus. It may be well to interpolate here that manufacturers of dog foods have made real progress in making their products precisely what is needed.

The pregnant bitch should be given daily exercise until a few days before parturition is to take place. The amount and kind of exercise depends on the physical condition of the bitch. On the whole, after the third week of pregnancy, all hard running, jumping, or jarring should be prevented, especially during the last two weeks. This is recommended although there are some hunters who like to work the pregnant female until late in the gestation period. Do not allow the pregnant bitch to become overly fat because of too much food or too little exercise.

Two weeks before parturition is to take place, provide a separate, dry, roomy, warm enclosure, away from other dogs or other animals, making sure that it is worm-egg and -larva free. Do not allow fleas, mosquitoes, lice, flies or ticks to infest the dam, or later the puppies. Place the bitch in these quarters ahead of time in order to allow her an ample period in which to become accustomed to her new surroundings. Supply a liberal amount of clean bedding and watch her actions from day to day. If she is constipated, keep her bowels regular with a small, daily dose of milk of magnesia or a mineral oil. Feed her no bones during the last three or four days of pregnancy.

A few days before the puppies are to arrive, most brood bitches will fuss with the bedding, scratch and nose it around, making a bed in anticipation of the coming event which heralds its arrival by manifestations of some uneasiness and a little nervousness, and then shortly by mild contractions of the abdominal muscles.

The contractions gradually increase in strength and the interval between them shortens, and soon, usually within one to six hours, if parturition is proceeding normally, the first puppy arrives at the vulva, usually preceded by the so-called bag of waters. The bitch proceeds to tear open the water bag, if it is not already broken, or does so shortly after the puppy is born, or while being born. After the puppy has been born, the bitch severs the umbilical cord, if it has not already been broken, with her teeth. Most times the afterbirth follows immediately, as it is attached to the umbilical cord and the cord in turn to the puppy. At other times, because of the cord breaking during parturition, it is expelled shortly after, or just before the birth of the next puppy.

During parturition an attendant should be close at hand to assist the bitch and to be sure that there are as many afterbirths expelled as there are puppies. The attendant takes hold of the puppy with one hand as it is being delivered, and if the water bag is not broken, breaks it, releasing the puppy, and applies gentle, steady traction; the expulsion of the afterbirth is usually hastened by the efforts of the bitch. A smooth-edged forceps, clamped on the placenta end of the cord, helps in holding on to the placenta if the puppy is separated from the placenta before it is expelled.

When the puppy and the afterbirth have both been expelled intact, the cord is severed about 1 to $1\frac{1}{2}$ inches from the belly. One does not have to be hasty in severing the cord, as a few minutes' wait will cause coagulation of blood in the cord and little if any hemorrhaging will follow. It is seldom necessary to apply ligatures to the cord to prevent hemorrhage, and ligatures are likely to encourage the bitch to lick and nibble at the cord to the extent of causing damage to the abdominal wall. However, if it is desired to do so, a sterile thread can be tightly applied between the puppy's belly and the to-be-severed end of the cord.

The bitch will usually proceed to eat the afterbirths soon after they are expelled, if not watched. While eating the

In addition to inanimate matter, the Hunting Dog will frequently pick up hitchhikers in the form of fleas or ticks while out in the field. He should be sprayed regularly, powdered, or dipped in a good insecticidal mixture regularly, particularly after every outdoor excursion.

SALLY ANNE THOMPSON

afterbirths appears to be quite a natural trait of carnivora, it is best not to allow it in the bitch as experience evidences that she does better and is more free from sickness and bowel trouble after parturition if not permitted to eat the after-births.

It is a good practice to take each puppy, which has been rubbed dry with a clean towel, away from the bitch as soon as the next puppy is about to be born, so as to prevent her from stepping or lying on the puppies and injuring or killing them during her labor. Dry and cover the puppies, keep them warm and far enough away so that the bitch will not hear them crying.

After all of the puppies are born, give the bitch a drink of fresh milk containing a tablespoonful of corn syrup, and in a few hours give her a light feeding of cooked meat and cereals. If parturition extends over a rather long period, she can have an occasional drink of milk if she cares for it, but do not allow her to fill her stomach.

After all of the puppies have arrived, clean up the dam's bed, supply new, clean fabric for bedding, wash off the mamma and vulva with soap and warm water, then with clean, warm water. Dry her skin well and place the puppies with her. Do not use straw, hay, sawdust or excelsior for bedding the whelping bitch and very young puppies.

Watch the dam, without molesting her, during the first day after the puppies are born to see that she takes kindly to them. After she has settled down and the puppies have started to nurse, leave her pretty much to herself and litter, except to feed her or to allow her to go out for necessary relief, or perhaps to give her a little exercise several times during the day after the second day.

Do not douch your bitch after a normal parturition, or do any unnecessary manipulation with your fingers during parturition. Your hands, and all instruments and pans, should be clean. If labor is delayed, that is if no puppies make their appearance after from four to six hours of labor, or if the bitch has retained some of the afterbirths, procure the services of a reliable veterinarian without delay. Such precaution will help you to save puppies, as well as preventing possible grave infection of the bitch.

After the litter has been whelped, the nursing dam should have the quantity of her food increased gradually. The amount of food and frequency of feeding depends upon the number and age of the puppies. A bitch feeding from seven to ten or more rapidly growing, vigorous puppies, as well as supplying enough sustenance for her own needs, has a rather heavy nutritional demand and she should be fed generously enough to meet this demand. The feeding of yeast during the lactation period seems to help to increase the volume of the milk secreted.

For the average Setter or Pointer bitch, raising seven or eight puppies, say when they are two weeks old, five to seven pounds of food daily, not including milk or bones, is not too much, and some will require even more.

Do not allow the nursing bitch to go hungry for a long period, feed her well, pay due respect to kennel hygiene, give the bitch more consideration than you think is due to her—and both the bitch and yourself will profit.

18   In conclusion

American Pointers and Setters are a development exclusively of the sportsmen and breeders of this country. The dogs are excellently suited to hunting conditions in various sections of our land. And there is no doubt at all that these breeds are now at the crest of an amazing popularity.

The average American hunter has found it necessary to get himself a good hunting dog if he expects to bag such prized game birds as bob-white quail, ringnecked pheasant, ruffed grouse, prairie chicken—the upland varieties that may be taken legally.

More and more sportsmen have turned to Pointers and Setters. While these pointing breeds have been our most popular hunting dogs for over a century, today they must be better than ever to achieve success in the shooting field. Extra effort has gone into the breeding, rearing, development and training of practical gun dogs, and it is safe to say that a good Pointer or Setter is really a gilt-edged investment for the hunter.

Setters are not just hunting machines, they are also companions and friends, and lots of fun to be with and to play with.

SALLY ANNE THOMPSON